It was now clear to Barbara that the wound sustained by Mateo Mendoza was no accident. This van they rode in was expertly equipped to treat it. There were racks of surgical supplies—dressings, sponges and instruments—all in sterile packaging. Across from her, the man called Julio had donned surgical gloves and seemed to know something about what he was doing. Mendoza had either done this to himself—something she couldn't quite believe—or had another inmate do it to him, to facilitate his escape. And now he wanted her to pull the knife out.

"I say *pull* it, bitch!"

CHRISTOPHER NEWMAN

K I L L E R

VISTA

First published in the USA 1997 by Dell Publishing

First published in Great Britain 1997
as a Vista paperback original

Vista is an imprint of the Cassell Group
Wellington House, 125 Strand, London WC2R 0BB

A catalogue record for this book is
available from the British Library.

ISBN 0 575 60240 6

Printed and bound in Great Britain by Caledonian
International Book Manufacturing Ltd, Glasgow

97 98 99   10 9 8 7 6 5 4 3 2 1

This one is for Susan.

ACKNOWLEDGMENTS

I would like to thank the following people for their invaluable assistance in the research and preparation of this novel.

First Deputy Superintendent Charles Greiner, Sing Sing Correctional Facility; Dr. Roger Rose, M.D.; Dr. Arthur Boyd, Jr., M.D.; Lieutenant William Caunitz, NYPD (Ret.); Larry Marren, NYPD (Ret.); Sergeant Al Singleton, Metro-Dade Homicide Bureau; Officer Gene Kowalski, city of Miami PD; Knox Burger, Kitty Sprague, John Talbot, Bob and Patience Mason, Ethan Sprague, and my wife, Susan. The DEA agents who helped Dante find his way in Miami must remain unnamed, but Joe would have been lost without them.

"Then everything includes itself in power,
  Power into will, will into appetite;
  And appetite, an universal wolf,
  So doubly seconded with will and power,
  Must make perforce an universal prey,
  And at last eat up himself."

> Wm. Shakespeare
> *Troilus & Cressida*
> Act I:3

PROLOGUE

Cali, Colombia
1975

Lucho Esparza was the closest thing to a father that Teo Mendoza had ever known. Don Lucho treated Teo's little family very well. They had color television. Both Teo and his brother, Freddy, wore good clothes to school. In turn, their mama treated Don Lucho much better than Doña Esparza ever would. Lucho was in the bedroom with their mother now, as ten-year-old Teo and his brother quietly amused themselves in the other rooms of their rooftop apartment. It was pouring great buckets of rain out on the terrace, killing the noise of traffic on Avenida Sexta below, but not drowning the grunts and moans of their mother's lovemaking.

The game the boys played was Monopoly, a gift from Don Lucho after one of his trips to the Estados Unidos. Freddy loved it with a passion rivaled only by his interest in girls. Between rolls of the dice and contemplation of his real estate holdings, Freddy would cock an ear toward the bedroom door. While still on his knees, he'd thrust wildly with the forward rocking motion Teo had seen one goat perform on another in the marketplace.

"Uh, uh . . . ooh," Freddy finished, his eyes still closed in communion with his fantasy. He relaxed back on his heels, sucked in a breath deep, and opened his eyes. The smile he gave his little brother was heavy with superior knowledge. "You hear that in there? The same as me, with Amparo Salamanca last night. I am like a stallion, and still she beg me for more."

Freddy was fourteen. Teo suspected him of great exaggeration on many fronts. Teo knew Amparo Salamanca from the next class below his brother's at school. A mestizo with strong Indian features, she had immense *tetas* for a girl of thirteen and was the lust object of every boy who'd recently hit puberty.

"Roll the dice," Teo begged. Freddy and his fantasies could drag these games on for hours. "I saw Amparo with two of her friends last night on the pla—"

His sentence was cut short by the clump of heavy boots on the stairs outside their door. The boys knew the sound of those boots, and their hearts were suddenly in their throats.

"El capitán!" Teo was on his feet in a blur and racing for the terrace door. Through the rain he could see the red-and-yellow DAS, federal police van parked with two tires on the sidewalk. The captain's driver sat behind the wheel with the window down, smoking a cigarette. Behind him, Teo heard the captain's heavy fist on the door.

The DAS *capitán*, Ramirez, did not treat the family as well as Don Lucho did, but he too came here regularly. Indeed, it seemed to the brothers Mendoza that Don Lucho encouraged their mother to receive the captain.

Their mother appeared from behind the bedroom door, her face a mask of panic. She clutched a bed sheet to cover her nakedness. "Ask who," she hissed. "Say I am sick."

From behind her, Don Lucho emerged zipping his fly,

shirt in his teeth and shoes beneath one arm. He dashed across the room, scattering little green houses and red hotels from the game in progress. Lucho passed Teo where he stood in the pouring rain and started over the parapet wall for the roof next door. Capitán Ramirez hammered again on the door as Teo watched Don Lucho's progress.

"Who is it?" Freddy called.

"You know damned well who it is, you little bastard," Ramirez snarled. "Open up."

"Mama says to tell you she is sick."

Down on the street, the captain's driver spotted movement and looked up. Don Lucho had dropped the ten feet to the clay tile roof below and started across it. The shirt in Lucho's teeth and a shoe in each hand told the story. The driver scanned farther up toward the rooftop apartment, saw Teo watching him, and began frantically honking the horn.

Capitán Ramirez kicked the door open to hurry across the room and out onto the terrace, his face twisted in a scowl of irritation. He leaned out to make contact with his driver. The man was pointing excitedly to the fleeing Senor Esparza, and Ramirez instantly understood. When he turned back toward the little apartment he was reaching for the flap of his holster.

Teo rushed after him in panic, but stopped when the captain's Luger barked, one quick shot after another. From beyond the bedroom door, the hysterical screams of his mother were cut dead, mid-wail.

"Run!" Freddy implored, trying to push Teo back out the door. The fierce look of urgency in Freddy's eyes snapped Teo out of his stupor. In the next instant they were off across the terrace in the rain to leap the parapet wall.

Teo's ankle gave on impact with the roof below. He went down with a sharp cry of pain.

"Come *on*!" Freddy cried. "Hurry!"

Teo tried to stand, and fell, as Capitán Ramirez appeared

above them. Freddy ran back across the rain-slick tiles to grab Teo's hand and pull him.

"Tit-sucking little *bastards*!" Ramirez screamed. He took aim.

Teo realized the captain's intention and tried to push his brother away. "Run, Freddy!" he begged. "Go!"

The captain's first shot shattered a tile only inches from Teo's head. Then Freddy threw himself to cover his younger brother. Paralyzed with fear, Teo huddled under Freddy's weight. The next crack of the captain's pistol was muffled by the rain. Teo felt the bullet impact his brother and heard Freddy cry out in pain. Then Ramirez cursed as his gun clicked empty.

An eternity passed before Freddy rolled off Teo with a moan. His ankle forgotten, Teo raised his head to look at his brother. Freddy's face had gone white and his right side was bright red with blood.

"Get help," Freddy whispered. His fingers reached to clutch Teo's arm. "Find Don Lucho."

TWENTY YEARS
LATER . . .

ONE

Sing Sing Correctional Facility
Ossining, New York
Wednesday, November 22
5:11 P.M.

"**L**" gallery, level four, "A" block. Teo Mendoza shuffled from his cell, headed toward the mess hall for evening chow. On approaching the south-end staircase he watched José Cerrato from the corner of one eye. José waited. When Teo passed, Cerrato fell in step behind and passed him the knife. Teo tucked the weapon, with its locking four and one-half inch blade, under the cuff of his work shirt.

"Jus' like we say," Mendoza murmured. "Soon as we get on the stairs."

It was five weeks since Mateo Mendoza learned his brother, Freddy, had been killed by police in a shoot-out on Manhattan's Upper East Side. Freddy and Cali cartel chemist Benjy "The Biker" Pollock were trying to take out a snitch, and news reports said a cop named Dante had saved the snitch by pulling the trigger on Freddy. When Teo heard this cop's name, he swore on his mother's grave to avenge Freddy's death. Teo hated all cops, but this one was special now.

Other inmates gave José Cerrato plenty of space as he fell back to join two other Colombians. All of these Cali cartel soldiers were Central Monitoring Case—or CMC-A— inmates; the baddest of the bad in a house jammed to the rafters with society's worst nightmares. Because they hung tight, nobody messed with the cartel Colombians. They were like the gang Chinese, their unity giving them power.

The south-end staircase leading to the mess hall descended two flights from the fourth level to the second. There, the corridor crossed an open chasm between "A" block and the mess building via an enclosed bridge. At the foot of that bridge, a lone guard monitored the flow of traffic. José and the other Colombians moved ahead of Teo now to create a screen between him and the guard's watchful eye.

Halfway into his descent, approaching the third level, Cerrato spun on one of the others to shove him hard against the wall. "I *see* you take it!" he screamed. "I don' get it back, I gonna cut your fucking *cojones* off!"

The other "L" gallery inmates quickly jammed the stair-well on all sides of the combatants, the noise level of their hoots and taunts deafening. Below, the bridge officer could see little beyond the first rank of onlookers. He could not see Teo Mendoza where he crouched just behind the crowd, down low, two steps up. Mendoza knew he had maybe fifty seconds to execute the next phase of his plan. The bridge officer had surely pulled the pin on his portable radio by now, creating a "red-dot situation." In less than a minute the block sergeant and guards from the surrounding area would respond in force. Teo knew this because he and the others had stolen a stopwatch from the recreation office, created three similar disturbances, and checked the response times.

During the past month, Teo had displayed a keen interest

in human anatomy. In particular, every Sunday during visiting hours he'd been briefed exhaustively on the subject of open pneumothorax, or sucking chest wounds. In his cell he'd studied and then destroyed every Spanish-language document on this medical condition that his outside sources could convey to him. He now considered himself something of an expert on pneumothorax, its diagnosis and treatment. He hoped he was, because he was about to inflict one on himself.

Grim determination, fueled by hatred of the man who killed his brother, drove Teo as he set his back to the stairwell wall and pulled the blade of the so-called "007" open to lock it in place. In one slashing motion he drew its razor-sharp edge across his solar plexus. It created a quarter-inch-deep cut, ten inches long, which instantly began to burn like the flames of hell. Teo prided himself on his ability to control pain, but he bit his tongue hard as the fingers of his left hand guided the tip of the blade to a spot directly above his right nipple. He'd probed to find that spot so many times over the past few days that the skin was tender to his touch. Without looking, he gripped the knife handle with both fists and jerked it into himself in one quick thrust.

When the red-dot situation startled him from his reverie, Block Sergeant Clarence Nixon had been tying himself in knots trying to figure out how to convince Dalawa Rainey to quit calling his house. Dalawa was an inmate's girlfriend. Her boyfriend had caught her in the bathtub with another man and put a bullet in her playmate's brain. The boyfriend was doing five-to-fifteen for manslaughter, which left Dalawa plenty of spare time to find other playmates. Last week, a month after Clarence first met her in the visitors' room, she began phoning his wife to make anonymous, obscene taunts. Clarence regretted ever visiting Dalawa's Ossining welfare hovel. He swore to his wife this was the work of some prisoner with a hard-on for him, trying to make trouble.

Clarence had just decided to get a new, unlisted, number, when his radio blasted out his call numbers and informed him that a red-dot situation existed. The incident was located on "A" block's south-end staircase, and as block sergeant he was responsible for support of the men responding from other areas. Radio in hand, he called the bridge officer for his report while setting off from his office at a dead run.

"From here, it looks like a couple Colombians mixing it up, Sarge," the bridge man reported. "I ain't seen no metal flash or no blood yet. Everyone's kinda all knotted up."

Nixon and the red-dot response team converged at the south end of level two. Clarence led the way into the stairwell with the response team close at his heels.

"Against the walls, you scoundrels! Now!" To Clarence, the fight seemed to have de-escalated of its own volition. As soon as he and the red-dot team appeared, individuals began to loosen their knot, hands spread in gestures of innocence.

"Yo! Guard! This dude, he stuck bad!"

It came from up the stairs, behind the crowd, and everyone turned to look as Nixon bulled his way toward the source. The instant he saw blood, he reached for the rubber gloves in his belt pouch. These days, the risk of HIV infection was always in the back of a prison guard's mind.

"Get a stretcher down here! Fast!" He yelled it up to a pair of guards coming down from level four. "And call the infirmary. Tell 'em we're headed their way." It was then that Nixon realized who the injured man was, and wondered who was crazy enough to stick a mutt with so much juice. Mateo Mendoza was reputed to be a close friend of the Cali cartel overboss, Lucho Esparza. He was the cartel's number one enforcer on the eastern seaboard, doing this stretch for weapons possession only because district attorneys in New

York and Florida had failed to assemble enough evidence to convict him of homicide. He was slippery, this one, and bad to the marrow.

Clarence took hold of one shoulder to ease Mendoza from his side onto his back. It was then that he saw the knife planted to the hilt in the man's chest. "Holy shit," he murmured. And then he bellowed. "Get these mutts cleared outta here! Where's that fuckin' stretcher!"

Whenever agency nurse Barbara Jo Kelly worked fill-in shifts at Sing Sing, word spread like brushfire that she was on duty. Every Romeo in the joint came down with gut pains. This evening she'd already treated three and she'd only been there an hour and a half. Blond and petite, with some dramatic curves that even her loose white tunic dress failed to hide, Barbara Jo wondered how desperate this sorry collection of miscreants thought she was. If she needed a date—which was hardly her problem—the last place she'd go trolling was behind bars. Only because her rent was due next week had she canceled tonight's date with a cardiology resident at the Westchester Medical Center. A steady parade of sociopaths, each with a wittier blue-ball complaint than the last, was little consolation.

Barbara Jo's patience was further put to the test when a call came in from "A" block. A stabbing victim was headed their way. She'd spent a year right out of nursing school working that sort of emergency at Lincoln Hospital in the South Bronx, and now she steeled herself.

The moment Barbara Jo saw the knife sticking from Mateo Mendoza's chest, and all that blood pouring from a gut wound, her self-pity evaporated. The Lincoln Hospital emergency room nurse took over.

"Let's start an IV! *Stat!*"

Barbara had to nudge her partner, Linda Tuttle, who had gone white. Linda *liked* it when these misfits mooned over her. As far as nursing skills went, Barbara Jo thought Linda would make a better cosmetologist. Once Linda started to move, Barbara grabbed a pair of scissors to cut the hurt man's shirt from his torso. All that blood made it hard to see if he'd sustained any other stab or slash wounds and right now her primary objective was to stop as much bleeding as she could.

"Someone get on the phone to Phelps," she commanded. "Tell them we've got a pneumothorax on the way. Knife still in him. Better get a van ready too. No time to wait for an ambulance."

Phelps Memorial Hospital was located in North Tarry-town, four miles to the south down Route 9. There was no way Barbara Jo would touch the knife sticking out of this guy. It looked huge, the handle protruding like that. This was a job for a chest surgeon.

Accompanied by the evening captain overseeing the shift, the prison superintendent rushed into the infirmary. "What's the status here?" he demanded.

"Nurse says we gotta get him outta here," Block Sergeant Clarence Nixon reported.

The superintendent took one look at the bleeding inmate strapped to the gurney and nodded. "Who is he, Captain?"

The duty desk sergeant stepped up, computer printout in hand. "CMC-A, sir. Drug-related weapons possession. Suspected shooter for the Cali cartel."

The superintendent turned to the nurses. Barbara Jo was now helping Linda get the IV of lactated Ringer's solution started in the injured inmate's left arm. "This man is extremely dangerous, Nurse. You sure we can't treat him here?"

Barbara's nostrils flared as she swung her head around to dead-eye him. "Dangerous? He's got a knife in his chest. I want to keep my license—you think I'm going to pull it out?"

Barbara was looking on the bright side as she turned away to slap a blood-pressure cuff on the man's opposite arm and pump the rubber bulb. A nurse would have to travel with the patient in the van. She'd be damned if it would be Linda. The last time Barbara worked Phelps Memorial there was a real cute neurology resident working the evening shift. Tonight might be her lucky night.

Lyndon "Sonny" Reed couldn't help himself. Here he sat, about to commit a crime that would make him a hunted man for the rest of his life, and he was thinking about calling his bookie. His gambling obsession was what got him into this mess in the first place. He thought about either making those calls, or the bets he'd already placed, most of his waking hours.

Sonny's sunburned and freckled bulk—all six foot three inches and two hundred forty pounds—was wedged behind the wheel of a rented Ford Escort parked outside the Sing Sing Correctional Facility gate. Even with the seat run all the way back it felt tight in there. After forty minutes cooped like that he was getting antsy. Tomorrow was Thanksgiving, and the Lions were playing the Cowboys in a big one. In his judgment, Detroit could cover the eleven-point spread. He needed to get to a phone.

Between the prison and the Conrail commuter station a few hundred yards away, joggers plodded up and down a grassy recreation area overlooking the Hudson. Reed ignored them and concentrated on the prison parking area and a gate just beyond. The prison would evacuate Teo Mendoza in either an ambulance or one of their own vehicles, and as Sonny waited he searched for some last-minute deliverance.

Sonny's problem was simple enough. He owed his pal Julio Mesa three hundred thousand dollars. A gambling scandal involving athletes and boosters had come to light at the University of Florida last summer, and Sonny was booted from the New York Giants' training camp. The Ferrari he'd bought with his signing bonus was stolen from the driveway of his rented condo. He hadn't bothered to get it insured. To make ends meet he'd sold cocaine fronted by Julio, some to acquaintances on the sporting scene and more to associates of his girlfriend, Bebe, an exotic hostess. But rather than pay Julio for the dope, he'd used the proceeds to pay his bookmaker. Now push had come to shove. Julio was the nephew of Cali cartel kingpin Lucho Esparza, and Uncle Lucho needed a favor. Sonny had agreed to it rather than have his genitals fed to him.

Mesa was parked a mile away on Route 9, across from the Ossining Junior/Senior High School. Now, as one gray prison van emerged from the gate, followed by another, Reed raised a portable radio with the latest scrambler technology to his lips. There wasn't much doubt that Teo had done just what he'd planned to do.

"Stalker, this is Bird Dog. They're on the fly. Company vans. No frills." Sonny hailed from a neck of the Georgia backwoods where a man was expected to take his lumps and hold his counsel, but purposely sticking a four-inch blade into his own chest put Mateo Mendoza in a whole other league.

"How many bodies, Jim?" To Julio, everybody was Jim. He drawled it frosty cool.

"Windows all around in them vans. I see a nurse plus two guards. Two more uniforms in the chase wheels. Nobody actin' like they think he's goin' nowhere."

"You know the drill, Jim."

Reed felt that familiar surge of adrenaline he'd always felt at opening kickoff on game days. It worked on him as he twisted the key in the ignition and got the little Escort in gear. The radio off his right hip crackled.

"And remember, Jim. I'm sitting here blind. Pretend you're a commentator. Talk to me."

"They're rollin' up Hunter to Main, just like you figgered."

"I want to know the second they hit Church."

How many times had they gone over this? Sonny concentrated on staying far enough off the chase van's tail to avoid arousing suspicion. Those two in the follow vehicle would be his. He needed it to be a complete surprise.

Sergeant Clarence Nixon was none too easy about this latest development. As the "A" block supervisor, security in that cell block was his responsibility. An inmate getting himself stuck and maybe dead meant a shitstorm that was sure to hit him full in the face. If the inmate lived, there would be a lawsuit. The institution had failed to protect Mendoza, and therefore his civil rights had been violated. The command chain at Corrections liked to spread blame around like jam on toast, and Clarence was on the lieutenant's list. As far as any hope of promotion went, it might be best if this mutt died.

Once the two vehicles conveying Mateo Mendoza to Phelps Memorial climbed out of downtown Ossining to Route 9, a local cop was on the scene to hold back rush-hour traffic. They made the right turn to streak south. The prison had notified both local and state police that a Central Monitoring Case prisoner was en route to the hospital. Nixon guessed that because Phelps Memorial was so close, any state police investigator responding wouldn't catch up much before the emergency room.

"Damn, that took some *cojones,*" Andy Sepulveda marveled. Seated behind the wheel of the chase van, his eyes on the vehicle ahead, the young guard shook his head.

"What's that?" Clarence asked. "To stick a dude like Mendoza?"

"Damn straight, Sarge. Word I hear, that man's untouchable. Him and Lucho Esparza? The Cali cartel honcho? They supposed to be like this." He held up a hand, index and middle fingers intertwined.

Nixon thought about it. Lucho Esparza was a businessman. If this job had taught Clarence anything, it was that the human animal first looked out for himself. "Could be Esparza, he know how much this dude know. Don't like the feeling of being that exposed."

Sepulveda scowled. "This man, he supposed to be the cartel's number one enforcer. A crazy motherfucker, one who'd cut his own mother's throat for Lucho Esparza."

"Ain't no use to anyone in stir," Nixon replied. "Besides, the fact he took the fall might mean he's losin' his edge. It's the kinda thing could make a drug emperor nervous, his number one gun goes off his game."

Traffic moved slowly to the side of the road in response to the van's flashing red light as they passed from Ossining into the high rent, less densely populated Briarcliff Manor. It was then that Sepulveda noticed the little red Ford in his rearview.

"Why is it some asshole always does that?" He nodded toward the mirror.

Nixon glanced at his own side view and smiled. "Human nature, I guess."

The car had slipped in behind them, like they'd both seen countless times down in the city. While other drivers pulled grudgingly aside to clear the way, there was always one who had to slip in and ride on a speeding ambulance's or fire truck's tail.

"This one got something burnin' on the stove," Nixon continued. "Been on us ever since we clear town."

They were approaching the gate to the Sleepy Hollow Country Club, scene of one or another of the major PGA tournaments that past summer. To Clarence, all that wrought iron and those stone pillars demarked a world he couldn't imagine. He wondered how those members with their Jaguars and designer wives would handle it if some irksome piece of side tail started calling their old ladies on the car phone or whatever. It was easy to imagine what he would do if he had that much juice.

The taillights of the van they were following lit, and the rear tires started to smoke as it skidded. Only because Andy Sepulveda's van had worn brake pads did it track a straight line. The lead van, meanwhile, wound up crosswise in the lane, the nose of Sepulveda's van thudding hard into its right flank.

Andy's knuckles were white on the wheel. "What the fuck!" he gasped.

Nixon was already releasing his shoulder harness and reaching for the door lever. "Move, man! It's a fucking ambush!" He'd been watching the car on their tail in the side view when the van first started to skid. It was how the driver of the red Ford reacted that set off an alarm in the back of Clarence's mind. That car hadn't skidded at all, but seemed to fall back just an instant before all hell broke loose . . . like the driver knew what was coming.

By the time Nixon had a foot on the pavement and could drag the Remington 870 twelve-gauge pump across his lap, one huge white boy had erupted from that little red car and was running at him. He held a machine pistol outstretched in one freckled hand. Clarence barely registered dread before the first burst, like a swarm of angry hornets, tore into him.

So far, it was all working just as Julio Mesa had so carefully planned. After establishing himself in the lead position, traveling a hundred yards ahead of the prison van, he'd started to slow as if pulling to the side of the road. Then, as the van began to accelerate past, he swerved back onto the road, into its path. It forced a panic stop. The van's occupants were still trying to figure which way they were headed when Julio appeared at the passenger-side door. Mesa doubted the man in that seat even knew what hit him as a first burst from his Uzi blew out window glass and tore off half the guy's face. He reached inside to unlock the door, jerked the handle, and dragged the dying man onto the street. The driver was groping in panic for his holstered .38 Smith & Wesson when Julio triggered a burst of slugs, tearing into his torso. He didn't kill the nurse tending Teo. They would need her. It wasn't until Sonny arrived to clear the dead man from behind the wheel that she finally recovered enough of her breath to scream.

TWO

Lieutenant Beasley "Jumbo" Richardson was curious about the look on his partner's face as Joe Dante hung up the phone. It was late in the workday and both men were preparing to leave their Special Investigations Division office to start the Thanksgiving weekend. Richardson was outside in the hall when the phone rang. Now, on his return, he found Joey eased back in his chair, his eyes staring off into some unseen distance.

"Who was that? You look like you just seen a ghost."

A slight smile tugged at the corners of Dante's mouth. "A friendly ghost. You remember Janet Lake?"

It was going on three years now, but a lot more time than that would have to pass before Jumbo Richardson forgot Janet Lake. A former fashion model turned successful actress, she also had her own line of clothing, produced by a major label. They'd met Janet—gracious, stylish, and rich—in the course of a homicide investigation. She and Joey had fallen briefly in love, but when the initial fireworks were over they realized how impossible their romance was. Joe would always be a cop's cop. Janet would always belong to the world.

A sense of foreboding came over Beasley as he dragged

his chair out to sit. "How long's it been?" It was all he could think of to say.

"Over two years. She's stopping over on her way from Milan to L.A. Some rag-trade meeting. Gonna meet me at my place, and we'll go on from there. Have an early dinner."

"Rosa will be thrilled."

Joey didn't look as fearful of his current girlfriend's wrath as maybe he should have. "I'm asking her to join us." He paused, looking to that far-off place again. "They met once, you know. I ever tell you that?"

That "once" was after one of several breakups in his long off-again, on-again affair with Rosa Losada. Lately, Joey and Rosa were on again. Dinner with Janet didn't have to mean disaster, but Richardson feared his friend was tempting fate.

"That wasn't the best time for you two," he reminded Dante. "You and Rosa, I mean. How happy's she gonna be, you asking Janet to your pad?"

"Her flight leaves at eleven, Beasley. Tonight. Dinner at seven-thirty and she's off to the airport by nine-thirty. How much could happen?"

"You always been fast, friend. I remember things I shouldn't."

Dante scowled. "Nothing I ever told you."

Beasley stood and grabbed his jacket off the back of the door. "I'm a *detective*, remember. Promise me you'll stay outta trouble."

Dante reached for the phone and punched out Captain Losada's number at the D.A.'s Investigation Squad. "Happy Thanksgiving, Beasley. You try not to burn your turkey, I'll try not to burn mine."

A mile east of Route 9, on Sleepy Hollow Road, Sonny Reed pulled the Corrections vehicle into a turnout providing access to a state parks-and-recreation trailhead. An hour earlier they'd left a Pontiac Transport parked in the clearing, as any day hikers might. It was outfitted with a rolling ambulance stretcher and all the medical supplies needed for emergency treatment of an open pneumothorax. Four hours from now, the Colombian doctor who'd shipped those supplies north would land at a remote New Jersey airstrip to evacuate the escapee. Until then, all that Reed, Julio Mesa, and the prison nurse had to do was keep the patient stabilized.

Reed shut the engine off and hurried to retrieve the stretcher from the Transport's windowless cargo bay while Julio prodded the nurse with the muzzle of his Uzi. Three minutes had elapsed since they'd left the scene of the hijacking. Police pursuit couldn't be far behind.

"As long as he stays alive, you stay alive. You're gonna help me and my buddy get him into that other van. Fast. You drag your ass, I'll make you wish you didn't. You dig?"

Barbara Jo Kelly stared at him, almost too scared to breathe. Minutes ago she'd seen this man execute two prison guards with all the cool of a kid shooting aliens on a Nintendo screen. "He needs an emergency room." It came out too brusque and she froze, afraid it might provoke him.

Mendoza lifted his head from the stretcher. "*El cuchillo*, Julio." He was fast slipping into shock, with only sheer orneriness sustaining him. "Pull the fucker out."

Julio eyed that bloody knife handle as Sonny Reed hauled open the back door, the rolling stretcher pulled up outside at the ready. "Soon as we're moving again, Jim." Mesa handed Barbara the rolling IV stand, the bottle of Ringer's dangling from it. "Take this, sweet meat. And don't drop it. What do you hear, Jim? Any sirens?"

"Not yet." Sonny reached to grab Mendoza's shoulders, handling him like a toy as Mesa lifted both feet. " 'Nother thirty seconds, we're history, and they're scratchin' their balls, wonderin' where we disappeared."

Captain Rosa Losada was still at her desk at One Hogan Place, plowing through an investigative report on a recidivist child molester, when Joe Dante called. The news of Janet Lake's presence in New York blindsided her. That time in her life, when Janet was a part of Joe's, was one she would rather forget. The day, three years ago, when Janet answered Dante's front door was the first time Rosa really regretted leaving Joe. She could still taste the jealousy that had surged up like bile.

"I see. She's never been to your new place, so you invited her to meet you there for drinks." It was hard to keep the sarcasm from her voice. She wasn't even sure she wanted to. "I think I'll take a rain check, Joe. You've got a lot of catching up to do."

"Brian and Diana are joining us too, Rosa."

Dante's closest friends and upstairs neighbors had become friendly with Janet Lake while she and Joe were involved. The idea of having them in the mix brought Rosa's anxiety level down a notch. "What time are you meeting?" she asked.

"I'm leaving right now. Brian's delivering some new pieces to his gallery. They'll be coming down from there. We'll all hook up at my place for a drink, then head out for an early dinner. Janet's got an eleven o'clock plane."

"How early?"

"Seven-thirty."

Rosa looked at the file before her. She'd barely gotten into it and had at least another hour's work to do. "I'm still buried here, Joe. Tell me where, and I'll meet you at the restaurant."

"La Metairie."

"You remembered to take the turkey out of the freezer this morning?"

There was a pause on the line. "Shit."

She kept her voice calm. "If it'll fit, give it a couple minutes in the microwave, then put it in water. That speeds up the process." Before he could reply she replaced the receiver in its cradle, then rubbed her face and stared back down at the child molester's file. The upcoming long weekend was starting to look longer than Rosa had planned. Then again, if Dante fawned too much over his movie star friend, at least she would have plenty of time later to kill him.

Because the new van had no cargo area windows, Barbara Jo had no idea where they were headed. Rather than worry about something over which she had no control, she concentrated, instead, on the situation at hand. The gorilla-size white man had an accent from somewhere down South. The cold-blooded killer who watched her every move looked Hispanic, but had none of Mendoza's accent. His English was almost *too* hip, and he drawled it a bit, like he'd spent significant time in the South. All the same, he spoke fluent Spanish with the escapee.

It was now clear to Barbara that the wound sustained by Mateo Mendoza was no accident. This van they rode in was expertly equipped to treat it. There were racks of surgical supplies—dressings, sponges, and instruments—all in sterile packaging. Across from her, the man called Julio had donned surgical gloves and seemed to know something about what he was doing. Mendoza had either done this to himself—something she couldn't quite believe—or had another inmate do it to him, to facilitate his escape. And now he wanted her to pull the knife out.

"I say *pull* it, bitch!"

For a man who'd lost that much blood, the grip Mendoza had on Barbara's upper arm was surprisingly strong. He was only of medium stature, and because he insisted on being kept alert, she'd hit him with just fifty milligrams of the Demerol they had on hand. Administered intramuscularly, it couldn't have kicked in to full effect yet, and still he demanded she pull the knife out now.

"My uncle wanted to know why this vendetta can't wait," Julio addressed him. "He knows how much you loved Freddy, but he's worried about your condition, Teo. After this." He pointed to the knife.

"Pull it!" Mendoza seethed. He turned to Barbara, fixing her with a steady glare. "My friend, he think I must hurt too much with this knife to avenge my brother's death." He turned back to Julio. "Never."

Mesa nodded to Barbara. She gritted her teeth to steady her nerves as she focused on the knife handle. She'd begun to secrete excess saliva as nausea threatened to overwhelm her. If she gave in to it and vomited, the man called Julio would make her pay.

"Now!" Mendoza roared.

Barbara wrapped her fingers around it and yanked straight upward just as the van hit a bump. The knife blade encountered unanticipated resistance before it came clear. Mendoza gasped with the pain of it as blood flowed freely again.

"Sponge! Now!" Barbara snapped.

Julio grabbed one from the rack full of dressings behind him, tore the package free, and handed the sponge across. The knife thudded to the carpet as Barbara tossed it aside and started to mop the wound.

"Antiseptic swab first. Then the compress," she ordered. "Once it's in place, I hold, you tape."

As Barbara worked, Mendoza's wound tried to suck air into his lungs each time he drew breath. Drug or no drug, he had to be in agony. When she got the compress in place,

Julio tore off strips of adhesive to tape it. A radio on the floor crackled with gibberish Barbara couldn't comprehend.

"I'm busy, Sonny," Julio told the driver. "You get it."

From where she knelt, facing forward, Barbara saw the gorilla reach onto the passenger seat to retrieve his own radio unit. She could only pick up snippets of the ensuing conversation. By the time it ended, the compress over Mendoza's pneumothorax was in place and the wounded man was breathing almost normally.

"They just refueled outside Greenville," Sonny reported. "The tower there? They sayin' they could hit snow squalls, anywhere from Lancaster on up to our airstrip. No accumulation, but it could get a little hairy."

"What about the schedule, Jim? They gonna be on time?"

"Ten o'clock, Bubba. Just liked you planned."

Mendoza clutched at Julio's shoulder. "What about my cop? Where is he?"

"It's workin' as we speak," Mesa replied. "How you feel?"

The veins in Teo's forearms popped prominently as he tightened his grip. "You just fin' him. The time, when it come? I feel good enough."

Julio wrinkled the discarded dressing wrappings into a ball. "Okay. But that chest tube is gonna hurt like a motherfucker."

Barbara Jo's face creased with sudden confusion. "What chest tube? You need a surgeon to insert a chest tube."

Mesa reached into one of the racks behind him to extract several more sterilized packages of equipment. One held a trocar: a surgical steel tube with one razor-sharp end. The other contained what looked like a pliable rubber diaphragm enclosed in a glass cylinder. There were places to attach rubber tubing at either end. Julio held this unfamiliar object out to her.

"It's called a Heimlich valve. Paramedics in Vietnam put them in all the time."

"But—"

"No *buts*, babe. You've seen them use the trocar to cut the tube hole?"

Barbara's nausea again fought to get the better of her. She gritted her teeth as she nodded. "But—"

Julio held up a hand to stop her. "Once you got him swabbed, ready to cut the drain? Teo, he'll point you to the spot."

The instant that New York City's chief of detectives, Gus Lieberman, broke his car phone connection with the state corrections commissioner in Albany, he dialed his office at One Police Plaza. On his way home, Gus had learned en route of Mateo Mendoza's escape, and he wanted action fast. A month earlier, NYPD had made both Corrections and the FBI aware that Mendoza had mailed a threatening letter to Detective Lieutenant Joe Dante. In it, Mendoza swore to see Dante dead.

"Detective Bureau. Detective Moore."

"It's the chief, Larry. Gimme Frank."

Lieberman's exec, Captain Frank Bryce, was still there when Gus had left. He was trying to get Detective Bureau affairs squared away for the long weekend and sounded harried when he picked up. "Yeah, Gus. You hear about Mateo Mendoza?"

"News travels fast."

"You kidding? Four dead guards and a kidnapped nurse? The wires are smoking."

"We need to find Dante, Frank. I doubt he's in danger, considering the shape this mutt's in, but I'd want to know if I were him."

"Read your mind, boss. Operations is paging him as we speak."

Back when dinosaurs still roamed the earth and Gus Lieberman was a young cop wearing blues, he and Frank Bryce had worked together as partners out of the 102 station house in Richmond Hill, Queens. That was twenty-nine years ago and this wasn't the first time one had read the other's mind.

"You find him, tell him to watch his ass and call me. Then check the lists and see what kind of protection detail we can put together. I don't care if he wants it or not."

"One step ahead of you there too. I read the FBI report on this mutt, same as you. Sonofabitch is wired different than your average Colombian shooter. Blood runs cold instead of hot. Makes him less predictable."

Lieberman's driver had them crawling north on the Brooklyn Queens Expressway, starting over the Kosciusko Bridge. After Gus hung up with Bryce he sat back in his seat to stare at the mid-Manhattan skyline and think about Mendoza. The story had it that both Teo and his dead brother, Freddy, were raised by Lucho Esparza, the Cali cartel overboss. Esparza was in hiding somewhere in the Amazon now, but still controlled the disciplined distribution system he'd masterminded. While Freddy Mendoza had overseen Esparza's entire metro-area network for six years, it was thought that Mateo had gotten closer to Esparza than Freddy had. When Freddy was killed by Dante and his partner, Beasley Richardson, Mateo had already been inside for three months on a weapons possession conviction. He'd been implicated in seven cartel killings that law enforcement knew about, in Florida and New York. Knife in his chest or not, the idea of him being on the loose made Gus nervous. Very nervous.

Janet Lake never seemed to age. Tall and slender, with hardly a line in her face, she looked even better to Dante now than the last time he'd seen her. That was a time of great stress in her life. Her brother had been murdered; she'd gone through a divorce; and she was fighting to save the clothing label she'd created. Tonight, as Joe handed her from a cab outside his West Twenty-seventh Street building, she looked rested. He closed the door and kissed her cheek.

Dante's loft building, located on the corner of Eleventh Avenue, was already known to Janet as the home of rock singer Diana Webster and Diana's sculptor husband, Brian Brennan. They were two of Joe's closest friends and resided on the top floor. Up there they had views of both the Hudson River and midtown. After dark, the sidewalk out front often looked as it did now; populated with loitering prostitutes in their usual freakish garb. Walking past them, Janet hooked a hand in the crook of Joe's arm. "I've never been kissed by a lieutenant before. What's with the limp?"

As Dante walked them toward the front door, he was noticeably favoring his left knee. "Sprained it a month back." He'd hyperextended it, actually, as he tackled a suspect on an East Seventy-fifth Street sidewalk to prevent her from being shot. "The older I get, the longer these things take to come around."

"Don't say that word."

He inserted his key in the lock. "Huh?"

"Older. God, it seems like we saw each other just yesterday."

He got the door open and held it as she entered first. "Yesterday? Not for me. It seems like I've lived lifetimes since."

The elevator off the lobby was an old freight job, which Joe had to release with another key. It shuddered as they started the journey to the fourth floor. "How's Skye?" he asked.

Skye Lake was Janet's daughter. "She's modeling now, you know. Following in her mother's footsteps."

"What happened to school?" The last time Dante saw Skye, she was starting college and studying dance.

"I begged her to finish, but I'm only her mother, right? She's making phenomenal money, and swears she'll go back once she's run out her string. I was lucky. Maybe she'll be lucky too."

When the elevator stopped one floor from the top, Dante hauled back the mesh gate so Janet could enter his loft. The sprawling living room dead ahead was still unfinished, but getting close. The built-in bookshelves along one wall had recently been stained and tung oiled, the odor of it still in the air.

Accustomed to Dante's old Greenwich Village garden apartment, Janet marveled, "It's huge."

"Same size as the west half of their place, upstairs," Joe replied. His friends and landlords had another five thousand square feet of workshop and art studio space, complete with a kiln for firing wax casts, and a small foundry.

"Are they coming down or we going up?" she asked.

"They're on their way from something at Brian's gallery. Should be here any sec. Glass of wine?"

"Only if you want to carry me to dinner," she replied. "My body thinks its later than yours does. Club soda? Wedge of lime?"

Joe's cat emerged from his bedroom, saw company, and abandoned his usual indifference to cross the room and rub against her leg.

"That's Toby, my roommate." He led the way to the kitchen as Janet scooped the white Turkish Angora into her arms to scratch him between the ears. Joe filled her glass, then opened a beer for himself and a can of Friskies for the cat. Janet wandered.

"So catch me up, Joe. It's lieutenant now. I had dinner with Diana in Aspen last February. That's how I heard you and Rosa are back together. You're happy?"

Dante followed her into the living room and sat across from where she stood, reading the spines of books on his shelves. "Yeah, I am. We both seem to have grown up a lot; worked some things out. She's a little nervous about having dinner with you tonight."

She sipped her soda and frowned. "Because of us? That's history."

"I think it's because of who you are. And sure, history or not, we were what we were."

Her eyes gleamed, the light of sun reflected off ice. "She's never had to make her living dressing in lingerie for a million people to see. There are pros and cons to this life."

Joe grinned. "I'll have to remind her of that." He felt his pager start to vibrate and reached to tug it from his belt. The display window carried Gus Lieberman's office number. "Damn," he muttered.

"I see the routine hasn't changed," she observed. "At least you're home. You won't be asking if you can borrow a quarter."

THREE

Gus Lieberman's house on the waterfront in College Point, Queens, was a sprawling old fieldstone-and-clapboard affair with a huge veranda and lush, mature landscaping. As the chief's driver pulled the company car into the drive, Joe Dante connected with Lieberman's car phone. Rather than loiter in the late November chill, Gus carried his portable unit up the front walk toward the stoop.

"You talked to Bryce?"

"Uh-huh. Creative way to bust out of the joint, don't you think?"

"The man made a threat, Joey. I want you off the street until they catch him."

"The way I hear it, he's got a knife stuck four inches deep in his chest."

As Gus mounted the short flight of steps to his veranda, his wife, Lydia, opened the front door, a finger marking her place in a book. Lieberman held the phone aside to kiss her cheek. "Your favorite hotshot," he murmured.

"What's that?" Dante asked.

"Never mind. Where are you? They killed four guards, Joey."

"I'm at home, but if it makes you feel better, I'll spend the night at Rosa's."

"What are your plans tonight?"

"I'm having dinner with the neighbors, Rosa, and Janet Lake. La Metairie on Bleecker and Tenth. Seven-thirty."

Gus grunted, wondering but not asking how Janet happened into the formula. "I'm gonna assign some bodies, Joey."

"Fine, Gus. It's hopeless, arguing with you."

"Say that again, please. I wanna get it on tape."

Across the entry hall from where Gus loitered, the phone on a table at the foot of the main staircase rang. Lydia moved to get it as Gus punched the *end* button on his cellular. He set the unit on a side table near the door to the library, while Lydia held the receiver of the other phone out to him. The fire she had crackling on the hearth in the library looked inviting. If this kept up, it would be out by the time he got to it.

"Who?" he asked.

"Special agent-in-charge Charles O'Roark. DEA, she told him. "What's going on, Gus? Is Joe in danger?"

Lieberman took the receiver from her hand. "Gimme a sec—I'll fill you in." He wedged the instrument between cheek and collarbone to shrug out of his overcoat. "Yeah, Charlie. I know about Mendoza. What's up?"

"The kidnapping of the nurse makes some of it the FBI's jurisdiction, Gus. Al Dyson is insisting they take the reins." Dyson was the bureau's New York agent-in-charge, a man prone to push his weight around rather than play a team game, at least in Charlie's opinion. He didn't have much respect for how Dyson handled a crisis situation. "If it makes you feel any better, we've got an interest too. We're taking the threat Mendoza made against Dante seriously. Where is he?"

"Right now? He's at home. Having dinner later with Captain Losada from the D.A.'s Investigation Squad and some friends. One is Diana Webster, the rock star. Another is Janet Lake, the actress."

"Wonderful. Dinner where?"

"La Metairie, in the Village. Seven-Thirty. I'll make you a deal. You run interference with the Feebs, we'll handle protection."

"You know Dyson better than that, Gus. How would it look, this mad dog makes a try and he's got nobody within three miles? He'll want to cover his fanny. Trust me."

Gus must have looked like he needed a drink when he hung up. Before she asked any questions, Lydia handed him a Scotch on the rocks.

All the time Barbara Jo Kelly held that trocar poised to cut a drain tube opening into Mateo Mendoza's chest, she was nearly paralyzed by fear. Her pleural cavity anatomy was vague at best, six years out of school. She knew the area surrounding the lung had to be drained in the event of pneumothorax, but the question was how deep should she drive that razor-sharp surgical tube to avoid hitting the lung? If she went too deep and hurt this guy worse, or—God forbid—killed him, she would be killing herself as well.

In the final analysis, Mendoza had more than enough pleural cavity anatomy for the both of them. She was mesmerized by his concentration, by his total detachment from the pain he experienced.

"*Bueno,*" he murmured, guiding the instrument. "Now push. Slow. I tell you when to stop."

Sweat trickled from Barbara's hairline into her eyebrows as the tip of her instrument pierced flesh to enter the fifth intercostal space at the midaxillary line. Julio stood by with a sponge and started to mop as soon as blood began to flow.

"Steady," Mendoza growled, teeth clenched. "You doin' good."

She watched the trocar slip down into the pleural cavity maybe an inch past the ribs before Teo stopped her.

"There. Loose the clamp. You'll see."

Sure enough, when Barbara released the clamp from the rubber tube threaded down the hollow inside of the trocar, bloody fluid from inside the cavity surged down the tube's length. She removed the trocar quickly, leaving the tube in place. With the clamp reaffixed down low, she waited for Julio to finish mopping up and to tape the insertion in place. Then she affixed the Heimlich valve and opened the clamp again.

The valve did just the job it was designed to do, allowing fluid trapped in the cavity to drain freely while preventing any air from being sucked back into the void. Fifteen minutes after Mesa finished taping, the amount of blood flowing through the valve slowed to a trickle and then stopped, just as they assured her it should. Through all of this she was astounded by the clarity of the wounded man. With only fifty milligrams of Demerol in him, he displayed an unnatural tolerance for pain. Heck, he'd watched himself being skewered and had hardly winced. He was breathing almost normally now.

"You don' believe Teo, do you, pretty nurse?" He forced a gruesome smile. "Now there is the blood plasma. Julio, he get the other IV for you."

Barbara continued to marvel at their preparedness while Mendoza looked over at Mesa. "Dante." Teo spat the name like it was a foul taste in his mouth. "What is the word on him?" he demanded.

The man called Sonny was speaking softly into the Securenet radio as he drove. He shot a glance over his shoulder as he replaced the radio on the passenger seat. "Get this. He's at home now, but havin' dinner later with some movie star bitch. Lives on the corner of Eleventh Avenue and West Twenty-seventh. Headin' out to dinner, prob'ly 'bout quarter past."

A little over a month ago, when lieutenants Joe Dante and Beasley Richardson killed Freddy Mendoza, the Cali cartel's metro-area structure was thrown into turmoil. Freddy was Lucho Esparza's number one man in the Northeast. His death had left a hole in the power structure, undoubtedly since filled. What both the FBI and DEA wanted to know was, by whom? Teo Mendoza's escape from Sing Sing was too well orchestrated not to have been run from the very top. No doubt Esparza himself had a hand in it.

FBI agent-in-charge Alan Dyson hated having Charles O'Roark of the Drug Enforcement Administration insist on sticking his nose in. Then again, he didn't see that he had much choice but to let him. Teo Mendoza was high-level Cali cartel, which made him DEA business too. And O'Roark *had* made a good point. While police agencies, including their own, had a blanket thrown over the entire tri-state area, they had no idea what the fugitives were driving. The best hope anyone had of apprehending Mendoza quickly was the long-shot chance he'd try to hit the man he'd threatened. Both Dyson and O'Roark knew if they could get their hands on any of Mendoza's accomplices, a direct line into the new metro-area command structure might open up. They could save themselves months of investigative man-hours, and the man who saved his agency millions in overtime pay would be a hero.

O'Roark now sat alongside Dyson in the backseat of the bureau's command car. Charlie was Boston College Irish-Catholic, while Dyson was University of Utah Mormon. Their outlooks on life and law enforcement mixed about as well as oil and water. Just being around Dyson made O'Roark antagonistic. He gestured to the single sedan parked ahead of them at the curb, sixty yards on a diagonal from La Metairie's front door. "Four is all you could manage, Al?"

"From our UN antiterrorist detail," Dyson defended himself. "This is a crapshoot, Charles. How many men can I justify sitting around all night twiddling their thumbs?" Dyson hated being called Al. Earlier, he'd persuaded O'Roark that any attempt on Dante, unlikely as it was, wouldn't happen soon. It was seven o'clock already, the ambush in Briarcliff Manor took place at five-thirty, and the city was over an hour away under the best traffic conditions. For the time being, the FBI was willing to leave the protection of Dante at home to the NYPD.

Charlie shook a cigarette from his pack, not intending to light it, but just to give Al's blood pressure a little goose. "They the same bunch that did such a bang-up job preventing the World Trade Center bombing? No pun intended."

At five minutes past seven, Brian Brennan called to say they were running late. Dante suggested they meet a block east of there, at his garage. Ten minutes later, he and Janet emerged into the cool November evening, Joe grateful for a chance to walk and loosen his bad knee. Janet linked her arm through his as they set off.

"So this bad guy who sent you the letter; it wasn't even you who killed his brother?"

"Nuh-uh. I knocked down the woman they were trying to shoot; I was on the ground with her. I did get another guy, inside their van, but it was Beasley got Freddy himself."

"So why the confusion?"

The expression of resignation on Dante's face had become almost second nature. "You should know better than most. How often does the media twist even the simplest facts pretzel-wise? Joe Dante was on the scene, it had to be him who killed them all."

"Ah. The price of past glory."

"Something like that."

Because the weekend was getting an early start, the whores were already out in force, loitering in pools of street light. In the passing cars, lurking furtively behind window glass, their johns looked like caged zoo monkeys.

Sonny Reed jabbed a finger at the windshield, pointing. "That's him!"

Julio Mesa leaned forward over the back of the passenger seat to get a better look out the sloping windscreen. "Where, Jim?"

Reed indicated a couple moving up the opposite sidewalk just ahead. With his other hand he was reaching for the ignition key. "The blond bitch *is* a movie star, just like your boy said. Damn. I recognize her. What's her name?"

Sonny depressed a button to run the passenger-side window down, an Intratec machine pistol cradled in his lap. He spun the wheel to ease the Transport away from the curb, while behind him, Julio had one hand on his Uzi and the other on the door handle.

"No!" Teo Mendoza snarled. "I gonna do this!"

"How?" Mesa countered.

Teo made an impatient grab for the Uzi in Julio's hands. "Gimme that."

Mesa relinquished the Uzi and drew a 9mm Beretta from his belt. He watched for Sonny's signal as Teo, wincing, hauled himself up onto one elbow. Julio was amazed. With that hole in his chest, and all the Demerol in him, Teo should have been semicomatose.

Dante and Janet reached the opposite sidewalk before Joe spotted the protection Gus had assigned. From their position, parked directly across the street from his front door, they were backing their Plymouth sedan toward him against the one-way flow of traffic.

"Oh, look!" Janet blurted. Her face lit with delight as she pointed to a wall plastered with movie posters and music event bills. "That's my new film."

She disengaged her hand from Joe's arm to start away for a closer look when Dante saw a white Pontiac Transport pulling into the curb alongside. There was something too abrupt about the way it stopped. Then, even more abruptly, the side door was jerked back on its track. One part of Joe's brain refused to believe what was happening while another was already reacting. He grabbed for Janet and missed. In her enthusiasm she'd moved away too quickly. In the next second, when Joe set to dive for her, hoping to drive her to the pavement, his bad knee buckled.

Julio hauled the side door open and got the hell out of the way just as Teo opened up. To Mesa's eye it seemed as though the target started to crumple even before that hail of lead raked the scene. The blond actress was hit while turning toward their target. Surprise caught her open-mouthed as slugs impacted her torso.

"Cops!" Sonny yelled from up front. He jammed the accelerator to the fire wall, the tires screaming as they lurched away from the curb. Through his open window he sprayed lead at two plainclothes detectives in a blue Fury sedan that was backing toward them. He tore a gash in the van's rear quarter panel in squeezing past.

Julio hurried to the rear of the van to see one of the cops trying to struggle from behind the wheel. The windshield of the Fury was shot out, and the other detective slumped forward. Mesa took careful aim through the rear window glass and fired. The way the cop jerked sideways, Mesa didn't know if he was hit or diving for cover.

By the time they reached the corner and started south on Eleventh Avenue, their nostrils were clogged with the stink of cordite and their ears were deadened by the quick, short claps of noise-suppressed gunfire. Teo had collapsed onto his back, his face gone a scary gray. The nurse, huddled in terror, was worthless right now. Once Julio got the side door slammed shut, he checked the tape securing Mendoza's chest tube. It still held fast. As Mesa started to turn away to keep an eye out for pursuit, Teo clutched at his arm.

"I get him, no?"

Julio shook the hand loose, happy to be done with this craziness. His mind was on disappearing. Fast. "Oh, yeah. You got him, Jim. Got him good."

FOUR

After thirty minutes spent sitting alone at Dante's reserved table, Rosa Losada's simmer became a rolling boil. Her waiter had passed three times in the last ten minutes, eyeing her unopened menu and the empty chairs. Now Rosa stopped him.

"Yes, ma'am?"

"Could I have the check, please?"

He heard the iciness in her tone and replied with caution. "There's a phone near the rest rooms, if you need to make a call."

"I don't think so. Just the check, thanks."

Rosa had spent a long day trying to tidy up her paperwork for the extended weekend. On arrival here, she'd ordered a glass of wine, consumed it too quickly, and ordered another. As angry as she was, she regretted putting that much alcohol into an empty stomach.

The check that came was small enough that she paid cash. With her pocketbook slung over one shoulder, she started to rise when the pager clipped to her waistband commenced vibrating. The display showed a number Rosa didn't recognize. Instead of heading for the front door, she veered right toward the pay phone. If it was Dante, calling with some lame excuse for why he'd stood her up, he was a dead man.

Rosa dropped a quarter, punched in the number, and waited through three rings before her call was picked up. She was surprised to hear Chief Lieberman's voice rather than her boyfriend's.

"Rosa?" He sounded anxious, which wasn't like him.

"Yeah, Gus?"

"I think you better get over to Bellevue Emergency, quick as you can. Joey's been hurt."

Her heart was suddenly in overdrive. "Hurt how?"

Lieberman evaded. "They got him in radiology. Doin' an MRI."

Magnetic resonance imaging could mean any number of things. Whatever came immediately to mind just pushed Rosa's anxiety level higher. She pressed him. "*What* happened, Gus?"

"Grab a cab, Rosa. I'll tell you when you get here."

The funky-reggae band Urban Blight had re-united recently and was playing at the Ritz all that weekend. It was almost eight o'clock; they'd finished loading their equipment, then eaten a quick Chinese dinner, and bass player Wyatt Sprague was in a hurry to return for the sound check.

The band parked their two vans at a public facility atop the Pier Sixty-three Ports and Terminals building at the end of West Twenty-third Street. When Sprague arrived there driving one of them, he had a lot on his mind. The sound check would barely be squeezed in before the club opened its doors, and their new trumpet player had had only three days rehearsal. Wyatt worried that the guy's solos were still a little rough. He worried about his own left wrist, sprained slightly playing tennis that afternoon.

Thus preoccupied, Sprague drove across the chain-link–enclosed street-level compound, then headed for the rooftop access ramp. He failed to notice the shattered glass littering the pavement around the attendant's booth until he was almost on top of it. Then he focused on the booth itself and saw all that blood. It gleamed a wet near-black, spattered across the interior and reflecting the ambient security light like someone had thrown a can of paint in there. As he looked once more out his window and then to the ground, he spotted several bright brass bullet casings and swallowed hard to keep tonight's lo mein dinner down.

"Aw, fuck." He couldn't see him yet, but knew there was a man in that booth, either dead or badly hurt. His first impulse was to throw the damned van into reverse and jam. His second was to park it and *then* get the hell out of there. The third, and strongest, was to do the right thing.

It took a lot of nerve to climb out, get the booth door open, and stretch the crumpled attendant straight enough to feel his neck for a pulse. The man's eyes were glassy, even if his blood was still wet. Searching for any sign of life, Wyatt came up empty. There was a phone in the booth. As he picked it up to dial 911, Wyatt wondered if he should have touched the receiver. Evidence, and all. Then, as the police operator came on the line, another thought struck him. What if the cops thought *he'd* done this?

Janet Lake and one of the detectives from the protection detail were dead. The other plainclothes man was critically injured. In the sense that Joe Dante was still alive, he was lucky. Rosa Losada stood in a fluorescent-lit hallway outside Bellevue's radiology department, absorbing this news and feeling suddenly unsteady.

"From what our guys found at the scene, and what witnesses report, he tried to turn and grab Janet but missed," Gus Lieberman told her. He clutched coffee in a paper cup and looked harried. The other wounded cop was several corridors away, in surgery. "It looked to one witness like that bad knee went on him. One round hit him in the temple, but we think it was a ricochet, come back up off the pavement."

Rosa's head swam. "Let me get this straight. You called and warned him that Mendoza was on the loose, and still he insisted on walking out in public?"

Lieberman reached for his smokes with his free hand, remembered where he was, and put them back. "What can I tell you? We were taking precautions, but who knew this mutt would make a try like that? With a knife planted in his chest?" He paused to shake his head. "What I don't get is how they knew right where to find him. Less than two hours busted outta stir, fifty miles upstate, they drive right up and start blastin', like shooting fish in a fucking barrel."

Jumbo Richardson hurried in, accompanied by Diana Webster and Brian Brennan, the three of them carrying cups of coffee. "Forget about finding them in that white Transport van, boss. They killed the attendant at a parking lot over on the river. Switched wheels. Prob'ly had the spare there, waiting."

Diana moved to join Rosa, putting her arm around her. "How're you holding up?" she asked.

"I've been through this before," Rosa replied. "Janet has a daughter, Di. She shouldn't have to hear about this on the news."

Ten years ago, Rosa had learned via the news about her own parents' murders. Diana knew this, and nodded. "Name's Skye. I'm not sure who represents her, but she's been doing a lot of modeling work lately."

"Which means she could be almost anywhere."

Better known to the world for the second-skin jumpsuits she wore onstage, Diana Webster, Queen of Beasts lead singer, dressed down in public to camouflage herself. She reached into her bag to dig out change. "Give me a minute. I'll make some calls, see if I can find her."

Diana disappeared beyond a pair of swinging doors and

was gone less than a minute when two doors in the opposite direction banged open. When Dante was wheeled through on a gurney, the sick feeling that had gripped Rosa's stomach squeezed with renewed intensity. She took in Joe's ashen color and the swath of bandages wrapping his head, wondering how many times in the six years she'd known him; she had seen him hurt.

Gus closed on the radiologist. "What's the story, Doc?"

A stout, unusually tall woman with glasses and red hair tied back in a ponytail, she held a large manila envelope and a clipboard in one hand. "The bullet glanced off the skull rather than penetrate it. There's no fracture, but any blow like that ruptures a considerable number of blood vessels. Your Lieutenant Dante is one very lucky man, Chief."

"You're saying he's gonna be all right?"

"In a word." The radiologist's movements were tired. "A blow to the head like that can be dicey. We gave him an injection of Decadron to reduce swelling inside the cranial cavity, and we'll keep him overnight for observation."

Rosa stepped up. Something else she'd seen was puzzling her. "What was all that going on with his left knee?" As Joe was wheeled past, the leg looked huge, with something bulky wrapping it.

The radiologist's expression livened in an obvious attempt to put Rosa's mind at ease. "We x-rayed it while we had him in there. I'm no orthopedist, but it doesn't look like he retore any ligaments. He did strain them, though. That was an ice pack you saw."

"Can we talk to him?"

The doctor shook her head. "Not for a while. We had to sedate him to keep him still. An hour from now, when he's settled in his room."

Once the radiologist turned away, Brennan and Richardson joined Gus and Rosa. In contrast to the heavyset, tough-guy black lieutenant, the sculptor was distance-runner slender and boyishly handsome, with curly, salt-and-pepper hair.

"Sounds like we've got time to grab a bite, get some air," Brian offered.

"Suddenly I'm not hungry anymore," Rosa replied.

Gus laid a reassuring hand on her forearm. "You heard the doctor." His touch was surprisingly gentle for a man so big. "He's gonna be fine."

Rosa wasn't so sure. "Does he know Janet's dead? He had to be knocked out cold. You know how crazy he was about her, Gus. Maybe better than I do."

Lieberman's expression sobered. He turned to Beasley and Brennan for support. "That was a long time ago."

Those two stood there looking helpless, and Rosa forced a smile. "Attachments come in all shades, guys. Rarely black and white."

"He was delirious when they brought him in here," Brian told her. "I was right there. I don't think he knows." He turned to Gus. "Join us?"

Lieberman shook his head. "I've gotta head over to surgery. A car from the Six-Eight is bringing Byrd's wife in. She'll be here any minute. You go ahead. I'll grab something from the cafeteria."

Gus left to his duties, the other three met Diana as they emerged into the corridor beyond a set of double doors. The singer was closing a Filofax, which she stuffed back into an oversize shoulder bag. "What gives?" she asked. "I just saw them wheel him past."

"They say he'll be okay," Rosa reported. "How about Skye? Any luck?"

"She's represented by Elite. I called a photographer I know, who called someone at the agency *he* knows. Right now, Skye's in South Miami Beach."

"You got a number?"

"My friend's working on it. I asked him to call your operations desk soon as he gets something. He'll have them page you."

The weather began to deteriorate as soon as Sonny Reed drove out the west end of the Holland Tunnel. Nothing he'd heard on local radio, or seen on the Weather Channel earlier that day, had said anything about the snow squalls mentioned by their pilot. What they were getting now, as they sped along I-78 through central New Jersey, was a cold, light rain that turned heavy at times, pushed by a nasty wind gusting out of the Northeast.

The new van was a burgundy Plymouth Voyager; one of two they'd left parked on opposite sides of Manhattan for just this purpose. Its cargo bay was outfitted much like that of the abandoned Pontiac Transport, complete with racks of sterile dressings, bottles of disinfectant, and painkillers. Aside from a cache of ammunition for their weapons, and the high-tech radios, the wounded fugitive and his kidnapped nurse were all Sonny and Julio had transferred from one van to the other. As Sonny drove, squinting at the road through the rural New Jersey night, he reflected on how much Lucho Esparza's fortune could buy. It had bought Sonny and his willingness to commit murder. It was buying an American-educated Colombian chest surgeon to fly up here and treat one of Lucho's most valued friends. Indeed, it seemed to Sonny that there was very little Esparza's billions couldn't buy.

"You got that turnoff, Jim?" Julio asked. Mesa sat behind the front passenger seat, perched on a folding camp stool with one eye on the pretty blond nurse.

"Route 513, just past Clinton." How many times had they been over this? Sonny had driven over this route to Hunterdon County twice since last Friday, the last time not needing a map. In this weather, what he needed was an airboat.

"You 'bout ready for a taste?" Julio wondered.

"I thought we was gonna wait for the plane t' land."

"Just figured it might help you stay alert, Jim. I know it would help me. All that adrenaline pumping takes it out of you. Feel like I been up a week."

The first time Sonny Reed met Julio Mesa was over a snort. As an undergrad at the University of Florida in Gainesville, Julio had lived a more lavish lifestyle than most college students could manage. Sonny was taken to one of Mesa's parties in the Duck Pond section of town by a coed from Lauderdale. It wasn't a jock party, and most of the guys Sonny met there had more money than him, but none had made seven solo tackles and gotten a sack in the Auburn game. Julio invited Sonny and his beach bunny date to the den, where he laid out some lines. They started talking sources of anabolic steroids and action at the Jacksonville dog track. Before they knew it, they were deep into a three and a half gram eight-ball, the party outside forgotten. That was four years ago, almost to the day.

Sonny reached out behind him, offering Julio his fist. "What the fuck. Do me."

Sonny steered one-handed into the driving storm. Mesa, using a matchbook cover, shovelled a pile of coke onto the side of Reed's hand. With practiced ease Sonny lifted his fist to his face and dragged the dust deep into his nasal cavities.

"What about you, sweet meat?" Julio asked the nurse. "You're along for the ride, just like the rest of us. Why not make the best of it?"

Barbara Jo Kelly stared, wide-eyed. "What are you going to do with me?"

Mesa lifted the matchbook cover to his face and snorted.

"I don't know. Use your imagination. Maybe I'll let you suck my dick."

The drug had a foothold in Reed's consciousness by the time the turnoff to Route 31 and Clinton came and went. His synapses fired more brightly now and he sat up straighter behind the wheel, alert for the exit onto 513. "Got that turnoff comin' up," he announced. "How's our man ridin'?"

"Rock-a-bye baby," Mesa replied. "Got enough Demerol in him to keep an elephant down."

The airfield was called Sky Manor, located in rolling countryside to the south and west of a tiny, picturesque burg called Pittstown. The first time Sonny had driven out here with Julio to scout the place, he was struck by how affluent the area seemed. There wasn't a major metropolis for miles and he wondered where the residents of all those big houses worked. Tonight, all he cared about was getting Teo Mendoza to their destination, and seeing himself safely deposited beyond the reach of the American law. The coke he'd snorted was making him feel invincible, while an irksome awareness tucked to one side insisted that life would never be the same again.

The first snowflakes started sticking to the windshield as Sonny turned onto the approach road leading back past the north end of the airfield. "Shit." In the near-blinding swirl he was able to pick that single house out of the gloom, to the right of the road. He used its several lit windows as a guide. At nine-thirty it wasn't all that late, but considering the weather, he expected everything farther along the road to be buttoned up tight: the several maintenance buildings and an administrative office. Sky Manor also featured a restaurant, but that closed at six, weeknights. The runway itself was equipped with lights controlled by radio, enabling aircraft to take off and land twenty-four hours a day. "They gonna think we crazy, comin' out here in weather like this."

"To make a pickup, Jim. Not to land a plane. The pilot's who they'll think is crazy."

For twelve years Eddy Sandts had flown a U.S.-registered Beechcraft King Air out of Kendall-Tamiami Airport on special assignments for Lucho Esparza. They were money runs mostly, shuttling cartel cash from the States to offshore banks. He harbored no illusions about how all that money was generated, because all his illusions had crashed and burned in the mid-sixties. Eddy had survived six years of flying out of Vientiane for Air America during the Vietnam conflict, and back then the cargo was heroin, the profits split between Southeast Asian warlords and enterprising U.S. military intelligence personnel. Only his mortal coil had survived, and with it, his skill as a rough-terrain pilot. On the ground, he ate, slept, drank, and fucked. In the air, he sold his skills to the highest bidder. In the 1990s, there was nobody anywhere who could outbid Lucho Esparza.

On hearing the weather report out of Greenville, the Colombian doctor had broken out in a cold sweat. Eddy assured him that it was nothing compared to a Laotian monsoon. That had cut about as much ice as his deicing fluid and wipers were cutting now: not enough, fast enough.

"You cannot see anything," the doctor complained. Educated in American schools, he'd taken his M.D. at the University of Iowa. "Call them on the radio. Say there is no way."

Truth was, Eddy *couldn't* see much. He flew on instruments as he traversed the Delaware River north of Easton, trying to adjust to a sudden wind shift. Half an hour earlier, as they flew north into Pennsylvania, they'd worked against a headwind blowing out of the Northeast. Since then, the flow of moisture up off the Gulf had started to dominate, slamming into the Canadian cold air and pushing it east. That forced him to make his approach to tiny Sky Manor from out of the Northeast, which meant avoiding the high-tension wires indicated on Eddy's map as running perpendicular to, and a mile north of, the runway.

"Oh, there's a fucking way, Doc. That's one of Lucho Esparza's dearest compadres on the deck down there, probably bleeding to death right now. I think maybe we should *find* a way."

"Don Lucho's nephew Julio is capable," the doctor argued. "I coached him myself. Shipped him medical supplies enough to treat *six* pneumothoraxes. Nobody is bleeding to death, Senor Sandts."

"Yeah? And twelve hours from now, what sort of shape'll he be in? By then they could have a foot of snow on that runway."

"You are sure the lights will come on?" The doc was looking for any excuse to abort. Clutching at straws.

"It's an automatic system. I call in, bring up the intensity with a few clicks of my mike. Why don't you stick to doctoring, *hermano*? Let me do what I do best."

FIVE

While Rosa Losada, Beasley Richardson, and Brian Brennan waited at their table in an Indian restaurant close to the hospital, on Second Avenue, Diana remained in the car parked outside with Rosa's cellular phone. Skye Lake's agency had provided a reach number for her in South Miami Beach. When the singer returned, her face was pale.

"Always new firsts." She collapsed onto the banquette across from the two cops, her husband slipping an arm around her shoulders. Face buried in her hands, she rubbed hard. When she eventually looked up, she found them all staring back. "I don't *ever* want to do that again."

Rosa reached across to take one of her hands. They locked fingers. "She coming up here?"

"Uh-huh. Said she'd call the airlines soon as I got off. I told her we'd pick her up, to leave a message on our machine." She paused to glance at Brennan. "I said she can stay with us."

Rosa's grip on Diana's fingers tightened. "Whatever we can do." She nodded toward Richardson.

Diana knew how hard this had to be for Rosa. She and Joe had only recently gotten their personal lives back in sync again. Now there was this. Diana wondered how Rosa would react to meeting Skye Lake. The kid looked so much like her mother, it was scary. "Thanks. She'll probably need help with whatever arrangements she wants to make." Diana paused to take a deep breath, then let her head loll to one side, coming to rest against Brian's shoulder. "There were voices and music in the background, like she was having fun down there. I feel like shit."

"I'm going with you to the airport." Rosa's tone was soft.

"I wish Joe could go too," Diana replied. "There was more than shock in Skye's voice. She was angry. Maybe if she saw him . . ."

Rosa looked again to Richardson.

"You know him," Jumbo rumbled. "The man can walk? He'll be there."

Barbara Jo Kelly heard the airplane first. She'd complained about needing to pee and was forced to squat in the swirling snow, back turned, under the watchful eye of Sonny Reed. The coat she wore was too light for these conditions. She hugged herself, shivering. No snow was sticking to the asphalt yet, but at the rate flakes were falling—big, fat, wet flakes that were fast getting smaller and drier—it wouldn't be long. And through them, on the wind that drove the storm, the first remote drone reached her ears.

Barbara Jo stood and turned to peer at Reed's face. Usually when she encountered a man this big, she assumed he was thick clear through. This one, she wasn't so sure about. The man called Julio treated him like a lackey, but something was going on there. He wasn't just a stooge.

"Sounds like your ride is here."

"Huh?"

She lifted her chin toward the sky, her face pointed toward the far end of the runway. North?

Sonny scowled into the snow, the wind at his back, then lifted his wristwatch close to his face. "On time, even."

"Do me a favor?" she asked.

He had started toward the van, but stopped. "What's that?"

"If I'm going to die, I'd rather you do it than him."

He shrugged those huge shoulders. "Ain't my call, Sugar." Was that sympathy she caught in his tone?

Barbara watched him jerk open the van's side door and heave it back on its track. The plane's engines were louder now as it bore down to make a pass overhead. All along the runway, lights set at twenty-foot intervals suddenly sprang to life, each reflected in a larger globe of blowing snow. Barbara couldn't see the plane, but it sounded bigger than the little single-engine jobs parked behind her on the tarmac. She couldn't imagine how a pilot could hope to land in these conditions, but this was an age of smart bombs and all manner of unfathomable technology. Big jets flew in and out of JFK and LaGuardia in bad weather all the time.

Julio Mesa emerged from the van to join Sonny on the runway verge. The way he clutched his jacket to his throat and hopped from foot to foot told Barbara he wasn't much for the cold. As a nursing student at Columbia-Presbyterian in the upper reaches of Manhattan, she'd met Hispanics from all over the Caribbean like him. To his tropical metabolism, thirty degrees was as bad as thirty below.

"You see him when he flew over?" Julio asked.

Reed shook his head. "Nuh-uh."

Mesa turned to Barbara. "Ever been to South America?"

She frowned. "No. Why?"

He chuckled. "Be a shame to waste perfectly good pussy."

"So don't." Barbara hoped she sounded braver than she felt. "Once you're gone, what harm can I do you?"

"I'm thinking more about the good you could do me. What kind of hot, sweaty jungle fuck you might be."

Barbara wondered how much she wanted to stay alive. If

the choice was death or living out the rest of her days with this jerk in some remote Colombian hellhole, maybe her short life had already been rewarding enough.

The sound of plane engines grew more distant as the pilot finished his pass and turned to start his approach. He was lower now, and lined up to come straight at them.

For an instant, a brilliant flash lit the landscape north of them like midday. It coincided with the plane engines going dead. And then, amid a shower of sparks made fuzzy by a scrim of falling snow, a fireball hurtled to earth. It exploded on impact, a bright orange glow relighting the horizon seconds before a muffled thunderclap reached their ears.

"Fuck me," Mesa murmured.

"Hot *damn*!" Sonny echoed.

While the bigger man continued to stand and stare, Julio was already cutting his losses. He elbowed Reed and reached to grab Barbara, dragging her toward the van. "C'mon, Jim. Move. Let's get the fuck outta here."

It all came back to Joe Dante as he struggled up from the depths of drug-induced torpor. The van. Janet turning away. His knee, unable to take the sudden demand put on it. Muzzle flashes and the image of Janet crumpling to the pavement. Then, the last toehold his consciousness could find—the bright splotches of crimson on Janet's white blouse as her coat flew open.

When Dante opened his eyes to the harsh fluorescent light of a private hospital room, his surveying gaze met the worried faces of his five closest friends. Staring into Rosa's eyes, he remembered he'd invited her to join Janet and him for dinner. How long had she waited? Down at the foot of the bed, Beasley Richardson and Gus Lieberman contemplated him like they might a corpse at a wake. To his left Diana Webster stood, one hand stroking his arm where it lay atop the blanket. Her husband, Brian Brennan, had an arm around her shoulders.

"She's dead, isn't she?" He'd shifted his eyes to Gus as he asked it. The chief's tough-guy countenance told all.

"Aw, fuck." The knowledge was like a knife blade twisting in his guts. He blinked, then squeezed his eyes shut as tears welled up and spilled down his cheeks.

Gus tried. "There's no way you coulda—"

"Bullshit, boss!" Dante's eyes were open again. The knowledge of his own stupid arrogance overwhelmed him. The weight was a pressure so heavy, he found it hard to draw breath. Mateo Mendoza wasn't some loose-focus fanatic. He was a Colombian cartel shooter. Everything Joe knew about the street told him he should have known better. A guy like Mendoza makes a specific threat, he intends to follow through. "The guys in that detail you put on?" Joe's head throbbed as he coughed. "What happened? I saw their car coming from up the block."

"Mendoza got the jump, Joey." Lieberman reported how one detective was dead and the other, recently emerged from surgery, would likely be paralyzed from the waist down. "They had another set of wheels stashed in a lot at the end of Twenty-third Street. Killed the attendant. We got the Crime Scene Unit going over the van they left behind. Looks like a MASH unit after a firefight in there."

Dante shifted his attention to Diana. "I've gotta reach Skye."

"Done, honey. She's coming up from Miami in the morning. Staying with us."

Joe looked to his buddy Brennan, the sculptor's fingers unconsciously kneading the tensed muscles of Diana's neck. "When you pick her up, I'm going with you."

Brennan glanced to the others. "You haven't seen a mirror yet, friend. One step at a time, huh?"

Dante was aware that his head was swathed in bandages.

The drugs he'd been given pushed the pain of his injuries to the far corners of perception, but that bolt of pain when he'd coughed told plenty. Concentrating, he could feel his left knee immobilized, a dull, burning ache there too. He remembered it buckling on him again. He'd probably hit his head on the pavement when he fell. "No way I'm gonna lay around in a hospital bed with that animal on the loose."

"You were hit in the head, Joe," Rosa told him.

"I've been hit in the head before."

"By a bullet."

Dante frowned; the contraction of his facial muscles caused another stab of severe pain. His face felt puffy, swollen. But he was thinking as clearly as a drug hangover allowed. He had motor function. He could wiggle his fingers and toes. "*Where* in the head?"

"Left temple. A graze, but it gouged pretty deep. One centimeter to the right and they say you would have been lobotomized."

Lieberman stepped to Rosa's side. "They did a brain scan, Joey. You've been severely concussed. Right now, the best you can do for yourself is rest."

When Dante was awarded the gold detective shield sixteen years ago, Gus was his first squad commander. Over the time since, through his climb up the command chain, Lieberman had become Dante's "rabbi" and friend. Gus already knew how Dante felt, and what Joe knew he had to do, but it couldn't hurt to reiterate it now. "This fucker's ass is mine, boss. I don't care if I've gotta crawl after him . . . all the way to Colombia."

The earlier snow squall had turned once again to a cold, driving rain. It was a nasty night to be called to the scene of a plane crash, but Hunterdon County Sheriff Everitt Stanton looked at these things philosophically. What other sort of night would invite a disaster like this one? A twin-engine

Beechcraft King Air, making an approach to Sky Manor air-field, had hit the high-tension wires strung a mile and a half north of the runway. The big steel-skeleton power-line towers each had a blinking red beacon atop them, but Stanton could barely make out their glow against the stormy sky. In a snow squall, they'd be all but invisible. What he didn't understand was why any maniac would attempt a landing in those conditions.

With rivulets of rainwater streaming from his slicker, Stanton finished filling the second of two plastic foam cups with coffee from his thermos and carried the steaming bev-erages back toward the wreckage. There he handed one cup to Cooper Richland, an FAA investigator flown out by chopper from Newark. Both sipped gratefully.

"What was that?" Stanton asked. Richland had just returned his cellular handset to the pocket of his jacket. "Anything?"

Tall, slender, and raw-boned, Richland nodded. "Plane's registered to a Florida outfit headquartered at Kendall-Tamiami." He talked with a Chuck Yeager drawl. "Ever-glades Avionics. A one-rig operation, owned by a fella named Sandts. Edward Sandts. They think it was prob'ly him flying it."

Two individuals had been found badly burned in the wreckage. Stanton's deputies were still searching for ID.

"Your people are in touch with Miami?"

"Yep. No news yet on who the other fella might be. Ten minutes ago I talked to the manager of Sky Manor." Rich-land glanced toward a Jeep Cherokee parked alongside a cluster of volunteer firemen's cars. "He says they were con-tacted Monday by some fella, said he was with a film com-pany. Location scout. They had a plane flyin' up tonight from South Carolina, carrying a director or some such."

"And landing in this kind of weather?" Everitt's coffee was fast growing tepid and he thought about a shot or two of something medicinal once he got back home to his warm bed.

The FAA man shrugged. "Musta been on an awful tight schedule." He sipped his coffee and frowned at it. "Funny thing is, the manager reports seein' headlights. On the airport access road, about ten minutes before the crash."

"Like someone showed up to collect this guy?"

"Uh-huh." Richland surveyed the rain-swept landscape. "So the question I gotta ask is, where'd they go? The manager was in his house, still pulling on his boots, when they went past again, goin' t'other way. He figgered they was headed here."

Each man catalogued those members of the assembled company. In addition to sheriff's deputies, volunteer firemen, and the airstrip manager, several neighboring residents and a couple of reporters from Flemington and Raritan loitered at a distance from the smoldering wreck. There wasn't a face Everitt Stanton didn't recognize.

SIX

Audrey Stumpf was dreaming. In her dream, the jump area beyond the stables of her rural Berkeley County, West Virginia, horse farm was occupied by Audrey's fifteen-year-old daughter, Brittany, perched atop Slim Jim, a twelve-year-old hunter-jumper. Brittany, with her chestnut ponytail flying from beneath her riding helmet, rode around the training course with steady assurance while a faceless, shirtless man leaned on the training-ring fence and watched. He had a beautifully muscled back, and as he watched Brittany with a hungry, predatory leer, Audrey watched them both; first her slender, beautiful daughter, every precisely conditioned fiber in tune with her mount, and then this man who ate her daughter with his eyes. Part of Audrey was filled with revulsion for the obvious strength of the stranger's lust. Another was hit by wave after wave of jealousy. That perfect, tight little fanny of Brittany's lifted gracefully from the saddle with each flex of the knee and thigh as she and the horse took hurdle after hurdle. And while Audrey watched this spectacle, she both loved her daughter and hated her. She was unable to help wondering what it might be like to feel her hands on the stranger's glistening back, and the more he ignored her presence behind him, the more she hated Brittany. Silently, her own insecurity begged him to turn. Why wouldn't he? She rode for hours every day too, didn't she? And slaved to keep her thirty-six-year-old physique in peak condition.

Then, as the man finally did start to turn, Audrey realized she was all but naked out there, wrapped only in a sheet. A sudden fear gripped her as she saw the stranger's back muscles ripple, hands planted to push off the fence. When he turned, it was as if he'd been aware of her all along. He locked eyes with her, took a quick step, and reached to jerk the sheet away.

Audrey awoke with a start to find herself lying naked on her bed, blankets stripped aside and a stranger looming above her, a gun held to her temple. The sudden surge of adrenaline was so powerful she feared her heart might explode. Don also came awake.

"What th—"

The gun left Audrey's temple to flash sideways. Don cried out in pain, gunmetal crushing cartilage with an audible crunch. Audrey screamed, but only got the edge of it out before a hand clamped over her mouth.

"You want to die, bitch?" She felt the stranger's hot breath as he pressed close. "I'm gonna take my hand off your mouth and you and your old man are gonna get the fuck outta bed. Slowly."

Audrey had forgotten her nakedness in that initial rush of fear and the attack on her husband. Suddenly aware of it now, embarrassment flushed through her. Beside her, Don lay with a hand to his face, blood pouring between his fingers. A powerful ex–bull rider, he'd never looked scared in all their sixteen years of marriage. Right now he looked terrified. His voice was muffled by his hand.

"Wuh? Wuh d'you wan'?"

"I want you to get the fuck out of bed *now*, asshole! Move!"

The stranger had turned on the overhead light. In its bright glare Audrey felt his eyes roam over her, lingering on her breasts and pubic area. Don watched him too, and started to rise. Blood ran in rivulets down his neck and through his chest hair as he tried to pull the blankets toward Audrey and cover her with them. For his efforts, the stranger shot him. The automatic pistol, with a four-inch noise suppressor screwed into its muzzle, was strangely subdued in its report. It jumped in the man's hand, each of three jerks punctuated by a flat whap, like an open palm slapping wood. Don lurched as though clubbed. Three crimson blotches appeared among the rivulets down his chest.

Audrey's scream was involuntary, but as soon as she heard herself, she remembered the stranger's first words. Even before he reached her, with his free hand connecting hard with the side of her face, she'd managed to strangle the wail rising in her throat.

"I said *up*, bitch!"

She'd bitten her tongue when he hit her, and could taste blood. No longer gripped by any impulse but the will to survive, Audrey scrambled, her bare feet finding carpet as her head rang with the blow.

"Ah. So you *do* understand English. Who else is in the house?"

For only an instant, Audrey considered lying to him, then realized it was only a matter of time before he found Brittany himself. "M-my daughter."

"Where?"

"H-her room. D-down the h-hall."

She forced herself to take a good look at the man. Unlike the one in her dream, this one was pig-faced and swarthy. His bright green eyes sizzled with malice, set close in a wide, fleshy face. His wavy jet hair was swept back from a low brow. With nostrils that were large for his pushed-in nose, he had full lips too fat to be sensual. They only looked cruel.

He saw her study him. "How old?" he snarled.

"What?"

"*Who*. Your daughter, bitch."

It froze her.

"I asked how old."

"Fifteen." It came out almost a whisper.

The man chuckled, his fingers now unconsciously caressing the fat metal cylinder that made his gun so much longer. Audrey stared at his fingers, riveted to them, the focus of her fear for Brittany suddenly galvanized. "W-what d-do you want w-with us?"

"Your daughter's titties. They like yours?" His fingers left the gun barrel, now aimed at her stomach, to reach and fondle her left breast. His thumb and forefinger were rough as he pinched the nipple.

"Julio." It was another man's voice, coming from the hall outside.

"In here, Sonny."

Brittany, clad in an oversize West Virginia Mountaineers T-shirt, was shoved stumbling through the open bedroom doorway, followed by a young man considerably broader and every bit as tall as Don. This one had freckles, short-cropped red hair, and spoke with an accent from somewhere in the deep South. The big man pulled up short, a sudden scowl taking in the spectacle of his partner fondling a naked woman at arm's length, a dead man on the floor behind. When Brittany saw her father collapsed at a crazy angle against the side of the bed, his chest soaked with blood, she stared to scream.

The one called Julio, glancing back over his shoulder, spun to hit Brittany in the stomach with his fist. She gagged on her scream, doubled up, and fell to her knees, fighting for air. Audrey saw him wet his lips as he stared at her daughter's backside. What had possessed Brittany to wear the scandalous panties now seen beneath her nightshirt? Mostly black lace, they were cut high to leave both cheeks of her fanny exposed.

"Anyone else?" Julio asked.

The partner's expression remained disapproving. "Just her. This her mama?"

The pig-faced man grinned. "Hard to believe, huh? Got such a nice, tight ass on her."

"Damn, Bubba," the bigger man complained. "Y'all don't *never* give it a rest? We got us a situation here."

Brittany finally found her breath and began gulping it with huge, blubbering sobs. "Mommy, help," she moaned.

Julio kicked her in the ribs to send her sprawling. When his attention returned to the one called Sonny, there was an even brighter spark of malevolence in his eye. "I call the shots, Jim. Not you. Shut her the fuck up and get her outta here. Take this one with you. I'll get Teo. Cold as it is out there, our little nursie's probably freezing her ass off."

When the plane crashed, Barbara Jo Kelly had been shoved into the back of the van. She had her wristwatch, and once they wound their way back to some sort of main highway or interstate, they'd driven steadily for a little over four hours. To prevent her from reading road signs through the wind-shield, Julio had forced her to ride facing rearward, her knees to his. Through the first hour of the drive she'd watched him cleaning his fingernails with the tip of his knife blade. Once, he'd reached with the knife to toy with the top button of her blouse, clearly getting off on her initial panic. But when it went no further, she began to understand something. Whoever Mateo Mendoza was, he was clearly very important to some-body. When that plane went down, these two desperadoes were stranded with Mendoza. They needed her. Julio had only a partial knowledge of medicine; one with some very large gaps. Should a crisis arise, Barbara was their only chance to save the wounded fugitive's life, and until Mendoza was safely in the hands of someone with more medical expertise, Julio wasn't about to hurt her. With that knowledge, Barbara had begun to feel just the faintest glow of hope.

It was 2:20 on Thanksgiving morning when they finally pulled off the highway and onto a series of side roads. From the conversation between Sonny and Julio, it was obvious they were on the lookout for some secluded, out-of-the-way place to lay over. Julio had gone forward to kneel on his camp stool and scan the storm-swept landscape through the windshield. From what Barbara could gather, the approach to the house they eventually picked was a long private drive. Sonny killed the lights and crept forward with the van for what seemed like an eternity.

Gagged and bound hand and foot, Barbara was left with Mendoza in the van when they arrived at their destination. Any warmth in the van began to seep away the minute they eased the doors shut and stole off. In his drug-induced unconsciousness Mendoza couldn't have cared less, but Barbara's teeth began to chatter after fifteen minutes. She tried to pull her knees up beneath her chin and hug herself, but with her hands tied behind, and the space so cramped, she had trouble holding herself in that position. Her circulation to all her extremities was cut off, and they burned as if plunged into ice water.

Another eternity later, Julio reappeared. He tugged open the side door of the van, hair glistening with rainwater, and reached in with his gravity knife to cut Barbara's bonds. She could barely move.

"C'mon, babe. It's not *that* cold. Shake a leg. Help me get the man inside."

She clawed at her gag with numb hands, her fingers refusing to feel the fabric. Once she managed to work it free, she plunged both hands into her armpits. "I'm g-going t-to n-need a sec. Okay? I c-c-can't f-feel my f-feet."

"You're gonna feel *my* foot, you don't get a move on."

Barbara felt an excruciating surge of pins and needles as circulation returned. The earth seemed spongy when she swung her feet out the door to plant them. Julio grabbed her by the upper arm to jerk her upright, but she couldn't hold her own weight, and fell. Enough was enough.

"I said *give me a minute*, you bastard!" She struggled to her knees, wind-whipped rain beating cold on her. Light poured from an open door across the drive, and by it she could make out the shapes of large, leafless trees and the shadows of barns or outbuildings. The house looming before her seemed large. The walls to either side of the front door were constructed of fieldstone.

By the time Barbara had gained her feet and could walk, Julio had the back door of the van open and was tugging at Mateo Mendoza's stretcher. She limped around to help lower the contraption to the ground and unlock its wheels. While Julio pulled the tow strap, Barbara hurried alongside, one hand on the stand with the IV drip and Heimlich valve, the other on the injured man to steady him. Mendoza groaned but remained unconscious.

The hall Barbara entered faced a wide staircase leading to the floor above. The surrounding walls were hung with prints of hunt scenes; horses and hounds in full chase across English countryside. She'd smelled horse manure on the way to the house and guessed at least one of those outbuildings housed stables.

"There's a bed in the room opposite the girl's," Sonny called from upstairs. "We'll put him in there."

"Send them bitches down here," Julio replied. "We need a hand."

Barbara stood gazing through a wide archway into a large parlor. It contained a fieldstone fireplace and an impressive collection of old, period furniture. What period, she wasn't sure. Whoever they were, these people were affluent. Long private driveway, stables, big stone house with rooms like this.

Sonny appeared at the head of the stairs herding two women.

"Aw, you're a fucking pussy, Jim," Julio complained. "You let her get dressed."

The older woman was handsome in a well-scrubbed, outdoorsy way. Blond, about five-six or -seven. Mid-thirties. The younger one had to be her daughter. Tears streamed down the girl's cheeks and her chestnut hair was sleep-tousled. The shapely young legs that protruded from beneath her nightshirt filled Barbara with foreboding. Julio had rapist written all over him, and it was unlikely this youngster had any of the medical skills necessary to ensure her safety. Apparently Reed was made uneasy by his partner's appetites as well.

"What?" Sonny started the two women down the stairs. "She's gonna be any use t' me, walkin' around here bare-ass nekkid? You oglin' that and thinkin' clear as flood mud?"

Reed, the mother and daughter hauled the stretcher upstairs to an empty room across from one decorated with trophies and ribbons from show-jumping events. Barbara glanced into the room in passing and spotted a large, poster-size blowup of the girl hunched over the neck of a jump horse, frozen in mid-flight over a hedge hurdle. The intense look on the girl's face was impressive. Barbara hoped the kid had that iron in her, clear to the core. She was going to need it.

Bedside, Sonny lifted Teo from the stretcher in one effortless scoop and set him on the mattress. Barbara then stood the drip stand at the head of the bed, and once the patient was settled, she checked the chest tube dressing. The wounded man began to mumble incoherent Spanish.

"We better hide that van outta sight somewhere," Sonny told Mesa. "Y'all need anythin' from it, nursie?"

"The blood pressure cuff," Barbara replied. "And more of his pain meds. He needs his rest."

"Gimme the keys," Mesa told Reed. "I'll move the truck, then you take the first turn watching the bitches. I'm too tired to even fuck."

Before dawn, Chief Gus Lieberman had reached Jumbo Richardson at home, in bed. Twenty minutes later, the chief and his driver collected Richardson from the curb outside his Fort Green, Brooklyn, town house. Now, after a sixty-mile drive west into rural New Jersey, they climbed from Lieberman's car as the sun appeared through a line of leafless trees to the east. Overhead, the high-tension wires running across the surrounding countryside from one giant steel-frame tower to the next were under repair. Power company emergency vehicles sat parked, yellow roof-lights flashing, with support and supervisory personnel seen here and there across the terrain. Linemen hung a hundred feet overhead while generators powered work lights. Portable radios squawked.

Lieberman pointed to a group of men clustered in parkas, drinking coffee. "There's Charlie O'Roark." Last night's rain had stopped; the sky at daybreak was scattered with straggling clouds.

Richardson trudged across the trampled undergrowth at the chief's side, his collar up against the chill. DEA special agent-in-charge Charles O'Roark stepped away from the others to join them.

"Gus. Lieutenant. You made good time."

"Tell me everything, Charlie. What's this about a Colombian doctor?"

Jumbo got his first look at the wreckage of the twin-engine plane as O'Roark led them down a steep incline, speaking as he went. Strewn across a fifty-yard stretch of charred underbrush, most pieces of the craft were twisted and burned beyond recognition. In a stroke of pure luck for

FAA investigators, a large chunk of the tail assembly had been thrown clear on impact. The registration numbers found there were as distinct as the day they were painted.

"All the FAA knew until three hours ago? Owner of the plane, where the flight originated, and who the pilot likely was." O'Roark stopped at a spot with a good vantage of the whole scene. "They had to wait until the cockpit debris was cool enough to sift through before they found the pilot and his passenger. Fried extra crisp, still strapped in their seats, but the stuff in the passenger's back pocket was intact. Colombian passport, identifying him as Arturo Sesin, M.D. Age thirty-eight. Address in Bogotá."

Gus lit his first Carlton of the day and Jumbo watched the way he savored that initial drag. "You ran him?"

"I called our Bogotá office," Charlie replied. "Med school at the University of Iowa. Did his internship and residency at Jackson Memorial in Miami. Chest surgery. Considering the pilot, and the good doctor's specialty, I think we hit a home run here."

Jumbo thought so too. He turned to watch a light plane land at nearby Sky Manor, his expression thoughtful. "Mendoza and his crew are stranded out here."

"Either that, or holed up somewhere back in the city," O'Roark speculated. "It's only ninety minutes away, and we've got no idea what they're driving. There's no reason they couldn't slip back into New York."

Below them, FBI agent-in-charge Alan Dyson and another man appeared from behind a piece of the wreckage to start up the incline toward them.

"The gang's all here," Lieberman murmured. "What's his mood?"

"Not happy," O'Roark replied. "A high-profile victim like Janet Lake means extra heat . . . from the media, and his bosses in D.C. It doesn't help he elected to set up two miles from where the hit went down." He turned to Jumbo. "How's your partner, Lieutenant?"

"Knowin' him?" Richardson asked it distractedly, still thinking about where he might try to get lost if he were Teo Mendoza. "You'll prob'ly see him back on the street before the day is out. On crutches, or in a wheelchair, if that's what it takes."

O'Roark's expression was uncertain. "I thought he was banged up pretty bad. Hospital-time bad."

Jumbo looked to Gus. "You explain it, boss."

Lieberman flicked an ash and took another drag. "A bullet meant for Joey killed someone else," he replied. "Someone he cared for."

"I know he's tough . . ." O'Roark admitted, a dubiousness in it.

"And smart, and the stubbornest sonofabitch I've ever met." Gus butted his smoke on a rock while clearly trying to organize his thinking. "I want to form a joint-agency task force, Charlie. Along the lines of the homicide force we have with you in Queens, or that Red Rum op you're running with Metro-Dade."

"What if Mendoza didn't run back to the city?" O'Roark asked. "You've considered that?"

"If he ain't on my turf, he'll still be on yours. If I can't attach Joey to you, he's liable to take personal time and go after this guy on his own. From my end, I can promise all the technical support at my disposal. Warm bodies, anything you need."

O'Roark lifted his chin toward the approaching Dyson. "What about his end, Gus? He's gonna be all over this like stink on shit. He'll want to run everything."

Lieberman fixed the SAC with steady, unblinking regard. "Fuck him. Do we have an arrangement? *Outside* the ring of that asshole's circus?"

O'Roark got a twinkle in his eye. "Your guy starts

stepping on Feeb toes, Al'll make trouble for me, Gus. Washington trouble."

"I know that."

"Fine. The information gets channeled both ways. Through me to you, and you to me. Anybody asks, Dante is NYPD's liaison to the DEA's investigation." He started away to intercept Dyson. "Joe needs anything, have him give me a call."

A nine A.M., after six hours sleep, Julio Mesa awoke in one of the guest rooms to a bellowing from somewhere down the hall. Suddenly alert, he grabbed his machine pistol from the pillow next to him and leaped from bed. The room was flooded with light streaming through sheer curtains. He barely registered that last night's storm must have passed, as he ran to the door in his briefs, weapon clutched cold against one thigh.

The bellowing was a string of epithets spewed in Spanish by Teo Mendoza. His gutter-tutored eloquence was focused on the hole in his lung. He was in pain. He wanted that worthless *puta* of a nurse to do something about it. Now. He babbled something about *aguardiente*, the anise-flavored Colombian national drink, but Julio figured he'd be better served by Demerol than firewater.

Mesa found Sonny standing alongside the injured man's bed, his pistol in one hand and the nurse with him, a syringe held at the ready. The two women of the house were seated side by side on the floor, against the wall opposite the door. It amused Julio to see the girl's expression register a new kind of fear when he appeared. A Latino stud, in bikini briefs, carrying an Intratec machine pistol, had to be an unsettling eyeful. The mother's expression of pure, smoldering hatred was unchanged.

"So give him the fucking shot," he commanded. "Shut him up."

The nurse turned to him, too preoccupied with the task at hand to register anything but frustration. "He won't hold still!"

Teo saw Julio now. "This fucking drug, it make me *stupido*! *Aguardiente!* Where is this place? Not Colombia, *si*? Why, Julio? Where is this you take me?" Teo got louder with each question, his outrage noisy enough to leak outside the house.

"The plane crashed," Mesa replied. He turned back to the nurse. "He okay? I mean, considering?"

"Blood pressure's been steady all night," she replied. "But he needs his rest. He's got to stay calm."

Julio stepped up and nodded to Sonny. "You pin his hands, Jim. I'll take his legs." His gun set on the coverlet where it would be handy, he grabbed hold as Mendoza started to scream again.

The nurse swabbed Teo's forearm, spiked a vein, and drove the plunger home with crisp efficiency. In the process, Teo spat in Sonny's face. The drug was already taking hold as Reed backed away and crossed to the adjacent bath for a towel.

"Ungrateful sumbitch. Mean as a fuckin' snake, ain't he?"

"How these ladies behave themselves, Jim?"

"Quiet as churchgoers. You get a look outside yet?"

"Nuh-uh." Mesa stepped to one of the room's two windows and cautiously pulled down a slat in the shade. The house sat on the floor of a wide rural valley. Off to the right, he was pleased to see, it was situated far down the tree-lined drive from the road. At least three hundred yards. The fields on both sides of the drive were dotted with big round hay bales. Closer in, there was a horse pasture enclosed by hundreds of feet of neat fencing. The barn he'd used to park the van out of sight was on his left, south of the house.

"You expecting any help to show today?" he asked, turning. It was the mother he addressed, and he got that same sullen, burning hatred in return. "I asked you a question." When she stubbornly refused to answer, he crossed to slap her.

"No!" the daughter blurted. "Nobody! It's Thanksgiving. Please don't hurt her."

Julio backed away, his glare still locked with the hatred in the mother's eyes. "I'm gonna take these two across the hall, Jim. So Teo can have some quiet, and you and the nurse can catch some z's."

"We gotta talk," Sonny countered. "Figure our next move. Bein' hung out t' dry like this gives me the creeps."

"Sure thing, Jim. But whatever we do next, we're gonna need you rested. Both of you."

"Uh-huh. Soon as I close my eyes, she cuts my throat an' crawls out a window."

Julio winked. "So tie her to the fucking bed, Jim. I bet she'd like that."

Sonny looked too tired to argue further. As he and the nurse left for the room next door, Julio herded his charges across the hall to the girl's room and eased the door closed. He stood a moment, admiring that poster of the girl on board the jumping horse, and clucked his tongue. He tore his attention from the poster to look at her. The fear in her young eyes excited him, almost as much as the challenge of her mother's clear hatred. He grinned from one to the other and wandered over to flop onto the bed, bouncing to test the firmness of the mattress. He'd left his knife in the pocket of his pants, but they could play with it later. For inducing fear, the Intratec he cradled with one hand had all the impact he needed. He began fondling the big, cylindrical noise suppressor at the end of its barrel as he leaped back to his feet, delighting in the way the move startled them.

"Either of you familiar with the expression 'hard as gunmetal'?" He hooked a thumb into the waistband of his briefs and started to peel out of them.

SEVEN

Skye Lake was due to arrive on a 10:15 flight from Miami into LaGuardia. Rosa Losada appeared at Bellevue at nine with Diana Webster and Brian Brennan to find Dante out of bed and staring out his window at a bright Thanksgiving day. When he turned, Rosa thought he looked awful. Overnight, his left eye below where the bullet struck had completely blackened. His skin tone was almost gray.

"How you feel?" She advanced as she asked it to put a clean shirt, pants, and change of underwear on the bed. Brennan tossed Joe's Brooklyn Dodgers warm-up jacket alongside them, and set a pair of sneakers on the floor.

Joe tried to force a smile and couldn't pull it off. "My doctor was just in. She wishes I'd spend the next week watching the soaps and twiddling my thumbs. I don't think she understands what happened last night."

"You're sure you want to do this?" Diana asked him.

He grunted. "I'm sure I *don't* want to do it. But what difference does that make?" He started for his bedside, his limp pronounced as he favored his injured left knee. Brennan stepped forward to lend a hand and Joe waved him off. "Thanks. I've gotta at least try to go it alone. I'd rather not do crutches again if I can help it." At the bed, he paused to flex the leg and winced. "Believe it or not, it ain't as bad as I feared."

"Something's come up," Rosa told him. She reported on last night's plane crash. "The DEA thinks the pilot worked for Lucho Esparza. Both he and the chest surgeon were killed."

Joe collected the shirt and underwear and headed for the bathroom. He stopped there, fingers gripping the doorjamb. "So Mendoza's stranded."

"That's right. The big question now is, where?"

Brittany Stumpf hated herself for wearing that silly underwear to bed last night. They were a present from a girlfriend; part of a dare. Ray Lundy had asked her to a party Saturday. All her friends thought he was the sexiest guy at school, and if he asked, she *had* to sleep with him. She took the panties as a joke, but had tried them on in front of her mirror last night and decided she looked pretty hot. Enjoying the game, she'd worn them to bed. Now, as she sat against the wall of her bedroom with the bare cheeks of her fanny deadened to the floorboards beneath, she loathed those goddamn panties. The animal who loomed before her had seen them, and he hardly needed the extra stimulation. He stood so close she could smell him, his gun in one hand and his thing in the other, shaking its flaccid, uncircumsized length in her face. It made her whole body go cold, an icy sweat oozing from every pore. She'd never really thought about rape in practical terms: what exactly she'd do. Right now, she was about to throw up.

"Leave her out of this," her mother growled. Brittany was surprised by the strength she heard there.

"Yeah?" The naked man took a sideways step to confront her.

Audrey looked up at that pig face and into those green, lifeless eyes. "You want to fuck somebody, fuck me." The challenge was clear. "Unless the idea of a *real* woman scares you." Her chin was up and she reached to loosen the sash of her robe. Brittany couldn't believe it. This man had killed her father.

"By the time I'm done with her, she'll *be* a real woman," the pig man replied. "Guaranteed."

Audrey peeled the robe from her shoulders and tucked her legs to come forward onto her knees. "Go shut yourself in the bathroom, honey," she told Brittany.

"I think she should watch," he countered. "Maybe pick up a few pointers."

The sheen of sweat that covered Brittany's body had glued her T-shirt to it. She had started to shiver. When her mother turned to her, she saw the hatred was gone from her eyes. They were pleading, begging her to go. A slight tilt of the head toward the bathroom urged Brittany with all the directness she dared. Then her mother turned to face her tormentor again.

"I do my best work without an audience."

The killer's expression changed. He was less amused, more cruel. His breathing came a little faster. In his agitation, he tugged at his penis. "Get the fuck outta here," he snarled at Brittany.

She stood on shaking legs and started tentatively toward the bathroom.

"Hold it!"

Brittany froze, acutely self-conscious of her nakedness beneath that T-shirt. But instead of shifting his focus to her, the killer hurried ahead into the bath and stood on the toilet lid. He lifted the lower sash of the one little window up there with its frosted glass and peered down into the driveway past fifteen feet of sheer fieldstone exterior wall.

"Okay," he growled.

Brittany realized she'd been holding her breath, waiting for him to look up. When he passed her, headed back toward her mom, he ran his hand down her back and across her bottom. She wondered if he was about to change his mind. Then he turned to see Audrey out of her robe and climbing onto the bed.

Knowing what her mother intended to do sent a flush of shame through Brittany as she stepped into the bath. The killer stopped the door with his bare foot as she started to close it.

"You want to watch?" he sneered. "Try the keyhole."

Skye Lake was numb throughout a sleepless night and then the flight north. She had flown into and out of LaGuardia a hundred times in her young life, but today when she landed, everything about her surroundings felt surreal. Even the act of walking seemed strange. She was disconnected from this world, and as she emerged through the gate into the crowded terminal, the sight of Joe Dante, standing there with Diana, Brian, and another woman, hit her like a hammer blow.

Diana stepped forward to hug Skye, her embrace gentle in its attempt to reassure. But reassure her of what? That all was *well* in the world? "We're so sorry, Skye. If there's anything you need, *anything* we can do . . ."

"I feel like I'm in a bad dream, Diana." Skye started forward, the singer's hand resting lightly on her shoulder. Dante looked awful, and while part of her heart went out to him, a bigger part held him responsible for her mother's death. The last time she'd seen him, nearly three years ago, she was a high school grad of eighteen. She'd had a sort of teenage crush on him then, so tall and handsome in his rugged, capable way. It had looked for a while like he might become her stepfather, and the confusion of those old emotions she'd felt were thrown into further turmoil now. There were tears in his eyes.

"Why?" she asked. She'd stopped directly before him.

"On the news they're saying they called to warn you, Joe. Why did you go?"

He spread his hands in a gesture of helplessness. "I'll ask myself that question as long as I live." He squeezed his eyes shut and winced. The way his head was wrapped and his face was bruised, it looked like he was in a lot of pain. "It won't bring her back, but I swear it, I'm gonna get the people who did this, Skye."

"You didn't answer my question, Joe. Why?"

He glanced to the woman at his side, a stranger to Skye. There was an intimacy in his wordless exchange with her. The way she took his hand made Skye angry all over again. "I've survived as long as I have at my job by trusting my gut instincts," he replied. "Last night I was wrong. I didn't believe a man with a knife in his chest was a threat.

"And because you were wrong, my mom is dead." She meant it to hit hard. It did. "The bullet that killed her was meant for you, Joe. How does that make you feel?" She had the knife in and was twisting it now. It was a shitty thing to do.

He drew a breath deep, released his lady friend's hand, and pointed to the garment bag Skye carried. "That your only luggage?"

Before she could reply, he moved closer, seeming to favor one leg, and took the bag from her.

"I've gotta live with it." There was unmistakable anger in his voice. "Same as you."

Sonny Reed was usually a heavy sleeper, but with the nurse tossing fitfully beside him, hog-tied wrists to ankles, what sleep he'd gotten was merely a veneer over consciousness. He had no idea how long he'd been drifting in and out when he came to, all of a sudden. Some uncharacteristic noise had disturbed him. It came from the drive outside. All was quiet now, but a dreamlike memory of the disturbance hovered. And then there was the noise again. A quick *clip-clop*, then several more in rapid, staccato succession.

Sonny leaped from bed and bounded to the window, where he jerked back the curtain in time to see a horse and rider disappear around the end of the farm's main barn. In his skivvies, he bolted through the doorway into the hall outside. In the next room, Teo still slept undisturbed in his Demerol daze. Julio had taken the two hostages into the girl's room, and Reed gave that doorknob a violent twist to shoulder his way inside.

"Get outta here, you asshole!" Mesa roared.

Sonny's jaw dropped. Julio sat straddling Audrey Stumpf's head, his gun held at her temple and his limp member in her mouth. "The girl!" he blurted. "Where the fuck she at?"

Julio swung his pistol up to hold it outstretched, aimed at Sonny's chest. "I'll kill you, you don't blow *now*, Jim!"

Reed ignored him to race toward the closed bathroom door. He yanked it open and found the room vacant, an icy breeze blowing in through an open window over the toilet. "Fuck! Where'd you put the keys to the van?"

It was the icy breeze from the open window that made Mesa understand what had happened. He came off Audrey fast and searched frantically for the clothes he'd left elsewhere. "That's crazy, Jim! It's fifteen fucking feet to the ground!"

Reed was headed for the hall, where he crossed to the room opposite and lifted Teo from bed to stretcher. "How 'bout the roof, asshole?" he hollered back over his shoulder. "Go cut the fuckin' nurse loose. That little bitch saddled a horse." Sonny had Mendoza under way, the drip stand carried in one hand as he tugged the stretcher's tow strap with the other. He'd made the turn toward the stairs when he heard the single *blat* of a suppressed pistol shot. Julio, in his briefs, hurried from the girl's room and toward the rest of his clothes, up the hall. Sonny grabbed him by the arm in passing. "Why?" he demanded. "Because she couldn't make your dick hard?"

The knuckles of Mesa's gun hand whitened. "You're on thin ice, Jim. It occur to you she could identify us?"

And so could the girl, Reed thought, and she was either on a neighbor's phone or halfway to Martinsburg by now.

Joe Dante's return to the scene of last night's attack hit him like a new blow to the head. Outside his loft, the West Twenty-seventh Street sidewalk was cordoned off with yellow plastic tape, the bloodstains turned an ugly black. With Skye upstairs with Brian and Diana, he stood out there in the harsh glare of midday, Rosa at his side. Ten minutes later, when he stepped off the elevator, his mind's eye was filled with an image of Janet, smiling and relaxed as she sat on his sofa with a glass of soda in her hand. At peace with herself and the direction her life was taking, she'd never looked better or seemed more content. That was who had been killed on his sidewalk last night; a woman just hitting her best stride in life.

Rosa read the look on Joe's face and slid an arm around his waist. "I'm with you through this, Joe." She hugged him. "Whatever it is you've got to do."

He hugged her back and started forward, the throb in his knee not too bad if he went easy. Thank God he didn't need crutches again. He would want mobility. "I feel like I did when Sammy was killed, only worse," he confessed. Sam Scruggs was his former deep-cover partner. They'd both worked Narcotics together. "When he got it, he knew the score going in, who we were up against. But Janet? Five minutes before she was hit, she was sitting here in this room without a care in the world."

Rosa was on the scene when Scruggs was killed. The two men had been close as brothers.

"You mind feeding my boy?" he asked. Toby was rubbing insistently against his ankles. "I'm gonna shave and see if I can take some sorta half-assed shower." He started away toward his bedroom and stopped. "That kid upstairs. Skye. She used to like me, Rosa. We were pals. You got any idea what it feels like, to have her hit me with that much hatred?"

"You're the easiest target right now, Joe. She doesn't hate you. It's part of her grief."

In his bathroom, Dante ran hot water into the wash basin and surveyed the damage done to his face. His body bore the numerous scars of battles past: the whitened trail left by a knife from shoulder to jaw, the path of a bullet seared deep in scar from front to back across his right rib cage. The damage from yesterday's bullet seemed mostly superficial. The flesh around his left eye had turned a mottled purple from his cheekbone to the dressing encircling his head. He'd been prescribed Tylenol with codeine for his various aches, and any minute now he was going to need more. His knee actually felt better after having had a chance to loosen up.

He wet his face, lathered it, and began to scrape it clean of whiskers, then heard the distant ring of his bedroom "hot line." That second phone was installed to separate the two halves of his life, and when the hot line rang, he couldn't choose to ignore it. "Get that for me?" he called out.

The ringing ceased, mid-chime. He was rinsing his face when Rosa knocked. "It's Frank Bryce, Joe. Gus wants to talk."

Dante emerged clean shaven, his loins wrapped in a towel. He lifted the receiver from where she'd left it on the bed, and sat. "Yeah, Frank."

"Hang on a sec," the chief's exec instructed.

There was a click, then Lieberman's gruff voice. "Joey? I guess you know how pissed off your doctor is."

"I'll live, boss. What's up?"

"I've convinced Charlie O'Roark to set up a kinda quasi-official task force, outside the usual talent pool."

"You mean, without the Bureau butting in?"

"You're attached to their investigation, as our liaison. I hate to ask this, but you feelin' up to a little travel?"

Dante felt his pulse quicken. "What've you got?"

"Charlie just called. A fifteen-year-old girl, lives outside Martinsburg, West Virginia, called the cops from a neighbor's place. In hysterics. Blurted a story 'bout being held hostage by a couple homicidal crazies. One's a big, muscled-up white guy. The other's Hispanic. They've got a wounded man on a stretcher, babbles Spanish, and a little blond nurse with them."

Dante dug into his nightstand drawer for a pen and notepad. "Martinsburg. Where's that?"

"Down I-81, 'bout sixty miles west of D.C. The kid escaped out a bathroom window while the Hispanic was raping her mother. The cops found both the mother and father dead, in two different rooms. Him shot in the chest, her in the head."

His shower forgotten, Joe crossed to grab a fresh shirt from his closet. "And no sign of Mendoza."

"Cleared out. The state police down there don't think they could have gotten far. Pennsylvania, Virginia, West Virginia, and Maryland have a net out. The girl says she saw a van parked in the barn. No make, but some kinda burgundy color. That's better than nothing."

Dante guessed there were a lot of burgundy vans in the greater Washington area. He switched the receiver from one shoulder to the other as he pushed his arms into sleeves. "D.C. That's four hours down 95. I can hit I-81 past Allentown, quicker. Head south that way."

"The shape you're in? We'll get you a flight down to National, hook you up with O'Roark from there."

"I'll feel better with my own wheels, if I have to keep going, Gus. It sounds to me like they're headed south."

"You're our liaison, Joey. The DEA's got helicopters."

"Let O'Roark know I'm coming," Dante replied. "I'll call you when I get there." He hung up the phone before Lieberman could protest further, crossed to his dresser, and threw fresh underwear onto the bed. He saw Rosa at the door, reflected in the dresser mirror, her arms folded across her breasts.

"I'm coming too, Joe."

"You can't. I'm gonna need you and Beasley here." As he dressed, he told her about the girl's escape and what she said she had seen. "Those two guys with Mendoza? They're cartel connected for sure. I'm betting they set up Teo's escape from somewhere here in the city. That means either our Narcotics people, or the DEA, probably have a line on them, even if they don't know it yet."

"So let them handle it." She drew herself up taller, hands dropped to her sides and clenched into fists.

"Nuh-uh." He shook his head. "I keep asking myself how Mendoza knew right where to find me last night. My address. The fact that I was here, and planning to go out. I've got a bad feeling about this. I need you and Beasley close, working the inside."

Jim and Tillie MacPhearson had a wide variety of travel books in the library of their Itasca Sunflyer motor home. Every November when they hit the road, headed south from Syracuse to escape winter, Tillie read about opulent resort hotels and quaint country inns while Jim steered them southward. The fact was, on their budget, they never stayed at those places. But Tillie liked to dream. They never ate at any of the fancy restaurants she read about, either. For lunch

they always found a place that gave good value, usually rec-
ommended by a AAA tour book. For dinner they almost
always shopped close to whatever RV park they selected,
and Tillie cooked while Jim watched TV.

Because today was Thanksgiving, tonight would be an
exception to the rule. The tiny oven in the Sunflyer's galley
was too small for a turkey. On the road it was hard to make a
proper crust for pumpkin pie, and on Thanksgiving, especially, both MacPhearsons liked all the trimmings. Cranberry
sauce, definitely. Candied yams, if they could get them. To
hold them over, they'd made a typical lunch stop off I-85
near Winchester, Virginia. The China Gourmet might seem
an odd choice for lunch on Thanksgiving, but the MacPhearsons were eclectic in their tastes. Jim had worked around the
world as an oil company chemist before settling in Syracuse
to start his own oil reclamation business. They'd raised their
two boys to like foods from all over.

Predictably, Jim grabbed two mints and several tooth-
picks from in front of the cash register on their way out of
the China Gourmet. It was early yet—just noon—but Jim
liked to put miles on the odometer early. They'd left the
campground on the Chesapeake at dawn, their next destinations the Shenandoah National Park, Blue Ridge Parkway,
and then Dollywood, in Pigeon Forge, Tennessee. Ultimately they'd wind up at their winter digs in Tarpon
Springs, west of Tampa, but Jim and Tillie were in no rush.
Each year they chose a new route and took up to three
weeks to traverse it.

While Jim stepped up to unlock the side door of the Sunflyer, a big, healthy-looking kid climbed out from behind
the wheel of a nearby Plymouth Voyager to hail them. He
had a tin of dog food in one huge hand.

"You folks got a can opener I could borrow? Musta left
mine behind at the campground."

"Sure thing, son," Jim replied. He had the latch unlocked

and the door pulled open, waiting for Tillie to climb in first. "You hang on a minute, we'll fix you right up." Once inside, Tillie reached into one of the galley drawers as Jim gained the top step. "Big fella like you, I bet you played some football, huh?" He turned to the kid as he spoke, and that was when he saw the gun.

"Don't do nothin' dumb, y'all won't get hurt," the boy told him. "Keep movin' on inside."

Both Jim and Tillie were more astonished than frightened. They couldn't believe this was happening. This wasn't some ghetto mugger, preying on travelers at a Florida rest stop. This was rural Virginia, and the boy was a clean-cut white kid, for lordsake.

"Let's have you'n grandma up there in the seats," the kid directed. "Get her started up, pops, an' when that van of mine heads out? You follow."

EIGHT

Barbara Jo Kelly drove with Julio Mesa holding a gun to the nape of her neck. From the restaurant parking lot in Winchester, she followed signs to US 50 west, then went ten miles along it to the Chambersville exit. The surroundings got rural in a hurry out there, and it being Thanksgiving, there were few other cars on the road. All the while, the lumbering motor home in their wake filled her rearview and side mirrors.

"So." Mesa prodded her with his pistol. "You and Sonny boy get it on this morning?"

She scowled, not favoring his trash talk with a reply.

"What? He had you tied up like that, and didn't make his move?" Julio snickered, shaking his head. "Figures. It's all them steroids, turned his balls the size of peas. Next time, it's you and me, good-looking. *I'll* show you a good time."

"You mean like you showed that woman back there?" Mateo Mendoza was still her insurance policy.

"Damned straight I showed her a good time. I show all my bitches a good time. Before I shot her between the fucking eyes? She was begging for more."

Sure she was. Barbara cringed. Next, this asshole would claim he'd made it with the poor woman three or even four times. All sexual contact was conquest, and his hatred for his victims fairly oozed from his pores.

He suddenly leaned forward to scrutinize the roadside ahead. "Slow down." He pointed to a dirt road that ran off into a copse of trees. "Turn there."

Barbara swung the wheel, easing the van down a deep rutted dirt track into a clearing alongside a tumbledown old barn. There were scattered patches of snow from last night's storm, the day having failed to warm much despite a crystal-clear sky.

"Park it and shut it down," he directed. "Then get your ass around back and help me with Teo."

Sonny had two geriatrics with him in the motor home. The woman was probably in her early seventies, and he looked a couple years older. They stared in dumbfounded shock while Teo was carried from the van to be hoisted up through their side door. The woman made eye contact with Barbara, albeit wide.

"Oh, my word! Has he been shot?"

"Meet Jim'n Tillie MacPhearson." Sonny introduced his captives. "From Syracuse, New York."

Inside the MacPhearsons' thirty-foot rig, Julio surveyed his surroundings with a mixture of contempt and grudging satisfaction. "That the only fucking bed?" He nodded to a big, full-size mattress next to a shower stall and toilet, aft.

"The banquette converts," Tillie blurted.

"Real cozy, huh? C'mon, Jim. Help nursie here get Teo into the rack."

The old man started to rise from behind the wheel, and Reed placed a heavy hand on his shoulder to stop him. "Not you, pops. Everyone's Jim t' him."

Mendoza's last hit of Demerol was wearing thin, and as Barbara checked the IV drip and chest tube dressing, he started to moan and writhe.

"Let's load up a spike and stick him again," Julio told her. "That ain't what we need right now."

"I need him conscious awhile," Barbara argued. "To see how his breathing is. Last time I listened, I didn't hear too much fluid. Still, I want to make sure it's not worse."

"Not right now you don't. Once we're back on the road. Don't dose him so heavy. Just take the edge off. Next couple hours, I don't need that asshole screaming in my ear."

Twenty minutes later, back on I-81 headed south, they encountered their first roadblock. Fortunately for Mesa and Reed, traffic was backed up for several hundred yards from where law enforcement vehicles were parked on both shoulders, roof lights flashing. It gave him time for Julio to prep Jim and Tillie, the only occupants of the RV who were visible.

"Understand this, Jim," he growled in MacPhearson's ear. "My buddy and me? We've already killed a shitload of people. They catch us, we're gonna kill you first. Heck, we're already dead meat."

MacPhearson flicked a nervous side glance at Tillie. She didn't look so good, her color all funny. "What'll you have us do, mister?"

"Just drive right up there, Jim. Like the no-care-in-the-world geezer you are. Smile at the nice officers. You so much as squirm like there's a problem, I'll be right down here on the floor behind you. My gun'll be aimed at your old lady's back. The first bullet's hers."

Mesa turned to look at Reed. Seated opposite the refrigerator, Sonny had a map spread on his knees, with one eye on Barbara Jo and Teo. The nurse was propped at the head of the bed with a pillow at her back, and sound asleep. The curtains over both the big back windows were drawn, but to prevent it from looking odd, they'd left the four smaller windows, amidship, with the shades pulled back.

"Time to hit the deck, Jim. If Teo so much as farts back there, stuff a cork in it." He pointed to the map. "What you got for us?"

Reed slid to the floor, wedged against the icebox. The space was so tight, his chin nearly rested on his knees. "You ain't gonna like it, 'cuz it's slower. Still, it might be a stroke of genius."

"What's that?" Julio's tone said he doubted it was any such thing.

"The Shenandoah National Park. It ain't the express route, but what kinda fugitives take a windin', two-lane road, speed limit thirty-five? Fugitives wouldn't, but a couple old-timers out enjoyin' their golden years might."

"Thirty-five? For how many miles?"

" 'Bout eighty. You take 66 east, maybe twelve miles south a' here, then go south again t' the Front Royal entrance station. Once we're through the park, we can take the Blue Ridge Parkway clear on down to where it intersects I-26, outside Asheville."

"How much farther's that?"

Sonny placed his index finger against the scale of miles, then marked off the distance. "Past the park? Two hundred fifty miles, plus or minus."

The motor home crept toward the roadblock, and Julio peeked over the dash to monitor how far they'd progressed. They were ten car lengths back now from where a half dozen county sheriff and Virginia state trooper cars were parked on the verge. Cops in Smokey the Bear hats stood between the lanes of traffic, scrutinizing the occupants of each vehicle before waving them on.

"Steady as she goes, Jim," he growled. "How you doin', grandma? You gonna have a heart attack on me or what? Smile, for shitsake!"

He dropped his head and was back with Sonny on the subject of route. "You might be right about the heat through there, Jim. And what the fuck?" He waved at their surroundings. "We got all the comforts of home."

"I can't do this," Tillie blurted. "I'm going to wet my pants!"

Mesa scooted to a spot directly behind her. "So piss them, grandma. And *smile* while you're doing it. I put a hole in the back of this seat, you won't *have* to pee no more. You won't have a fucking bladder!" He looked over at MacPhearson. "How far, Jim?"

"Two cars." Despite his wife's outburst, MacPhearson had control of himself. He sounded determined now.

"It's a beautiful sunny day, not a care in the world," Julio crooned.

As MacPhearson approached the cop in his lane, he reached over to slide his window open and nodded to the man alongside. Mesa and Reed stopped breathing. "What's going on, Officer? Anything the missus and me should be worried about?"

"No, sir. Please keep moving," the cop replied.

Jim slid the window shut, accelerated up to an even fifty-five, and reset the cruise control.

"Jesus kee-rist!" Sonny whooped. "You get a load a' him? Academy-fucking-Award material!"

Mesa grabbed the map and hoisted himself off the floor to sit on the banquette. "Not bad," he agreed. "Route 66 east and then follow the signs to Front Royal, Jim. We're taking you on a National Park tour."

Brian Brennan would forever stand in awe of how quickly women were able to find the same wavelength in times of crisis. Throughout a simple lunch, ordered in from a neighborhood deli, and now afterward, as he, Diana, and Skye Lake sat together in the living room of his loft, he felt like a relative caveman. Emotionally, he could empathize with Skye and the tragedy that had befallen her, but he was helpless to comfort her in her sadness. Diana, on the other hand, was remarkable. She hardly knew the younger woman but seemed unhindered by any chasm of unfamiliarity that stretched between them.

"It isn't quite accurate that Joe broke it off with her," Diana was saying. "That's probably the way it seemed to you at the time, but it was mutual. Not because one cared less than the other, but because both of them knew it wasn't going to work."

"But she was so sad afterward," Skye argued. "I don't think I've ever seen her that down, not even when she and my dad broke up."

Diana looked back three years, her smile faraway. "He was down too. Your mother wanted him to quit the work he loves, to come live with you two in L.A. But Joe's a cop. His father was a cop. His life is governed by old-fashioned ideas about honor and purpose. He couldn't imagine himself *not* doing the job he does."

Skye remained curled on the sofa with her legs tucked, her bare arms, tanned dark by the Florida sun, folded tight against her. "Then why did he lead my mother on?"

"I don't believe he did," Diana countered. "And I doubt Janet thought he did, either. They spent six months trying to fit their lives into each other's worlds. Both of them wanted it to work. That's just not how it happened. Some relationships work. Others crash and burn. Theirs crashed."

When Skye glanced over at Brian, he was hit by something in her face that dared the world to reckon with her. It was the thing a fashion photographer's lens freezes for fashion to flaunt as its banner: perfection in an imperfect world. He wondered for a moment if it would be possible to capture that essence in bronze. "I know he tried," he told her. It came out sounding lame.

"Right now, I can't *help* but hate him," she said. "Not totally, but so much that I wanted to kick him in the balls and scratch his eyes. My mom's dead and he's still got your friend Rosa. It isn't fair. She'd still be alive if it weren't for him."

Brian held her gaze. "And Diana would be dead now if it weren't for him. Six years ago, I would have sat where you're sitting now, furious with some force in the world over which I had no control. A psychopath straddled Diana with a knife at her throat and I watched helplessly, not a thing I could do to stop him. I never realized how much I loved her until those eternal seconds right before Joe Dante shot him dead."

Dante's buddy Brennan had been executing a commission for Nissan corporate headquarters in Tokyo when he helped Joe get a deal on a new Nissan 300ZX, two years ago. The car had an automatic transmission, which under current circumstances Joe viewed as an unforeseen blessing. Otherwise, every tollbooth and freeway access ramp would be a real nuisance, his left leg in the shape it was in.

Before his departure, Dante had plugged in his radar detector, made sure he had an extra battery for his portable cellular phone, and brought along a forty-channel CB radio, just for good measure. He didn't have time to explain his business to a legion of state troopers patrolling the roads between New York and West Virginia, and he needed to get there fast. Instead, he would depend on the network of truckers on highways all over America, who warned each other of cops via their CBs. Joe chose "Speed Demon" as his handle as he joined them on the airwaves, figuring it appropriate for a dark gray 300ZX going a hell-bent hundred M.P.H. for points south.

He reached Martinsburg, West Virginia, in under four hours, and pulled off at the exit to Route 15. Signs told him he was pointed toward downtown, and once past a large Factory Outlet mall, he pulled into a gas station. There, he filled the tank and used his phone to call Charlie O'Roark's

DEA reach number. The New York field office reported that O'Roark could be found at the local federal building in Martinsburg. They gave him the FBI office number there, and when Joe tried it, he was patched through to O'Roark in a car, somewhere on the road.

"It's Dante, Charlie," he told the SAC. "How do I find you?"

"I thought Gus said you were driving."

"I'm parked for the moment. At a filling station off Tuscorora Road." He heard O'Roark murmur something to another occupant of his car. When that person replied, the SAC grunted.

"Jesus. How's that possible?"

"You're a sworn officer of the law, Charlie. Don't ask."

"I'm headed for a funeral home, just east of you. It's this big Victorian mansion, doubles as the county morgue. It'll be on your right. Tuscorora turns into King, and it runs all the way to the middle of town."

"When are the autopsies scheduled?" Dante asked.

"Ten minutes ago. The Bureau flew a pathologist in from Quantico. I'm already late." O'Roark paused. "Oh, by the way. The Feebs are all over this thing. You'll run into Dyson."

"How surprised will he be to see me?"

"Very, I'd imagine. He gets in your face, you're with me."

The funeral home was one of a number of opulent residences lining the main drag of Martinsburg. These suggested that the city was once a center of commerce. There wasn't much of a skyline further east to suggest recent prosperity, but clearly this had been a place to be.

On arrival, Dante was shown downstairs to where the county coroner, assisted by that FBI forensic pathologist, was already well into the Audrey Stumpf autopsy. The coroner droned into a microphone dangled overhead while the pathologist scraped samples from the area surrounding and inside the dead woman's vagina. He smeared each sample on a separate slide, and an assistant labeled them.

Charlie O'Roark had anticipated Joe's arrival, and when Dante appeared, he eased over to greet him in hushed tones. "God, I hate this part of the job."

"You know anybody who likes it?" As Joe stepped up to view the corpse, he was struck by how young and pretty the dead woman was. He'd heard the victim was a West Virginia farmer's wife and the mother of a teenage daughter. He had conjured a different mental image. A bullet had entered her forehead up high near the hairline and blown off a chunk of the skull in back. It left most of her face curiously serene; almost accepting.

"You look awful," O'Roark said. "How you feel?"

"About time for another couple Tylenols." Joe watched the pathologist's assistant carry slides to a microscope set on a bench. FBI agent-in-charge Alan Dyson finally looked up and noticed Dante's presence as the pathologist bent to examine his first tissue sample.

Dyson backed away from the action to hurry around the slab to where Joe and O'Roark stood. "I'm sorry about what happened to your friend, Lieutenant, but who authorized you to be here? This isn't your jurisdiction."

"I did, Al," O'Roark told him. "He's here at my request."

Dyson gave the New York SAC a quizzical look. "I don't understand." He had the habit of coming up on his toes and bouncing slightly when he was agitated. He was doing that now.

"DEA is operating on the assumption that Mendoza's escape was orchestrated from inside the Cali cartel. Probably through their New York network. Chief Lieberman has designated Lieutenant Dante as their liaison to us."

Dyson bounced some more, the fingers of one hand getting into the act now as they tapped against his palm. "He's *personally* involved."

O'Roark remained impassive. "With what we've got from the victim's daughter, the quickest means of identifying Mendoza's accomplices might be via New York's Narco division. I want their full cooperation, Al. The lieutenant is part of the package."

"No evidence of penetration, no traces of semen," the pathologist announced. He was still bent over the microscope as he spoke.

The county coroner placed a hand over the microphone. "I thought the daughter claimed her mother was raped."

Studying the face of the corpse, Dante noticed a slight bruise along Audrey Stumpf's right jaw. "What about her mouth?" he asked. "You check inside it yet?"

The coroner, who Joe put well up in his sixties, looked ill at ease. "We're looking for evidence the man *forced* himself," he countered.

"Yeah? And?" Joe asked. "Rapists are confined to the missionary position in West Virginia?"

The pathologist was already at work wedging the woman's mouth open, his spatula in hand. Joe turned back to O'Roark.

"What did you get from the daughter?"

Charlie was watching the pathologist's hands, the rubber-clad fingers manipulating the spatula with precise little movements, scraping and then withdrawing it to smear another sample on a slide. "She described two men, the one she says raped her mother, and another who matches descriptions of the guy who shot the two prison guards in the chase van. We've got names now too. First names, anyway. The rapist is called Julio, and the big guy built like a pro linebacker is either Sonny or Jim."

"Either?"

"She says Julio called him both. Sonny's probably a nickname."

"You gave Gus this?"

O'Roark turned away from the pathologist to nod. "My office and your Narco division are both doing file searches. We put it on the Teletype to all our other offices too. And the Bureau is working on it from their end."

"Rung any bells yet?"

They watched the pathologist carry a new batch of slides to his microscope. "Still waiting." O'Roark lifted his chin in the pathologist's direction. "The mouth was a good call."

"Maybe. He strikes out there, you may want to have them open the esophagus. When can I see the girl?"

The SAC glanced at the bandage wrapping Dante's head. "You sure you're not pushing it?"

"Damned straight I'm pushing it, Charlie. It's me who's supposed to be dead right now, not Janet Lake. Where is she?"

"Staying with a neighbor. The one she ran to when she escaped. They've got a daughter she goes to school with."

While O'Roark continued to watch as the first of those new slides was placed under the microscope, Joe stared at the naked corpse of Audrey Stumpf, then at the other gurney across the room, a sheet draped over it.

Tillie MacPhearson wasn't feeling better, but once Jim got them through the Shenandoah National Park entrance at Front Royal, she started to collect herself. She was still frightened, but with that initial rush of adrenaline long spent, she no longer had the energy to be terrified. She'd heard last night on the late news about what these men had done up in New York. She knew the nurse was along because she'd been kidnapped. The possibility existed that Tillie, Jim, and the nurse might all be dead by morning, or at least sometime in the relatively near future. Tillie thought of the two grown sons she might never see again, of the one daughter-in-law she loved and the other she tolerated, and her three beautiful grandchildren. She had to focus all her resources, and try to find a way out of this predicament.

The nasty one, Julio, was in the way-back, as she called it, reclining across the end of the bed where she could see only his feet. The nurse was still asleep back there, all propped up like that. The poor thing had looked exhausted. Sonny Jim was stretched on the banquette, with that ugly little machine gun cradled in his lap. He was reading a map, trying to stay awake, and was the one Tillie couldn't figure at all.

"What exactly are you people up to?" she questioned Sonny. She twisted in her seat to better face the boy, and saw the look of alarm register on her husband's face from the corner of her eye.

"Huh?" Sonny hadn't heard her question. He was trying to figure a way to make his next call to his bookie. The game between Detroit and Dallas was over by now, and he'd either won big or was back in the hole.

"I asked what you think you can accomplish?"

He smiled. "Stay alive, ma'am. And if y'all keep your cool an' act like a good granny, maybe y'all will too." He held up his map, gesturing to it. "Just where is it you was headed, you'n Jim?"

"Pigeon Forge, Tennessee," she replied. "Dollywood. Jim just loves Dolly Parton. After that? Maybe the Grand Ole Opry, in Nashville, then south on I-65 to the Gulf."

Reed nodded, scanning the map. "Who knows your schedule?"

"It's never like it's carved in stone," she replied. "That's the point of these trips. Our son Richie—he runs Jim's oil reclamation business now?—we call him every night, just to let him know where we are."

Reed saw the scowl MacPhearson flashed his wife at the same time Tillie did. He swung his legs over to plant his feet and rose. Easing up behind MacPhearson, he leaned forward, looming over him. "That's just the kinda cute trick y'all could pull, y'want t' get both you an' your old lady killed, Jimbo. *Not* makin' that call t' your boy, and havin' him get the cops out lookin'? Be the dumbest fool move y'all could make."

"You heard him, Jim," Julio called from the way-back. He sat forward on the bed so they could see him. "Make no mistake. You fuck this up, you're the first two people to take a bullet in the brainpan."

Tillie shuddered. While his eyes burned into her like evil lasers, she couldn't avert her gaze. It was as though he knew her thoughts, and his eyes were saying, "Don't try it."

NINE

The beautiful young woman whom Joe Dante met at the Hinkle farm was still too deep in shock to fully comprehend what had happened to her. Raised in a tranquil world where violence was something she watched on television or saw in a movie, she couldn't comprehend how that other world had just invaded hers. The neighbors who sheltered her were longtime friends. They now offered the only continuity in her otherwise shattered life. As Dante sat with Brittany in the Hinkle living room, he could smell roasting turkey emanating from the kitchen. It was Thanksgiving. They already had the bird, and had to eat something.

While Bob Hinkle was off with neighbors, feeding and watering the animals in the Stumpf stables, his wife Terry and daughter Beth hovered in the kitchen doorway as Joe asked his questions. They'd self-consciously avoided staring at the dressing wrapping his head and that nasty black eye. It was all over the news, what had happened in New York last night, his name figuring prominently in many media accounts of those events.

Shortly after Dante started his questions, Charlie O'Roark was summoned to his car to take a call.

"Describe Sonny to me," he asked gently. "The big guy."

Brittany closed her eyes, the images more vivid for her that way. "He wasn't a Yankee. He talked like someone from south of here. Way south. I can't say where."

"And he had red hair?"

"Uh-huh. Cut the way a lotta jocks are wearin' it now. Y'know, like almost shaved on the sides and then real short on top? I forget what they call it."

"Did he do or say anything that struck you as odd? Something to help us get a handle on him? Who he is?"

She opened eyes bright with anger. "They murdered my mama and daddy. What do you call *that*?"

Joe took the brunt without trying to deflect it. He knew what fueled it. "Believe me, Brittany. I'm on your side more than anyone else in this world. I'm gonna get these guys for what they did." He leaned forward, keeping his voice subdued but earnest. "Think, please. Something he said to his partner, maybe?"

She closed her eyes again, brow knit, cheeks reddened from crying a day's worth of tears. "Wait a minute," she murmured. "He made a phone call."

Bingo. "When?" He tried not to sound as excited as he was.

"That's the strange part," she replied. "He waited till after that Julio guy left him alone with us. My mama, me, the wounded Spanish man, and the nurse. He didn't even do anything then. Not till the nurse fell asleep."

A call that Sonny didn't want the others to know about. To whom? Where? "The nurse fell asleep, and then what happened?" he prodded.

Brittany remained with her eyes closed, as if in a trance. "I don't think she even knew she did. I mean, she was just so tired, like. She put her head on her arms, and the minute Sonny knows she's nodded out, he stands up and goes over there to give her a little push with his knee, like."

"Where was the phone?" Joe asked.

"On a table near the bed. We were in one of the guest

rooms. He used a credit card, and said he couldn't talk long." She stopped, frowning. "Murray, I think he called him." She nodded. "Uh-huh. I'm positive. He said, 'Murray, m'man!' Then he started talking numbers, and the names of football teams."

Dante reached to touch her arm, stopping her. She opened her eyes. "Talking numbers how? As close as you can remember."

"Like, Bengals by four. Packers by three, fifteen hundred. Stuff like that. He had this folded piece of paper he was reading from. Kept it in his shirt pocket."

Dante's heart was pounding now. The damned fool had called his bookie.

The front door opened and Charlie O'Roark stepped back inside. "Sorry, Joe. I need to talk to you a minute." He had the collar of his coat turned up and glanced toward Mrs. Hinkle, reluctant to return to the cold. "Is there someplace private we could use?"

She led them to a den replete with buck heads and bowling trophies. With the door shut, O'Roark spoke as he paced, his voice hushed but excited. "We've gotten a break. Two of our guys in Miami were working undercover a year or so ago. They met a man we think is our Julio, at a party. At the house of a Cali cartel lieutenant in Kendall."

Dante's Miami geography was bad, but the pilot killed in last night's crash was based at some place called the Kendall-Tamiami Airport.

"He's the nephew of Lucho Esparza, no less," Charlie continued. "And get this. He was there at the party with a couple of football player buddies from college. The name Lyndon Sonny Reed mean anything to you?"

The guy's size, the accent, and the call he'd made to his bookie all fit. Sonny Reed was a consensus all-American linebacker from the University of Florida. The New York Giants had taken him in the first round of last spring's draft, and late last summer, after two solid preseason exhibition games, Reed was named in a point-shaving scandal. It was big news at the time: the Giants best hope to bolster the linebacking corps, bounced from the squad by the league office before he played a single regular season down.

"You bet it does," Dante replied. "And get this. He's still got the disease."

O'Roark looked confused. "What disease?"

Joe was idly inspecting a row of shotguns and deer rifles in a locked cabinet. "His gambling addiction. He made a call last night. To his bookie."

"He did what?"

It was Joe's turn to pace now. His knee twinged as he turned from the cabinet and took his first step. Through his progress across the room and back, he limped slightly. "It was something Brittany blocked out when she talked to the local bulls. She didn't realize what he was doing; only that he'd made a call using a credit card and talked to someone named Murray. All she heard were the names of NFL teams, and numbers."

"God*damn*," O'Roark marveled. "How dumb could he get?"

"He's got an addiction," Joe reminded him. "Which means he might call that bookie again."

O'Roark was animated. "This is beautiful. We locate this Murray from phone records. Set up on him, and wait for Reed to call again." He'd found a golf ball on a shelf and was tossing it. Now he stopped. "You understand, there's no way we can freeze the Feebs out on this. I run with it on my own, without telling Dyson, he'll have my nuts."

"How about, I never told you? I give it to Gus, let him run with it?"

"Sorry, Lou. No can do. There's got to be as many Murray the bookmakers in Miami as there are in New York.

Who knows where this guy's at? I sit on this now, it'll come back to bite me later."

Dante eased himself into a chair. "I guess you're right. What else do we know about Julio and Reed?"

O'Roark resumed tossing the golf ball. "We know Julio's last name is Mesa. He was expelled from the University of Florida when a coed accused him of attempted rape. The charges were dropped, but the Florida Department of Law Enforcement wants to talk to him about those rape murders they had in Gainesville a few years back. FDLE hasn't been able to find him."

"What about Lyndon Reed? Where's he been since August?"

"We're working on that. It's a holiday, it's late, and the information gathering goes slower than we'd like."

"His being in New York kinda suggests he might have stayed there, once the Giants let him go," Dante reasoned.

"If that's the case, maybe your Narco people can help."

Joe nodded, started to rub an itch beneath the bandage covering his forehead, and winced, wondering when he'd learn not to do that. "I need a few more minutes with the kid."

"Fine. You hungry?"

"Starving."

"When you finish up, there's a restaurant in town the sheriff recommends."

Barbara Jo Kelly was taking Teo Mendoza's blood pressure and checking his breathing with her stethoscope when Jim MacPhearson announced they were getting low on gas. Julio hadn't planned on the current turn of events and the IV drip was long exhausted. The Heimlich valve had functioned well, with very little fluid draining from the chest cavity any longer. The rattle Barbara heard now was not fluid from outside the lung, but inside; not a lot, but enough to cause concern. Julio hadn't stocked any antibiotics, either. Barbara was worried about infection and pneumonia.

"Find us an exit off this pike," Julio ordered Reed. "With something like a McDonald's."

A few minutes later, Reed got MacPhearson off the Blue Ridge Parkway and onto a road headed toward Roanoke, then only a dozen miles away. Once within view of the city's skyline, MacPhearson pulled off at an interchange among an array of tall, brightly lit signs. There was a Wendy's opposite a Texaco, where they turned in and pulled up to an outer pump island.

"I'm gonna stick out less than you are," Julio told Sonny. "Keep an eye on the rest of them while Mac here shows me the routine. Then I'll run across there and grab us a bag of food."

Reed tapped the face of his watch. "Ten minutes, it's the six o'clock news. Be a good idea, we give a look, see what they're sayin' 'bout us."

Julio focused on MacPhearson with his best don't-fuck-with-me stare. "Let's do it, pops. One wrong move, I squirt you with gas and flick my Bic. Show me how you fill this hog."

Barbara called forward to where Tillie sat. "I need a thermometer, Mrs. MacPhearson. You happen to have one somewhere?"

"In the medicine cabinet, dear. Above the commode."

Mesa stopped before opening the side door. "There a problem?"

"Maybe," Barbara replied. "He should have had a course of antibiotics by now. I hear a rattle in his lungs, and he feels like he's burning up."

Dante and O'Roark had a pleasant, surprisingly good meal at a place called Redfield's, a couple blocks off Queen Street in the heart of Martinsburg. Six o'clock was early for

Joe to be eating dinner, but the place was jammed with family groups, all feasting on the special Thanksgiving fare. That night, the turkey and trimmings could have been meatloaf for all he cared, but he was hungry and ate well.

Over coffee, O'Roark told Dante he was staying at the Sheraton, on King Street at the intersection with the interstate. He was sure they had vacancies, and knew they had a whirlpool. "Judging from how you're favoring that left wheel of yours, it might do you good to soak it awhile."

"Guess I have to sleep somewhere," Dante replied. They'd left it to the FBI to lean on the phone company for a record of the call made by Lyndon Reed. Gus Lieberman and O'Roark's second-in-command at the New York DEA office were digging up everything they could on Mesa and Reed. Until they called back, Joe and the SAC were stuck in a holding pattern. "But you don't know how itchy I am, Charlie. They're out there somewhere, less than a day's drive away. Mendoza's gotta be in bad shape. That has to be slowing them up."

O'Roark leaned back in his chair and slurped the last of the coffee in his cup. He replaced the cup in its saucer and nodded. "I think they're close too, Lou. I've been trying to figure where they would run." Their waiter set the check between them and O'Roark reached for it. "There are pockets of Colombians up and down the East Coast. The closest one to here is probably Washington."

"Then why didn't they cut over on I-70?" Joe countered. He pointed at the check. "We're gonna split that. Your guy saw both Julio and Sonny partying in Miami last year. They both went to the same school in Florida. My gut hunch says that's where they're headed. They know the players there, and they know the turf."

"But how? The state and local law threw out a net today over a two-hundred-mile radius. Roadblocks. Light plane and helicopter patrols. Probably close to a million bucks in holiday overtime pay, and they didn't find shit. Checked every rolling burgundy van in four states."

Joe almost rubbed his forehead again, catching himself in the nick of time, and realized how tired he was. "Then they've changed wheels again. Only this time they had to either hot-wire or hijack them."

"We're monitoring reports of thefts and missing persons," O'Roark replied. "So far we've turned up nothing even *slightly* suspicious."

"You take a hostage, there's no one to report a vehicle stolen," Joe reasoned. "You take the *right* hostage, there's no one to report *him* missing, either."

Twenty-four hours had passed since Teo Mendoza's last vivid recollection. His life had become a drug-obscured blur. He was in a van, after being moved from another somewhere in New York. He could recall killing the cop and the woman walking with him. After that, there was the transfer from that van to the next, and then everything went fuzzy. They'd hit him with something for his pain. Too much of it. Now, as he started to regain consciousness, his head was a jumble of confused dreams. It was dark outside the curtain he lifted, and he was moving. He was in a bed, not on a stretcher anymore. A clock on the paneled wall before him said seven-thirty. The nurse from the prison was still there, sitting at his side.

"¿Dónde está Lucho?" he murmured. It was hard getting his breath as he asked it. His mouth was parched. *"Tengo sed."*

"He's awake," the nurse announced. "What's he saying?"

Julio appeared at the nurse's side. "He wants to know where my uncle is, and says he's thirsty. Go get him some water."

The nurse rose to fetch a glass.

"The plane crashed," Julio told him. "In a snowstorm.

We're still in the States, *hermano*. Any sec now, we cross into North Carolina."

The nurse arrived with water, and Teo drank gratefully. He was in much more pain now than he'd been in last night. When she lowered the glass from his lips, he gasped and closed his eyes, absorbing what he'd just heard. When he opened them again, he reached for Julio, gripping his shirt.

"What this is?" He waved a hand at his surroundings.

"Motor home."

Teo looked puzzled.

"You know," Julio insisted. "An RV. *Coche.*"

"Ah. *Sí.*"

"He's got a fever of a hundred and three," the nurse reported. "Without antibiotics, we've got nothing to check it. Tomorrow we need to do something."

"Like what?" Julio demanded. There was a sneer in it. "Drop into the local emergency room? Ask if they can spare a penicillin IV drip? Maybe throw a couple bags of lactated Ringer's in, while they're at it?"

The nurse was undaunted. "That Heimlich valve? It's designed as a temporary measure. He needs hospitalization. Badly."

Julio barked a laugh and leaned close to her. "Well, he ain't gonna *get* hospitalization, sugar lips. Not till we get where we're going. And try to keep in mind, you ain't worth fuck-all to me if he don't get there alive."

Barbara continued to press her case. Teo's water glass was still in her hand and she had to fight the urge to break it over Mesa's head. "We can order the antibiotic from a pharmacy. Nobody has to know it's for him."

Julio laughed again. "Nice try. You want to pull a fast one, you'll need more imagination that that. What kind of fool you think I am?"

Barbara was angry, but it was her tone that provoked Mesa more than her words. She talked like she was reasoning with a simpleton. "We're talking antibiotics, not heroin, you asshole. I've phoned in enough prescriptions to know how a pharmacy will react. I tell them I'm calling for a doctor, from whatever town it is, and ask if they've got any Rocephin. I think it comes ten vials to a box. If they say yes, I tell them I'm sending my messenger over to pick it up."

Deep suspicion clouded Julio's glare. "You think I'll forget you called me an asshole? What's Rocephin?"

"A fast-acting, broad spectrum antibiotic. You inject it intramuscularly, one to two grams a day. Two, at first, for someone in his condition." She nodded toward Teo. "We've still got half a dozen disposable syringes left for the Demerol."

Mesa continued to regard her with wariness. "Don't you need some kinda doctor's license number or something?"

"A DEA control number, but only if the *substance* is controlled. Otherwise, they might ask for a phone number, but they almost never call back. Not if somebody who sounds like they know what they're talking about places the order."

Julio was no longer menacing, but his voice still carried an edge. "We try, and it doesn't work, you know what I'll do to you. You're dead meat."

"It doesn't work, *he's* dead meat. But it *will* work," she insisted. "You don't have any choice. You've got to trust me. Your friend will only get worse."

"I don't trust you no further than I can throw you." He turned back to Teo. "She says you're developing an infection, *hermano*. How you feel?"

"No more, this *stupido* drug you give me," Teo growled. "*Aguardiente*, Julio."

Julio turned toward Reed. "You find anything to drink in this crate, Jim?"

"Whole fuckin' liquor cabinet. What's your pleasure?"

"Anything licorice? Anisette, maybe?"

"Whole bottle of Sambuca."

"It'll do. Get it for me."

"Alcohol impedes the body's recovery processes," Barbara argued. "You can't let him drink."

"Fuckin'-A bet I can. *Aguardiente* ain't killed this bad boy yet, it ain't gonna kill him now."

TEN

Ellwell Crescent in Rego Park, Queens, was quiet, with draperies drawn and Thanksgiving turkey long put away by the time Lieutenant Jumbo Richardson and Captain Rosa Losada turned onto it off Alderton Street.

"I hear Al Dyson flew back up here from West Virginia," Rosa told Beasley. "Soon as he heard the call was made to the 718 area code."

It was 8:45 P.M., and they were en route to observe an FBI raid on the home of bookmaker Murray Glass. It was Glass whom Lyndon Reed had phoned from the Stumpf house using his AT&T calling card.

"Pretty predictable," Richardson growled. "Al wants bumped up to an assistant director's job in Washington so bad, he'd step on his own mother to bring Mendoza in. He does, it's gonna be hard for them t' keep him down. Nobody knows that better'n him."

Murray Glass was no stranger to NYPD's Public Morals Division. He'd been in their files for years, but neither they, nor the IRS, had ever been able to hit him with anything that stuck. Glass was careful, always keeping his runners and the cash they collected at arm's length. A federal judge had thrown the last charge against him out of court, and had ordered all monitoring of his phone lines to cease. It constituted harassment. But now all the rules had changed. Murray Glass had received a call from a fugitive wanted for homicide and interstate flight. His failure to report that contact could be construed as aiding and abetting. That was the charge the United States Attorney, Southern District of New York, would threaten to level against Glass should he fail to cooperate.

When the two cops rounded the crescent, they found the rendevouz point at the corner of Sixty-fourth Road empty. The reason why was a hundred yards farther up the block. There were a half dozen squad cars from the One-Ten and One-Twelve parked in the street, their light bars flashing. Another dozen unmarked cars jammed the crescent from one curb to the other, some with dash-mounted gumballs streaking the night red. The sidewalk and driveway outside one house on the northeast side of Ellwell were jammed with loitering law enforcement personnel.

"What the hell?" Richardson murmured. If he and Rosa hadn't rolled with their squawk box switched off, they would have been tipped to this. But there wasn't suppose to be any action. Not yet. They were all to rendevouz before the show started.

"That little snake made his move without waiting," Rosa concluded. "Why do I have this really bad feeling?"

Jumbo pointed to an ambulance, parked backward in the drive. "That got anything t' do with it?"

Dante limped toward the Jacuzzi alongside the indoor pool at the Sheraton Motor Inn when he experienced a sudden wave of dizziness. If there hadn't been a chaise nearby to fall into, he might have hit the deck. As it was, he dropped the beer he was carrying and nearly dropped his cellular phone. A minute later, the dizziness passed and he threw what remained of the spilled beer into the trash. Considering how he'd pushed himself that day, and the shape he was in, he supposed he shouldn't be drinking anyway.

It was quiet there in the pool area, with no other guests availing themselves of the facility that holiday night. He sat chin deep in the frothing whirlpool waters, his injured leg extended in front of one jet, while another jet worked on the tension between his shoulder blades. He'd taken another Tylenol with codeine before leaving his room, and the dull ache in his head was pushed into the distance for now. What he couldn't push from his mind were the stark, sharp-lined images of Janet's surprise as he dove for her, of the pained loathing in Skye Lake, and of the FBI pathologist scraping the inside of Audrey Stumpf's mouth.

"You awake?" It was Charlie O'Roark. He approached across the pool enclosure, dressed in jeans, a sweatshirt, and sneakers. "Just got another call from my office. We did some digging in both Florida and New York. The picture's coming clearer on Mesa and Reed."

Dante lifted a hand from the water to indicate a row of deck chairs. The SAC had two cans of beer and offered one.

"No, thanks. I *will* fall asleep. Fill me in."

Charlie dragged a chair over and sat. He popped the tab on one of the beers and took a pull, smacking his lips. "You remember any of the particulars about Reed? Why he was bounced from the Giants?"

"I remember it was big news when it happened. You lose your number one draft pick, it's bound to make people sit up. But, nuh-uh, not specifics."

"Beginning of his senior year at Florida, Reed got in deep to a bookmaker in Jacksonville. A group of rabid Gator boosters helped bail him out. Then the bookie was busted for something unrelated, and as part of his plea bargain, he spilled it that Sonny had bet heavily against the spread when his own team was favored."

"That's right. Point shaving."

"Yep. Those Gator boosters were called before a closed-door session of an NCAA investigative committee. We don't know what happened in there, but no sanctions were ever levied against their football program. We think one or more of them gave the committee everything they wanted."

"You mean, Reed's head on a platter."

O'Roark took another long pull, draining his beer, and nodded. "His NFL career was history."

"Where'd he go when the Giants dumped him?"

Charlie crushed the can in his hand and opened the next one. "That's what I'm hoping your narcotics division can help us with. My agents in New York are still checking with them." O'Roark eyed the pool across the way. "Now that I see all that sparkling blue water, it's hard to resist jumping in."

"You pack a suit?" Joe asked.

"I wish." Charlie stood, his expression wistful. "Maybe I'll check, see if the front desk can help me. You plan to be here long?"

"I'm outta here at *al dente*," Dante replied. "Maybe another half hour."

O'Roark started off in search of a swimsuit. "Maybe I'll see you, I have any luck. You hear anything, keep me posted."

The SAC was gone less than five minutes and Joe was just getting a good, meditative mull going of recent events when his phone, set on the pavement behind his head, chirped. He sat higher in the water and dried a hand before picking up. "Still alive, but not exactly kicking," he answered.

It was Beasley. "Dyson and his crew moved on Glass before our team was in place, Joey. When the man didn't answer his bell, they forced entry and found him with a hole in his head, right there on the entry hall floor. Corpse was barely cooled below body temp."

"Damn," Dante muttered. Another wave of dizziness washed over him, but this time it wasn't physical.

"There's another new development, too, Joey. Reed's got a girlfriend. According to a couple guys at Queens Narcotics, he's been livin' with her right here in Manhattan since the end of the summer."

"Why would they know?" Joe asked.

"Good question. They say she's this hostess at Dallas Direct. That fancy strip club, midtown. I guess she really likes her nose candy, and has lots of friends of like mind."

"You mean she deals?" Dante shifted in the water to get more comfortable, while taking care to keep the phone out of the soup. Dallas Direct, like a number of similar Manhattan establishments, was a new kind of skin club, which featured beautiful young topless hostesses and catered to a high-roller business clientele. From what Dante had heard, they had stage shows, but the hostesses didn't dance. Instead, for a reportedly handsome base wage and anything they made in tips, they worked the tables bare breasted. Touching them was out. They were objects to be admired from a distance.

"According to these Narco guys, Reed owed a couple hundred grand in gambling debts that Julio Mesa paid off. Mostly to this dude Glass. Sonny'd bought a Testarossa that was stolen, and his money was so tight he hadn't insured it."

"Jesus."

"I know. After the Giants bounced him, he was so deep in debt, him and his girlfriend went to work for Freddy Mendoza, to pay Julio back. Ounces, mostly, a couple keys at a time."

Dante thought about the implications of such an arrangement. "If Reed had that kind of gambling monkey, I'm surprised he didn't go *further* in the hole."

"Who says he didn't?" Beasley asked. "We need to find this girlfriend, Joey. Fast."

"And keep a lid on her, once you do. Reed calls his

bookie, he could try to call her too. She might be our inside line to him."

"That's what Rosa and me are thinkin'. There's a chance she might even know who he'll turn to next, t' take his action now that Glass got hisself whacked." Beasley paused and Joe heard a muffled exchange. "Hang on, Joey. Rosa wants t' say something."

Rosa sounded anxious when she came on the line. "Don't lie to me, Joe. How do you feel?"

"Tired," he replied. "Soon as I drag my sorry ass from this whirlpool, I'm gonna take it to bed, see if I can sleep."

"This Murray Glass homicide has given us all the creeps," she told him. "You know how cops hate coincidence."

"I doubt it is one," he growled. "No more shared information, Rosa. Not before we've had a chance to run with it first. I'm talking about Reed's girlfriend."

"We're leaving now to see if we can locate her," she replied. "Go to bed, Joe. Please."

Seventy miles of paralyzingly slow progress down the Blue Ridge Parkway beyond Roanoke, Julio Mesa's patience finally wore thin. The road, which was nearly five hundred miles long, followed the crest of the Blue Ridge mountains, often climbing to altitudes where a blanket of last night's snow covered the shoulder. Two lanes, with a speed limit of forty-five, it left Mesa feeling like a sitting duck. At Fancy Gap, near the North Carolina line, he blew.

"Fuck this tourist bullshit, Jim! Find us some way off this!"

Sonny eventually got them onto I-77 headed south, but not without difficulty. The parkway wasn't like a freeway, with regular on and off ramps. Two hours later, as they bypassed Charlotte and started southeast on I-85, Mesa wandered forward to kneel on the floor between Jim and Tillie MacPhearson. Since they'd hit the interstates, Jim had set the cruise control at sixty. Compared to the Blue Ridge, it felt like they were flying.

"How you holding up, Mac? Can't have you falling asleep at the wheel on us."

"The man is seventy-two years old!" Tillie snapped. "He's been behind that wheel for close to sixteen hours. How would you feel, buster?"

Julio reached to prod her ample, sagging bosom with the muzzle of his gun. He grinned without good nature. "I'd be dead-ass tired, Tillie. That's a fact. And that's why I'm asking. I thought we might start looking for a rest area, pull in and grab a few winks." He mimicked the inflections of his pal, Sonny, without much credibility. "That sit all right with you? Couple of geezers, out much later on the road, just ain't gonna look right." He turned to face Reed, still seated with his map. "How we doing, Jim?"

"South Carolina, any time now. Not much b'tween here an' Greenville. Somethin' called the Kings Mountain Military Park. Beats me what it is, but there's gotta be a rest stop somewhere along here."

Propped in bed, before turning out the light, Dante used the room phone to contact Gus via Operations. "I'm fine," he replied to Lieberman's initial inquiry. "Listen, Gus. I need to talk privately. What kinda line you on?"

"The phone in my car. I'm still at the Glass scene."

"No good. Find a land line somewhere. Call me back." Joe gave him the number.

"What's up, Joey?"

"Not on the phone, boss. Call me."

Ten minutes later Lieberman came back at him. He called from the detective squadroom of the One-Twelve, on Austin Avenue in Forest Hills. "So what's this bug you got up your ass?"

Dante had the TV on without sound, tuned to local news.

On-screen, they were showing taped footage of police at the Stumpf farm, a coroner's stretcher being wheeled out the front door, either Audrey or Donald Stumpf in a body bag. "Last night, when Mendoza knew right where to find me? It seemed like too big a coincidence. Now I'm sure of it."

"I'm with you there, hotshot. Seems pretty clear we've sprung a leak."

"We've had the Bureau, DEA, and our own people all over this from jump street, Gus. All three agencies had access to where I was last night. Same story now. All three knew who Sonny Reed called."

"And ain't any of them going away, neither," Gus grumbled. "The media's all over this like maggots on a corpse. You got an idea?"

Dante had been thinking about little else since Jumbo gave him the news about Glass. "Not yet, but how much more damage can we afford to sustain? Who else knows about Reed having a girlfriend?"

"Nobody but us and the deep-cover guys who delivered it. I instructed the Borough Narcotics Commands to report to Beasley directly."

There was a clip of Janet in her latest movie, playing on-screen now. As Joe listened to Gus, he forced himself to watch. "The minute you find out who she is, she's gotta have round-the-clock protection, boss. Reed's got the gambling disease bad. It ruined his career and put him to work for Freddy Mendoza, and now Lucho Esparza. Glass may be dead, but who says Reed won't go elsewhere with his action?"

"You wanna lean on the girlfriend, find out what she knows?"

"Just hard enough to spook her, but not enough to scare her off." The TV news went to a commercial and Joe hit the *off* button on the remote. "And keep it quiet, whatever you do."

"You got it, Joey. When you headed back?"

"Let's talk in the morning. Right now, I'm so tired I can hardly think straight."

That afternoon, Sonny Reed had stretched out in the back of the coach and finally got some decent rest. The trade-off was the first watch at the rest stop. He was now positioned up front in Tillie's seat while the others slept aft. The banquette in the galley folded down into a double bed and was occupied by the MacPhearsons. Julio had joined Teo and the nurse on the big bed in back.

Sonny still had no news of who'd won the day's NFL games. After making his call to Murray Glass that morning, he'd done some fine-tuning of his overall betting strategy. Now he needed to find another phone. As the digital dash clock marched one painfully slow minute to the next from eleven to midnight, Reed listened to the sounds of slumber behind him and stared outside into the moonlit night. The truck section of this roadside rest area, perched on a knoll above the south bank of the Broad River, had quite a few tenants that time of night. From where he sat, Sonny could see enough in the moon glow past trucks on either side of them to make out the water's edge, off to his right and below. This place reminded him of where he'd spent many boyhood summer days; a swimming hole in a creek not far from his home in Gray, Georgia. God, how he missed that time. He'd played both ways, linebacker and fullback, and made the all-State team twice. Everybody patted him on the back and wanted to be his buddy. Girls died for him to ask them out. He'd been a star.

Last summer, Sonny thought he was going to die after the phone call from his daddy. The message of that terse conversation had been simple. Sonny had disgraced his father and his whole family. All across the landscape of his life, the backslapping and glad-handing stopped. Sonny was sealed off from his former world, a bank vault door pushed shut in his face. If it hadn't been for his girlfriend, Bebe, and later, Julio, there wouldn't have been a soul in the world who cared if he lived or died.

Sonny had the rearview set where he could observe any movement behind him from the corner of his eye. He caught a shadow shifting and spun the swivel seat sideways to see Mesa slip soundlessly past the slumbering MacPhearsons.

"Where the fuck *you* goin'?" he snapped.

Julio held a finger to his lips and whispered. "Cooped up like this makes me stir-crazy, Jim. I need to get some air."

Sonny had watched the weather turn warmer as they progressed south. Julio wouldn't suffer too adversely, dressed in a turtleneck and sweater. "Try not to fall in the river, you decide to go that far."

"You okay here?" Mesa asked. "Can't have you falling asleep on me, Jim."

"I'm wanted for kidnapping in six states, murder in two, Bubba. I'm just peachy."

Dallas Direct's bar manager, Steve Lombard, had sent his two tenders home at ten that night and was working the duckboards himself. Likewise, the floor manager had let half his staff go home early. Thanksgiving was not a hot night in the titillation trade. The few guys at tables tonight, scattered thinly around the room, were the hard-core obsessives.

Lombard thought he had an eye for his clientele, but the couple who approached the bar a few minutes before midnight fooled him. A salt-and-pepper pair, she was a long, tall stunner—Brazilian, maybe?—and he, a nasty-looking heavy. Steve figured the guy for her pimp, but the threads made no sense. He was big and tough enough, but the suit was strictly off-the-rack. Their body language was definitely not master/meat. Lombard was still trying to figure them when the little leather cases came out.

"Captain Losada," the woman introduced herself. "This is Lieutenant Richardson."

Both hands planted palms down on the mahogany, Lombard's expression was wary. A few years younger, this captain could get work here in a minute. He wondered if she was some sort of vice cop, and if this was a roust. "What's the trouble, Officers?"

The captain removed a photograph on fax paper from her pocketbook and slid it at him. "You recognize this man?"

The picture was one of those press release shots that the professional sports teams circulate to the media. It pictured a crew-cut guy in a New York Giants jersey, crouched and looking formidable as only pro football players can. "Yeah, sure," Steve replied. "That's Sonny Reed. The girls haven't talked about much else around here." He shook his head. "Jesus. Did that jerk step in it or what?"

"The girls. You mean the hostesses?" the captain asked.

"You got it. Reed's been dating one of them for quite a while now. Close to six months."

"Who would that be?" the big lieutenant asked. He turned to scan the room.

"Bebe Masaryk. You've missed her by a couple hours."

"How's that?"

"It's Thanksgiving. Everyone's got a bad case of family values, night like this."

He saw the captain watching one of the other girls, Kristina, work a table where two suits tried to engage her in conversation. It is hard to come off suave when you are as tight as they were.

"How can we get in touch with her?" she asked.

Many of the girls who worked the tables and danced in the floor show, including the statuesque Colombian who the captain was watching, were into coke. Since she'd hooked up with Sonny Reed, Bebe Masaryk suddenly seemed to have access to an inexhaustible supply. She was running a nifty sideline business among her coworkers, and early on, Lombard had taken her to task about it. Then a couple of Colombians had paid him a visit. They wanted to make sure he had no problem with Bebe and her extracurricular activities. The fact was, Steve liked his legs the way they were, more than he wanted to fight for a drug-free workplace. He'd assured them of his willingness to look the other way.

"Sorry, Officers. There's a strict policy about revealing girl's addresses or phone numbers. A kind of sacred trust we share, y'know?"

The big black cop leaned closer. "We're the police, remember? This woman's boyfriend is wanted for multiple homicides. Or don't you watch the news?"

ELEVEN

It was 7:15 A.M. The last fuzzy vestiges of sleep pushed aside, Rosa Losada and Jumbo Richardson were sipping coffee across the street from Bebe Masaryk's building. Located on East Seventy-seventh Street, one address from the southwest corner of Lexington Avenue, the topless hostess's apartment was on the fourth of six floors, in the rear. The bar manager at Dallas Direct had described their subject as an immigrant from Prague, close to six feet tall, white-blond, and the biggest tip earner on the wait staff. Last night, before departing for her Upper West Side apartment, Rosa had contacted Chief Lieberman and requested a wiretap warrant.

"Gus called right before I left," Rosa reported. "A judge signed the warrant at four o'clock. By now, the wire should be hung." She nodded toward a laundry truck parked at the curb, around the corner on Lex. "That'll be our unit there."

Beasley sipped his coffee and considered their options. "Let's lean on her enough to scare her, but we don't want her t' panic. Reed's got another bookie, we want her t' call him, not burn her bridges."

"How long does she have to stay on the line for us to get a trace?"

He smiled. "You *have* been outta the loop awhile. Long as she's not smart enough to use a blocking code, they have instant access to calling numbers now. Even if she is, we'll grab the number right as she dials."

It was a rare work night when Bebe Masaryk got home as early as ten-thirty. Last night she'd taken full advantage, jumped into a cab outside the club, gone straight to her apartment, and climbed into her tub. There, with a glass of wine and a couple of lines, she'd watched the eleven o'clock news. They were saying Sonny and Julio had raped a woman and killed her and her husband outside a town in West Virginia. She'd heard about the plane crash earlier and had no idea where they were going now, but was sure it wasn't Sonny who'd committed that rape. The only thing that bothered her about the idea of joining Sonny in Colombia was that Julio would be there too. But at least their drug supply would be assured there, while here it dwindled rapidly. She was already rationing herself.

Bebe had finally crawled into bed and was deep in a dreamless sleep when a pounding at her front door woke her. She opened her eyes to see daylight leak in past her bedroom shades. When the hammering persisted, she gave up trying to ignore it, threw back the bedclothes, and swung her long legs over to plant her feet. The bedside clock read 7:35.

"Bastard!" she seethed. Crossing the room, she snatched her robe from the hook on the back of the bathroom door. She was knotting the sash with one hand when she jerked open the front door, ready to rip someone's head off. "What this is!" she snarled. "Who you think you are?"

"Ms. Bebe Masaryk?"

She was confronted by a large black man in a suit and tie and a very pretty, raven-haired woman. It was the black man who asked her name, a capable-looking specimen with a tough, broad face. The woman wore slacks, a sweater and jacket, and as Bebe looked at her, a small leather case fell open to reveal a gold police badge. The man had one too.

"I'm Lieutenant Richardson and this is Captain Losada," he introduced them. "Looks like we woke you, Ms. Masaryk. I'm sorry."

"What do you want?" she demanded.

"We want to talk to you," the lady captain replied. "May we come in?"

For an instant Bebe feared she'd left her hand mirror, dusted with cocaine, on a lamp table in the living room. Then she recalled carrying it into her bedroom before turning in. "You have—what is it called?—the warrant?"

"We only want to talk," the captain pressed. "It's no secret that you and Sonny Reed are close. Or that he is in a lot of trouble right now."

Bebe started to ease the door shut. "Sorry. I cannot help."

The black man planted a palm on the panel, stopping her. "You came here to go to NYU on a student visa. I'll bet you ain't been to a class all semester. Want us to call the registrar?"

Bebe stepped back and the lieutenant eased the panel inward. He waited for the captain to enter first, then followed.

"Nice place," he commented. "For a college kid."

"You know what I do," she growled. "Say what you want."

"Has Sonny tried to contact you since Wednesday night?" Captain Losada asked.

Bebe shook her head. "I hear nothing. I have not seen him since Sunday."

"But he lives here, doesn't he?" It was Lieutenant Richardson now, alternating with the captain.

She shrugged. "Maybe sometime. He spends a night, you know?"

"But not since Sunday," the black man pressed.

Bebe tugged her robe tighter around her and dropped into an armchair, fumbling for a cigarette and her lighter. The policewoman stepped back in.

"Did you know that someone killed his bookie last night? Murray Glass?"

Bebe felt surprise cross her face before she could catch herself. "No." She said it too quickly. "I've never heard of him."

"Sure you haven't." The black man reached into an inside jacket pocket and produced a card. "If you do happen to hear from Sonny, we'd appreciate a call." He looked her over with slow purpose. Her robe was a slinky satin, the thin fabric revealing as much as it hid. "Nice place you work, Ms. Masaryk. You must make a bundle in a place like that. The IRS might be just as interested in you as Immigration."

The fugitives and their hostages left the rest area at dawn to start south again on the interstate. They'd been on the road for a little more than an hour when Barbara Jo Kelly got adamant. She was seated in the back of the motor home, on the edge of the bed alongside the pale and sweating Teo Mendoza. Overnight, the wounded man's temperature had risen to a hundred and four. The hole in the lung tissue itself had sealed, but the entry wound made by the knife through muscle tissue and between his ribs was an ugly, inflamed red. Thus compromised, Mendoza showed signs of developing pneumonia. He'd consumed an entire bottle of Sambuca last night, which hadn't helped matters. His blood pressure was the only good news. It held steady.

"Listen to me, goddammit!" She held the thermometer up for Julio's inspection. "You can't wait anymore. He needs antibiotics *now*."

Instead of confronting her, Mesa stared out a side window at the landscape. They were bypassing Greenville, with its graphic evidence of the region's recent prosperity. Heavy machinery carved up the surrounding red earth at every turn. They'd just passed a huge new BMW plant, and now Julio looked out on Michelin's North American headquarters. He asked himself why his uncle had to care so much about this peasant orphan, a man who wasn't even blood. Anyone other than Teo, Julio would be content to let nature take its course and cut his losses. With Teo, he didn't have that choice. "He dies, you're dead," he murmured.

"Then why not just shoot me now?" Barbara snapped. "I'm telling you, he *will* die if you don't do something for him soon."

Julio tore his eyes from the landscape and turned to Reed. "What say, Jim? You think we could find us a drugstore, somewhere off the beaten path? The kinda place a local boy like you might blend in?"

To Barbara, it looked like Sonny could barely keep his eyes open. Mesa must have left him with the guard duty all night. Sonny had the map spread on his lap again, a coffee cup clutched in one thick-fingered mitt.

"I was thinkin', we should try 'n avoid Atlanta anyway," he replied. "On account a' what we heard on the news last night. The heat won't be so hot, I don't think, we drop south, here, at Commerce." He traced a theoretical route with a forefinger. "Head straight on down t' Macon, takin' secondary roads."

Mesa faced Barbara again, thoughtful, as he continued to speak to Sonny. "There'd be a drugstore somewhere along that route, you think?"

"Oh, sure. Gotta pass right through Athens. That's Georgia Bulldog country. Big university town like that's gotta have somethin'."

Julio jabbed a finger at Barbara. "You pull any shit, I'll be right there. And remember, you jerk me off, I'll kill you."

At eight o'clock Friday morning, Joe Dante didn't feel much better than when he went to bed ten hours earlier. Not as dog-tired maybe, but in every bit as much pain. Dressed in a T-shirt and a pair of gym shorts still damp from his previous soak, he limped to the elevator and rode downstairs to the whirlpool, grabbing a cup of coffee from the lobby en route. Thankfully, his phone didn't ring until he'd been immersed for close to an hour. By then, two Tylenol with codeine were starting to kick in. When the phone did ring, it was Charlie O'Roark.

"Where are you? I tried your room."

"In soak mode. Trying to loosen up enough to move. What's up?"

"I'm on my way back to New York. What are your plans?"

Joe flexed his left knee. It felt better than it had when he first climbed out of the sack. "Can't say. I need to call Gus, see what Narco division's managed to turn up for us on Mesa. After that, I don't know. I'm still thinking about it."

O'Roark told him to be in touch. At half past nine, Joe straggled into the Sheraton coffee shop. No sooner had he ordered breakfast than Gus called.

"Thought you would have checked in with me by now," Lieberman complained.

"Funny thing about getting hit in the head, boss. I'm moving a step or two slower than usual. Got a late start."

"Where you at?"

"You're the second guy who's asked me that today. I'm at breakfast. When O'Roark called, I was still in the whirlpool."

"I just heard from him, somewhere over Pennsyvlania. He's headed home. Wanted to know what luck we've had with Narcotics."

"What did you tell him?"

"That Rosa and Beasley are riding them hard, but so far they've come up with nothin' new. We talked about the Glass homicide. Nothin' useful there, either."

The waitress brought Joe's bacon and eggs. He pierced a yolk with his fork and tore a piece of toast to dip it. "I've decided to keep heading south, Gus. Soon as I check out. Call it another one of my hunches, but I think they're headed for Florida."

"There's pockets of Colombians all up and down the East Coast," Lieberman countered. "They could be headed anywhere."

At the surrounding tables, at least half the diners looked like snowbirds to Joe: people headed south to escape winter's chill. Judging from the cars packed with luggage he'd seen yesterday on I-81, it was a main conduit for this annual migration. "A DEA deep-cover guy saw Mesa and Reed partying in Miami last year. Both of them went to school in Florida. It's the turf they know, Gus. I'm gonna roll the dice." He heard his old friend sigh.

"I think you're nuts, as beat-up as you are."

Joe nibbled a piece of bacon. "The whole world's gone mad, boss. Why buck a trend? I need to think about conserving my phone batteries, but I'll leave it switched to *roam* the first quarter of every hour."

"Tell the truth. How you feel today?"

"After my nice long soak in the whirlpool? Now I feel like *warmed over* shit."

TWELVE

For the increasingly anxious Barbara Jo Kelly, the journey south from I-85 to Athens was uneventful but maddeningly slow. She was at war within herself, half of her demanding to know why she even cared about saving the wounded killer's life when Julio would certainly take hers anyway. The other half insisted that if she could buy more time, there was a chance of deliverance. The pessimist in her called the optimist a sucker. Neither side knew where her captors were going, other than south. The stress of her ordeal was making her light-headed, almost giddy. That giddiness contradicted Barbara's physical exhaustion. Her mind was afloat while her limbs felt leaden. Even if an opening to escape developed, she wondered if she'd have the presence of mind or the energy to take advantage of it.

Route 129 was two lanes wide. Five miles along it, the motor home got stuck behind an old pickup loaded with firewood. It took them nearly an hour to travel twenty miles through the Georgia backcountry, all scrub pine and red clay. When they finally reached the Athens campus of the University of Georgia, they found it a virtual ghost town, with most students away for the holiday weekend. There, Julio used a campus directory board to learn the whereabouts of the health center, and then had Jim MacPhearson park out front of the clinic while he wandered inside to learn which physicians were on duty. When he returned, he looked pleased with himself, carrying a bundle under one arm. He tossed it to Sonny.

"There's only one doctor, this being a holiday weekend and all. His name's Milton Rainford." He pointed to the white garment, now unfolded in Reed's hands. "Try that on, see if it fits. It's the biggest I could find."

Sonny shrugged into the lab coat and tugged it closed as Mesa turned to Barbara. "It's your play now. I hope to hell you're ready."

All Barbara could do was nod. That lab coat was a size too small for Reed and he looked like somebody's pet gorilla in it.

The main east-west drag through campus was Broad Street. West of the university it widened to traverse an area of strip malls and fast-food restaurants. Sonny was the first to spot the big new Kroeger's supermarket, complete with deli-bakery, restaurant, pharmacy, and First American bank, all under one roof. In its parking lot, Reed kept watch on Jim and Tillie in the RV while Barbara and Mesa crossed to a row of pay phones outside the supermarket entrance. None of the three phones was engaged, and as Julio pressed a slip of paper and a quarter into Barbara's hand, he leaned close to whisper, "The health center's number. Don't fuck this up."

Barbara called information to get the number of the pharmacy inside the Kroeger's The woman she reached there had a pleasant but crisp manner. Barbara had grown so accustomed to Reed's slower-than-winter-molasses speech, she'd started to assume everyone down here spoke that way.

"Hi. I'm calling for Dr. Milton Rainford? Over here at the campus health clinic?" She didn't mean for it to come out with questions on the end of each phrase, but was letting her nervousness get the better of her. She made a conscious effort to control it. "We're down to our last vial of Rocephin and need a box. Can you help us?"

The pharmacist put her on hold while she checked. Julio didn't look as cocky now as when he'd returned to the motor home with that stolen lab coat. He was out in the open here, and seemed almost to vibrate with anxiety.

"I do have a box," the pharmacist reported. "Of the one-gram vials. Y'all want them sent over?"

"I've got a man here, ready to jump in his car," Barbara replied. "We need more sodium chloride, too, to mix the injections. With the holiday and all, I'm afraid there's no one here to cut us a check. You want, we can pay cash."

"No problem. I'll put it on your account. Send your fella right over."

As Barbara hung up, she gave Julio her best smug look, hoping he couldn't tell how fast her heart was beating. "See? She didn't even ask for a phone number."

Ever since learning on the morning radio news that he'd won his Dallas-Detroit bet, Sonny Reed had been preoccupied with getting in touch with Murray Glass. He was on a mini-roll, and could feel his luck starting to change. If he let his winnings ride, he could fatten them up with his Sunday NFL wagers, and finally get into that groove he knew was out there. When he stepped up to the pharmacy counter, a quarter hour after Barbara Jo Kelly made her call, and the businesslike woman told him it would be a few minutes, he started to look for a phone.

There was a fast-food eatery off to one side of the pharmacy, and as Sonny scanned it he spotted what he needed, on the back wall. It looked like everyone in town was at home, with plenty of leftover turkey. The restaurant was deserted. He had the place to himself as he dug into his back pocket for his wallet and phone card.

Murray Glass's number in New York rang half a dozen

times before an unfamiliar voice picked up. "Murray Glass. Hold, please."

That was strange. Eleven-fifteen wasn't early. Murray always answered his own phone, and had more call forwarding and line switchover capacity than most mid-size corporations. "What the fuck is this?" he murmured. He knew he was rubbed raw with paranoia about now, but this was bogus. A deep sense of foreboding gripped him as he stood there waiting. After fifteen seconds he depressed the cutoff flap. When he got a dial tone again, he punched in another number, this time remembering to key in the three-button *call-restrict* code. Using it, he blocked any instant access to the number from which he was calling.

When her phone rang at eleven-twenty, Bebe Masaryk was back in bed but wide awake. It was early for any of her drug customers to be calling, and she considered letting her machine pick up. Then again, the cops were on to her about Sonny, and could be listening. She needed to talk to those customers, tell them not to call, and not to leave messages. She rolled over and grabbed the receiver on the third ring.

"It's me." Sonny's voice was hushed, almost a stage whisper. "Call Murray for me, baby. Find out what the fuck's goin' on. I just called over there. Some stranger put me on hold."

"We cannot talk, Sonny. The police, they maybe are listening."

"What?"

"Murray is dead. Somebody shoots him last night."

She heard a grunt. "Fuck. He owes me money." He paused. "Do me a favor then. Call Boone."

"Please, Sonny. We cannot talk."

"Just call him, goddammit! Tell him I got some plays I need t' make. Then get the number off a pay phone, somewhere I can call y'all."

"I try, Sonny. But—" The line went dead.

Bebe removed the receiver from her ear, stared at it, then replaced it slowly before opening the drawer of her nightstand to haul out her stash. She thought about Prague, about jumping on a plane. Then she weighed that option against the little pile of sparkling white powder dumped onto her hand mirror. If she ran, where would she be tomorrow? She would be left dry, but not at all high. No, she would wait until Sonny called her to join him. He'd sworn to her that his friends would be grateful for whatever he was helping them do; that their world would be his oyster, and hers too.

"No good." The Intelligence Division's Investigative Support Section technician shook his head and pulled off his headset. Still hunched over the electronic equipment crammed into the laundry van, he glanced in Rosa's direction. "Sorry, Cap. He used the call-restrict code to block us. All I could get was the area code."

"*What* area code?" Rosa had a code map and list spread before her.

"Seven-oh-six."

She found it on the list and then on the map. "It's somewhere in north-central Georgia. Let me hear it again. Sounds like he's looking to connect with his backup bookie."

The technician hit a button. "Yep. What it sounded like to me too. Somebody named Boone."

Rosa reached for the phone on her left. "I'll give OCCB a call, see if Public Morals has anybody by that name in their files."

Fearful for her own safety, the pharmacist waited until the big redhead disappeared out the front door of the store before she raced to a rack of newspapers near the checkout. The guy was young enough to be a student, but that lab coat was at least a size too small. The media had published pictures of the fugitives from that prison break in New York, Wednesday night, and of the nurse they'd kidnapped. It seemed crazy that they could be in Athens, but she knew the moment she looked at a paper that she'd just seen the man identified as Lyndon "Sonny" Reed.

"Call the police!" She yelled it to a nearby checker, then ran for the supermarket doors.

Business was slow and the parking lot outside the Kroeger's had fewer than two dozen cars in it. None were moving, and none were occupied. The pharmacist searched up past the supermarket toward Alps Road and saw eight vehicles idling in a line at the Broad Street intersection. When the light changed, they started to move: a pickup, three small foreign cars, something big like a Cadillac or Lincoln, a motor home, a Ford Taurus station wagon, and a minivan. Not one moved as if its driver was running from anything, and she began to doubt what she thought she'd seen.

Twice in the last twenty minutes, Dante had been warned by truckers that Smokey was lurking in the bushes ahead. He'd left Martinsburg at 10:15 with an estimated four hours between him and Charlotte, North Carolina, moving at roughly ninety M.P.H. He'd traveled close to a hundred and thirty miles and just switched his phone back to *roam* again when Gus Lieberman called at 12:03.

"Where are you?" the chief asked.

"Fifty miles short of Roanoke. Why? What's up?"

"Sonny Reed called his girlfriend, trying to reach his bookie—from an area code somewhere in north Georgia. Less than fifteen minutes later the Georgia State Police received a pretty credible sighting report. From a pharmacist in Athens. She'd been scammed for an antibiotic prescription, and claims she recognized Reed as the guy who picked it up."

Dante ran his road map past his mind's eye, gave up, and

pulled onto the shoulder. With the map spread across the steering wheel, he found Athens off Interstate 85, maybe an hour east of Atlanta. "I guessed right, didn't I? They're on a beeline for Florida."

"And Mendoza prob'ly ain't in very good shape. No other reason for them t' pull a risky stunt like that."

Joe shifted his phone to wedge it against his chin. God, his head hurt. "Any chance this pharmacist saw what they're driving?"

"Negative. Claims she checked the parking lot, but I guess they were outta there."

Joe studied the roads leading out of Athens. "What about roadblocks, Gus? The main road headed south, at least so far as I-20, is only two lanes. Their straightest shot is down 129 to I-75 at Macon."

"Reed's from around there, Joey. His hometown's Gray, fifteen miles north a' Macon. He'll know all the back roads."

"What about aerial surveillance? An area sweep?"

"Lookin' for what?"

"Any car or van with out-of-state plates. Athens looks like it's in the middle of nowhere. They could draw a fifty-mile radius and throw a net over the whole area."

"There's a million cars down there with outta-state plates, Joey. And it's Dyson's call. The Air National Guard scrambled a trainer out of Stewart to fly him down there."

Dante swung back into traffic, accelerating diagonally across the interstate to start eating miles again. "You get anything useful from Reed's call?"

"A name. Rosa thinks it's another book Sonny uses. She's checking it with files at OCCB."

"We're on them now, Gus. I can smell it. I'll leave the phone switched on, so keep me posted."

He heard Gus grunt. "Shit. You're a day's drive away."

Dante glanced at his speedometer, the needle pegged at ninety-eight. "Not the way I'm moving, I ain't."

The feeling of exposure Julio Mesa had experienced, standing outside the Kroeger's pay phones with Barbara Jo Kelly, had spooked him. The idea of driving another eighty miles to Macon over a two-lane road was suddenly anathema to him. A big, lumbering beast like the Sunflyer motor home would be a sitting duck; easy pickings for any cracker sheriff who saw New York plates and decided to pull them over, just for fun. Julio wanted off the two-lane and back onto the interstate as fast as possible. The quickest route was to retrace their steps back to Commerce, going north. Sonny thought he was crazy, but Julio was vehement, and Julio was in command, crazy or not.

Ninety minutes later, having bypassed Atlanta and merged with I-75, they ran into the second roadblock of their trip. Traffic, at twenty minutes past one, was light. Julio was in the back with Barbara, monitoring Teo's condition an hour after she'd given him his first Rocephin injection. Sonny Reed was slumbering on the banquette, the radio tuned low to a local country station so they could keep an ear out for news bulletins. Jim and Tillie were riding quietly in their seats when Jim suddenly braked.

Sonny's reflexes were surprisingly quick for a man dead asleep. He was wide awake and off the banquette before Julio could rise from the bed. On his knees between the MacPhearsons, he peered out through the windscreen. "Cops! Whole shitload a' them." His left hand touched Jim's elbow. "Easy, ol' timer. Slow an' steady, just like yesterday. You're a coupla retirees, headed for Florida, as loose and relaxed as Sansabelt slacks."

Behind Reed, Julio scrambled on hands and knees to the galley cabinet where they'd stored the Uzi and ammunition. He worked the action of the gun, then stuffed an extra clip into his waistband. Easing up behind Sonny, he threw a quick glance back at Barbara. "On the fucking floor, bitch! Looks like someone in that supermarket recognized you, Jim."

Sonny had his own Intratec machine pistol in hand, two extra clips on the deck in front of him. He studied the state police cars, parked on both verges. This time, rather than scan cars in all the lanes as they passed, they sought to funnel the traffic into a single lane past a group of lawmen in a cluster. Several of them were armed with twelve-gauge pump guns.

Julio nodded toward their driver, addressing Reed. "If Mac here tries to John Wayne it, I'll shoot him and you jerk him the fuck outta there. While I grab the wheel, you open up right through the skin of this crate. The way they're standing, all knotted up, I bet you can get most of them with your first burst."

Sonny rolled his eyes. "Sure I will," he muttered.

After an hour trip in a jet trainer, New York agent-in-charge Alan Dyson had gone back up in an FBI helicopter to scour the Georgia pinelands. Four hours after the pharmacist in Athens reported seeing Lyndon Reed at her drug counter, Dyson had his pilot set him down again at Atlanta's Hartsfield Airport. When his feet hit the tarmac, he saw Charlie O'Roark start toward him from a nearby parked car.

"How long you been here, Charles?" Dyson found it hard to keep displeasure out of his voice.

"An hour or so. Been monitoring reports from the road-blocks. No luck, huh?"

Dyson refused to honor the observation with any comment. "*Why* are you here, Charles?"

O'Roark stared off toward the south horizon. "There's a nasty rumor a few boys from the Cali cartel's New York operation passed this way a couple hours back. Thought I'd come down, watch you bloodhounds work." A jetliner took off, its roar deafening. A moment later, Charlie continued. "And by the way, just so you know, in the interest of interagency cooperation and all. We've sent an advisory to all hospitals in the Broward and Dade areas. That drug they purchased in Athens is a broad spectrum, fast-acting antibiotic. Mendoza must be in bad shape."

Dyson shifted with impatience from one foot to the other. "*You've* sent an advisory?"

O'Roark nodded. "Not that it'll do any good. They'll seek treatment inside the Colombian community, once they get down there."

"And meanwhile, Miami's still a long way off, Charles. More than six hundred miles. They haven't gotten there yet."

O'Roark watched a tractor towing a string of baggage carts as it raced past. "My parents make the drive from Yonkers to Captiva in two days, Al. They're both in their seventies. If you miss Mendoza here, how long you think it'll take them to get there?"

THIRTEEN

At four o'clock, with the sun just an hour from plunging behind the Great Smoky Mountains, Joe Dante hurtled past Fair Play, South Carolina. He was only a few miles from the Georgia border now. By heeding trucker's CB warnings, and then using bursts of speed, he'd managed to average ninety M.P.H. throughout the 180-mile stretch between Roanoke and Charlotte. It was time to call Gus for an update.

Joe had his cellular handset in his lap to speed dial Lieberman's office number when he spotted a green Buick parked along the freeway ramp he'd just shot past. The car started down the ramp, blue dash light flashing, as Captain Frank Bryce came on the line.

"Hi, Frank. Dante. Gus might have to clear up a problem I'm gonna have with local enforcement down here."

"That you're *gonna* have?" Bryce replied. "What kinda problem, Joe?"

"There's an unmarked on my ass. No bleep on my radar detector, but I went past him doing ninety-seven."

"Where?"

"Maybe five miles from the Georgia line, on I-85. Just past the exit to someplace called Fair Play."

"Poetic."

"Yeah. I've gotta deal with this. See what you can do."

Rather than provoke a roadblock at the state line, Joe took his foot out of it and let the pursuit close. As they pulled within several car lengths, he eased over onto the shoulder and rolled to a stop. But instead of pulling up behind him, the unmarked went past to cut in diagonally, skidding to a stop just feet from his front bumper, to block his way.

Something wasn't right. There were two men in the unmarked, unusual for cops pulling speed-trap duty. Standard operating procedure was to approach a stopped vehicle from the rear, where the officer could observe a vehicle's occupants and anticipate potential trouble. This kind of cutoff was strictly TV stuff. Dante hadn't been stopped by cops, and knew it.

Before his pursuit could come to a complete stop, Joe reached for the shift lever, shoved it into reverse, and got his tires smoking. The 300ZX—the most stolen car on the eastern seaboard—shot backward twenty yards before he hit the brakes, spun the wheel hard, and brought the car around with the trunk half buried in a kudzu-choked thicket. At the same time he reached for the door handle, Joe triggered his belt release and grabbed his Walther from the passenger seat. With the door open just enough to allow exit, he rolled out and scrambled at a limping crouch into the woods.

Running footsteps could be heard as Joe dove into the kudzu behind his car. On his belly, gun extended out in front of him in both fists, he watched two men come on fast around the front bumper, brandishing automatics. Both were angry and agitated as they looked right and left.

"Where the fuck'd he go?" one yelled. Short and heavyset, with a beer gut hanging over his belt, he had a Marine Corps emblem tattooed on one forearm and a crew-cut. His partner was taller and raw-boned, with a moth-eaten little mustache and greasy blond hair tied back in a ponytail. Dante drew a bead on them.

"Freeze!" he yelled. "You move, I'll blow your nuts off!"

The shorter man whirled and fired blindly into the woods, the round going six feet too high. Unwilling to risk hitting a passing car, Joe held fire as the gunman started forward. The fat little cracker seemed convinced that a failure to return fire meant his quarry was unarmed.

"Keys in it?" he asked as he advanced. His brow was knit as he squinted, trying to penetrate the thick kudzu growth. He was within three feet of Dante, and still coming, when his partner replied.

"Nuh-uh. Fucker took'm wit'm."

Joe waited. When the crew cut was almost stepping on him, he reached up and jammed the muzzle of his pistol hard into the man's crotch. His opponent's gun hand dropped, and Dante latched on to the weapon with an iron grip, wrenching it free.

"Tell your pal to be smart," he growled.

"L-L-Lester," the squat man stammered. A wet stain appeared in the blue jean fabric around the P-5's muzzle.

The rangy man hurried over. "Ya find'm, Billy?"

"He sure did." Joe came to his feet, his captive's weapon aimed at the slender man's belly as he emerged from the thicket. "If you wanna crap into a little bag the rest of your life, go ahead and try me."

The taller man absorbed the specter of Dante, one eye blackened and his head wrapped in bandages, and slowly extended his gun hand to set his weapon on the roof of Joe's car.

"Good. Now reach inside the car and get my handcuffs from the glove box."

As he herded his two captives back up the freeway shoulder toward their Buick, Joe wondered why there was never a cop around when you needed one. If passing motorists thought there was anything strange about one man prodding two others along the roadside at gunpoint, nobody bothered to brake and rubberneck. It might have meant getting involved.

"What're y'all gonna do t' us?" They'd reached the Buick and there was fear in Lester's voice.

"Open the driver's door," Joe directed. "The key in it?"

Lester nodded and did as he was instructed. Then Dante backed him and the other man off a pace, reached inside the car to switch on the ignition, and ran the window down. He looped the cuffs around the top of the door frame, ran the window back up until the cuff chain was pinched by it, and tugged to make sure the bracelets were held there securely. He removed the keys from the ignition, pushed the automatic door lock button, and slammed the door closed. Both cuffs now dangled outside the car.

"Step on up and clamp yourselves on, boys. One per customer."

"C'mon," Billy whined. "Y'all're gonna *leave* us out here?"

Dante turned and flung the Buick's keys into the kudzu. "You bet. Doors locked, windows up, fake cop car light on the dash and who knows what else you've got in there. Damn straight that's what I'm gonna do."

He turned and limped back toward his car. After six straight hours behind the wheel, it felt good to stretch his bad leg.

Gus Lieberman was seated at his desk, the shadows grown long over the East River outside his window, when Frank Bryce put Dante's call through. The chief had cut down to just five cigarettes a day and had one going now. It was his third, his late afternoon butt, and already he was thinking about his fourth. That would be his Scotch on the rocks butt.

"What the hell's goin' on down there, Joey? I just talked to the South Carolina State Police. They tell me neither them nor the local county bulls got any cars in that area."

"Call them back once we've finished here, boss. Let them know they've got a couple impersonators outside Fair Play, cuffed to a dark green Buick."

"Jesus. What happened?"

"I just thank God for kudzu."

"Say what?"

"Never mind. I think Mesa and Reed will spend the night in Gainesville, Gus. At least that's my bet. I'm gonna drive straight through."

Dante had been driving at breakneck speed all day, and his mental processes were in the same fast-lane mode. "Slow down, Joey," Gus begged. "How do you figure Gainesville?"

"They've stopped somewhere every night," Joe theorized. "Mendoza probably needs the rest."

"Okay."

"They can't make it to Miami tonight, at least I don't think they can, the rate they've been moving. That pharmacist spotted Reed in Athens at eleven, right?"

"Eleven-fifteen, and she made him wait." Lieberman had smoked his Carlton down to the filter. He butted it. "Man made a call from a pay phone there, which Rosa and the wiretap team intercepted. To his girlfriend, made at eleven-twenty."

"It took them a day and a half to run there from Martinsburg, Gus. That's only five hundred forty miles. Something's slowing them up."

Gus saw his point. "If I was wanted for ten homicides and counting, I'd want t' keep it under the speed limit. Take a few back roads. Today they beat a blanket aerial surveillance and a dozen strategically placed roadblocks."

"I'm betting Gainesville because both Mesa and Reed know it, Gus. It's where they went to school, and it's still another four hundred miles south of Athens. At their current pace, they'd pull in sometime late evening. Whether they take I-75, Route 129, *or* Route 441, they all converge there. It's a straight shot."

Lieberman did a quick calculation. If the fugitives averaged fifty M.P.H., it would take them eight hours to reach Gainesville from Athens. That would get them there around eight tonight. "Shit, the rate you're rolling, you'll almost arrive in a dead heat."

"That's what I'm thinking. Do me a favor?"

"Whatever I can."

"See what you can get on Reed's gambling scandal. Their names, if any other players were involved. And find out what the FDLE and Gainesville police have on Mesa. Why they want to question him about those rape murders."

Four hours after Barbara Jo Kelly injected Teo Mendoza with two grams of Rocephin, the wounded man's condition was not much improved. His lungs rattled with each labored breath. His body temperature was down a degree, but still hovered at the hundred and three mark. He sweated profusely, and Barbara Jo was concerned about dehydration. He was delirious and she could no longer coax him to drink. It was getting dark outside the motor home as Barbara Jo stood to approach Julio where he lounged alongside Sonny in the galley.

"If you don't get your friend to someplace quiet soon, you're going to kill him," she announced. "He can't get any real rest with all this constant motion."

Mesa looked up at her, his eyes red and glassy. He and Sonny had just done more coke. They'd done more this afternoon since the roadblock than they had all yesterday, and it worried her. She knew how the drug could cause radical mood swings.

"What do you think, Jim? A little whiff might loosen her up?"

"I'm serious! If you won't take him to a hospital, at least you can find him a night's peace and quiet."

Mesa turned, as cold as an old woman's feet. "We'll be in Miami tomorrow. He'll live until then."

"I wouldn't bet on it." She stepped past Julio to Sonny. "Talk sense to him," she pleaded. "What's the purpose of what you've done, if you deliver a dead man?"

Sonny spooned a little pile from the bag to his nose, sniffed quickly, and wiped his nostrils with thumb and forefinger. "She's got a point, Bubba. I can think a' one place I wouldn't mind stoppin'. Big house. Nice big barn we could hide this rig in too."

Julio's skepticism was pushed aside by the grin that slowly lit his face. "This ain't got anything to do with a certain score you'd like to settle? Would it, Jim?"

"Two birds, one rock, ol' buddy."

Mesa's grin broadened. "I bet it's *real* quiet out there in the country."

"Just what the doctor ordered." Sonny was animated now, his nostrils flared and lips stretched tight against his teeth as he savored the idea. "Y'all game?"

Mesa thought a moment, then slapped his thigh and grabbed for the dope bag. "Why not? Come to think of it, I could use a good night's rest myself."

Before resuming their surveillance of Bebe Masaryk, Jumbo and Rosa met Diana Webster and Skye Lake at the tiny Szechuan Kitchen on First Avenue for an early dinner. Diana had accompanied Skye to an appointment with a funeral director on Madison, five blocks west. At five o'clock, they had the often crowded East Seventies eatery virtually to themselves. Much had happened since they'd last spoken. The two civilians were eager for an update.

While Richardson listened, chewing on a spring roll and drinking tea, Rosa brought the others up to date. She related how bookmaker Murray Glass was found shot to death in his home in Forest Hills, how Sonny Reed had called his girlfriend from Athens, Georgia, and how the fugitives had eluded a net thrown over the area by the FBI and Georgia State Police. "Joe thinks they're headed for Gainesville. That's where Mesa and Reed both went to college. It seems as good a bet as any."

Skye leaned forward, animated, an appetizer plate of steamed dumplings untouched. "This Dallas Direct place? It's a boob joint for high rollers, right?" Her earnest expression was locked onto Rosa.

"That's correct," Rosa replied. "Floor shows, food and drink, topless table service.

The young model's expression remained intense. "Maybe I can help there."

Jumbo scowled. "How's that?"

She turned to him. "They'd hire me in a second. This Sonny Reed is paranoid about calling his lady at her apartment, right? Then there's a good chance he'll try to reach her at work. Maybe she's got friends there, ones she talks to. I could keep an ear out."

Richardson smiled while shaking his head. "That ain't all you'd have to keep out."

Her eyes flashed anger. "I'm only trying to—"

He held up a hand, stopping her. "I know what you're tryin' to do. I appreciate it. But we're not so desperate we need to clutch at *that* particular straw. What Rosa just described is some pretty promising movement. In every investigation, you look for cracks to develop. Then you drive a wedge into them. We've had three or four real good ones open up. You wait. We're gonna nail these sons of bitches."

Diana took one of Skye's hands and gave it a squeeze as the young woman slumped back in her chair. "Listen to him. Your heart's in the right place, but *I'd* go to work in that sewer before I let you do it."

"I've done nude work for photographers," Skye defended herself. "It's no big deal anymore. Everyone does it. It didn't bother me."

"You're talkin' about a whole different world," Jumbo told her. "There ain't no art in this commerce. It's a fuckin' meat market." Her defensive statement that nude modeling for fashion photographers hadn't bothered her came out a bit *too* defensively. He hoped that meant it had bothered her, at least a little. Most kids he met seemed born jaded these days. He didn't want to believe Skye was one of them. She had grit.

As their main courses began to arrive on the table, Rosa looked at her watch. "We're going to have to eat and run. Sorry. If anything happens tonight, how late will you be up?"

Beasley ate his first mouthful of Szechuan shredded beef and contemplated the long, ass-deadening hours of surveillance that lay ahead, while Diana told Rosa she could call anytime up to one o'clock.

When Dante hit the outskirts of Atlanta, he also hit rush-hour traffic and got bogged down for nearly an hour. By the time he reached Macon, he was famished and very low on gas. With the exception of his stop outside Fair Play, he'd been behind the wheel for nine hours. He needed a break, and when he saw a truck stop sign lit bright above an interchange ahead, he aimed for that exit. Truck stop fare generally beat the franchise fast-food chains. They nearly always had good soup.

Inside the restaurant Joe sat in a booth, with truckers jammed into other booths all around him. Once his waitress had filled his coffee cup, he washed down another pair of Tylenol with codeine and began to focus on the surrounding conversations. It seemed that he was the subject of one.

"Y'hear what that crazy fucker *did*? Just t' other side of the South Carolina line?" It came from one of three truckers in the booth at his back. "Some cracker assholes tried t' hijack him. Way Ernie Waycroft tells it, the sumbitch left 'em handcuffed . . . t' the door of their own fucking car. Who the hell is he?"

"They're sayin' he's that cop was with the movie star in New York City. He's after them animals that killed her."

A third man snorted. "A New York cop? Bullshit. No way. Who said that? He's been watchin' too much *NYPD Blue*."

Dante smiled to himself. When the waitress returned she was unable to refrain from staring at his black eye and the dressing wrapping his head. He ordered a chicken fried steak and mashed potatoes with gravy. When in Rome . . .

The waitress gestured at his wounds before withdrawing. "Wreck do that? Y'all're banged up pretty good."

Dante nodded. "Jackknifed in a gully washer last week. Lucky to walk away."

The chicken fried steak proved a good call, fat grams notwithstanding. The mashed spuds weren't from a mix and had the lumps to prove it. Only the gravy left something to be desired. It was the same wallpaper paste that places all over the South served with breakfast—clearly an acquired taste.

While Dante stood at the cash register stuffing his change into his wallet, he saw a trucker hurry in from outside. It was one of the three drivers from the booth behind him, and he rushed toward the other two, still seated at their table.

"You won't believe it! There's a gray 300ZX outside, caked filthy with road dirt, and with New York plates. Parked right here in the lot!"

Joe moved as quickly for the door as his lame leg allowed. Outside, a balmy southern breeze hit him with the scent of Georgia pine on it, and he felt the same disorienting dizziness he'd suffered at the Sheraton the night before. He grabbed hold of the front fender of a Peterbilt to steady himself. Was it the codeine hitting him, or had he gotten up from the table too fast? He needed to sit, and his car was twenty feet away. As he started toward it he noticed how filthy it was, and then the lights went out.

When Dante opened his eyes he was on the parking lot pavement, a cluster of faces crowded over him.

"You okay, fella?" a voice asked.

Joe squeezed his eyes shut and opened them again, images coming more clear. There was a stinging sensation along his right elbow and shoulder. He realized he must have passed out, and wondered if he'd hit his head again. "I think so. Felt a little light-headed there for a second."

"I saw you go down," another voice told him. "You drunk?"

"Had an accident. Somebody gimme a hand up, will you?"

Several strong hands gripped his upper arms as he sat, then got his feet under him. Fortunately, he'd fallen on his right side instead of his left. His bad knee felt no worse than it did before. His head still throbbed.

"Where's your rig, buddy?" a bearded man asked. "Looks like you had a nasty one. You sure you should be driving?"

"I'll be fine," Joe replied. "Too long between meals is all. Think I ate too much, too fast." He dug into his pocket for his keys and gestured toward the Nissan. "This is me, here."

The bearded man glanced quickly to one of the others, then back to Joe. "Then it's true."

"What's that?"

"They're sayin' you're the cop was with the movie star."

Joe looked from that man to the others in the circle. "If you guys know anybody who helped clear the way for me, tell them I appreciate it."

FOURTEEN

Dinner started later than usual that Friday night at the Chapel family's Crooked Steeple Farm outside Ocala, Florida. On this night after Thanksgiving, the Chapels were celebrating their son Wesley junior's engagement to Kim Trammel, his longtime girlfriend. Wes Chapel, Sr., had barbecued his famous all-day ribs, and those ribs got a later start that morning than Wes had intended. They hadn't sat down until eight, and it was nine-thirty now as they finished up.

Elizabeth Chapel had given the housekeeper the entire holiday weekend off, wanting this to be a quiet time in their usually hectic lives, with just family. She hadn't foreseen two of their grooms quitting, early in the week, to return home to Mexico. This was particularly inconvenient, with the trainer and their two other grooms down at Gulfstream Park. Then again, with Wes junior and Kim there for the weekend, she supposed they could manage. Monday the trainer would send up a couple new hires. Tomorrow the family would all travel up to Gainesville for a Gator booster barbecue before the game. Then they'd join the legion of Gator faithful to watch their team do battle with Alabama's Crimson Tide.

"They kicked our butts in my day, y'know," Wes told his son and future daughter-in-law. "Bear Bryant had the team back then. Won the national title outright in '64, my junior year. Shared it with Michigan State the year after that. Beat us pretty good, both seasons."

Wes liked the way his boy's fiancée seemed to hang on his every word. She was a looker, this one, taller than Liz— which meant their kids might be bigger—with the same fine-boned features. She had spunk, and Wes liked that in a girl. If she gave his son a few boys with some size on them, maybe there'd be hope for the next Chapel generation.

"Dad made eleven solo tackles in that last game," Junior told Kim. "Right, Dad?" Too puny for football at the big college level, Wes junior had nonetheless distinguished himself as a high school quarterback. He was still a bona fide major league baseball prospect, and to prove what a good sport he was, he'd become a Gator cheerleader. He yelled his head off at games, tossed pretty girls like Kim in the air, and balanced them on his shoulders.

"Best game I ever played," Wes contended, pride in his voice. "But it don't much matter if your offense can't get the ball in the end zone."

"Why not tell 'em how the fuckin' Colts cut you, third week of camp. Wes?"

Startled, the Chapels and Kim turned, as one, to gape at Sonny Reed. He stood in the dining room doorway with a machine pistol aimed at them. His hands opened and closed spasmodically on the gun, like it was hot.

"An' how y'all couldn't even get a tryout with the Browns or the Bears. How y'all had t' crawl home, marry a rich girl, an' go t' work for her daddy pourin' cee-ment."

Wes Chapel was rigid with fury. "What the hell are *you* doin' here?" he snarled. "How dare you walk into my house!"

"*How* dare me? You know fuckin' well how I dare, Wes boy. Ain't you been watchin' the news? I'm a fuckin' desperado. A homicidal maniac on a killin' spree." Reed broke into a sinister grin, lips stretched tight to show his teeth.

"Shit. Your place was right on my way, Wesley. I had t' pay my respects, didn't I?"

Chapel watched the gun muzzle and the way those hands worked. He didn't know that much about drugs, but it was clear that Reed was on something. It was also clear that Reed had come here to kill him. He looked at his wife's and son's faces. Liz was scared bad. Junior had known Sonny Reed a little bit at school. He wasn't sure what Junior was. Not yet.

"This is between you'n me, Reed," Wes growled. He nodded toward his family. "They ain't got nothin' t' do with it."

Reed moved around the end of the table to stand, feet planted, only a yard and half away from Wes. Chapel calculated the distance between them, and what kind of force he'd have to bring to bear to knock Sonny on his back. Reed was a recent all-American, but Wes stayed in shape with weight work and racquetball, and even at fifty-two, he still had that quick first step.

"It's got t' do with who *I* say, Wes boy," Sonny sneered. He lifted his gun barrel to point toward Liz and Junior, and that's when Wes launched.

Chapel figured that Reed's gesture had bought him maybe half a second. He gambled half a second would be enough. As he came up off the seat of his chair, Reed surprised him with the reflexes of a cat. Wes's quick first step was good against in-shape forty-year-olds, but against a world-class athlete of twenty-two, it was worthless. Sonny brought that barrel back around like striking lightning and shot him. The noise-suppressed report of his gun made a flat, fartlike noise in the close quarters of the dining room.

Knocked onto his backside with the force of the impact, Wes stared down at the bright red hole in his orange-and-blue rugby shirt. It was a couple inches above his belt, and didn't hurt yet. "Damn," he gasped. Only when both entry and exit wounds started a slow burn did he realize the bullet had gone clean through.

Sonny loomed over him now. "Serves y'all right, asshole. I'd be in 'Frisco, playin' the 'Niners this weekend, y'hadn't ruined my life." He forced Wes's chin up with the barrel of his gun. "Lookit me when I talk t' y'all."

Wes glanced toward Liz and saw she was pale as milk. He then turned his eyes on Reed, his jaw set in defiance. "You never tol' me you bet against your own damn team, boy. Fuck you, Sonny. You're trash."

Reed leered. "Y'all tryin' t' get me t' shoot you dead, Wes? End it quick? Cuz you're outta luck there. You're gonna bleed out slow."

"Jesus, Sonny," Wes junior protested. "He needs a doctor."

With terrifying quickness, Sonny whirled to advance and club him to the floor. Junior tried to scramble, but Sonny planted a foot in the middle of his back.

"Y'all wanna take a bullet too? Jus' do somethin' stupid like your daddy did, Junior." With Junior still beneath his foot, Reed faced Elizabeth. "I'm gonna ask y'all a couple questions. If I think you're feedin' me shit, I'll put another hole in Wes."

Liz tried to be strong. She tore her panicked attention from her husband, there on the floor, to face Sonny.

"Anyone else on the property t' night?"

Her voice quavered slightly as Liz told him about the trainer being away, losing the two grooms, and the housekeeper visiting her family in White Springs for the weekend.

"So there ain't nobody s'pose t' show here till Monday?" Reed's tone dripped suspicion.

"Nobody. The kids and I were going to handle the feeding. Tomorrow we're supposed to go up to the game."

Sonny seemed satisfied, at least for the moment. "Fine. Now tell me. What are they sayin' 'bout us on the news down here? All of it."

Elizabeth Chapel was unable to look defiant. Sonny held all the cards. She took a deep breath. "That you killed those guards outside Sing Sing . . . to help a Colombian escape. That you killed Janet Lake, and a policeman, in New York City." She stopped, a hand covering her face. "Oh God, I don't remember. You killed a parking lot attendant, right? An airplane crashed. In a snowstorm." Wes groaned and she couldn't keep it together any longer. She started to sob.

"Go on," Sonny crooned. "You're doin' just fine."

"Y-you killed a husband and wife in West Virginia. Raped the wife—"

"I didn't rape nobody," Sonny snarled.

"That's what they're saying on the news. That she was raped, then you shot her in the head."

Teo Mendoza's fever started to break around eight o'clock that night. By the time Jim MacPhearson pulled them to a stop, lights out, a hundred yards from a house and barns on a private road, Mendoza's temperature had dropped below one hundred. His breath still rattled badly in his chest, but Barbara Jo now had reason to hope he wouldn't die on her. At least not tonight. If they did as she said, and got him a good night's rest—more, if she could persuade them—he might make it to Miami alive.

The moon was bright outside the motor home and Barbara could see the shapes of horses grazing in a fenced pasture. Sonny knew the people who lived here, and held some sort of grudge against them. Until now, he'd seemed the more stable of Mendoza's two accomplices, but as they approached this place, Reed had started to manifest more and more cocaine psychosis.

The radio in Julio's hand had broadcast Sonny's progress reports to them. He'd whispered he was inside the house about ten minutes ago. Now his voice crackled through the little speaker again, much louder this time.

"You an' me, we gotta talk, Bubba. We're all clear here. Have Mac pull that rig right up t' the front door."

Julio lifted the radio to his lips. "What's the problem, Jim?"

"We'll talk about it when y'all get here. I'm waitin'."

If Mesa was concerned by Reed's tone, he didn't betray it. He ordered MacPhearson up the drive and around the top of a loop that brought them to a wide veranda. Barbara Jo, Jim, and Tillie were herded up the front steps to the door, where Sonny waited inside. Reed had their latest hostages huddled together in one corner of a big living room. The furnishings were all in shades of white, a stark contrast to the bright red blood seeping between the fingers of a wounded man on the sofa. He clutched at his abdomen, his face another shade of white, and filmed with a sheen of perspiration.

Julio wandered in behind Barbara Jo, prodding her in the fanny with his Uzi. "What the fuck's your problem?" he asked Reed. He surveyed the room as he spoke.

"You and your fuckin' dick is my problem. It's all over the news how *we* raped and shot that gal in West Virginia. I did what I had t' do up North, but this other shit ain't what I signed on for."

Mesa might just as well have been confronted with a charge of shoplifting. He shrugged and started to wander around the room, fingers fondling the noise suppressor of his gun. "It's the tension, Jim. We're both wound up tighter than teenage twat. We need something to eat. Take Tillie to find the kitchen and see what she can pull together. I'm starving."

"Y'all didn't hear what I'm sayin', Julio." Sonny stood his ground. "We go down, I ain't takin' the rap for no rape-murder."

Mesa stopped his pacing, his expression gone stone cold. "We aren't going down, Jim. Get that into your thick head."

He started forward again, circling Sonny's female prisoners. "My, my. So what have we here?"

By the time Dante rolled into Gainesville at ten-thirty that night, he just couldn't go anymore. He was too tired to think. His whole body vibrated from twelve hours of high-speed driving. His car probably needed the rest as much as he did. If the fugitives didn't stop here, or left at the crack of dawn, those were the breaks. He needed sleep.

The first motel he pulled into off exit 74 gave him a story he would hear repeatedly over the next half hour. The University of Florida Gators were playing Alabama's Crimson Tide tomorrow. Gainesville was in the grips of Gatormania. Every motel room in town had been booked since the Southeast Conference football schedule was announced last spring.

At eleven o'clock Joe gave up hope of spending the night in Gainesville, climbed back behind the wheel, and continued on to Ocala, thirty miles south. They were in the grips of Gatormania, too, but not to quite the same extreme. All he wanted was a bed, and that's all he managed to get, at a mom-and-pop cabin cluster west of the interstate on Route 40.

Dante had no reason to believe the phone in his cabin was any more secure than his cellular unit. He'd seen a switch-board in the motel office. Anyone so inclined could listen in. After an examination of his scraped right elbow—not too bad, just a little bark off—he showered and carried his cellular phone to bed.

Eight miles from where Joe Dante climbed between the sheets, Kimberly Trammel was frozen with fear on a cream leather sofa in the Chapel living room. The wounded man whom Junior and the hostage nurse had carried in was propped up with pillows on a sofa bed in Wes senior's den, across from the living room. He looked awfully weak to

Kim, and the others seemed surprised he was able to sit up and talk. Not that she cared. She was much too preoccupied with the way Julio had looked at her before he left the house.

Wes senior was in deep shock now. While Sonny Reed had allowed the nurse to bind heavy gauze pads to the gunshot entry and exit wounds and inject Wes with Demerol, he steadfastly refused him further help. He was a fugitive wanted for murder, and wasn't about to call an ambulance. Wes shouldn't have tried to jump him. After ratting him out, he probably deserved to be gutshot, anyway. Mrs. Chapel had her husband stretched flat on the sofa now, with a bunch of towels set under him. There was a lot of blood, and if Kim wasn't so scared, she might have been sick.

While Julio had gone to park the motor home, Tillie MacPhearson carried in microwave-warmed leftover ribs, mashed potatoes, turkey, and stuffing and set them on the coffee table with a stack of plates and handful of flatware. Sonny stood half in and half out of the kitchen doorway, one eye on Tillie and the other on the end of the room where the Chapel family was grouped. The front door banged open as Julio reentered the house.

"Damn, that smells good!"

"Y'all find a place t' hide it?" Reed demanded.

Mesa grabbed a rib and began to gnaw, talking around it. "Big barn back there; I just swung open the doors and drove it right on in. They've got a pick-up, two cars in the garage, and a brand-new Cherokee. Jeep still has its temporary plate."

Liz Chapel winced when Julio threw the rib bone to the floor before grabbing up another.

"The motor home's been fine up till now," Mesa continued. "But we're gonna lose even more time here, if this bitch gets her way." He glared into the den at the nurse.

"You got your eye on the Jeep?" Sonny's tone was wary.

"It's just the ticket. Rear seat folds flat and it's got tinted glass all around."

Reed gestured with his gun toward Teo on the sofa bed. "She's sayin' he needs a day, minimum, an' don't let how quick he seems t' be comin' 'round fool y'all."

Julio looked at Kim and sighed. "Bummer. Think we can find anything to keep ourselves occupied?"

When the phone at Gus Lieberman's elbow rang at 12:05 A.M., he started awake in his chair. He was expecting a call from Dante and had sat up reading in the library. The fire in the grate had died, and without looking at the mantel clock, the stiffness in his neck and shoulders told him he'd been out awhile.

"I'd about given up, Joey. Where are you?"

"Ocala. It seems Albert Alligator and his merry band of morons have booked every motel room in the greater Gainesville area."

"Huh?"

"The local football faithful, boss. A plague upon this land. Sorry it's so late. What've you got for me?"

Lieberman closed the book in his lap and set it aside. "You ain't the only one came up with the idea they might be headed for Gainesville, Joey. Dyson flew down there from Atlanta."

"Shit."

"Knew you'd be happy to hear that. But it *is* where the two of them went to college, so it didn't take an Einstein. He's at a Holiday Inn. One right close to the university."

"How the hell'd he get a room?" Joe wondered.

"Who knows? Man never has no trouble throwin' his weight around."

"You find me any leads? Ones Dyson doesn't have?"

Gus had a notebook on the little table at his elbow, and grabbed it. "Could be. When I talked to Al, I couldn't get much outta him. He's playin his cards pretty close to the vest. But we got you one possible toehold, though. The former athletic director."

"What's his story?"

"He retired, right after the scandal involving Reed hit this past summer and the NCAA finished raking them over the coals. He's still in town, and might know who Reed's booster friends were. The ones with the deep pockets who ratted him out."

Dante asked him to hang on while he wrote down the athletic director's name and address. "What else?"

"O'Roark tells me the town you're in now, Ocala, is popular with retired Colombian dopers. Ones who've become gentlemen farmers."

"Farmers of what?"

"That's horse country. A big-time breeding ground for Thoroughbreds, quarter horses, Arabians, you name it. Colombians have a passion for Pasofinos. Horses trained t' do all kinda fancy parade prancing, shit like that."

There was an extended silence as Dante digested this news. "If Mesa's the nephew of a heavyweight like Lucho Esparza, the politics of him making an approach for asylum could get sticky, Gus. Esparza is Cali cartel, and most of those retired guys would be Medellín. I think they hate each other."

"Interestin' point," Lieberman replied. "O'Roark tells me Dyson has requested the names of all the Colombians from the Miami DEA field office."

"I guess I'll try the retired A.D., then. First thing in the morning."

"If they're playin' Alabama, I suggest you start early."

FIFTEEN

The only bookmaker in the Organized Crime Control Bureau's files with the surname Boone was an Eric Boone, on Fifth Avenue in the Seventies, one of the most expensive stretches of real estate in the city. Eric Boone was a high-class, heavy-action act. Some Public Morals detectives were surprised that he would handle Sonny Reed's action, but Reed had reportedly wagered, and lost, huge sums since arriving in New York. The numbers were right, and as long as Sonny was flush, any bookmaker would be a fool not to take his money.

Late Friday, after making a call from a pay phone on a corner near her building, Bebe Masaryk took a cab to Boone's address and was admitted by the doorman. That was enough to persuade a judge to authorize a wiretap on Eric Boone's phone. Rosa Losada and Beasley Richardson sat on that tap until midnight, waiting for Reed to call. Then they left the surveillance to others and went home to their beds.

Jumbo's head had barely hit the pillow when his phone rang. He fumbled for the receiver in the dark and nearly dropped it, then dragged it to his ear. "Richardson. Yeah."

It was one of the cops from the surveillance detail. "Reed

just called him, Lou. With action for a whole slate of Sunday's games."

Jumbo was wide awake now. He propped himself up on one elbow, reached for the bedside lamp switch, and then a pen. His wife, Bernice, growled in her sleep and pulled the comforter back over her bared shoulder. "Play it back to me," he said.

There were several clicks, a hum, and then:

"Seven-two-three-eight. It's late. Who's this?"

"Sonny Reed, Eric. Bebe talk t' y'all?"

"Umm. I've been watching the TV news, Lyndon. Since you went South, CNN's given you more airtime than they gave Tonya Harding. So far as I can tell, you're a dead man."

"I ain't dead yet, good buddy. I got some plays I need t' make, on Sunday's games."

"You lose, how will you pay? You were into Murray for almost a quarter mil. Not to speak ill of the dead, but he was a fool to carry a negative balance that large."

"I squared it. Y'all know that too."

"Umm. But can you square it again?"

"You think I'm on this joyride for my health? People gonna *owe* me after this. Big. Influential people."

"So what's your pleasure, Lyndon?"

"I used a blocking code when I called y'all, but I been on too long. I'm gonna hang up and call right back."

The line went dead.

"Damn," Jumbo muttered.

"There's more," the tech told him.

"You get the number?"

"Nuh-uh. Blocked us again. Just the area code and prefix. Hang on."

Once more, Richardson heard Boone's voice first. Then

Reed, quickly rattling off his picks in Sunday's games, and dollar amounts on each. It was over sooner than the first conversation by at least ten seconds. When the wiretap technician came back on the line, Jumbo asked if he'd called the chief with this yet.

"You said to call you first."

"Where's the area code?"

"Nine-oh-four. That could be anywhere from Jacksonville to Pensacola, but the prefix narrows it more, to a few thousand possibilities in and around Ocala."

"Where's that?"

"Thirty miles south of Gainesville."

"You go ahead an' call the chief," Jumbo told him. "I'll call Captain Losada."

Teo Mendoza wasn't the only one in need of sleep. Barbara Jo Kelly would get her shot at some shut-eye tomorrow, but tonight Julio Mesa used duct tape to lash her to one of the dining room chairs. He even apologized for taping her mouth shut, which was more courtesy than he showed the other hostages, including the man with the belly wound. They'd been restrained in the chairs alongside. Barbara Jo was too exhausted even to care about the discomfort of being taped and having to breathe through her nose. Still, she knew too much about Julio by now to sleep at all soundly.

When Barbara Jo awakened, it was still dark. She tried to move, then remembered where she was and why she couldn't.

"Go back to sleep," a voice growled in her ear.

Startled, Barbara Jo jerked her head sideways to find Julio beside her, bent over the Chapel boy's girlfriend. She saw metal flash and realized that Julio was cutting the girl's bonds.

Her eyes slowly adjusting, Barbara Jo could now see

Tillie, Jim, and both Mrs. Chapel and her son watching helplessly from across the table. For all she knew, the man slumped in the chair at the head of the table had bled to death by now. She saw Julio pause in his cutting to pull aside a strand of the girl's corn-silk hair and trace the line of her jaw with the tip of his knife.

"Ah," he whispered. "I see everyone's awake. It's all your fault, Barbara Jo. Me being forced to look at that sweet ass of yours and not be able to touch it." He turned the girl's tear-streaked face in Barbara Jo's direction. "Look at this doll, will you? She's got a sweet ass too."

Julio grabbed one of Kim's freed hands to force it inside his open fly. Wes junior began to buck violently against his bonds. The chair legs thumping against the thick pile carpet made little noise, but Mesa was on him, fast. Junior gave up his bucking with a grunt when Julio hit him upside the head with the handle of his knife. Mesa then returned to the girl, jerking her to her feet.

"Everybody quiet in here now," he whispered. "Sonny needs his sleep." He started the girl toward the kitchen door.

The dressing Dante inspected as he shaved that morning looked about ready for an overhaul. He contemplated taking the thing off, but had no idea what his head looked like beneath. The bruise that spread below it and down around his left eye was starting to yellow at the edges. His head still hurt like hell, but he planned to wean himself off the codeine today and go with plain ibuprofen.

Once he shaved, and got as clean as he could feel with his hair still dirty, he was on the road by seven o'clock. He wanted coffee, but decided he had no time for it. Once he hit Gainesville, it would take him a while to get his bearings, and every minute was precious. The former athletic director's address was on Northwest Seventh Road, wherever that was.

Three-quarters of an hour after leaving his motel cabin, Dante passed a picturesque pond surrounded by trees hung with Spanish moss and saw his first great blue heron. It rose out of the morning mist into a tree, surprising him with its size. He'd stopped near the university to ask directions, and his inquiry led him here, to what was clearly an affluent residential section of town. Three minutes later he turned into the driveway of a large, rambling ranch-style house set up off the road.

Elsworth Short was still in his robe when Dante parked out front of his garage. He had an empty coffee carafe in one hand as he opened his back door off the kitchen and stepped out onto the brick stoop. On seeing the condition of Dante's head, he frowned.

"Help you with something, fella?"

Joe dug into the pocket of his rumpled chinos for his shield case and presented his ID. It was hot down here, and he wore a polo shirt, no jacket. "Detective Lieutenant Joe Dante. New York Police Department, sir. I'm a bit off my turf, but I wonder if I can have a word with you?"

"Up bright and early, huh? This have something to do with the Lyndon Reed situation? I already talked to a fella from the FBI about it, last night."

Joe couldn't help feeling disappointment. Al Dyson had beat him to the punch. "I'm the guy they were trying to get when they killed Janet Lake."

The reason for Joe's slight limp and bandage came clear. Short nodded. "I'm awful damn sorry, Lieutenant. They said on the news, she was an old friend of yours."

"And a good friend, sir." Joe pointed to the empty carafe. "You think you could spare a cup of that, once it's made?"

Short apologized for his manners and invited him inside. "We'll need to be quiet. My wife's a late sleeper, weekends. Let's sit at the table in the kitchen. You hungry? I'll fix you some flapjacks and grits."

"I could skip the grits," Joe replied. "But thanks. Flap-jacks sound great."

They talked while Short got to work. He heated his griddle and mixed the ingredients for pancake batter.

"You mind me asking what you and Agent Dyson talked about?" Joe asked. "What he wanted to know?"

"He wanted to know who loaned Lyndon Reed the money to pay off his bookmaker. I told him I don't know . . . which is the truth. The NCAA investigators held closed sessions." He lifted his spoon and let its contents run out into the bowl, evaluating the batter's consistency. "All I know is a group of our more rabid boosters was involved, without me, or any other university official, being aware of it. That's what saved the program from sanctions. The school was absolutely in the clear. Still, I was so disgusted with the whole lot of them, I quit."

"But you can guess who was responsible, I bet."

Short tested a small dollop of batter on the griddle. It started to sizzle. He allowed himself a slight nod. "But the FBI fella didn't want my opinion. He just plowed ahead, said he could subpoena those records from the NCAA." Short paused. "A little officious, that fella, don't you think? Or do you know him?"

"Oh, I know him," Dante replied. "What *did* you tell him about Reed? Anything?"

Ten healthy-size pancakes were spooned out onto the greased griddle, where they started to cook. The aroma made Joe's stomach growl. The smell of coffee, dripping into the pot, was in the air too.

"He wanted to know who on the team Reed was friendly with, and if any of them are still in town. I gave him half a dozen names, of boys who are still on the squad."

"If you *were* to guess, who would those boosters be? Those responsible for the loan, Mr. Short?"

"Call me El." He flipped the pancakes one at a time.

"Couple fellas come to mind. Former players, mostly. Men who've made a few bucks since, and like to throw their weight around. Jed Beene would be one, for sure. He played tackle here in the late fifties. Wes Chapel. And probably Billy Dean Tibbet. Those two played in the same line-backing corps in the mid-sixties. Chapel married into dough. His wife's daddy's in concrete. Tibbet is beef cattle."

Dante scribbled the names in his notebook. "They all live in the area?"

"Oh, sure. Couldn't be such a huge pain in the fanny if they didn't. Tibbet's got a big spread up north of here. In Live Oak. Both Beene and Chapel have places outside Ocala. That's horse country. Chapel's serious about it. Horse breeding, that is. Had a horse run in the Preakness this year."

"You think all three of them will be at the game?"

"You kidding? Matter of fact, you'll probably find them all at the booster's barbecue first. It's a big shindig the alums throw in the parking lot outside Ben Griffin Stadium. Cheerleaders, pep band, the whole shebang."

Dante eyed the flapjacks. They were golden brown as they came off the griddle. "How much time do I have before this event?"

Short chuckled. "Relax, son. You got a couple hours yet. You look kinda peaked. Maybe I should fry up some bacon. And you think again about those grits."

Sonny Reed usually awoke with the sun, but this morning, stretched facedown on a living room sofa, he overslept the dawn by two hours. When he sat up, dressed only in his Jockey shorts, he rubbed the sleep from his face and saw daylight streaming in from a sun already high in the sky. "Shit," he muttered as he rose.

Reed padded barefoot to the powder room to pee,

splashed water in his face, and rinsed the night from his mouth. When he emerged he passed the den and poked his head in before moving on toward the dining room. Teo was still asleep on his back, and seemed to be breathing more regularly now. Julio was on the other side of him, curled up in an open recliner. Sonny would get him moving in a minute, but first he'd check on the prisoners. He'd felt bad about Julio taping the nurse up with the others last night. She'd been a trooper, and they needed her rested too.

Wes Chapel was dead, of that he was certain, and he felt no remorse. Why not kill somebody who deserved it? Chapel sure did. He was a rat, and a sanctimonious rat at that.

As Sonny's gaze left Chapel to travel the room he found Jim MacPhearson still dozing, then saw the hatred on both Barbara Jo's and Tillie's faces. When his eyes fell, finally, on Kim's empty chair, Sonny spun and raced back through the living room to the den.

"You sick, sorry fuck!" he yelled, grabbing Julio by the front of his shirt to shake him violently. "Where is she?"

Julio came awake like a dog playing possum. One second Sonny was shaking him, and the next, Julio jammed the muzzle of his 9mm Beretta up beneath Reed's chin. "Back off, asshole!"

Sonny froze. He released the fabric of Mesa's shirt. "This one didn't crawl out no window and run for help," he seethed through clenched teeth. "Somebody cut that tape off her."

"You're a regular Sherlock Holmes, Jim. We took a ride in Mac and Tillie's rig." Julio wore a broad, leering grin. "Damn, buddy. I'd forgotten how good that coed pussy can be."

Sonny backed away from the gun at his chin and stalked from the room, rage boiling inside him. He'd forgotten how hot the Florida sun could be in November until he stepped off the veranda and into the drive. The horses in the adjacent paddock winnied and started for the stables. Reed went past, to the largest barn, and rolled back the heavy main door.

Julio had driven the Sunflyer straight in through those main doors and parked it. Sonny approached from the rear and stepped around to yank open the side door. It couldn't have been more than a matter of hours, but the smell of death was already heavy through the motor home interior. He took a deep breath of comparatively fresh air outside the RV and planted a foot to haul himself up into the interior. The moment he gained the galley area, he went lurching for the sink, his stomach racked with great heaving spasms.

Kim Trammel had been bound spread-eagle on the galley dining table. She had bite marks on her breasts and blood smeared inside her thighs. Half of her beautiful face was missing where a bullet had torn it away. Sonny looked only once before he turned and vomited, but that image would burn in his memory as long as he lived.

There was a message from Rosa on Dante's cellular voice mail when he returned to his car after leaving Elsworth Short's house. She asked him to call his own desk, and when he dialed the number en route, back south toward the university campus, she picked up.

"Captain Losada."

"The D.A.'s squad's loss is my gain. Beasley there too?"

"You bet. Gus, Frank Bryce, and most of Bureau command are upstairs too. How are you?"

"Better. Finally got some sleep. Any luck with those wiretaps yet?"

Jumbo joined them on the line. "Hey, Joey."

"Tell him what you've got, Beasley," Rosa urged.

"You're gettin' warm, Joey. Hot, in fact. Reed called his backup book last night. Twice. Tryin' t' avoid a trace. We got him as far as the area code and prefix."

Dante steered one-handed to turn onto NW Thirty-fourth Street. Traffic toward campus wasn't too heavy yet, but he could imagine how it would get, not too much later. "That pins it down some, doesn't it?"

"Reed's call originated from where Gus says you spent the night. Ocala. Without the last four numbers, it's not too specific. There's at least thirty weathy Colombians got horse farms, or big estates, around there."

"That's the angle Dyson's working," Joe replied. "I found a different one, and you just helped narrow my possibilities from three to two." He went on to explain about the boosters. "How did Reed sound when he called?"

"Kinda hushed, like he didn't want t' be overheard. And panicked that Boone might not take his action."

"He's got the fever bad."

"Wouldn't be in this jam if he didn't."

"Either of you talked to Brian or Diana? What's going on with Skye?"

"They released the body to the mortuary yesterday," Rosa replied. "We had dinner with Skye and Diana, right after they left there."

"The kid couldn't be in better hands, Joey," Jumbo added.

Dante knew from an earlier conversation that Janet would be cremated. He learned now that it would happen later that morning. The finality of it came at him hard. He was stopped behind a row of cars at a light, eyes closed. A horn startled him back to the here and now. His light had changed and the cars ahead of him had passed through the intersection.

"Dyson's got thirty leads to check out while I'm down to two," he told them. "Wish me luck."

"Charlie O'Roark told Gus yesterday that he's worried about you," Rosa told him. "The way you looked when he left you in Martinsburg."

"Tell him I'm touched by his concern. The leg feels much better today."

"It's not your leg I'm worried about."

"Good. Neither am I. Keep me posted." Joe removed the phone from his ear, glanced down as he pushed the *end* button, and tossed the unit onto the passenger seat. Ahead, past the intersection of NW Thirty-fourth Street and West University Avenue, Ben Hill Griffin Stadium loomed above a corner of the University of Florida campus. Everywhere around him, cars trailed orange-and-blue streamers from their aerials. Gator mania was building a head of steam.

SIXTEEN

Barbara Jo Kelly, freed from her bonds, had Teo Mendoza sitting up in the den when Sonny Reed stormed back into the house. The front door flew open with such force, it crushed an antique umbrella stand before crashing into the wall behind.

"You slime-wallowin' mother*fucker*!" he screamed. He came to a stop in front of Julio, seated in that den recliner with a map spread on his lap. It was then that Barbara saw the tears. They streamed down both Reed's cheeks as he turned to address Mendoza. "This fuckin' asshole? He's outta *control*!"

Mesa slid his Beretta from beneath the map and aimed it at Sonny's chest. "Back off, dickhead. You can't handle the road, you shouldn't have come along for the ride."

Reed was trembling, too outraged to care about the gun. "You ain't never seen nothin' like this," he told Teo. "The man's a fuckin' cannibal!"

A shiver ran the length of Barbara Jo's spine. Her stomach squeezed spasmodically and she tried in vain to cover her mouth. Stomach acid, mixed with undigested food, surged up to burn her nasal passages. Tears came to her eyes as she bent, choking.

"Put the gun *down*, Julio!"

The voice came from close by, cold, stern, and not open to negotiation. Barbara jerked her head up in surprise. It was Mendoza—his face, just yesterday pale as death, now red with anger.

Julio gaped before he could recover. "He insults my manhood, *hermano*. I cannot forgive this."

Teo was not mollified. "You do this thing he says?"

Mesa bristled. "It ain't his fucking business what I do."

Eyes closed, Mendoza shook his head and clucked his tongue. "I don' think so, Julio. I think he is right."

Julio looked over his shoulder to glare at Reed. "All them steroids, they make his balls like a little boy's. He's jealous."

Mendoza shrugged, and winced for his trouble. "You get me home firs'. Then you kill your friend, or he kill you. *¿Comprende?* Not today. *Manana.*"

Unable to tolerate criticism from any quarter, Mesa stood abruptly. He stuffed his pistol into his waistband and dropped the map at Sonny's feet. "Back the fuck off, Jim. You been paid to do a job. What? You're a moralist now?"

Reed stood his ground, the muscles of his forearms knotting as he flexed his hands at his sides. For a moment, Barbara believed Sonny was going to go for Julio's throat. When he spoke, his voice was tight. "From here on? I don't care *who* your fuckin' uncle is. Stay outta my face, asshole."

The parking lot to the west of Ben Hill Griffin Stadium was already filled with barbecue brunch revelers as Dante handed a note written by Elsworth Short to a parking attendant. The man read it and glanced first at the filthy 300ZX with New York plates, and then at the bandage wrapping Joe's head. Short's note requested that the event staff and Curtis Lolley, president of the alumni boosters, show Lieutenant Dante every courtesy. It got Joe a parking slot twenty feet from the three huge barbecue rigs. The boosters had a soundstage set up on a flatbed truck festooned with crepe paper in Gator orange and blue. A pep band sat in folding chairs alongside, huffing through a brassy rendition of "Swanee River." A group of cheerleaders loitered nearby, jittery with pent-up pregame energy. Between them and the pits, several hundred boosters sat at picnic tables, ready to feast on Polish sausage, chicken, and ribs.

A booster in a straw boater and official-looking orange-and-blue armband pointed out Curtis Lolley. He stood in conversation with a knot of people, all gathered on the opposite side of the truck from the band. They had to lean their heads close to hear each other above the music. Joe watched Lolley, trying to size the man up. He'd expected somebody fleshy and florid-faced. Instead, Lolly was tall and spare, his seersucker jacket hanging from bony shoulders. His swept-back hair was almost white, but his face was boyish, tanned deep by the Florida sun.

"Mr. Lolley?"

The booster president turned, a questioning frown creasing his brow as he failed to recognize the injured man who addressed him. "Yeah?"

"Detective Lieutenant Dante. NYPD. El Short says you're the man I should see here." He handed across the retired A.D.'s note.

Continuing to frown, Lolley scanned the slip of paper. His expression shifted to curiosity as he looked back at his visitor. "It doesn't say what *kind* of courtesy, Lieutenant. I'm afraid game tickets are pretty tight, if that's—"

"It isn't," Joe cut him off. "I need to talk to two of your boosters. Mr. Short figured this barbecue would be my best bet."

"Sure. I'm kinda busy at the moment, but once I climb up and say my piece, I'll be glad t' try and help. We're late getting started here. A couple of cheerleaders haven't showed up, but we can't wait any longer."

"How about you just point them out to me? Jed Beene and Wes Chapel."

Lolly frowned again. "Let's see. Jed was right here a minute ago. I don't see him now. Chapel's boy, Junior, and his girlfriend are the cheerleaders who aren't here yet. Wes, neither, for that matter. That's not like them."

The booster president gaped as Dante turned abruptly and bolted through the crowd.

Captain Frank Bryce buzzed Gus Lieberman in his office to say he had Dante on the line. It was urgent. Gus had Charlie O'Roark with him, the two of them going over a list of Colombians who resided in the greater Ocala area. The purpose of their exercise was to pinpoint potential Lucho Esparza allies among the names on the list. So far, there were few who Charlie would consider even vaguely sympathetic to Mateo Mendoza's plight.

Gus punched the blinking button on his phone. "Yeah, Joey. You talked to the athletic director?"

"I think I know where they are, Gus. I'm gonna need FDLE backup." Dante went on to relate what he'd just heard from booster president Curtis Lolley, and what he'd learned earlier from Elsworth Short. "The man owns a horse farm. It's Thanksgiving weekend. The son and the girlfriend probably went home to visit. Chapel's one of my three possibles: boosters the NCAA questioned during their investigation. Two of them live in Ocala, and Chapel didn't show up for this rally today."

Gus covered the mouthpiece and looked to O'Roark. "We might be on to something." He spoke into the phone again. "You call there? See who answers?"

"Twice. Got a machine. It's the same 263 prefix we got from Reed's trace."

"Al Dyson's gonna make it the Feeb's show, Joey. The FDLE can't keep him out. He'll force you and the state cops to sit on the sidelines."

"Not if we move fast. I'm already on my way."

Stripped to the waist, his fleshy torso gleaming with sweat, Julio Mesa entered the Chapel house sucking on the middle finger of his left hand. He ignored the sullen Sonny Reed to address Barbara Jo Kelly.

"Get me a goddamn Band-Aid."

He then turned to Reed. "Let's get Tillie and Mac into the kitchen, rustle us up something to eat. I'm fucking hungry as a starved dog." While Reed sat there, unmoving, Mesa dug one-handed into his travel bag to produce a half ounce of cocaine. He poured a small pile onto the glass-topped coffee table and looked once more to his sullen partner. "Want some, Jim?"

"I thought y'all wanted t' kill me." Sonny had perked up some when he saw the coke, but still eyed Mesa warily.

Julio grinned around the finger he sucked. "I got a Latin temper, Jim. Gets me into almost as much trouble as my dick. Truce, dude. We can't be at each other's throats like this." He used a single-edge razor blade to chop through the pile and offered a short length of plastic soda straw as an olive branch. "With all the algae and shit growing in that pond out back, ain't nobody gonna find the little bitch's Beemer."

Sonny slid to his knees before the table and took the offered appeasement with his old enthusiasm. "What happened t' that finger?"

"Cut it on a fucking license plate. I put the one from her car onto those new wheels, tore off that temporary."

Reed rocked back on his heels to ask Tillie how the Chapels were fixed for bacon and eggs. Barbara advanced toward Julio with a bottle of antiseptic, gauze, and a roll of tape. "Hold out your hand," she commanded.

While Barbara swabbed and wrapped Mesa's finger, Sonny led the MacPhearsons to the kitchen and stood half in and half out of the dining room doorway, one eye on their progress toward breakfast. Tillie got Mac to frying bacon while she broke eggs and beat them to make omlettes. When the telephone rang for about the eighth time that morning, all of them ignored it until the caller hung up rather than wait for the machine. Immediately after the ringing ceased, it started again, two rings, and stopped. When it rang a third time, with a ten-second interval between each call, Mesa picked up.

"Yeah."

"You've got five, maybe ten minutes to clear out," a voice told him. "Don't know how they found you, but a joint federal and FDLE net is set to drop any second."

Julio slammed the receiver down and dug into his waistband for his Beretta. "They're on us, Jim!" He shoved Barbara toward Teo in the den. "Drag that fucking stretcher out here and get his shit together." He was moving toward Reed and the hostages in the dining room as he spoke. "Those two are yours, Jim. Then get the car around front." He leveled his weapon to place it against Liz Chapel's temple. When Sonny didn't move quickly enough, he got excited. "Move, goddammit! Shoot them and get the fucking wheels!"

Wes Chapel, Jr., and his mother were wide-eyed with panic as Reed disappeared behind the kitchen's swinging door. Julio continued to hold the gun on Liz while tearing the tape from Junior's mouth.

"Think fast or I blow your mama's brains out. There any back road off this farm?"

Junior tried to get enough moisture around his tongue to speak. "D-down past the paddock. A-at the south end. It crosses our neighbor's place and hooks up with 326, going toward Silver Springs."

Mesa nodded and pulled the trigger, the report of his gun echoed by two quick reports from Sonny's pistol in the kitchen. As Reed emerged again past the swinging door, eyes averted from the horror of Liz Chapel's death and moving fast, Mesa grinned and turned his weapon on Junior.

The address Joe Dante had for Wes Chapel was off Jacksonville Road, or business US 301, headed north of Ocala toward Anthony. Game day traffic had slowed his exit from Gainesville, but once he hit US 441 he was able to open it up. The first indication that he was nearing the Chapels' Crooked Steeple Farm was a cluster of state police cars parked on the shoulder, behind a copse of pines. He pulled up where he wouldn't be boxed in, and climbed out to be approached by a uniformed officer, moving at a trot.

"Police emergency, sir. You'll have to move on."

Joe showed him his tin. "Lieutenant Dante. NYPD. Who's running the show?"

"Major Criswell, sir." He indicated a bald man in a suit, with several other suits and a half dozen men in navy blue SWAT team gear clustered around him.

Three days after reinjuring his knee, Dante could almost walk normally now. He crossed to Criswell's position, apologized for interrupting, and introduced himself. The major absorbed the condition of Joe's rumpled clothes and three-day-old head bandage as they shook hands.

"Your reputation precedes you, Lieutenant. Agent Dyson claims you have no authority."

"He's right. I don't." Dante peered through the pines, trying to make out what held the attention of several state police plainclothesmen with high-powered spotting scopes.

The radio in Criswell's hand came alive. He raised it to his lips. "Yeah, Tommy. Tell me what you see."

A tinny voice crackled through the speaker. "Everything's quiet as a tomb, Major. The front door's hangin' wide open and there's an empty ambulance stretcher in the drive."

"Vehicles?"

"Three that we can see. A Dodge three-quarter-ton pickup by one of the barns. Two cars in the garage, a Jag and a Lexus. I've had a scope on the house for five minutes now, but ain't seen no movement."

"Hold on, Tommy." Criswell lowered the radio and looked down the road to where several unmarked sedans were pulling in. "Here's the cavalry now."

Dante watched Al Dyson hurry from the lead car. Behind him, his troops gathered around the open trunks of their cars, handing out vests and automatic rifles. When Dyson spotted Dante, he turned ornery.

"What's this, Major? I thought we understood each other. The lieutenant's got no jurisdiction here."

"His chief called, requested that we let him observe," Criswell replied. "I don't see any problem with that."

Dyson stared at him. "I'm assuming command here, Major. You got people in the field, call them back."

"My instructions are to work *with* you, sir, not to pull out." As Criswell held his ground, his radio came alive again. He raised it, eyes still locked with Dyson's. "Yeah, Tommy."

"I sent Gallagher into the barn, Major. Found a motor home with New York plates parked inside. No bodies, but he says it stinks like a slaughterhouse and looks like somebody butchered a pig on the kitchen table."

A motor home, Dante thought. Of course. The roadblocks had been on the lookout for a van or station wagon. A motor home explained why they'd made such slow progress, Thanksgiving Day.

"That the house?" Dyson demanded. He squinted through

the trees and across a private road to a cluster of buildings at the end of a long drive.

Criswell nodded. "I've got a three-man surveillance team over there, crawling the perimeter."

"I'm going to ring the house and hail them," Dyson told him. "The longer we wait, the greater the risk of them spotting movement out here. They might do something stupid."

"They're gone." Dante was staring past pine trunks toward the house. His voice was hollow, faraway.

"What?" Dyson demanded.

"You won't find them there," Joe replied. "They've already flown the coop."

"Major?" Criswell's radio crackled with his man Tommy's familiar voice. "Colson's got two survivors."

Criswell keyed his transmit button. "Who? Where?"

"An old couple named MacPhearson. Claim they were kidnapped up north in that RV. The old lady says the family here are all dead. Her old man don't look so good. Face a bad shade of gray, and smells like he's crapped his pants."

SEVENTEEN

Matilda MacPhearson was getting angry, and Joe Dante couldn't blame her. Less than an hour ago, Lyndon "Sonny" Reed had pointed a machine pistol at her head, moved it slightly to one side, and pulled the trigger. Twice. Her ears were still ringing. Instead of coming unglued at the prospect of imminent death and then being spared it, she fought to remain collected. Her husband was being tended by paramedics, embarrassed at having messed himself in his fright and still none too steady on his pins. Meanwhile, Tillie spoke to the authorities with a forcefulness that surprised Joe.

"I told you twice. I never saw the car they left in. How can I describe what it looked like? You keep beating on this like you didn't hear me the first time." She addressed agent-in-charge Al Dyson, clearly not giving a damn who he was or what his station in the federal law enforcement power structure implied. "Julio told Sonny Jim to get the *wheels*. That's how he talked. And like I told you, we were on the floor till long after they left."

Dyson gave up and turned to FDLE Major Criswell. "I still don't understand why Reed didn't kill them. It doesn't make sense."

Tillie scowled at him. "It makes perfect sense. That's not

the kind of boy he is. I know he did all those other horrible things, but it's as if Julio has some kind of hold over him. When he discovered that little girl missing this morning, then found her dead, something snapped."

"He and his buddy had killed eight people to that point," Dyson countered. "Nine, including the man you say Reed gutshot and let bleed to death. What? Suddenly he lost his appetite?"

Tillie turned to Major Criswell. "Can you make this man understand? We don't seem to be speaking the same language. I've got this awful headache, and he's making it worse."

Before Criswell could speak, Dyson was defending himself. "I need to know where they're headed, and all I've gotten here is, maybe Miami. That's a metropolitan area of close to three million. Where in Miami?"

"She's told you a dozen times that she doesn't know," Criswell replied. "I believe her. Same as I believe she doesn't know what kind of car they took."

"I think my husband should see a doctor," Tillie told Dyson. "I want him taken to a hospital. You try driving up to a roadblock, a gun to the back of your head. That poor man did it twice in the past three days. He's seventy-two years old."

Dante turned and left the room, unable to watch Al Dyson's travesty of interrogative technique any further. Outside, Bureau and FDLE personnel were searching the grounds in search of Kimberly Trammel's corpse. In the dining room, two state police pathologists were examining the bodies of the Chapel family, the mother and son both fresh kills, each executed with a single bullet to the head. Joe wondered how much more he could learn here, suspecting that no matter their conveyance, his quarry was quick putting miles between them and him. Most disturbing right now, aside from the carnage left in their wake, was

how they'd known to flee when they did. Tillie MacPhearson was very clear on that point. They'd received a phone
call and known it was for them via some prearranged code
of hang-ups and rings. Joe needed to find a phone, and not
one here on the Crooked Steeple Farm.

Late Saturday morning, Rosa Losada drove Diana Webster and Skye Lake to the funeral home to pick up Janet's
ashes while Jumbo oversaw the Bebe Masaryk surveillance.
Afterward, as they rode south on Fifth Avenue, Diana asked
if any of them was hungry.

"I suppose I could eat," Rosa replied. "Skye?" She glanced
over her shoulder into the backseat, where the young woman
slumped, an unfocused gaze aimed at the world outside. The
package of her mother's ashes, wrapped in brown paper and
sealing tape, was cradled in her lap.

"Sure." Skye said it without inflection.

"Got something in mind?" Rosa asked Diana.

"Yeah. We need a little lift. How about Union Square
Café? My treat." She paused. "I think it's odd that Joe
hasn't called yet today. Don't you?"

"He will," Rosa assured her. "Soon as there's any news."
She got impatient with a dawdling Volvo station wagon
wearing New Jersey plates, saw an opening, and shot past.
No sooner had she settled back down to her previous brisk
progress along one or another of the three middle lanes, than
the flip-up cellular phone in her handbag rang. "Grab that
for me, will you?"

Diana got the phone opened and answered it. "Hi,
Beasley. Sure. Hang on a sec." She handed the instrument
across.

"What's up?" Rosa asked Richardson.

"The shit hit the fan again, Cap. Big-time. Joey gave me a
number he wants you to call, but not from your cellular. Get
to a land line."

"What happened?"

"I'll let him tell you. How soon can you find a phone?"

"A minute, tops."

They'd swung southeast at the intersection with Broadway and were approaching Sixteenth Street as Rosa handed the cellular back to Diana. She made the left turn, searching for a hydrant. When she spotted one directly opposite the restaurant, she glided in to park. Inside the eatery, Diana and Skye were shown to their table while Rosa headed for the pay phone. It wasn't until she'd finished dialing the number that she realized the 904 area code also carried the same 263 prefix trapped by the Eric Boone wiretap last night.

"Rosa?"

"Yeah, Joe. Where are you? Beasley said the news isn't good."

"I'm at a feed store," he replied. "About three miles north of Ocala." His voice sounded tight in his throat. "Mesa and Reed spent last night right where I thought they had. Left a few ugly calling cards."

"Oh God. Who?"

"A gung-ho Gator booster named Chapel, and his family, along with his son's fiancée." He explained how Julio Mesa had apparently raped and murdered the young woman outside the house, in the middle of last night. "They're still searching the grounds for her."

"If they haven't found her, how do they know she's dead?" Or, Rosa wondered, that she'd been raped, for that matter.

"That's probably the strangest part," Joe replied. "Sonny Reed let two of their hostages go."

Rosa listened in disbelief to Dante's quick recap of how something seemed to have snapped in Reed when he discovered the young Chapel man's fiancée butchered in a motor home, parked in one of the horse farm barns.

"Good God," she murmured at his story's conclusion. "What a nightmare. What kind of shape are they in?"

"The woman is claiming her husband was like a rock through the whole ordeal, but you wouldn't know it looking at him now. Poor bastard's pretty wrung out. Her major complaint now is that her ears won't stop ringing."

"So why a feed store, Joe?"

"They were tipped. I'm sure of it. The Chapel son and his mother were still warm when we swarmed the place. Then we learn from the MacPhearson woman that they got a phone call. They left a couple grams of coke on the living room coffee table, and the front door was hanging open."

The Saturday after Thanksgiving was traditionally the first major shopping day of the Christmas season. Around Rosa, restaurant patrons in their holiday shopping finery headed to and from the rest rooms, their realities and Rosa's a universe apart. "Tipped by whom, Joe?"

"That's what's got me bugged. FDLE is out. They just came on board. But Dyson and his gang knew, and so did DEA. Gus had Charlie O'Roark in his office when I called. They're all the same players, been in the mix from jump street."

It seemed outrageous that someone in enforcement would aid and abet these killers. "If they abandoned this motor home, what are they driving?"

"FDLE is checking how many cars are registered to Chapel. They probably took something from here."

"Headed where? Miami?"

"Be my bet. Any chance you could break away, meet me there? I'm not quite ready to hop on a plane to Cali."

Many of Rosa's Cuban relatives lived in the greater Miami area. Several of them were influential in the Hispanic community. They could be an important resource. "I'll need to make some calls. How much time do I have?"

"It's three hundred miles from here to there. What? Four hours?"

"I'll call you on your car phone, let you know my flight number."

"No. Call and give me a land line number. Nothing more about where I'm going, or what I'm doing, over the air-waves. And reach out to Beasley for me. From here on, he's our only link to the chain of command."

Dante didn't fall this time, but another wave of dizziness swept over him while crossing the parking lot outside the Ocala feed store. He gathered himself as he got seated in his car, the road map in his lap. With the law so close on their heels now, Mesa, Mendoza, and Reed would waste no more time meandering. They would make tracks.

The fugitives had at least an hour's head start by the time Joe was able to slip away from the homicide scene. Another half hour had passed while he made contact with Rosa. He got back on I-75 for the first thirty miles of his journey southward, then veered off toward Orlando at the start of the Florida Turnpike. His quarry was driving a vehicle with Florida plates now, but their photographs had been on the TV news and in newspapers all up and down the East Coast for days. US 27 was less trafficked but still a direct two-lane artery running right down the middle of the state. Joe had to roll the dice when I-75 and US 27 crossed. Gambling, he took the faster road.

Two hours into his trip, Dante slipped past Fort Pierce, the Atlantic less than fifteen miles off, when Rosa made her second contact of the day. He found a filling station and called her back.

"I talked to my uncle Tico," she reported. "He and Aunt Esmerelda have a big place in Coco Plum. That's where we'll stay."

"What's your ETA?"

"I'm leaving for LaGuardia now. My flight's at 3:46. Delta. Arrives Miami International at 6:05."

Dante checked the time. It was just three. "Perfect." At the rate he was moving, he was only two and a half or three hours out. "I should get there a couple minutes before you. We're squared away with Gus?"

"He and Beasley are both right with us. As far as the rest of the world is concerned? You've fallen off the face of the map. Al Dyson's already called once, wanting to know where you disappeared."

"I'll have to stop using this phone card," he told her. "Start paying my bills with cash. The only way to plug this leak, and keep it plugged, is to work undercover as much as we can."

"It would be handy to have an enforcement contact down there," she ventured. "Maybe Tico can help. He knows everybody."

Joe appreciated the thought, but hadn't met Uncle Tico. "We'll hold him in reserve. There's a homicide cop at Metro-Dade who I think I'll call first. He flew up to New York when Freddy Mendoza was killed. We talked again on the phone when Teo made his threats."

"I forgot to ask how you're feeling today."

"Not much different from yesterday. The knee's better. I'll see you at 6:05."

Sonny Reed liked the feel of this brand-new Grand Cherokee Limited. Most of today's cars didn't accommodate a man of his bulk. Not unless they were full-size. This rig had a smaller, sportier feel than that, but the leather driver's seat hugged him like a new best friend. The ride was smooth, not Jeep-like, and the 4.8-liter V-8 had plenty of power.

Why Mesa had decided to opt for US 27, rather than the turnpike, Sonny couldn't imagine. They were in a hurry now. Still, they'd made a steady sixty miles an hour if you factored in all those stoplights between Minneola and Lake Wales. Since Sebring he'd been able to hold it at seventy, still going with the flow of traffic. They were skirting Lake Okeechobee now, the sun low on a horizon of sugarcane as far as the eye could see. A couple small towns on the south end of the lake were all that lay between here and a straight shot to Hialeah. Easy money.

Julio turned in the seat next to him to face backward. The rear seat was down and Teo lay stretched beneath a blanket, a pillow under his head. Barbara Jo was wedged in alongside him, sitting cross-legged.

"Ain't heard a peep from him in over an hour, sweet meat. He riding all right?"

"He's asleep." It came out flat. Lifeless.

"You slip him something?"

She looked up, her eyes an emotionless void. Julio waited, but there was no reply.

"I asked you a question, bitch."

Sonny could see Barbara Jo's face in the rearview as she continued to stare. When Julio's hand flashed out to slap her, all she did was close her eyes, tears trickling down her cheeks.

"Let her be," Sonny murmured. "There was a problem, she'd tell us."

Mesa turned away from Barbara Jo to face Sonny across the console. "Say what, Jim?"

Reed had been trailing a pokey old pickup for over a mile, and now saw his opening develop. He jammed the accelerator to the firewall and whipped the wheel over, rocking Mesa off balance into the door. "I said, give her a break." He shot past the pickup and jerked the wheel back hard, straightening the Jeep once again in the travel lane. His jaw was set, his left hand poised to snatch his Intratec from where it was wedged between his thigh and the door.

Julio was crazy, but he was no fool. Sonny's blood was boiling, the little veins at his temples popping. Reed was quick and strong, and in these close quarters, Mesa knew he would be no match. "You look like you could use a snort, Jim. This pressure's getting to you."

Mesa fished his plastic bag of blow from inside his duffel while Sonny read the umpteenth roadside sign advertising a tourist trap barbecue joint in Clewiston. He was hungrier for something to eat than he was for another snort. "When y'all gonna make your call?"

"Pretty quick here. Why? You hungry?" Julio could read his thoughts.

"Food crossed m' mind."

"Well, think about this. We've got all the law enforcement in the whole fucking state with a bone-on for us. Some pimple-faced little prick at a Burger King window recognizes us, they'll call out everything but the Strategic Air Command." He jammed the corner of a matchbook into the bag and held it toward Sonny's face. "Lunchtime, Jim. Suck it up."

Dante caught the Airport Expressway past Hialeah and Miami Springs just as the heavens opened up. It had been dark ever since he hit the outskirts of greater Miami half an hour ago. Now, as he made his approach south toward Miami International, torrents of tropical rain reduced his visibility to only a few feet. Traffic slowed to a crawl, the taillights of the car in front of him mere crimson smudges. He arrived at the NW Twenty-first Street airport access ramp with ten minutes remaining before Rosa's flight landed, *if* it landed. Not only was it raining, but strong, gusty winds were kicking up, the torrents driving straight down one second and sweeping horizontal the next.

Joe's rumpled polo shirt and cotton slacks were soaked by the time he entered the Delta terminal a minute after six. He found a band of overhead monitors and was scanning an arrivals screen for Rosa's flight, when he heard her call his name. He turned and saw her crossing the concourse toward him, her pocketbook slung over one shoulder and a single garment bag in hand.

"You're early," he greeted her.

She dropped the bag to wrap her arms around his neck and hug him. Joe didn't worry about the effect of his wet clothes on her silk blouse and hugged her back, fiercely. Rosa stepped back, hands on his shoulders.

"Let me have a look at you." She gave him a once-over from bad knee to bandaged head, and sighed. "God, Joe. You look like hell."

"Yeah? You try living outta your car for three days. That your only luggage?"

"Yep. How bad's the driving?"

"About as bad as I look." He bent to retrieve Rosa's hang-up and was conscious of her studying the way he walked as they set off for the parking garage.

They were in his car, headed south toward Coral Gables on LeJeune Road as Dante finished telling Rosa about the Metro-Dade homicide detective he wanted to contact. He then steered the conversation toward their host. "Tell me about this Uncle Tico. He and your aunt have room? You're sure of that?"

Rosa's black hair was highlighted by streetlight refracted in the rain-soaked window behind her. She smiled. "You've never been to Coco Plum, I bet."

"Barely been to Miami. Flew down here once to testify at a trial."

"My uncle is the laundry king of South Florida. You stay in a hotel, eat off a table cloth in a restaurant, or towel off at a health club, there's a good chance his company washed, dried, and folded your linen."

"No kidding. So he *does* know everybody."

She nodded. "Oh, yeah. And wait till you meet my aunt Esme. The Orange Bowl queen, 1973. She and their nineteen-year-old twins are gorgeous."

"And you're trusting me in the same house with them?"

She chuckled. "I'll risk it. In your condition, the twins could outrun you."

There was no let-up in the downpour as they traveled the length of Coral Gables to the end of LeJeune. There, it emptied into a traffic circle that took them around to a guard house at the entrance to Coco Plum. Joe ran his window down and was greeted by a young cop in a slicker and Metro-Dade uniform hat.

"Yes, sir?"

Rosa leaned across the console. "I'm Tico Losada's niece. He told you we were coming?"

"Yes, ma'am. Go right ahead. You know where it is?"

She told him she did, and they rolled down a well-lit, divided thoroughfare. Dante peered out through the rain at the surrounding houses and whistled.

"Never knew there was *this* kind of money in dirty sheets."

The residences lining both sides of the street were of the eight- to twelve-thousand-square-foot variety. The architecture was a hodgepodge, with every style represented from Bauhaus to Greek Revival. Tico and Esme Losada's place was located on East Lago Drive, perched above the Lago Maggiore waterway, and looking as unlikely as a Georgian mansion with palm trees could.

A maid greeted the two refugees from the storm, and led them into a parlor of rich Spanish colonial textures.

"Rosita!" a dapper, white-haired man exclaimed. "It's only to chase killers that you come south anymore?" He embraced her affectionately, and turned to Joe. "Ah. The Lieutenant Dante I have heard so much about. A pleasure."

Dante took the extended hand and shook. "*My* pleasure, sir. We appreciate your hospitality."

Tico Losada seemed too young to have white hair; maybe fifty. He was of medium stature, trim, and wore a neat little mustache. All of his clothing, from woven leather loafers to navy blue jacket, looked European and expensive. "Not a problem, my friend. We are most happy to accommodate a guest or two around here. Allow me to introduce my wife, Esmerelda."

The realization that this aristocratic beauty who grasped his hand was the mother of nineteen-year-olds gave Dante pause. She was probably close to his own age, but looked at least ten years younger.

"Welcome, Senor Dante. We've heard of your ordeal from Rosa, and on the news. You must be exhausted."

"Give me your car keys," Tico directed. "You are soaked. I will send someone out for your luggage. After such a trip, you should rest." He turned to the maid. "Rita. Send Jorge out to the car, then show my niece and Lieutenant Dante to their rooms."

"I'm gonna need to use a phone," Joe told him. "And I've gotta ask you to tell no one we're here."

"My niece has explained, Lieutenant. There is a private line in your suite. Please. Relax. Take a shower. If you wish to join us, we have a dinner reservation at the Aragon Café for eight-thirty."

As they mounted the stairs to the second floor, Joe whispered in Rosa's ear. "Rooms. Plural."

She looked back at him. "They're Catholic, Joe. Devout. And we're not married. I'm his brother's little girl."

Dante's own Irish-Italian mother was just as Catholic. Were he and Rosa to visit her and her new husband in Arizona, the situation would be no different.

Rosa patted his arm. "I'll check for squeaky floorboards in the hall. Maybe we can work something out."

EIGHTEEN

There was rarely a quiet weekend night for Sergeant Mel Sullivan of the Metro-Dade Homicide Bureau. As whip of the Bureau's special squad attached to Operation Red Rum, Mel got calls no matter where he was on a Saturday night. The joint Metro-Dade/DEA task force investigated drug trafficker homicides. Saturday night was party night, and a prime hunting time. Players let their guards down, left themselves open at social clubs and discos. This particular Saturday night, Mel was hoping the shooters would hold off until late. He had tickets to watch the Heat play the Orlando Magic.

Mel and fellow homicide detective Oscar Cobian had paid their check at the Carolina Café, around the corner from the arena, when Sullivan's pager started vibrating against his hip. As he reached for it, all that good pork barbecue he'd just put away started to turn against him.

From a pay phone at the back of the café, Mel rang the Criminal Investigation Division switchboard. "Sullivan. Ernie Fontana's covering, isn't he?"

"Got a call for you, Sarge. A detective lieutenant from New York. Says it's urgent."

"Christ. Who? I've got seats three rows back of the Magic bench."

"Name's Dante. Left a number in Coco Plum."

That changed everything. Six weeks earlier, Joe Dante had busted the Cali cartel's New York operation wide open. He and his partner had killed Freddy Mendoza, Lucho Esparza's number one man in the area. Before Freddy moved north to take over that show, he'd been an ugly thorn in Metro-Dade's side. He and his brother, Teo, were implicated in a half dozen homicides that Red Rum had tried, but failed, to pin on them.

"Gimme the number," Mel told the operator.

Dante picked up on the first ring. "That you, Mel?"

"I see you made it. We've been hearing rumors," Sullivan replied.

"It's still a rumor, anyone asks. We had them in Gainesville, Mel. They were tipped."

"Shit. You're sure?"

"No doubt in my mind. I need somebody outside the loop who I can trust. Can you help me?"

"That depends. If the Fan Belt Inspectors decide Miami's where Mendoza's headed, it'll be chaos here."

"While Mendoza and his pals slip out of the country undetected. I've got to work fast, Mel. The weather forecast might be in my favor."

That evening, the Weather Channel had predicted several days of heavy rain and wind. A rare, late season southeaster was coming ashore off the Atlantic, and would rage clear up the East Coast. Mel had driven through the start of it on his way downtown tonight. Small craft advisories were up, and light planes were likely to be grounded for the duration.

"You know I'll do what I can, Joe. What do you need?"

"A guy who's tapped into the Cali cartel scene down here. Somebody with an ear to the rumor mill."

Sullivan eyed Oscar Cobian as the cherubic, easygoing

Colombian detective ogled a group of high-fashion black women at a table near the sidewalk. Cobian was a hopeless flirt, and ran the best string of informants in the Criminal Investigation Division. "I think I've got your man, Joe. Not that he'll be too happy about it. He's on vacation."

"He still in town?" Dante's tone was a mixture of hope and doubt.

Mel smiled to himself. As long as an inexhaustible supply of beautiful women existed in the greater Miami area, Oscar saw little reason to travel. "You're in Coco Plum? Give me an address. I'll bring him by within the half hour."

"I'm at my girlfriend's aunt and uncle's place." Dante gave Mel the address.

"Nice. Who's this uncle? Frank Rubino?"

"Tico Losada. I guess he's big in laundry."

Sullivan chuckled. "You *are* a stranger in these parts. Tico Losada *is* Miami laundry. Who's this girlfriend?"

Dante had asked Rita, the maid, for some adhesive tape, gauze, and an iron. She insisted that the house staff would press whatever he needed, and when she returned with his medical supplies, he traded her a rumpled navy blazer, dress shirt, and tan slacks. In the bath, he used his manicure scissors to cut away the tape wrapping his head. It hurt like holy hell to peel it from the tender, bruised skin.

What he found beneath was gruesome. The ricocheting slug had burrowed a groove diagonally through the flesh of his temple, from hairline to half an inch above the middle of his left eyebrow. The doctor had closed the wound with twenty-eight precise little stitches. The surrounding area was in the yellowing stage of bruised, and stained an amber color from disinfectant. Joe hoped the gash was healed enough now to be waterproof, because tonight he planned to go the whole nine yards: shave, shower, *and* wash his hair.

Julio Mesa called the cartel's main man in the Miami area from a phone booth on the south end of Lake Okeechobee, and was told that with the weather deteriorating so quickly, there would be no plane to extract them tonight. After what happened to Eddy Sandts on Wednesday, every cartel pilot in the hemisphere had the foul weather jitters. By the time they reached Miami, all local airports were expected to be closed to small plane traffic. The best they could hope for was an amphibious landing somewhere west of town in the Everglades, and even that would require a break in the forecasted storm.

Sonny Reed heard this with a growing sense of dread. His chances of surviving, cooped up with Mesa much longer, seemed slim. He wondered if his old buddy had intended to kill him all along, as soon as he had no more use for him. Julio had paid off all of Sonny's gambling debts, and wiped the slate clean for the money he owed for three kilos of coke. There was another quarter million forthcoming, when they reached South America, but Sonny doubted now that he'd ever see it. Julio probably assumed that Sonny would fail to grasp the reality of his predicament. Sonny was a football player, after all. And a dumb shit Georgia cracker football player at that.

It was seven-fifteen and had been dark for over an hour, with rain falling in gust-swept buckets, when Julio directed Reed off the Dolphin Expressway at LeJeune Road. Minutes later they turned into a gas station at the intersection with Flagler Avenue.

"You hang here, Jim." Julio searched his pockets for a quarter, his objective a pay phone in one of those pitiful little cutaway pods, the rain pouring down all around it. Sonny knew Mesa would have had him make this call if it was to anyone else but Eddie Ochoa. "This asshole best not jerk me around. We're sitting ducks in these fucking wheels."

No sooner did Julio jump from the passenger seat and run for the phone than Reed slammed the butt of his machine pistol into the overhead console, smashing the dome light. He looked back over his shoulder at the surprised nurse. "Ya wanna live as much as I do, I suggest y'all shift ass, sugar." He plucked the keys from the ignition. "When I open this door, he won't see no light now. He sees us anyway, an' starts t' shoot, I can cover y'all to a point. After that, you're on your own."

Barbara Jo knew she was dead if she stayed. Sonny had barely planted a foot after tugging the release handle when she was hot on his tail, clawing her way between the seats and tumbling headfirst onto the rainswept pavement.

From inside the Jeep, Mendoza cried out something unintelligible before Reed could get the door shut. In the howling storm, it didn't carry very far. Sonny reached down to grab Barbara by the collar of her blouse, jerked her to her feet, and started off at a run, one arm around her waist. A block west on Flagler, he turned south and slowed to let Barbara Jo get her breath, then continued down Forty-third Avenue at a brisk walk. He pulled his wallet from his back pocket.

"Here. Y'all won't get far on this, but take it." He thrust a twenty at her. It left him with four hundred and sixty, and some singles. "Hail a cab. I 'spect the cops'll be real happy t' see ya."

Barbara Jo stared at him as she hurried alongside. "Why are you doing this?"

"Survival, I guess. And you was just as dead as me."

"Where will you go?"

Rainwater streamed into his eyes beneath the bill of his baseball cap. "Nuh-uh, sugar." He still had the Cherokee keys in his hand, and flung them into the night. "Damn that cocksucker t' hell."

Joe had always been quick to mend, but at forty-two, he no longer bounced back with youth's accustomed ease. His leg was better than when he left the hospital, Thursday, but when he moved his head too quickly, Rosa saw his pain. It was there in the sudden flex of a jaw muscle, or an involuntary clench of a fist. His drive south had left him looking haggard.

She found him with a towel wrapped around his waist, shaving at the bathroom sink. The stitched head wound looked nasty with all the bruising around it. His short-cropped, sandy hair was finger-combed back from his face, still wet from his shower. "You look better, anyway," she told him.

"It's amazing what clean hair will do for a man. A head transplant and another twelve hours' sleep, I'd be good as new."

She considered a lecture and abandoned it as futile. As he studied her reflection in the mirror, she saw his expression soften.

"*You* look good enough to eat. You doing anything tonight, after the show?"

"Down, boy." Rosa wore a simple black pleated skirt, which flattered her small waist and showed off her slender, sculpted legs. Her long-sleeve red silk blouse was left open enough for a hint of cleavage to show. A strand of pearls gleamed against her light cocoa complexion. "How'd you make out with your Metro-Dade guy?"

"We might be in luck. He's got a man he thinks can help us. They're on their way now. Should be here any minute."

No sense asking why it couldn't wait until morning. Rosa stepped up to have a closer look at his head.

"What do you think?" he asked.

"A little antiseptic and a gauze pad. We can probably skip the Revolutionary War fife-player look." She reached for a sterile gauze packet and tore it. "You think you can hold still?"

Ten minutes later the job was done. Rosa relaxed in the comfortably appointed drawing room of the suite, watching Joe get dressed through the open bedroom doorway. Battle scars and all, she was terribly fond of that tough-guy body. The sight of him, standing naked and slipping into his briefs and slacks, gave her a delicious feeling of anticipation. A soft knock came at the door.

It was Rita the maid. "Two men to see Senor Dante, senorita. Detectives from Metro-Dade."

"We'll be down in a minute," Joe called from the bedroom. He emerged knotting his tie and sat on the settee to slip into his shoes.

Minutes later, a much refreshed Joe Dante preceded Rosa to the top of the stairs. With his forehead dressing reduced to an adhesive tape bandage, only the discoloration around his left eye betrayed how severe the blow to the head had actually been. In the entrance gallery below, Rosa saw two strangers, one lean and distinguished with neatly cut silver hair, and the other shorter, with curls of unkempt jet hair framing a wide, boyish face. They stood waiting with her uncle Tico. The slender Anglo watched Joe's descent; his Latino pal watched hers.

Halfway down the stairs, Joe lifted a hand in greeting and started to say something. Then he suddenly swayed, reached for the railing, and missed. Before Rosa could react to grab him, his knees buckled. He pitched forward and hit down hard on one side, flipped head over heels, and landed in a heap on the marble floor below. Rosa screamed and missed a step. Unlike Joe, she caught the rail, but still landed hard on a tread, her skirt up around her waist.

"Good God!" someone yelled.

Rosa managed to struggle to her feet and saw all three men on their knees beside Joe. They quickly got him onto his back, where the silver-haired cop put his ear to Joe's chest. Rosa had broken a heel, and frantically tore that shoe off, and then the other, to run downstairs barefoot.

"He's breathing. I've got a heartbeat," the man with the ear down announced. He looked up to his friend. "Call Jackson. Tell them to scramble the Medevac chopper."

"In this weather?" the Latino replied. "Forget about it, Mel. Let's get him an ambulance."

NINETEEN

In the fifteen minutes it took the cartel's Miami underboss, Eduardo Ochoa, to send a car to the corner of LeJuene and Flagler, time crawled like a glacier. Julio Mesa now stood in the living room of a large, Spanish-style Coral Gables house on the corner of Alhambra Circle and Sevilla Avenue, his clothing still soaked from standing at that pay phone. Across the sparsely furnished room, Eddie Ochoa paced the bare parquet floor.

"I'm telling you, Eddie, the fucker broke the light. I couldn't see him. He just fucking walked away."

"But this is crazy, no?" Ochoa countered. "He stay in this country, he is a dead man. Why, Julio? For this nurse?"

Every instinct told Mesa that even if Sonny let Barbara Jo Kelly go, she couldn't have gotten to the police in time. Not before Ochoa's people arrived to rescue him and Teo. If she had, he wouldn't be here now. Eddie was fearful that the cops might have set up surveillance; that they'd been followed here.

"For the nurse? I can't imagine," he replied. "You ain't seen his girlfriend." He paused, imagining what he would do in Sonny's shoes. "Besides, the nurse can implicate him, same as she can implicate me. The minute he got her some-place quiet, he put a bullet in her brainpan. Believe me."

Ochoa continued to pace. "On the television, they talk only about you, Julio. They say it was you did all these things."

"All *what* things?" Mesa demanded. God, he needed a snort.

Ochoa didn't care if Julio was Lucho Esparza's nephew. He had a show to run. He was all too aware of the problems Julio had brought here to his turf. *"El rapto."* He spat it, like it was a foul taste in his mouth. *"Y mutilación de mujeres."*

Mesa straightened, trying to reach for the right element of indignation. *"They* say?"

Eddie's eyes bore into him. "I think this is not the first time, *hermano*."

Julio stood his ground. How dare this lackey, this pissant, challenge him. "Careful," he warned.

Eddie grunted. "No, senor. I think *you* will be careful. Miami is my responsibility. You bring me trouble, I cut your *cojones* off."

For the first seconds after Dante opened his eyes, he had no idea where he was. The floor beneath him was cold as a tomb. Overhead, a monsterous wrought-iron chandelier loomed. Then he looked left, confronted the worried faces of two beautiful young women, and thought he was seeing double. Behind them, he recognized Mel Sullivan, and everything fell into place.

"Joe, honey?" It was Rosa. He felt his hand squeezed as she leaned over him.

"Yeah." His mouth was dry. It came out papery thin. "Damn. I blacked out again, didn't I?"

"Again?"

He closed his eyes and tried to take stock of the damage.

He remembered now that he'd been on the stairs. What? Maybe halfway down? That must have been quite a fall. Still, he had feeling in all his extremities; could wiggle his fingers and toes. "In a parking lot," he told her. "At a truck stop." He opened his eyes again, avoided Rosa's, and tried to sit. A half dozen hands gently but firmly stopped him, and eased him back down.

"Oh, no, you don't." It was Sullivan. "The ambulance will be here any minute. You're going for a ride."

Joe scowled. "I'm fine, for crissake."

"Sure you are. You just took a fall down a dozen stone stairs, and landed on a marble floor. You say this happened before?"

"It was nothing. I'd had a long day. Got a little dizzy is all. You brought your friend?"

"Don't worry about it. You're off the clock."

"Like hell I am."

Sullivan shook his head, amazed at Dante's willfulness. "Sorry, Joe. It isn't open to debate. I'll be damned, the most highly decorated street cop, from the biggest police force in the free world, is gonna buy it on *my* beat."

It was five miles, as the crow flies, from where Sonny Reed left Julio to where the MacArthur Causeway left the mainland for South Miami Beach. Through the stormy, rainswept night, Sonny Reed took a slightly longer route. In this weather, even crows were grounded. In an effort to blend in during the drive south, he'd worn casual clothes: shorts, sneakers, a T-shirt and Florida Gators cap. They made a perfect disguise now. Only a crazy jock would be nuts enough to go out for a run in this rain.

When Reed reached the Orange Bowl, he took advantage of a bank of pay phones out of the weather to call Bebe. It hardly seemed possible that the cops hadn't canceled his phone card, but when he dialed Dallas Direct, the call went through. Steve Lombard, the bar manager, had to recognize his voice, but didn't say anything.

"Where *are* you?" Bebe asked.

"Never mind. I need y'all t' contact Billy Pickering for me. He's in Cincinnati, playin' the Bengals. I think the Dolphins stay at the Westin."

"There is policeman here. He watches me."

"I bet he does. This is kinda an emergency, Beeb. Call the Westin. Get a number where I can reach Billy. I'll call you back, 'bout an hour."

Sonny cradled the phone and started east again at an easy trot. Within seconds he had the bill of his cap tugged low against the driving rain, thankful this wasn't New York. It might be wet, but at least it was warm.

Rosa told her uncle Tico and aunt Esmerelda that she would call the Aragon Café once emergency doctors had examined Joe. She rode in the ambulance while Sergeant Sullivan and Detective Cobian followed in Mel's car. Dante was in good voice the entire seven-mile trip to Jackson Memorial Hospital in downtown Miami. He insisted he was fine. He was an adult, capable of making his own decisions. He had too much work to do to spend any more time in hospitals. Rosa turned a deaf ear.

At Jackson, the fact that Joe was accompanied by two of Metro-Dade's finest seemed to carry weight. Ten minutes into his initial examination by the emergency room staff, a resident neurologist was called to consult. He ordered a CAT scan and complete set of head X rays. Dante was wheeled off to radiology, and Rosa and Sullivan were left alone. Cobian had wandered off somewhere, and returned carrying three plastic foam cups of coffee.

"I got black, black, and black. Coffee-mate and sugar in my right jacket pocket." He extended the cups toward Rosa first.

"Black is perfect," she said. "Thanks."

Cobian watched her move, and was clearly delighted. "You know, when we were waiting downstairs with your uncle and he tol' us he has a niece that's a captain with NYPD, I had a whole different mental image."

Rosa sipped her coffee and smiled. "We come in all shapes and sizes, Detective."

"Call me Oscar, Cap. I'll be crushed if you don't, and self-esteem is so important today."

"Down, boy," Sullivan growled. He turned to Rosa. "You've got to forgive Detective Cobian, Captain. He considers this Latin lover shit part of his heritage."

"I grew up in Spanish Harlem, Sergeant," Rosa replied. "I know all about his heritage, believe me." She paused. "Joe told you about the leak, right?"

Sullivan nodded. "He said he wants to go it alone down here. Wanted me to find him an ear into the Colombian community. That's our man Oscar here." He leaned closer to Rosa, confiding. "He's really less obnoxious than he seems at first."

Cobian grinned, Sullivan's words rolling like water off a ship's deck. "The way I see it? If Teo Mendoza's here in Miami, they're hiding him in one of two places. Either Kendall or Coral Gables. You've got a whole lot of *Caleños*, both places. Krome Avenue's possible, too, out past Kendall-Tamiami Airport. They've got some big estates out there."

"In other words," Rosa concluded, "they could be just about anywhere."

Oscar shrugged. "But pretty soon, the rumors, they gonna start flying. Saturday night is rumba night. Colombians go to discos, they drink *aguardiente*, and they start to talk. This Teo Mendoza escape has been playing big on the Spanish stations down here."

Rosa made direct eye contact with Cobian. "When Mesa and Reed slipped out from under the net in Gainesville this morning, Joe was convinced they'd come here. That your guess too?"

Cobian thought about it. "Where else? Considering what a hot potato Teo is. Ever since Lucho Esparza came to power, Teo's been the most feared soldier in the Cali army. When he went inside last year? Every doper in Florida heaved a sigh of relief. It's only Esparza's inner core down here that's gonna want within a mile of him, hole in his chest or not."

"And who are they? This so-called inner core?"

"Primarily? Eduardo Ochoa's the only name you need. He's at the same level Freddy Mendoza was. If anyone can get them out of the country, Ochoa's that man."

Rosa stared out a window streaked with rainwater. It glowed amber in the streetlight. "Joe thinks we have the weather in our favor; that the forecast might buy us another couple days."

Cobian shrugged. "Maybe. Nothing will fly in that shit. Not smaller than a 747."

Sullivan frowned and grabbed his pager off his belt. "Damn," he murmured. "What now?" He read the number in the message window and searched for a phone.

Sheltered, again, from the storm, Sonny Reed called Bebe Masaryk, this time from the Miami Metromover's Overtown Station. There was an event at the arena tonight, judging from the street hustler activity and police presence in the area. But Sonny felt curiously invisible. The last thing a cop had an eye out for in this revitalized ghetto area was some crazy white boy out for a run in the rain, especially one as big as he was. They were on the lookout for local kids with spark plugs in their pockets, out vandalizing the cars of event patrons too cheap to park in a lot.

At Dallas Direct, Bebe came on the line in less than a

minute. There was clear anxiety in her voice. "Billy, he want to know why you want to talk, Sonny."

"But y'all got his number, yeah? Give it to me." So Pickering and the Dolphins were indeed staying at the Westin in Cincinnati.

"They won't tell me his room. You must call the desk." She paused. "I am scared, Sonny. Policemen, they come to my apartment. Follow me. Everywhere I go, they go too."

Reed had a plan. As an illegal alien, Bebe was afraid to open a bank account, fearful the IRS might report her to Immigration. "How much cash y'got stashed, baby?"

Her tone went from anxious to cautious. That was the thanks he got for all that free coke. "Why do you ask this?"

"I'm kinda in a pickle down here. Julio went off his nut, and I had t' bail on him. If y'all been watchin' the news, y'know what I'm talkin' about."

More caution. "These things they say? They are true?"

" 'Fraid so, sugar. I'm gonna hole up a couple days, then get the fuck gone from here. Lucho Esparza owes me, but I only got one chance t' collect. I gotta get down there on my own."

"You want me to go with you?" Relief and excitement filled her voice. Colombia was the mother lode.

"I was gonna send for y'all once I got down there, right? There's just been a slight change of plan. Y'all gotta help, Beeb."

"But the police."

"Don't pack nothin', and don't say nothin'. Just make a reservation, and get your passport and cash t'gether. Then y'all walk out like you're goin' for cigarettes, hop on a subway, ride it a few stops, an' grab a cab."

There was hesitation, the silence heavy between them. Bebe was weighing her options. She had a good-paying job in New York. On the other hand, her unlimited supply of cocaine was fifteen hundred miles away, and headed farther south. Bebe could always get another job, anywhere men paid to stare at naked women and drool.

"How will you know, when I come?"

"Call me at Billy's. Down here. Y'all got that number in your book."

"He tell me he want nothing to do with you, Sonny. You are crazy."

Reed snorted. "Like hell he don't. Uppity sonofabitch. When y'all call me there, I guarantee I'll be answerin' the fuckin' phone."

When Sergeant Sullivan answered his page, the details were sketchy. Somehow, the nurse kidnapped by Julio Mesa and Sonny Reed had managed to escape. She walked into the Miami Police Department's South District substation at 2200 West Flagler, soaked to the bone. Rosa Losada remained behind, fearful of being connected to Dante and undermining his efforts in Miami, while Sullivan and Cobian hurried off to see this apparition in the flesh.

After an hour and a half spent watching the anxious faces of other emergency room friends and relatives, and thumbing back-issues of *People*, Rosa saw Joe's neurologist, Dr. Toller, emerge to approach her.

"Captain Losada? Your friend Lieutenant Dante has a stubborn streak, doesn't he?"

"I think that's safe to say. What's the story, Doctor?"

"He'll probably want to sue me when he regains consciousness, but I had him sedated for his own protection. What he needs more than anything right now is rest."

"He admitted blacking out last night, too, Doctor. What's causing it?"

"Swelling of the brain tissue, behind the spot where he was struck." Toller spread his hands, shaking his head. "There's no neurological damage that I can see. The X rays and CAT scan are pretty clear. I've prescribed a course of

Decadron. He'll take it in tablet form for the next week, to back up the injection we gave him. It should keep the swelling reduced, and give him time to heal." He reached into his jacket pocket for a card, and handed it over. "We can't force him to stay here, Captain. By the sound of it, he won't stay on his own. Give my office a call if you've got any questions. Maybe you'll get better results trying to reason with him than I did."

Shortly after Toller left, as Rosa contemplated calling a cab, Mel Sullivan and Oscar Cobian reappeared. They rushed through the doors from the sidewalk with their heads ducked, both shaking water from their clothes.

"You hear anything?" Mel asked.

"He insisted on leaving, so they sedated him."

"Any diagnosis?"

Rosa shrugged. "He's okay. No brain damage. What he needs is rest, and a chance to heal. So *is* it Barbara Jo Kelly?"

"Damnedest thing," Sullivan replied. "Reed let her go. While Mesa was making a phone call, at a gas station on the corner of Flagler and LeJuene." He went on to relate the nurse's story of how Reed and Mesa had a falling out. It was Sonny who'd killed Wesley Chapel, Sr., in Ocala, but he seemed to draw the line at rape and mutilation. When they reached Miami, Sonny knew that Barbara Jo would be Mesa's next victim, and he simply let her loose. "FDLE called right before we left. They found the Trammel girl's BMW convertible sunk in a pond at the Chapel farm, just where the Kelly woman said it was. The body was locked in the trunk."

Rosa felt a cold wind blow across her soul, and shivered. "How could Reed let the nurse go without jeopardizing himself?" she asked.

"Probably didn't figure he could." It was Cobian who answered her. "Which is mos' likely why he ran too."

Rosa stared at Cobian with surprise. "He what?"

"Mel forgot to mention that. *Both* of them split. Soon as they were clear, Sonny gave her twenty bucks an' kept on going."

"Just like that? Left her standing and ran off into the night?"

"That's right. So what can you tell us about the FBI's agent-in-charge out of New York? Name of Dyson?"

"Damn. He was there, huh?"

" 'Fraid so. Showed up an' tried to run us off, saying this is a Bureau investigation, and we got no jurisdiction. Mel and him got into it a little."

"Speaking of which," Sullivan interjected, "I'm going to leave you two. If Teo Mendoza and Julio Mesa are in Miami, my task force has a legitimate interest. This Fan Belt Inspector hot dog is kidding himself, he thinks there's only one guy can play hard-ball around here."

"We swung by the arena so I could collect my wheels," Oscar told Rosa. "I'll take you back to your uncle's. Or, if you want, I can take you someplace to eat."

"I'd forgotten I was even hungry," she admitted. It was a quarter to ten. There was no sense trying to join Tico, Esmerelda, and the girls at this late hour. "You already ate earlier, didn't you?"

"It don't matter. I can take you someplace quiet, you can eat and I can talk. I'm your Cali cartel expert, right?"

TWENTY

When the phone at Billy Pickering's Westin Hotel bedside rang at 9:45 P.M., central time, he'd finished debating whether or not to answer it.

"Billy, old son? That you, boy?"

Pickering played free safety for the Miami Dolphins, having made the squad this season as a third-round draft pick. He and Sonny Reed had roomed together for four years at the University of Florida.

"Why you doing this to me, Lyndon? You're fucking poison, man."

"Because y'all owe me, good buddy, and I need t' collect."

Pickering paced nervously, phone in hand, and regarded his reflection in the mirror across the room. Six foot one, two hundred and five pounds, and without an ounce of visible fat, he'd been nicknamed "Punishment" by the Miami media. Right now he felt helpless. "Jesus, man. It ain't like you're wanted for drunk driving or fishing without a license. You've killed twelve people, for crissake."

"Don't say no, good buddy. I'm out here hangin' in the breeze. Call your doorman. Say y'all got a buddy comin' by, needs a place t' stay. Tell him t' give me your key."

At the end of summer camp, after Billy won the starting free safety job, the Dolphins had negotiated a lucrative three-year contract. Billy had used some of the up-front signing money to buy an apartment on Ocean Drive in ultra-hip South Miami Beach. "You're crazy," he told Reed. "Your face is all over the place. You think you won't be recognized?"

"By who? Them stoned-out assholes in the lobby of your place? Y'all think they read? Or watch the news? Shit. They don't watch nothin' but MTV."

Pickering squared his shoulders to the mirror and straightened to flex his abs. "I do this, I become an accessory, Lyndon." He watched the washboard ripple with an uncharacteristic disinterest. "To murder."

"Only if they catch me, and they ain't gonna do that, boy. I placed them bets for all of us, Billy, but I'm the only one took the fall. Y'all are playin' football t'day, which is more'n I can say."

"You say that like *we* fucked you over, Lyndon. You fucked yourself."

Billy heard Reed chuckle. "That don't change how the Dolphins would feel, they know y'all conspired t' shave a sure-cover spread."

"Nothin's ever sure, Lyndon. That's why they call them odds."

"Suck mine, boy. You fuck with me now, y'all can kiss it good-bye."

Pickering was sweating, his hand clammy on the receiver. "All right. I'll call."

"That's the smart play, Billy boy. Oh, and by the way. Where'd y'all park your car?"

The Colombian doctor closed the door to Teo Mendoza's room and carried his bag through to the safe house living room. There, Julio Mesa, Eduardo Ochoa, and Ochoa's mistress, Andrea, sat lounging in chairs and smoking cigarettes. Two of Eddie's lieutenants could be seen in an adjacent room, watching television.

"So?" Ochoa asked.

"The antibiotic this nurse give him. It was the best thing, considering the circumstances. I have started a drip of the same drug, directly into his bloodstream."

"He look so weak," Eddie replied. "When can he travel?"

The doctor asked for a cigarette. Andrea shook two from her pack, handed him her gold butane lighter, and let him light both. He inhaled deeply while shaking his head. "To where? Don Lucho's? I don' think so, Eduardo. Not before this infection, it is under control. In the rainy season, such wounds do not heal well on the equator."

Mesa, quiet to that point, was suddenly on his feet. He flicked a cigarette butt to the floor and ground it beneath his heel. There were many such scars as the one it left in the parquet. "Fuck this noise. The weather clears? We're flyin' his ass outta here. It ain't just him hung out to dry here, Jim."

Eddie's expression was cold as marble. Turned away from Mesa, he extended a hand to the doctor. "*Gracias, amigo.* There is trouble, your nurse know what to do?"

"She is the best I have. I will return in the morning. *Buenas noches, señor.*" He faced and bowed to Andrea before starting for the door.

Ochoa lifted a Securenet radio to inform a man out front that the doctor was leaving. He sounded tired when he turned back to Julio. "In Miami, I give the orders, *sobrino.* Not you." His use of the Spanish for *nephew* was not uttered with respect. "When the weather clears, we talk, *si?*"

Ochoa's two henchmen had abandoned their TV program to join their boss. They regarded Julio with cold, bored stares that said they would just as soon shoot him as look at him, no matter whose nephew he was. Ignoring them, and Ochoa's intentional affront, Mesa turned to Andrea.

"I'm hungry. Fix us something to eat."

She stood and flipped her half-smoked cigarette at his shoes. "Eat shit." With a toss of her head, she started for the front door. "I'm going to get some air, Eddie. It stinks in here."

Oscar Cobian could see the exhaustion in Captain Losada's face as they sat in the Cuban restaurant he'd chosen off SW Twenty-fourth Street. Their dash to the door, through the persistent downpour, had gotten her hair wet. She shook her head, pulling that heavy black mane from her face.

"This is nice." She eased back in her chair to look around, taking in the high ceilings, rain-streaked skylights, and the privacy screens created by dozens of potted palmettos.

"I thought you'd like it. It's quiet. Low-key."

"I appreciate that. Thanks. I'm sorry you missed your basketball game. This is above and beyond the call."

The waiter approched to take drink orders. They decided they were in a wine mood. Rosa thought she would prefer white and asked Oscar to pick one from the list. Once the waiter departed, she focused on Cobian with fresh curiosity.

"You seem pretty acculturated for a guy with such close ties to the Colombian community. You born here, or there?"

"There. But I'm only half Colombian. My mother is Caleño. My father was American."

"Was? He's dead?"

Oscar nodded. "Killed by bandits. He was a geologist, working for Exxon in the mountains near the Venezuelan border. I was only three."

"When was that?"

"Nineteen sixty-five. My mother and I moved to Houston after that, to stay with my father's family. She got so home-sick for other Colombians, we moved here when I was five."

"There aren't any Colombians in Houston?"

Their waiter arrived with their wine and showed Oscar

the bottle, a Chilean chardonnay. He nodded and returned to Rosa's question. "Not as many in 1965 as there are today. And the majority of Colombians in Houston were black, even then. It's not the same culture."

The notion produced a smile with a frown wrapped around it. "I just learned something I didn't know. But of course. They would be different worlds. So you grew up in Miami's Cali culture."

The waiter poured the wine for Oscar to taste. He hadn't realized how much he wanted a drink until the first chilled sip ran back across his tongue. "People from all over Colombia banded together back then. From Cali, Bogotá, Cartagena, Barranquilla."

"Medellín."

Everywhere. Sure. But compared to the Cubans, or the Puerto Ricans? We went pretty much unnoticed, until Americans started their love affair with cocaine."

Her glass now full, she lifted it to her lips and sipped with her eyes closed. He watched her face. This was one good-looking *cubana*. Oscar was conscious of the envious glances from men seated at other tables around them.

"Tell me what you know about Mateo Mendoza, Oscar." Her energy was coming back. He could see it as she opened her eyes again. "Who his contacts would be. What the Cali cartel power structure looks like, here."

"The answer to that question is the same as to who would hide him. Eddie Ochoa. In Miami, Eddie Ochoa *is* the cartel power structure. If Teo Mendoza is here, Eddie is who he's being sheltered by. No doubt about it."

Rosa had her menu open and scanned it distractedly for a moment. "How's the ropa vieja?"

Literally meaning "old clothes," ropa vieja was as close as anything to a Cuban national dish; stewed flank steak, tomato, basil, and pimiento.

"Good. But you should try the langosta enchilada. It's

killer, here." Just the idea of it made Oscar's mouth water, and he wasn't even hungry; lobster chunks cooked in a sofrito sauce and served with pieces of fried bread.

"Ah. Good call. With salpicón, I think." Salpicón was a Cuban meat salad. "How hard is Ochoa going to be to track down?"

Oscar smiled. She wasn't easy to derail, once she got running in a direction. "That depends. He's naturalized, so he can't be deported. Without getting the goods on him, and making them stick, we've got no choice but to let him run free."

"And does he?"

"When he *wants* to be seen. Sure. You can find him most Saturday nights, out on the Colombian club circuit."

"But the problem is when he doesn't want to be seen, correct?"

"You got it. He keeps half a dozen houses all over the Miami area, and is always changing them. His official address, where his wife and kids live, is a walled estate out on Krome Avenue, back up to the 'Glades."

"Any special car he drives?"

Cobian signaled the waiter. The talk of food had made him hungry too. "That's another problem. He's got four identical Mercedes 600 sedans, all armored, with tinted, bullet-proof glass. When he wants to go somewhere? And doesn't want us to know about it? All four cars leave his place at once, headed in four different directions."

When the waiter arrived, Rosa ordered the salpicón and langosta. Cobian asked for a bowl of their black bean soup. Seconds after the man had left, Senorita Losada was once again back on track.

"What about Julio Mesa? You ever hear of him before this week?"

"Matter of fact, I have. He could be where we get lucky."

She heard something in his tone and sat forward, curiosity piqued. "How so?"

"It's something that happened a year and a half ago. That was the summer after he was arrested for attempted rape up in Gainesville. While Eddie Ochoa was busy intimidating the coed into withdrawing the charge, Julio spent the summer here in Miami, probably learning the ropes."

"Ah. The time-honored summer internship." She said it drily.

"You got it. Only there was this Colombian girl Julio met at a disco who wouldn't have nothing to do with him. No matter how hard he tried to impress her, he got nowhere. Then, two weeks later, they found her on the sixteenth green of the Riviera Country Club. Raped, and more."

"More what?"

"Ugly shit. You don't wanna know."

"Try me, Oscar."

Cobian needed to keep reminding himself that this was a cop-to-cop conversation; that she was an NYPD captain of detectives. "I'd only been working homicide for a month. When that one came in, what I'd seen up to then hadn't prepared me. She was opened up from groin to rib cage. There were bite marks everywhere." Oscar had closed his eyes as he spoke, and opened them now. The air temperature in the room suddenly felt ice-cold around him.

"You heard what he did to the girl in Gainesville?" she asked.

"Oh, yeah. We couldn't pin our homicide on him. His uncle got him out of the country before we could get teeth impressions, or blood samples for DNA testing." He paused, all of it fresh in his memory again. "The reason I say we could get lucky with him? Because that homicide really pissed off the Colombian community. It wasn't just another casualty in the drug wars. Lucho Esparza saved that boy's ass. If he hadn't? I honest-to-God think somebody would have cut his balls off."

"And eighteen months later, you believe there's still that animosity?"

The grin he flashed was twisted and slightly maniacal. "You kidding? You've heard about us Colombians. We're cold-blooded, obsessive, and carry a grudge to the grave."

Sonny was soaked, his clothes plastered to him like a second skin when he jogged in the door of Billy Pickering's Ocean Drive building. Given the weather, the doorman seemed surprised to see anyone come in off the street, Pickering's call notwithstanding. If there was any recognition, his reddened, stoned-out eyes failed to register it. The puddle forming on the slate floor at Sonny's feet earned more attention than his face, and to that, the guy gave hardly a glance before handing across the key and shuffling back to his chair. From the front desk CD player, the raucous noise of a Butthole Surfers tune filled the little lobby as Reed hurried toward a pair of elevators.

Billy's apartment was one floor below the penthouse, and decorated in the same minimalist style that Sonny had seen downstairs. The rooms were almost monastic in their sparseness, the living room entertainment center constructed of threaded pipe and commercial kitchen racks, and everything in the kitchen zinc and glass, including the eat-in table and chairs. Both of the bedrooms were identical, each with a king-size pedestal bed shrouded by white mosquito netting. The nightstand in one room had an open box of Lifestyle lubricated condoms to suggest that it might be Billy's.

Sonny explored the apartment naked, having pulled the sheer curtains and stripped from his rain-soaked clothes. He found Pickering's closet outfitted with more threaded pipe shelving, all of it crammed with neatly folded clothing. In college, Billy had been a neatnik. Like most pro athletes, he had an abundance of athletic wear. Half his shelves were stocked with brightly colored sweats, nylon warm-up out-fits, T-shirts, and shorts. Fortunately for Reed, Pickering seemed to favor clothes that ran big. He pulled on a pair of burgundy sweatpants that fit almost like tights, found a T-shirt that showed off his upper body development and a pair of thongs that would fit fine once he stretched them out. If he had to hit the street for any reason, there was a whole array of oversize black vests to wear with the T-shirt: the Ocean Drive uniform.

The phone rang as Sonny checked the refrigerator, where he discovered a whole slew of microwaveable meals and frozen pizzas in the freezer. He twisted the cap off a Bud and wandered into the hall to listen as Billy's answering machine picked up.

"Sonny? It is Bebe. Answer, please. I am at pay phone. It is cold."

Not for long, honey buns, he thought. He grabbed the receiver while punching the stop button on the machine. "Yeah, baby. That cop still followin' y'all?"

"He is, yes. In car, across street. I do like you say. Call airline."

"Good, baby. When?"

"Tomorrow. Seven o'clock, to Miami International."

"Perfect. Billy went and parked his fuckin' car at the air-port, so y'all gonna have to take a cab."

"But to where?"

"One forty-three Ocean Drive. That's a block south a' Fifth Street. On the beach side." He moved to pull a curtain aside and stared out across the storm-swept sand to the Atlantic. From seven stories up, he could make out the faint lights of ships at anchor, hidden by the rain. "Tomorrow, when it's time t' ditch that cop, baby? Don't forget, you're smarter than he is."

"I am out of coke, almost, Sonny. You can get it for us, there?"

He remembered the night when they'd met. He'd waited until she was leaving the party they'd both attended, and offered her a ride home in his new Ferrari 512 Testarossa. In the car, he'd dumped better than half a gram on the cover of a Spider Man comic and asked if her anatomy was all real, or surgically enhanced. Without hesitation, she'd unbuttoned her blouse, grabbed his free hand, and insisted he find out for himself. While he was thus engaged, she'd held her hair away from her face and stuck her nose in his stash. Without benefit of a straw, she'd horned down the whole damned thing.

"I'm the man, ain't I, babe? But right now, that's the least of our worries. Y'all just get down here. Daddy'll make sure everything's taken care of."

With his car pulled up beneath the side entrance portico of the Losada house, Oscar Cobian switched off the engine and turned to Rosa. "I'm gonna hit a couple discos, see if I can run into anybody. If the rumor mill's got anything grinding, they'll know about it." He paused, a slow smile spreading from the corners of his mouth. "Might be an easier task, I have a beautiful Latina on my arm. You like to dance?"

Rosa flashed on Joe, taking that headlong pitch down her uncle's main staircase. As much as she liked to dance, and thought it could help ease the tensions of a long, difficult day, she reached to release her seat belt. If the truth be known, she liked the kind of policework Oscar was suggesting; a late night of hanging out working the grapevine. There would be some harmless sexual tension, and that could be fun, too, but not with Joe in a hospital bed. "I don't think I'd be quite vivacious enough for your purposes," she begged off. "Thanks for all you've done, Oscar. For Joe, dinner, everything."

"My pleasure." He didn't press it, and Rosa was doubly thankful for that. "You want, I'll pick you up tomorrow, take you to see Dante. It'll give me a chance to report back."

"What time? Can we make it on the early side?"

He shrugged. "Say, eight?"

"Perfect. I'll see you then."

"Maybe, you're not in too much of a rush, you'll invite me in for coffee. With all that drama on the stairs, I barely got a chance to meet your cousins."

TWENTY-ONE

Eddie Ochoa wasted no time calling New York to ask the Cali cartel underboss there to keep an eye on Bebe Masaryk. Later that Saturday night, cartel soldiers Arsenio Fraga and Juan Trueba wandered into Dallas Direct to find the tall, voluptuous blonde on the phone at the bar. They settled at a table to ogle awhile, saw Bebe hand the receiver back to the bartender, and then go back to work for another half hour. Their own waitress was a six-foot Colombian named Kristina, who flashed a dazzling smile and leaned dangerously close each time she brought fresh drinks. To amuse themselves while they waited, the two men discussed which of the hostesses they'd most like to fuck.

Bebe received another call at 10:15, and shortly thereafter disappeared through a door signed EMPLOYEES ONLY. Arsenio approached the floor manager with a fifty-dollar gratuity to request that when the tall *chica* with the platinum hair returned from her break, she pay his table a visit. The manager apologized, saying that Bebe had left for the night. Fraga and Trueba raced for their car and reached it just as Bebe emerged from the club to hail a cab. They started to pull out to follow when two policemen got there ahead of them.

* * *

Brian Brennan was working late in his studio, with Skye Lake sitting for a series of charcoal-sketched studies while they talked. From Diana's music room, in another part of the loft, the repeated piano strains of a rock-and-roll hook line filtered in, faint on the air. Earlier, Skye had offered to help pick the tiny bits of casting material from a recently poured bronze. While she worked, Brennan had become fascinated by the look of studied concentration on her face, and asked if he could draw her. They'd been at it an hour now, Skye scraping at the heat-blackened metal with a dental pick while Brian sat across from her on a stool, sketch pad propped against his knees.

When the phone rang, Diana's muffled voice yelled that she would get it. A moment later she poked her head in through the studio doorway. "That was Beasley, wondering if it's okay to stop by. Should be here in another five minutes."

Rather than return to her work, Diana loitered in the studio until Richardson's arrival, then hurried across the living room to release the elevator. With the initial distraction, Brennan had set his pad aside. Now he stood to stretch.

"C'mon. Let's take a break," he told Skye.

"In a sec. I'm almost finished." With her hours of practice, her fingers now fairly flew, tiny bits of plaster dusting the front of her jeans and the table before her. "You can get into this."

He smiled. "You want a job as a studio assistant, you're hired."

With a final flick of the wrist, she set the pick aside and stood to step across, that same intent frown now studying his renderings. As she picked up his pad, her face softened. "God. Talk about wearing your heart on your sleeve. Do I really *look* that angry?"

"Um-hmm."

She turned to him. "I'm sorry. I appreciate what you and

Diana are doing. Putting me up, and putting up with me. I know how alone I'd feel right now, if I weren't here with you."

Brian heard the elevator door open and the gate rattle back in its track, followed by Richardson's growling, basso voice. He reached out to caress Skye's cheek with the inside of one work-roughened thumb. "It's what friends are for. People like us who don't have family? We have to choose it. We're yours now, and you're part of ours."

Diana led Jumbo into the room. The heavyset detective was in shirtsleeves. The strain of his weekend workload was etched in a slight puffiness beneath his eyes, and evident in the way his shoulders sagged. He and Brennan shook hands as Diana offered to get them something to drink. A minute later, they'd settled in the living room and Richardson, forever weight-conscious now, was enjoying a rare beer.

"Rosa flew down to meet Joey tonight," he reported. "I heard from her right before I left the big building In Miami. He took a bad fall at her uncle's house in Coco Plum." He went on to describe how Dante's injuries of Wednesday night, combined with the strain of his journey down the coast, seemed to have finally caught up with him. "A whole family on a horse farm in Ocala was killed last night. Joey's been going hell-bent. Admits to passin' out yesterday, in the parking lot of a diner."

Brian let his gaze drift from Beasley's face to Skye's in an effort to read her expression. Some of the anger was gone, replaced by a sober thoughtfulness.

"But he'll be okay?" Skye asked. It wasn't the question of someone filled with hate for Dante.

"What they're sayin' he needs most is rest. I doubt it's hit the news yet, but Reed and Mesa have had a falling out. Sonny let their hostage nurse go, then bailed on Mesa. He's on the loose down there somewhere."

"So what's his girlfriend done?" Diana asked.

"We're on her like glue. She took a couple calls at the strip club and went home half an hour ago. With Reed free-wheeling, she may try t' help him."

It was six the next morning when Bebe Masaryk emerged from her building on East Seventy-seventh Street, hurrying toward Lexington Avenue. The cops who'd followed her last night were parked facing west on the one-way block, as Bebe started east. They were forced to wait until she reached the corner of Lexington and disappeared around it before they could emerge unnoticed to pursue on foot. Arsenio Fraga, who had sent Juan Trueba home at four A.M. to get some sleep, was more fortunate. He was parked right there on Lexington when Bebe dodged down the entrance to the subway. As he started from his car, he felt the rumbling of a train, deep in the bowels of the earth.

At Grand Central Station, Bebe watched the platform exit from outside the turnstiles for five minutes before she was sure those two cops in the gray Plymouth hadn't followed her. Then she hurried upstairs into the predawn gloom of Forty-second Street and hailed a cab for LaGuardia. She arrived at the airport with fifty minutes to spare before the 7:03 departure on USAir for Miami International. She paid cash, checked no luggage, and, hyperalert, sat watching the concourse outside her gate. By the time it was announced that her flight was boarding, she was convinced her getaway was clean.

Beasley Richardson received a call from Gus Lieberman as he prepared to leave his Fort Greene, Brooklyn, home for a run at six forty-five Sunday morning. He usually slept later, weekends, but with Joey in hot pursuit of Teo Mendoza, this, like every other day of that holiday weekend, was going to be a workday.

"Bebe Masaryk's given our surveillance the slip."

"Shit. When?"

"Just after six. She left her building with no luggage. A Number Six train pulled into the Seventy-seventh Street Lexington stop, right as she reached her corner."

Jumbo saw his exercise program unravel on him, but continued to stretch anyway. With his cordless phone wedged between ear and shoulder, he reached out over his extended leg for his toes. "Sounds t' me like she knew we were watchin' her. Any movement on them phone calls she took last night?"

"A judge signed a court order in the wee hours. We took it to NYNEX. They got us the number of a hotel in Cincinnati, and we're still tryin' to find out who she talked to there. Soon as we do, I'll want you to run with it."

Jumbo had a leg up on the kitchen counter and continued to grip his toes, the tightness in his calves slowly giving way. "Where would she go at six A.M., Gus?"

"Good question. You told me she was dead asleep when you rousted her an hour later than that on Friday."

"That's right. You still got somebody on Boone's place?"

"Yeah, we do. But she coulda walked there. The subway doesn't fit that scenario. I think she might be on the run."

"Sounds like that to me too. But where?" Richardson dropped the leg and alternated standing on one foot and then the other, shaking the muscles loose. "Fact she don't have luggage don't mean shit, Gus. With Reed cutting himself loose like he did, I wonder if she's tryin' to help him?"

"You mean headed for Miami?"

"I doubt she went out for coffee and croissants. It wouldn't hurt t' have them keep an eye on the New York arrivals down there."

Once Arsenio Fraga was in the air, he used the in-flight service to phone Eddie Ochoa. His call was received at the cartel's communications center, located this week in the bedroom of a house on Eightieth Street across from Arvida Park in Kendall. It was fed through a scrambler and routed on to the bedroom of Ochoa's mistress, Andrea, via scrambled radio transmission. At eight o'clock that stormy Sunday morning, Ochoa left Andrea's to drive a light blue Honda Civic the ten blocks between her Coral Gables apartment and the safe house on Alhambra. When he arrived, his soldiers and the Colombian nurse were drinking coffee in the kitchen. Julio Mesa and Teo Mendoza were still asleep.

"Go wake up the nephew," he growled to one of his security men. Eddie joined the others in a cup of oily black Colombian coffee with several spoons of sugar.

Mesa wandered in still sleepy-eyed, scratching his belly. "Wha'?" Julio complained. "You know how much sleep I got these past three days?"

Ochoa ignored the grievance. "Your *amigo*'s woman is flying this way. She's on a plane that get her here roun' nine-thirty. You wan' to bet she knows where he's hiding?"

Julio's sleep-puffy face was suddenly alive. "This one's mine, Jim. Her *and* Sonny. He left me standing out there, my fucking dick in my hand. Which airline?"

Ochoa raised a hand. "Slow down, *sobrino*. Think about it. I let you have them, sure, but this woman, she know you, *si*?"

Julio was agitated. He stepped around behind the nurse, lifted the cup of coffee from her saucer, and drained it. "What about it?"

"Let my people handle the airport," Eddie reasoned. "Follow her, where she goes. Then you have them both, someplace not so public."

By the time Beasley Richardson could cut through the red tape at the Westin Hotel in Cincinnati to learn that the Miami Dolphins were all at breakfast, he had little patience left for the team's publicity director.

"I'm sorry," the man answered. "*Who* is this? We left specific instructions that we don't—"

"Lieutenant Richardson, NYPD/DEA joint homicide task force," Jumbo interrupted him. He hoped that mention of the DEA would catch the director's attention.

"DEA *homicide*?" There was a sudden wariness in the director's tone. "This is the team's motivational breakfast, Lieutenant. I don't underst—"

"I need Billy Pickering on the phone pronto, sir. No matter what kinda inspirational ham and eggs he's eatin'."

There was a pause, then the man came back sounding more composed and skeptical. "I'm sorry, mister. You could be anyone. Unless you can get someone from local law enf—"

"To do what?" Richardson snapped back. "Vouch for me? I gotta go that far, I can guarantee you, I won't stop there. Fifteen minutes from now, a couple U.S. marshalls'll walk in there and take your starting free safety out in cuffs."

Two minutes later, Richardson had Billy Pickering on the line. He sounded anxious, and he sounded defensive.

"New *York* police? What is this? I've got a game in four hours."

"You took a call from Sonny Reed's girlfriend, Bebe Masaryk, at eight-thirteen last night, Mr. Pickering. What did she want from you? She called your apartment in Miami too."

"I think I'd better call my agent, man," Pickering replied. "Maybe a lawyer too." He hung up.

Within a minute of first opening his eyes, Joe Dante began to reassemble the pieces and knew they must have sedated him. He was in a hospital room. The bed alongside contained an old guy stuck with half a dozen different tubes. He had no idea what time it was, but judging from how much noise the rain was making against the room's one window, the storm had intensified.

Stretched flat on his back, Joe took a moment for damage assessment. If his memory served, those stairs he'd fallen down were stone. He was lucky he'd broken no bones. His troublesome left knee felt no worse than it had before, while several tender spots up and down the right side of his body were new. With his second night's sleep in three days, he actually felt refreshed.

There was no dizziness when Dante took his first experimental step toward the bathroom to empty his bladder. His head still hurt, but the throbbing had subsided. Once he splashed water on his face, he gripped the basin to look in the mirror. His appearance was much improved by the removal of all that gauze that had wrapped his head. Rosa's handiwork had been replaced by a more professional dressing, and four days into his recovery, nearly all the bruising was yellowed now.

He left the bath in search of his clothes, and hoped that before he took his leave this morning, he could find himself a toothbrush.

Arsenio Fraga had made this flight from New York to Miami enough times to know the plane nearly always landed earlier than the scheduled arrival time. This USAir flight was the exception. Scheduled to land at 9:18 A.M., it was forced by the weather to circle for twenty minutes before it could put down at rainswept Miami International. To make sure he didn't miss the tall blonde as she departed the terminal, Arsenio was on his feet and headed for the door as soon as the *fasten seat belts* light went out. When he glanced back, he saw her duck beneath the outstretched arms of a passenger trying to open and overhead compartment, five rows back.

Once inside the crowded terminal, Fraga melted into a knot of passengers waiting to board other flights. Seconds later, as he feigned study of an arrivals monitor, the blonde appeared, pocketbook slung over one shoulder. She strode purposefully down the concourse toward the security checkpoint while Arsenio trailed, ten yards back. He wondered who Eddie Ochoa had sent to meet him. It wasn't until the blonde had passed beyond the security area that Fraga first saw the cop.

Tall, crew cut, and dressed in a jacket and open-collar shirt, the man stood off to one side, studying the faces of each female who passed him, until he locked onto the blonde. Fraga saw the portable radio held low against one leg as the cop started into the crowd after her.

Friends and relatives of arriving passengers thronged in the area outside the checkpoint. The atmosphere was a chaos of squeals, hugs, and hearty handshakes. Arsenio was so focused on the blonde, and her cop tail, that he failed to see Francisco Andujar until the taller, heavyset cartel soldier all but ran into him.

"Wha'sup?" Frankie murmured.

"Hey, man! How you doin'?" Arsenio bubbled it with ersatz effervescence and threw his arms around Frankie. "She's got a cop on her," he whispered in Andujar's ear. "The tall chump there, in the navy blue jacket." He already had Andujar by the elbow and was moving him along, never losing sight of his objective, now twenty yards away. The implication of the cop's presence was clear enough. They'd lost her in New York, but the stakes were too high to let her stay lost.

Thirty yards into the USAir main concourse, the blonde suddenly veered to her left, backed up against a pillar, and stood surveying the pedestrian traffic in her wake. The cop was caught out by this move and had no choice but to pass by. Arsenio watched him head for a newsstand and scan a rack of paperbacks. The cop eased around behind the stand to hide from view as he raised his radio to his lips.

"Gimme your knife," Arsenio snapped at Andujar.

"What?"

"*¡El cuchillo! ¡Rapido!*" He had ditched his own blade in a garbage can at LaGuardia before passing through the metal detector.

Andujar dipped into a pants pocket and palmed his weapon to Fraga. Arsenio's fingers closed around a gravity knife—handle five inches long, and slender. Perfect. It took four inches of blade to reach a man's heart. He had steel to spare.

Arsenio played the gregarious Latin male as he passed the blonde, en route toward the newsstand. He looked her up and down with a smiling leer and growled deep in his throat.

The cop paid the Colombians no attention as they entered the newsstand behind him. His eyes were riveted on the blonde as he murmured something into his radio. With Frankie screening Fraga from view, Arsenio plucked a book from the spin-rack and used it to hide the knife. The blade dropped and clicked into place. He focused on a spot eight inches down from the preoccupied cop's collar, two inches left of the center seam. In perfect synchronization, Frankie stepped forward to engage the cashier's attention as Fraga jammed the blade in to the hilt, and jerked it out again. Heart ruptured, the cop did little more than clutch in reflex at the sudden pain, then sigh before falling forward onto his face. Frankie was paying for a copy of *Penthouse* as Arsenio sauntered away, hands in pockets. The knife, once again retracted, rested cool against his thigh.

Delayed at her uncle Tico's house by a call from Jumbo Richardson, Rosa Losada arrived at Jackson Memorial Hospital with Oscar Cobian later than she'd intended. They pulled up out front of the main entrance to see Dante dressed and waiting inside the doors. Before she could dash through the rain toward him, Joe emerged and climbed into Oscar's backseat.

"Damn it, Joe! You *collapsed* last night!"

His hair wet, tie hung around his neck, unknotted, he reached across the seat to offer Cobian his hand. "We didn't meet last night. I'm Joe Dante. Tell me what's happening."

Cobian shook. "Oscar Cobian, Lieutenant. Sonny Reed sprang the kidnapped nurse and went AWOL on Mesa last night. Mel and I talked to her. Julio and Reed had a falling out."

"She say why?"

"The girl Mesa killed in Ocala. She thinks Reed bailed because Julio planned to kill him too."

The scowl that Rosa leveled at Oscar failed to penetrate. He, too, was obviously eager to press on. At times like these, she wondered how she'd ever fallen in love with a man as stubborn as Dante, or how she'd chosen this career.

"Let me get this straight." Joe tried to focus. "Reed just let the nurse go?"

"Like something snapped, is what she said. They left Mesa at a pay phone, Sonny gave her twenty bucks, and ditched her."

Rosa's more immediate concern was Joe's welfare. "The doctor was going to prescribe something for your swelling."

Dante held up a plastic amber bottle.

She gave up trying to fight him. "Beasley called. Just as we were leaving the house. Reed's girlfriend slipped her surveillance this morning. She might be headed here."

Dante stripped his tie from his neck to stuff it into a side pocket. "You two have breakfast yet?"

"There's more, Joe. From work last night, Bebe Masaryk called a Miami Dolphins player at the Westin Hotel in Cincinnati. Billy Pickering. He and Reed were roommates at Florida."

Dante pushed his wet hair back and chewed his lower

lip, deep in thought. "The Dolphins are playing the Bengals this weekend. If Sonny needed a place to lay low . . . Did Beasley talk to Pickering?"

Cobian got them rolling as Rosa nodded. "We're running into a lot of problems. It's the Sunday of a Thanksgiving weekend. Pickering wouldn't talk without his attorney. Probably scared shitless he'll be implicated."

"We have an address?"

"That's another problem," Cobian told him. "This Bebe called a number registered to Pickering in South Miami Beach. But the telephone company picked this, of all weekends, to transfer their service location information to a new data base."

"Yeah? So?"

"Pickering took this number with him when he moved from an apartment on Washington to somewhere else in South Beach, two weeks ago. As soon as the transfer's completed, they can tell us where. Right now, he's sorta lost in the cracks."

"What about the Dolphins? Wouldn't they know?"

Cobian lifted both hands from the wheel and shrugged. "They've still got him at his old address. Mel thinks our best bet right now is the post office. He's getting them to open up and check the forwarding address files." Oscar turned west on Twentieth Street, then south on Twelfth Avenue beneath the elevated Metromover.

"So where we headed now?" Joe asked.

"South Beach." Cobian jabbed a finger at the skyline to the east. "The FBI's got agents covering every flight from New York to the greater Miami area. Sooner or later, Mel is gonna call, and if we get lucky, Reed's girlfriend will show up too. Meanwhile, I figure we'll have breakfast with the trendies."

On the Dolphin Expressway, headed east, Frankie Andujar let the cab carrying the blonde run two cars ahead of them in the steady, gust-blown rain. Meanwhile, he spoke to Eddie Ochoa via scrambled radio hookup.

"We just gone past the Ninety-five innerchange. It looks like she's headed for the beach."

"She get where she's going, you sit tight on her, *hermano*," Eddie replied. "Julio wan' to do this personal."

"No problem, *jefe*. The *mona*, she pick up a cop at the airport. Arsenio was forced to do him."

"Just call us," Ochoa said. "Tell us where. Julio be on his way, the minute we hear."

TWENTY-TWO

It wasn't the first time that Sonny Reed had eaten a micro-waved frozen pizza for breakfast. This one was topped with sausage and peppers, the crust not thin or crisp enough. As he ate, he thought about his plan. Once Bebe arrived, she could get him some clothes that fit, then rent a room in one of the lesser flophouse hotels a few blocks off the beach. Billy would return from Ohio after the game today, and they wanted to be long gone from here. And he still hadn't fig-ured a way to get himself and Bebe out of the country. He'd never owned a passport before signing with the Giants, and he'd left it behind in his travel bag. There were always rumors floating around about the undetectable forgeries that could be had for a few hundred bucks. Sonny had heard of a biker in Tallahassee, and a printer in Tampa who ran a side business out of his garage. He didn't doubt that these forgers existed, but with his growing reputation, their ser-vices would undoubtedly come higher than a few hundred dollars. Maybe he'd have better luck obtaining documenta-tion offshore. But where? And how would he get there?

Reed wondered what size nest egg Bebe had tucked away. Dallas Direct was paying her fifteen hundred a week, and when she put her mind to it, she could carry away another five hundred a night in tips. She worked four nights a week, which would put her in the hundred and fifty a year range. Before he met her, she'd spent a lot of her money on happy dust. But since, she hadn't spent a dime. If she showed up on his doorstep with even twenty grand, Nassau was only a hundred and seventy miles away by boat. In Nassau, how much could a good U.S. passport cost?

The whole pizza was gone, and Reed was still running a myriad possibilities over the hurdles of his imagination when the doorbell rang. His pulse thundered in his ears as he leaped to his feet. He padded barefoot across the cool tile of the kitchen floor to the service area door while cursing himself for throwing the Intratec down a storm drain last night.

Once on the landing, he tiptoed to the internal hallway door, twisted the knob slowly, and peeked out. His heart rate automatically subsided as he pulled the door open wider and cleared his throat. Startled, Bebe gasped while twisting to turn toward the noise.

"C'mon," he urged, waving her toward him. "Quick now."

There were only two apartments per floor, but who knew where the other occupant was? Sonny had already dodged back out of sight by the time Bebe started in his direction. As soon as she entered the service area, Sonny had those big arms of his wrapped to hug her fiercely to him, her feet lifted clear of the floor.

"Y'all bring a snort, baby?" he whispered, lips pressed to her right ear, tongue darting in and out of it. "God*damn*, I need a snort right now."

She clamped her thighs around his waist and kissed him hard as he carried her into Billy's kitchen. Once he kicked the door shut, she broke the kiss off to draw her face back and study his. He grinned, his hands now on her beautiful backside, her breasts pressed warm against his naked chest.

A heat rose in his loins. Bebe was the best-looking woman he'd ever laid hands on, and she was nuts about him.

"Ooh," she cooed, alive with mischief. "You *do* miss Bebe." She rocked gently, thighs flexing each time she brought herself in contact with the hardening bulge in his too-tight sweatpants. While clinging with one arm around his neck, she used her free hand to unfasten the buttons of her blouse, and kissed him again, more slowly now.

Reed threw all thoughts of passports and escape routes to the wind when Bebe lowered her feet to the floor and pushed a hand inside his waistband. He released the clasp of her brassiere with practiced ease and pushed the fabric aside to caress her.

"In my purse. The vial," she whispered. She eased his pants down over his butt as he pulled the handbag from her shoulder.

"Put some on you," she growled, wetting her lips.

He lifted the flap of her purse. It was the sight of all that cash, in rubber-banded rolls, as much as the little vial of cocaine, that made his anticipation of pleasures to come complete.

The Eleventh Street Diner in South Miami Beach reminded Dante of Manhattan's Empire Diner, five blocks south of his loft, on Tenth Avenue. Pure deco in its shiny stainless and aluminum design, it catered to the same kind of crowd: young, wee-hours scene-makers who were ending their days at ten A.M., not starting them. Since leaving New York, Thursday morning, this was the first public place where the bandage on his forehead and bruised left eye drew no notice.

For a couple of moments after his coffee was poured, Joe enjoyed the presence of two willowy young women at a table to his right. Each had that prominent bone structure a camera loves, and was surely a hopeful fashion model. This was an area that teemed with models and photographers, all looking to make their mark.

Then Joe thought of Skye Lake, who lived somewhere here in South Beach, and crashed head-on into the reality of why he was here.

Oscar Cobian watched Rosa also studying the models. "You could have been one, easy, Captain. You ever consider it? With your height? And just the right hint of the exotic they always seem to go for?"

Joe wondered what Rosa and this openly flirtatious detective had talked about last night while he was down on phenobarb farm. They seemed friendly, at ease in each other's company. Rosa smiled, her expression maybe a little wistful as she looked out the window past the lush tropical foliage into the rain.

"You mean when I was still *young* enough? There were people who tried to push me, but I couldn't have cared less. Until my parents were killed, I wanted to get my MBA and make a quarter million a year. It was the eighties."

Cobian grabbed his pager from his belt and frowned down at the message window. "We might have to eat fast. It's Mel. He said he'd call, soon as he gets access to the post office."

While Cobian hurried off to use the pay phone, Joe reached across the table to take one of Rosa's hands. "I was thinking about Skye just now. Where she'll be after ten, twelve years in this meat grinder."

"I doubt she'll stay that long," Rosa replied. "Her mother tripped into a few pitfalls along the way. I think Skye's learned something from them."

Their waiter arrived to set breakfast before them just as Cobian came rushing back. "Food's gonna have to wait, people. One of the Feebs at the airport was on the radio, reporting he'd spotted Bebe Masaryk, when somebody stuck a knife in his back. The post office just gave us Billy Pickering's new address."

All that mosquito netting draped over the bed in Billy's guest room only got in the way. Sonny Reed, grunting like a buck deer in rut, tore it from its screw-eye mooring. Bebe laughed as she toppled backward onto the mattress, all two hundred and forty pounds of his hard-muscled eagerness sprawled atop her. The power or wealth of little men had never excited her. What thrilled her was this, another beast as big and beautiful as she was. Her pleasure receptors were alive with delicious electricity as Sonny stroked her flanks. Transported on a cocaine magic carpet, he was every sinew the worship that her perfect body was due. Lesser mortals could fill her drink tray with hundred-dollar tips and drool, their tailored trousers bulging with hopeless erections, but only earth-bound gods like Sonny Reed were admitted to worship at the altar.

In his eagerness, Sonny pawed, trying to force her legs apart.

"Not yet," she growled.

Mid-thrust, he quit his quest for ultimate release to bury his face between her breasts. Then he moved down her body in a slow, ritual journey of hot, wet kisses.

"I'm surprised, Jim. Never thought you had it in you, boy. Hot damn! You *are* a stud!"

Bebe was on her back, her lover's face buried between her legs, when that familiar voice froze her. She scrambled to cover herself, and all her fingers found was mosquito netting. Sonny was on the move too, rearing back in a low, wary crouch as Julio Mesa advanced, a noise-suppressed automatic held loose in one hand.

"C'mon, Jim. You can't *quit* on me. Ain't nothing I like more than watching a grown man eat pussy."

"Sonny?" Bebe's voice quavered.

"Leave her outta this, Julio," Reed murmured. "This is 'tween us."

"The fuck it is, Jim. It's between who I say it's between. You stole the nurse. Fine. I'll take Bebe here, in trade."

Julio stopped a few feet from the bed and Bebe saw Sonny tense. Rage broke the dam of prudence and he lunged, his whole mass thrown sideways in Mesa's direction. Julio displayed the cool of a matador, took a quick step back, raised his pistol to hip level, and fired. The first slug took Sonny in the chest, point blank. The second hit him in the neck. Sonny collapsed, both hands clutching at his throat, his face a mask of pure surprise. While he began to flop convulsively, like a mackerel dumped in the bottom of a boat, Bebe was too petrified even to scream.

Sonny still trembled in the throes of death as Julio stepped over him. The menace of his gun muzzle turned Bebe from grieving lover to survivor. The cold sweat that covered her now penetrated and wrapped her heart. She'd heard the news reports and knew who she was dealing with. If she let him have his way, even pretended to delight in his perversions, an opportunity to fight might present itself. She was four inches taller than Mesa, and while she didn't have his bulk, she spent two hours a day at the gym.

Mesa was reaching to prod her between the thighs with that fat cylindrical noise suppressor when the phone rang. It sent his eyebrows up in question. "Friend of yours?"

She swallowed hard. Maybe it was Pickering, calling to see if Sonny had gotten in all right. Sonny had said something about Billy having a game today. When was that?

On the second ring, the answering machine in the hallway picked up. Bebe could hear its magnetic switches click, the internal mechanism whir, then a silence. The caller had either hung up or was listening to Pickering's outgoing message. Then:

"Bebe? It's Kristina. You got to get away from there,

baby. Now. The cop, he knows you called Sonny's ball-player friend. From the club last night. They know where the apartment is."

A second cousin of his, who Freddy Mendoza had planted at Dallas Direct, Mesa knew Kristina as well as Bebe did. Her call to warn Bebe, after Sonny had so openly betrayed Julio last night, made him furious. He grabbed the hostess by the hair, the muzzle of that noise suppressor jammed into her rib cage. "We ain't finished having *our* fun yet," he hissed. "No such fuckin' luck." His breath was hot in her ear and she felt the barrel of the gun pushed to prod her right breast. "*Move*, bitch! You so much as squeak, it better feel good. It'll be the last sound you make."

He dragged her from the bed, hustled her naked along the hallway to the kitchen, and there Bebe realized how he'd entered the apartment. Sonny had kicked the door to the service stairs closed, but in his eagerness to get at her had failed to lock it. When Bebe hesitated at the door now, Julio jerked his fistful of her short hair. "Move!"

She was thrust, stumbling, to the stairs and started down them. How he expected to get her out of there, naked, she couldn't imagine. On the ground floor, the service stairs opened onto a hallway that led in two directions. Around a corner to the right, fifteen feet away, Bebe could hear sub-dued voices. When she'd entered the building, the British rock band Blur was playing on the lobby boom box. Now there was no music. Julio seemed to notice it too. He looked left down the corridor to another door at the far end. Through a six-inch panel of wired glass, gray daylight could be seen. He tightened his grip on Bebe's hair, jammed the gun against her neck as a reminder, and pushed her that way.

The door provided tenants with access to the beach. Directly outside it, a hard-packed dirt service alley ran north and south. A low, sea-grass-covered dune stood beyond, with a wooden walkway running across it to the beach. At the door, Julio peered through the unrelenting downpour for just an instant before propelling Bebe out into it.

A number of buildings along that stretch of Ocean Drive, south of Fifth Street, were under renovation, with chain-link construction fences blocking access to the street. Between buildings, police cars could be seen parked in a cluster. They forced Julio to give up on the service alley and shove Bebe toward the walkway over the dune. That way, he hoped to flank the entire row of oceanside buildings by striking out down the beach. In weather like this, the sand was the better bet, their progress hidden from view by the dune.

In the middle of the walkway, after climbing the short flight of wooden stairs, Bebe pretended to stumble. She grasped the handrail on her right with both hands and forced Mesa far enough off balance that he, too, had to grab for the rail. His other hand gripping her hair, he was forced to use his gun hand, and the instant the gun muzzle left her jaw, Bebe used the rail for leverage and drove a shoulder into Julio's chest. The balustrade hit him in the hip, functioning as a fulcrum. His momentum flipped him head over heels onto the dune grass below, a tuft of Bebe's hair jerked loose as she tore herself free.

Julio's howl of outrage was muffled by the storm as Bebe leaped rain-blind onto the sand from the top of the walkway. She sprinted pell-mell for the Atlantic and had no idea he was shooting at her until a bullet slammed into her right shoulder. It pitched her forward onto the beach, but adrenaline mixed with panic drove her on. No sooner did she land than she was up again.

At the tide line she risked a look back, the froth of the storm-buffeted surf coursing around her ankles. Julio was running straight for her, thirty yards away across the rain-packed sand. Another wave crashed ashore as Bebe took three more splashing, knee-deep strides, lowered her head, held her breath, and dove.

She swam beneath the water for as long as her air held, kicking and pulling with one hand until she believed her lungs would burst. Salt water burned the hole in her shoulder. Her right arm was numb. When her head broke the surface, she saw she'd gone north. She spotted Julio fifty yards away, searching frantically in the wrong direction. With each foot of headway, her spirits soared as she struck out parallel to the shore, headed farther away.

Dante stood with Rosa and Oscar Cobian in the guest room of Billy Pickering's apartment as the FBI's Alan Dyson raced through the doorway. The sight of Sonny Reed, buck naked in a pool of blood and staring at eternity with dead eyes, barely caught Dyson's attention. He pointed at Dante.

"What's he doing here?"

Lieutenent Gene Nichols, Miami Beach PD Homicide, rose from where he'd squatted to retrieve a 9mm shell casing with the point of his pen. He inspected the gold shield hung in its leather case from Dyson's breast pocket. "He's with Detective Cobian, DEA/Metro-Dade Homicide task force. They think this might be cartel related. Who are you?"

"Agent-in-charge Dyson, FBI. This scene is sealed forthwith." He squinted at the homicide cop's shield. "Lieutenant, I want you and everyone else cleared out of here."

"The hell it is," Nichols replied. He kept it cool. "This is a homicide. I'm a homicide cop, and this is my jurisdiction. You got a problem with that? Call my chief."

"I don't want these people here," Dyson protested.

"Yeah? Who I allow on my scenes is my business." Nichols pointed to the doorway. "Maybe you should try your entrance again, Mr. Agent-in-charge."

Dante turned so that Dyson couldn't see his smile. "I'm

gone," he murmured to Cobian. "If this turns into a pissing contest, we don't wanna be in the line of fire."

Cobian told Nichols he would be in touch while Joe and Rosa drifted into the hall. They found more Miami Beach detectives in the kitchen, busy examining the womens' clothing they'd discovered there. A lab man dusted the service door for latents. Back in the bedroom, a pair of pantyhose and panties had been found on the floor. A skirt was found in the middle of the hall. It wasn't a difficult scenario to reconstruct. What the evidence failed to explain was how it had ended. Dante was pretty sure that Bebe Masaryk hadn't killed that Fed at the airport, or Reed, here, in a praying mantis ritual of seduction and death.

They were in the elevator, descending toward the lobby, when Joe turned to Cobian. "You got a cassette player in your wheels, right?"

Cobian's car was a Chrysler Concorde, property of the county and part of a recent program that provided Metro-Dade officers with take-home cars. "You bet. I requested CD, but . . ." He shrugged.

"Why, Joe?" Rosa asked.

Dante slipped a cassette from his pocket and tapped it against an open palm. "The incoming message light was lit on Pickering's answering machine."

Cobian's cheeks bulged. "So you *took* it? From a homicide scene? That's a felony in this state, *hermano*."

Joe met him heads up. "Borrowed it. Reed was still bleeding out when we walked through that door. Whoever killed him got lost in an awful damned hurry."

"What are you getting at?" Oscar asked.

"Not what, who," Dante replied. "And why did they take the woman?"

"Who says she wasn't working with them?" Oscar asked.

"The fifty-two grand she left behind in her purse. The clothes, scattered all over. Our report from New York says

Bebe Masaryk left with nothing but that handbag. You saw how much room she had for a change of clothes in there."

The doors of the elevator parted and Rosa stepped off first, with Joe and Cobian in her wake. They crossed the lobby to the street doors through a crowd of Miami Beach uniformed personnel. Beneath the sidewalk canopy, Rosa guessed at what Joe was thinking.

"With Pickering away, they wouldn't risk picking up the phone, right? They'd let the machine do it."

Dante aimed a finger at her and winked, popping his thumb down like the hammer of a gun.

Parked at the curb on Ocean Drive, across the street in front of the Century Hotel, the three of them sat in Cobian's car with the rain hammering on the roof. Joe leaned forward between the seats to push the tape into the player. It started halfway through a message, and Rosa pushed the rewind button to take it back to the beginning. The voice of Billy's dad came on, saying that he'd be watching Sunday, via the new satellite dish, that he expected Billy to "kick some fanny," and reminding him to make his Christmas plane reservations, "before the rates go through the roof." That message ended and another began. It was a woman's voice this time.

"Sonny? It is Bebe. Answer, please. I am at pay phone. It is cold." There was a click, a beep, and then a different female voice. *"Bebe? It's Kristina. You got to get away from there, baby. Now. The cop, he knows you called Sonny's ballplayer friend. From the club last night. They know where the apartment is."*

That was it. Rewound, they listened to it again.

"So who's Kristina?" Dante asked.

"Definitely Hispanic," Cobian replied. "And the way she said *the club*? Maybe she's a coworker."

"That's good," Rosa agreed. "One with an inside line. The *cop* knew that Bebe had called Pickering. Which cop?"

Dante slouched in the backseat, face upturned and eyes closed. "We need to call Beasley. Have him find this Kristina." He sat up and leaned toward Oscar. "We'll give the tape to Mel, let him turn it over to Nichols and explain the delicacy of the situation. If Dyson's our leak, and if he'd found it first, nobody would have heard what we just did."

TWENTY-THREE

Jumbo Richardson and Gus Lieberman sat in the library of the chief's opulent College Point, Queens, home. A fire burned in the fireplace and the first flakes of a snowstorm crawling up the East Coast were starting to stick to the windowpanes. The chief's wife, Lydia, an unashamed New York Giants fan, had the game on low in the parlor across the entry gallery. No longer allowed to smoke in the house, Gus fidgeted with a plastic cigarette and drank a bottle of beer. Jumbo had hardly touched his diet Coke.

"Kristina," Gus mused. "They don't use their real names at a club like that, do they?"

Beasley's strip club expertise was limited. "Y'got me there, boss. The place don't open till five, and both the floor and bar managers are out in the Meadowlands. I talked to the bookkeeper, and she don't know shit."

"You said Joey called you with a plan. So feed it to me."

"It's simple enough, but that don't make it easy. It involves him calling here tomorrow morning, then monitoring all calls back out, from here, and the FBI and DEA offices in New York and Miami."

Gus grunted. "A cinch. Like passing gun control legislation."

"That tape he found? It *proves* we got a leak. So his plan is t' plug it by planting something hot in their pipeline."

Lieberman hoisted himself from his chair, grabbed a poker, and prodded the fuel of the fire. "Such as?"

"Word that his Colombian detective at Metro-Dade Homicide has received a tip about where Mesa and Mendoza are holed up. It's from inside the cartel, but he can't share the details because of the leak. He's getting set t' make his move, with Metro-Dade as backup."

Gus straightened, still gripping the poker, and wandered to a window to watch the snow. It was coming down hard now, unusual for so early in the season. "And spring the trap on this end," he concluded. "See who makes the call down south to warn them, and where. I like it."

"Our problem is gonna be with the Feds, Gus. There were a dozen people on the job who knew where Joey would be the night Mendoza made his try. But so did Charlie O'Roark and Al Dyson and God knows who else."

Gus turned away from the window. "It was the same story in Gainesville. Once Joey called me, half our own detective bureau knew where he was off to. Charlie was right there sitting with me. I called the FDLE, and they called Dyson."

"Monitoring our own phone traffic outta here is one thing, Gus. But throwin' a net over half of Justice's New York operations? Who's gonna authorize somethin' like that?"

Lieberman returned the poker to the fireplace stand. "My money'd be on the Attorney General. The Department of Justice hates bad press, and imagine the shitstorm, one of their own turns out to be dirty."

"Attorney General," Beasley repeated. "A city makes a request like that, it could take a week just to cut through red tape."

Gus was moving toward the phone. "I don't think so. I know you and Joey think our esteemed commissioner's an asshole, but Tony Mintoff gets a bug up his ass when dopers start shooting his cops. You watch him."

Until Beasley could detail Dante's plan to Gus, and then shepherd it through the labyrinth of law enforcement bureaucracy, Joe, Rosa, and Cobian would have to sit and wait. Having left their breakfasts uneaten, they were famished by the time they settled down for lunch at Crawdaddy's on Washington Avenue in South Beach. Two hours, a dozen oysters, and a tuna steak later, Joe suggested they move to the lounge so Cobian could watch his beloved Dolphins. When the Miami defense took the field after the kickoff, Billy Pickering was conspicuously absent from the secondary.

Cobian's pager tickled his hip early in the first quarter and for a moment he looked like he might throw it at the wall. His Dolphins were driving, first and goal, on the Cincinnati eight-yard line. "I hate this thing," he complained.

The message window displayed Mel Sullivan's number at Homicide. Oscar rose reluctantly from his seat as the Dolphins tried a play-action pass that floated harmlessly beyond the end zone. He found a phone and hurried toward it as Joe turned to Rosa.

"I guess Mel did right by us with this guy, huh?"

She nodded. "He's good."

"You got along last night. I can tell."

She took a sip of her Campari and soda. "The fact that I'm an NYPD captain helped."

"Did he tell you anything useful about the cartel scene here?"

"One thing in particular." Rosa swirled ice around her nearly empty glass. "The Colombian community is convinced that Mesa raped and killed a grocer's daughter, summer before last. She was found dumped on a Coral Gables golf course. Oscar also thinks Mesa did it. Julio disappeared before they could question him or do any tests."

Miami scored, on a toss over the middle to the tight end. Joe thought about the implications of what Rosa had just said. "So, no matter who the little shit's uncle is, it's possible someone on the inside hates him enough to rat him out. Right?"

"That's why Oscar didn't argue with your plan. It's probably more plausible than you knew."

Cobian came back from the phone, clearly preoccupied. He had their bar tab in hand and was peeling money from beneath a clip he kept in a front pocket. "They score?" And then without waiting for an answer, he tossed tip money onto the table and waved them out of their chairs. "The sarge says they might've found Bebe Masaryk. It's back over to Jackson. C'mon."

In his car, going west across the MacArthur Causeway, Oscar related the gist of his conversation with Sullivan. "The Miami Beach PD got a call from some surfer. He and his buds found a naked lady on the beach, with a bullet hole in her."

"How bad?" Rosa asked.

He shook his head. "Not too, I guess. She was conscious, and trying to crawl up the sand for help. Claimed she was jumped by Rastas, that she was out running on the beach in this soup. They tried to rape her, she fought them, they shot her and left her for dead."

"Where?" Joe asked.

"On the beach, like I said."

"No. Where'd they shoot her?"

"Up high in the right shoulder is what Mel tells me. Couldn't have wanted her dead all that bad, huh?"

"Just what I was thinking. Any bets the slug matches the two they take from Reed?"

Cobian nudged Rosa, seated next to him in the passenger seat. "You tell your friend how intelligent I am. I hate to brag."

Rosa looked over her shoulder at Joe. "Oscar's got a degree in mathematics from Columbia. The university, not the country."

Dante felt a little strange, walking back through the front doors of Jackson Memorial Hospital. At the admitting desk, they learned the wounded woman was out of surgery and now in Intensive Care. When they arrived on her floor, they found two FBI agents and a City of Miami uniformed officer guarding the door from the waiting room to the unit. Oscar approached the nurse's desk and asked to see the woman who was found shot on South Beach. The duty nurse looked toward the agents. Cobian had his shield case out, and the older of the two Bureau men crossed to examine it.

"Sorry, Detective. The lady is a secured witness, in an on-going federal investigation."

Oscar turned to introduce Rosa. "This is Captain Losada, NYPD. She was running a surveillance on the lady, up north," he lied. "Some boss-level Bureau dude named Dyson asked us to take her over here, make positive ID. You didn't get his call?"

Cobian was dead earnest, his full-steam approach catching the agent off guard. Rosa had her gold shield out for him to examine, and there was nothing in the play book about how to tell a New York police captain to take a hike.

"Uh, maybe I'd better make a call," the guy stalled.

"The captain's got a press conference with the governor and Senator MacKay, across the street at the Civic Center, in fifteen minutes," Oscar pressed. "Your call was supposed to be made half an hour ago."

Dante figured that mentioning the U.S. senator was what did it. Without further argument, the man nodded, turned, and led them through a pair of double doors. Joe had never seen Bebe Masaryk, but Rosa had. As they approached the groggy woman's bedside, Rosa registered recognition. Without makeup, Bebe's face with its pale eyebrows and puffy, colorless lips was devoid of most of its character. It was hard to imagine the person behind it.

"Bebe?" Rosa said it gently. "Remember me?"

"Just an ID, Captain," the agent warned. He sounded nervous.

Bebe's eyelids came halfway up, her expression one of dazed, postsurgical confusion. Then something clicked and those icy blue eyes, the spooky color of a Siberian husky's, came wide open.

"Who's Kristina, Bebe?"

"Hey." The Bureau man's hand was halfway to Rosa's arm when Dante clamped onto his wrist. To that point, the guy had paid little attention to Joe.

"You touch her, I'll break it," he warned.

The muscles of the man's neck bunched as he spoke through gritted teeth. "You're under arrest, mister."

"I don't think so," Joe replied.

Bebe had closed her eyes again, tighter this time, and Rosa turned away. "We can't exactly beat it out of her."

Dante released the agent's wrist. "But at least we're sure it's her now. Let's go."

"Wait a minute, pal."

Cobian's voice was level and reasoning as he stepped between Dante and the Bureau man. "It looks to me like he's had a rough weekend. I don't think you want to push it."

Teo Mendoza wondered what had happened to gravity. As he stood at the edge of his bed, the nurse with a grip on his elbow, he felt a heavy sluggishness in his legs. He took his first step.

"*Lento,*" the doctor warned from across the room. "Slowly."

Teo saw Julio in the doorway studying him like a wolf

studies a limping caribou. The little prick had returned from
South Miami Beach that morning in a murderous rage.
Francisco Andujar and the man from *Nueva York* said a
legion of police had descended on the scene. They arrived
while Julio was still upstairs, killing his friend and the
woman. When questioned, Mesa only fumed and stalked the
room in wordless fury.

With each step, some of the oppressive weight lifted. Teo
could not believe that a man could get so weak in so short a
time. "Much better, *si*?" he asked the nurse.

She agreed he was much improved. Once Teo had walked
to the opposite wall and back, he began a frank, personal
assessment of his condition. He'd been hurt before. Intense
pain was not new to him, and the pain he experienced now,
each time he drew breath, was nothing like he'd pushed
past, four days ago, to shoot the man who'd killed his
brother. His fever was gone now. The rattle in his lungs was
no longer constant, and was only an occasional discomfort.
By the time he reached the doorway to stand face-to-face
with the twisted son of Catalina Esparza and Rosario Mesa,
his knees no longer trembled.

"I think it is time we go home, yes, nephew?"

There was no life in Julio's expression. His were a
shark's eyes, the flesh around them puffy with the sleepless-
ness induced by cocaine. "No one calls me that, Jim. Not
even my uncle."

Smiling, Teo turned and walked away, each step firmer
than the last. He approached Eddie Ochoa, who stood, arms
folded, beside the doctor. "This storm. How much longer
does it last? The drug, I can inject myself. On the television,
la policia look everywhere for me. We must go. *Pronto,
hermano*."

"Nothing can fly in this," Ochoa told him. "They say the
rain may stop tomorrow, in the night."

Monday night wasn't soon enough. Mendoza had a bad

feeling about being shut up in this place, with Julio and his strange animal blood lust. Teo had killed more than two dozen men in his lifetime, but he'd only killed twice with passion. The first time was the DAS *capitán* who killed his mother. The second was that New York cop last week. Otherwise, when he pulled the trigger, pushed the knife, or tugged the garrote tight, the blood always ran cold in his veins. Julio was different. He was as dangerous as the rumbling deep in the belly of a volcano. Teo put on his killer's face, his expression impassive, like a stone carving of an Inca priest. "Tomorrow, Eddie. *No mas.*"

Jumbo contacted Dante and Rosa, Sunday afternoon, to report that the United States Attorney General had approved the monitoring of DEA and FBI phone traffic from their New York and Miami field offices, Monday morning. Meanwhile, there was nothing to do but wait. Relieved to see Joe enter their house on foot once again, Tico and Esmerelda invited him and their niece to join them at Carlos in the Grove for their usual Sunday repast. Dante didn't need to be pushed to take a nap, and woke at five, refreshed. He found a shower cap to cover his forehead dressing, and stretched much of the stiffness from his joints during a long, hot shower. The knee still caused trouble if he sat too long, but he'd experienced no dizziness all that day. He dutifully took his second Decadron after dressing in clothes that Rita, the maid, had once again pressed. In his absence, all the dirty clothes from his trip had been cleaned. Given time, he could get used to this life.

Sunday dinner in the Losada tradition turned out to be something special. Carlos in the Grove was an elegant, continental Spanish restaurant. The family that owned and ran it clearly valued Don Tico and his wife as friends, as well as customers. The Losada twins, Bianca and Mercedes, were seated one on either side of Dante, while Tico was seated between Rosa and his wife. The two men were the envy of every roving male eye in the place.

Mercedes noticed the scars across Joe's knuckles as he lifted his spoon early into the first course. "The sensei at our dojo has hands like yours. You're a karate fighter, right?"

Joe's attention left a mouthwatering crab bisque. He raised his hands to frown at them. "I'm not a fighter anymore. But yeah, I do study. You too?"

Mercedes nodded, alive with enthusiasm. "My sister, also. Kenpo."

"Tae kwon do, mostly," Joe told her. "But I mess around with other styles a lot. Some kung-fu, some judo. I used to box, so I'm hardly a purist."

Mercedes addressed Rosa, across the table from her. "He's good, isn't he? Awesome, I bet."

"Careful," Rosa cautioned. "His head is swollen enough as it is."

Bianca joined her sister. "What degree black belt are you?"

"I've never been rated," he replied. "In the style I study, you only earn belts in competition. I don't compete."

"Why not?" Mercedes demanded.

"Don't you think that is his business?" Esmerelda cut in. She turned to Joe. "I'm sorry, Lieutenant. They've been taking classes since they were twelve. It's an obsession."

Dante smiled. "I was obsessed once. I understand. And when I boxed, I enjoyed the competition." He turned back to Mercedes. "But then I stopped enjoying it, and I quit boxing. I still enjoy the discipline, and putting demands on myself. That's all I want from it now."

Mercedes sneaked a conspiratorial look at her sister. "We have a mat in the basement. If there's time, before you and Rosa leave, I mean, will you show us some things?"

There was an intensity in this slender nineteen-year-old that reminded Dante of himself at that age. If she'd been at it since she was twelve, she was a serious student. It wasn't a thing to be discouraged. He dipped his head to her. "I'd be honored. Sure."

In the living room of the Losada house, later that evening, Joe announced it was looking like a big day tomorrow and he was going to bed early. Rosa said good night to her relatives as well and joined Joe as he ascended the stairs to the second floor. Outside his room, as he took her in his arms to kiss her, Rosa leaned close to whisper in his ear.

"How is your energy level?"

"I can probably manage. Your place or mine?"

A smile deepened her dimples as she released him and backed away. "We don't want to make you work *too* hard. Give me ten minutes. I'll come across the terrace."

Dante's suite and the other guest rooms in that wing were connected by an outside sun porch. While Joe waited, dressed in a robe, Rosa slipped in past the terrace door and eased it shut. When she came into his arms, he caressed the small of her back beneath soft terry cloth.

"His and hers matching robes," he murmured. "They think of everything."

"You were quite a hit with the kids tonight, hotshot."

"The *kids*?"

Rosa sighed. "You're right. I don't think Tico is ready for this stage in their development. Not yet."

Joe snorted. "He'd better hang on tight, then, 'cause it's gonna be one wild ride."

She crossed to switch off the bedside lamp, leaving the only light in the room the soft glow of security lights outside, shining through the sheers. "I'll be gentle. I know how delicate your condition is." She tugged loose the sash of her robe and shrugged the garment off her shoulders.

"Screw my condition."

"You mind if I take a few minutes? Get in the mood a little first?"

"By all means."

"Fine. One of us is overdressed."

The only cartel guard inside the house had gone outside to join his partner for a smoke. Once Julio Mesa was sure the man was occupied, he crept to the door of Teo Mendoza's room. It was already open a crack, and he quietly pushed the door open a few inches more. Teo was out cold, no question about it. Stretched on his back, propped at a slight incline on several pillows, he slept with his mouth open. The blanket drawn across his chest moved up and down with a slow, steady rhythm. The sonofabitch had surprised Julio that afternoon, getting out of bed and walking. Instead of being overwhelmed by his exertions, he seemed to gather strength as he went. Uncle Lucho had once described Teo as the most stubborn man he knew. And Lucho Esparza knew a number of such men.

Five feet from the bed, on the far side, the soft beam of light from the bathroom down the hall fell across the nurse where she lay curled on a daybed. The skirt of her white uniform rode up on her thighs, the top of a stocking revealed, held in place by a garter. She might as well have worn a sign that said *puta*. As she breathed deeply, her breasts strained the front of her dress and Julio could already feel each button pop, with a flick of the tip of his knife. He wondered if she was a fighter. He would like that. The bitch Bebe would have been a fighter, and he was still incensed she had so easily duped him. It only made him all the hungrier.

He slipped past the door, down low in a crouch just off the floor. The knife in his hand was so eager it seemed like a part of him. As he crept up to stop within five feet of her, Julio watched her face. God, he loved that surprise, when the fear first sprang full blown onto their faces. This one, with her wide, flat nose and big, disgusting nostrils, was far away from that fear right now.

On his knees, Mesa tugged down the zipper of his fly and reached inside to caress himself while gravity sucked the blade from the handle of his knife. A sheen of sweat broke out all across his forehead, slowly beading up to run toward his brow as he savored the delicious pain of being forced to hold himself in check. He stared at the nurse, salivating, almost able to taste the salty sweetness of her blood. His breath came in short, gasping pants with the effort it took to force the knife down at his side, and all the while he continued to stare.

Outside the house, he heard the soft *whump* of a car door closing and realized the guard must have finished his cigarette. He tugged one last time at his flaccid member while rocking back on his heels to regain his feet. It was then that he felt the eyes, and a chill went through him. He jerked around to find Teo, wide awake, regarding him with the coldness of a coiled snake. Suddenly, the fear that should have been the woman's filled Julio's chest. With great force of will, he continued to rise until he stood at full height.

"What?" he demanded with as much indignation as he could muster. His voice was a hoarse whisper.

"You know, *sobrino*." Teo's regard was unwavering. He never even blinked.

Mesa retracted the blade of his knife and shoved it deep into his pocket as he turned to stalk from the room.

TWENTY-FOUR

The logistics of implementing Dante's telephone monitoring plan were a nightmare for Jumbo Richardson and the group assembled to assist him. From NYPD came a pair of Intelligence Division technicians, experts who knew their way around the job's communications network. The Attorney General hand-picked two Federal Bureau technical experts and flew them up late Sunday night from Quantico, along with four U.S. Attorneys with extensive clandestine operations experience. For them, the task of securing New York's One Police Plaza was the easy part. All phone communications ultimately passed through the computerized Telephone Control Section on the ninth floor. The federal agencies had similar centralized communications, but the problem there wasn't tapping them. The problem was getting the effort coordinated and implemented in four different locations, at opposite ends of the East Coast.

It would be impossible to monitor every conversation made on a busy Monday morning, but not impossible to analyze all traffic from a specific time period. That analysis would reveal the destinations of all calls made, and determine their sources. With the aid of computer technology, Richardson and his team aimed to isolate any call made from New York to Miami, and all those made from the FBI and DEA field offices to private exhanges once news of Dante's development was relayed to them. That meant putting personnel in place at Miami's DEA Field Division headquarters on NW Fifty-third Street, and the FBI Field Office on NW Second Avenue, overnight. Those facilities were at opposite ends of sprawling Dade County—while in New York, the logistics were only slightly less daunting. Richardson's task force had to be set up in three separate locations before thousands of city and federal employees descended on their workplaces.

Chief Lieberman arrived at One Police Plaza at six A.M. Monday to monitor progress. He found Jumbo in a sealed-off section of Telephone Control, a central table jammed with Nagra reel-to-reel machines, each patched into an electronic switchboard. Richardson looked tired.

"You set?" Gus asked.

"Can't get any readier, boss. The Miami teams reported in"—Beasley glanced at the wall clock—"ten minutes ago. Right on schedule. The friendly Feds at the Javits Building and over on Tenth Avenue have been ready for an hour. They're all taking naps."

"Speaking of which, you look beat. Why don't you crawl off somewhere for a couple hours?"

"Too wired," Beasley replied. "By the way, we were right about Kristina. She works with Bebe Masaryk at Dallas Direct. They don't have a current address for her, and Sunday was one a' her nights off."

Gus had his plastic cigarette out and was fidgeting with it. Jumbo wasn't the only one on edge here. The tip of the chief's ersatz butt was melted.

"She work tonight?" Lieberman asked.

"Nuh-uh. Club's dark, Mondays."

"Wonderful. C'mon. You've got some downtime, I'll buy you breakfast."

* * *

Dante awoke at dawn, Monday, from another dream about Janet. The odor of Rosa's perfume on the pillow helped remind him of where he was, but when he reached out for her, she was gone. He shut his eyes tighter, the memory of the dream flooding back. It was neither a nightmare nor erotic. He and Janet had been sitting and talking at a table in a house she used to own in the country, near Salisbury, Connecticut. Light poured in through a window off her kitchen, which overlooked a rambling flower garden and little brook. Janet was happy and content there, a universe away from this tropical Miami morning. Joe could hear rain, still whipped by strong winds, beating against the roof. The forecast had it moving north to collide with arctic Canadian air, and Salisbury was probably being buried beneath a blanket of snow right now. Janet had sold that house after her move to the West Coast, but Joe remembered their time spent there, and their talks at that table, like he could almost reach out and touch it.

He threw back the sheet and stood to limp to the terrace doors. The anger that had gripped him for fifteen hundred miles still smoldered, and he knew he had to focus it now. He had to use his anger, and not let it consume him. At nine-thirty that morning he was scheduled to place a call to Gus Lieberman in his office. Within five minutes of hanging up, Gus would contact Charlie O'Roark, just as he had on Wednesday evening, before Janet was killed. Then either Gus or Charlie would call Al Dyson. Those calls were their fishing net. When the net was pulled in, they were betting they'd find their shark, lurking among the tuna. Joe lowered himself to the cool tile floor. Saturday's fall had left him stiff. He would try to stretch some of it away here, and more in the shower.

Jumbo Richardson had headphones on to monitor Joey's call as it came into Lieberman's office. At exactly nine-thirty, the chief's exec, Captain Frank Bryce, was heard answering.

"It's Dante, Frank. Gus around?"

"Sure, Lou. Hang on. How you feel? Okay?"

"I've been better," Joey admitted. "But it could be, I've finally hit pay dirt."

Bryce buzzed Gus to tell him Dante was on the line.

"What's up, hotshot? Frank says you got news?"

"Might be the break we've been looking for, Gus." Dante couldn't be accused of just going through the motions. He sounded excited. "This guy Cobian? The Colombian detective Mel Sullivan found for us? He got a tip early this morning. From one of his people, a guy inside the Cali organization."

"What tip?" Gus pressed.

"The snitch claims to know where Eddie Ochoa's got Mesa and Mendoza."

"Where?"

"I'll let you know when I get there. Gotta run. Metro-Dade Homicide's getting set to move, with their Special Response Team in support."

"That's it?" Gus sounded peeved.

"I'd say more, boss, but this investigation's been leaking like a sieve. I can't risk compromising it. Not over an open line."

New York SAC Charlie O'Roark was at DEA Field Division headquarters, 99 Tenth Avenue, when he took Gus Lieberman's call. Downstairs in the communications section, the FBI man and U.S. Attorney monitoring phone traffic noted the activity with satisfaction. It had begun. Less than a minute after the call terminated, O'Roark dialed a toll-free WATS number that connected him to his opposite at the Miami Field Division.

"Carl Edgar," Miami's SAC answered.

"Charlie O'Roark, Carl. You hear anything from Metro-Dade about a Mendoza tip?"

"No. Why?"

"NYPD's guy, Dante, just called his chief. Says Metro-Dade knows where Mendoza's hiding, and is getting set to move on him."

"Where?" There was an edge of irritation in Edgar's voice.

"He wouldn't say. He's paranoid; believes there's a leak."

"Christ. Dyson know about this?" Edgar demanded.

"I told Chief Lieberman I'd call him, but I'll flip you."

Edgar grunted. "I'll do it. You've got him in your face more than I do. He'll want in, you realize. How long can I wait?"

"It's Metro-Dade's show and Metro-Dade's problem. Call him now. Those communications are all logged. We don't want the attorney general crawling up our asses later."

The phone call, to an art gallery in the Cocowalk Mall, Coral Gables, was made from Joe Dante's Special Investigations Division desk, eleventh floor, One Police Plaza. Jumbo Richardson hit the record button as soon as he saw the number flash onto the monitor screen. As the reels of a Nagra started to turn, he grabbed up headphones from alongside the unit.

"Galleria Pre-Columbia. Buenas dias," a cheery female voice answered.

"Gimme Alvaro, fast." It was the familiar voice of Captain Frank Bryce. "It's an emergency."

The cheery woman switched to English. "Hang on." Her accent was no further south of the border than Howard Beach, Queens. A moment later a man's voice came on the line.

"Why you call here?" Alvaro growled.

"Metro-Dade knows where Julio's hiding. You got maybe ten minutes, if that, to get them the fuck outta there."

The line went dead. Jumbo stood for a moment with tape hiss the only accompaniment to the disbelief that had frozen him. "Holy shit."

The two Intelligence Division techs stared at him as he pried the headset from his ears. "Holy shit *what*?" one asked.

"Isolate the phones in my SID office. Shut everything else down," Jumbo ordered. He was dialing Joey in Coco Plum. "Dante."

"We got him, Joey, and you ain't gonna believe who."

"Try me."

"Frank Bryce." Richardson's anger was barely controllable. "He called someplace called Galleria Pre-Columbia. Talked to a dude named Alvaro. You better get your buddy Sullivan on it, posthaste."

"Holy shit."

"That's what I said. Listen. You do what you gotta. I've gotta go tell Gus."

"Galleria Pre-Columbia," Joey repeated. "God*damn*, buddy. Go easy. This is gonna kill him."

The Cocowalk complex on Grand Avenue off the Dixie Highway was Monday morning quiet as Mel Sullivan and Oscar Cobian entered the Galleria Pre-Columbia. Cobian often visited the mall, to dance and flirt with women at the Baja Beach Club, to have a few beers with the boys at Hooters, or just to shop. He'd passed the Galleria window countless times, and never paused to look. Dopers had front businesses all over Miami. This seemed typical of them; a gallery filled with relics of his heritage, most of them dug up from ancient burial mounds, for sale to gringo collectors. Some called it archeology. Oscar called it robbing the dead.

Today, when he entered the place for the first time, Cobian saw a handsome redhead Latina behind the front counter display case. Her face tanned almost black, it was hard to guess her age. When they came into her sights, she lit up like somebody offstage had flipped a switch.

"*Buenas dias,*" she greeted them. "*¿Como esta? Bien?*"

"Oh, sure," Mel told her. "Wonderful." And as he spoke, he showed her his tin. "Tell your pal Alvaro he's got company. *Por favor.*"

Her brightness turned harsh. She spun abruptly and poked her head past a curtain behind her. "Alvaro. *Policia.*"

Dante's partner in New York had mentioned that the woman who answered the phone spoke fluent Spanish *and* English. Cobian wanted to call her on it, but played it according to the script. A dapper man in European-cut pinstripe emerged from the back room. Oscar bet his English was pretty good too.

"*Hola,*" he grumbled. "*Identificacion?*"

Once more, Mel displayed his shield. "You received a call this morning, *chico*. It was made by somebody at Police Headquarters in New York City. We'd like to know who."

Alvaro was a mediocre actor. Oscar watched his face. Mention of the phone call saw his eyes narrow just a hair, in reflex reaction.

"I wha'? I no know this call." Pure Ricky Ricardo. "Wha' call?"

"The one that told you to call Eddie Ochoa, *chico*, about Julio Mesa."

Alvaro frowned, then his expression brightened. "Ah. *Si, si.* The man, he talk so fast, I remember only this name you say. Julio. It was *numero erroneo. Si.* How you call it? Wrong number?"

"But you called Ochoa anyway, right?"

"I know no Ochoa," the man protested. "I am businessman." He waved a hand at the objects in the cases around his gallery. "Art dealer. You see?"

Mel turned to Oscar and frowned. "You believe this dirtbag?"

Cobian shrugged. "Ain't gonna win no Academy Awards with that *numero erroneo* bullshit. How about you?"

"Doesn't really matter, I guess. You talked to the phone company, right?"

"Less than ten minutes ago. Soon as they pinpoint that call, we'll have the man who made it, dead to rights."

"You have breakfast yet?" Mel asked.

"Nope." Oscar started for the door, then stopped to regard the gallery owner and shake his head. "Wrong number, my ass."

From a pay phone at the back of the diner where Dante, Rosa, Mel, and Oscar gathered, Joe placed a call to Jumbo in the Telephone Control Section. The chill he'd felt on learning of Frank Bryce's treachery was still with him. Bryce had violated something sacred, and Joe was at a loss to imagine why. For money? Would a man who'd risen to the rank of NYPD captain do that for money?

"Yeah, Joey. How'd it go?"

"Cobian says Sullivan should take up acting. The seed's planted. Nothing yet, huh?"

"We're on it. I think he'll run."

Behind Joe, the rattle and crash of plates and tableware, combined with a stream of Spanish invective, forced him to plug one ear. "An accomplice in a dozen homicides? He's got to run, Beasley. You need to stick to him like glue." He paused. "How's Gus taking this?"

"Not good. For a minute, I thought he'd walk in there and shoot the bastard. Thirty years they know each other, Joey. Gus trusted Bryce like a brother."

"What about Kristina? You catch a break yet?"

"That trail's colder'n yesterday's corpse. We traced down three South Americans, all work with her. They claim she's

Colombian, not Brazilian like them. She started livin' with some dude 'bout a year ago. No one ever sees her, 'cept at work."

Living with someone. Not Bryce, Dante thought. Frank was married. Joe had met his wife a dozen times. They had two girls, both in college. Again, he asked himself why. "Let me know, the minute you get anything, Beasley. Sullivan's C.O. is getting authorization for a wire on the art gallery. It'll probably be too late, time we get it hung. Bryce is our ace."

At 9:40 A.M., the cartel guards at the safe house on Alhambra received a scrambled radio transmission ordering them to evacuate. Their security had been compromised. Julio Mesa was amazed to see how quickly Teo Mendoza could move now. He'd risen from his bed in seconds, stuffing the remaining vials of antibiotics and a fistful of disposable syringes inside his shirt. He walked barefoot to the door without hesitation, his pistol in his hand. It seemed clear he hadn't survived as long as he had for want of decisiveness in a moment of crisis.

It was eight months now since Kristina Abrantes rear-ended Frank Bryce at a light on Metropolitan Avenue, driving that little Volkswagen Cabriolet of hers. She hadn't even scratched the back bumper of his Ford Taurus wagon, but was scared to death she would be deported, once she learned he was a cop. When she'd begged him not to call Immigration, his heart had melted. It intrigued him that she worked as a hostess at Dallas Direct. She was terribly grateful when he promised to forget the whole incident, and threw her arms around his neck and kissed him. It sent a jolt clear through him as she pressed her exquisite body against his chest. She'd begged him to come by, any night, for free drinks. A week later, on Virginia's mah-jongg night, he found himself seated alone at a table in Kristina's section. The shame he felt was overshadowed by his erection.

When Kristina kissed him this time, her breasts were bare as they brushed against him. She told him her car was still in the body shop, and he offered her a ride home. He called his machine to leave a message for his wife, saying he'd been summoned downtown. Something nasty was brewing and he was needed for damage control. Later, in Ridgewood, he was invited upstairs to Kristina's apartment, and then, to her bed.

From another desk in the Detective Bureau office, a detective held up the receiver of his phone. "It's some Spanish broad, Cap. On three."

Frank picked up and punched the button. Ever since Dante's call that morning, he'd been sweating ice water. "Captain Bryce. Help you?"

"You got to get out from there, Frankie," Kristina blurted. "My cousin Julio call me. *Policia*, they jus' roust Alvaro."

The ice water poured in rivulets now. This was it, the moment he dreaded. His life was over. "Pack some things for me, baby." He cupped the receiver. "Use the credit card I gave you. Call the airport. . . ." He searched his memory frantically. What airline was their best bet? "Call Delta. Book us a flight to Detroit. We'll connect from there to Miami. That'll buy us some time."

"Okay, Frankie. Jus' hurry."

Bryce hung up and sat a moment, trying to collect himself. It wasn't quite eleven o'clock. He called Alvaro when? Nine forty-five? They'd probably rousted him within the half hour, but Frank hadn't been busted. It had to mean they didn't know who he was yet. He had to move. God, he could use a snort right now.

Headphones clamped on his ears, Gus Lieberman stood with Jumbo Richardson, listening to the recording of his exec's conversation with the woman. Across from them, one of the two Intelligence Division men was on the line with NYNEX. The conversation ended and the chief removed the phones, his face unreadable. Jumbo puzzled it, concerned for his friend. Was it sadness? Dismay? Righteous fury? No doubt. But there was also something else.

"Lydia plays mah-jongg with Virginia every Thursday night. How are we gonna break this to her? I was best man at their wedding, Beasley." He blinked, and for an instant Jumbo thought he might cry.

"Got it," the Intelligence man barked. He hung up the phone and swiveled around in his chair. "Sixty-six twenty-one Forest. That's Ridgewood, Queens. And get this. The number is registered to a Fernando Mendoza. Jesus. What's your guy stepped in?"

"Shit," Jumbo murmured. "*Deep* shit."

"Let's get a warrant," Gus told the Intelligence man. "Hang a wire on this broad's phone." His gaze met Richardson's, clear of trouble now. It was time to dig in. "Call Detective Bureau–Queens. Find out who's available. Have them get a surveillance set up. Sounds t' me like he plans t' pick her up."

"T' hell with finding someone else," Jumbo replied. "I want this one."

"You ain't had any sleep in a day and a half," Gus argued.

"True. But how'm I gonna feel, some other joker loses them? Nuh-uh, Gus. His ass is mine. I'll sleep on the plane."

"You get on a plane with him, he'll spot you," Lieberman reasoned. "We'll put somebody he *doesn't* know on the plane. You can fly direct."

TWENTY-FIVE

Not forty-eight hours after Teo Mendoza had stood at death's door, Eddie Ochoa could almost detect a bounce in the killer's step. Maybe all that health shit Teo preached *did* pay off. Mendoza was famous for keeping in peak condition. He ran up to ten miles a day and did hundreds of repetitions with light weights. It was rumored that he'd kept up that regimen in stir, running endless laps of the "A" block yard and paying outsiders to bring him special foods to supplement his prison diet. Today, Mendoza was not only cocky again, he was adamant. He didn't like this new safe house, nor events that had prompted the panicked move. It implied sloppiness in Eddie's security. He wanted out of here. He wanted to go home.

"It's *loco*, Eddie. The *policia*, they trick you. They don' know shit. This *capitán* from New York? *He* trick you. And now he comes here? I don' think so. You kill him, and the *puta* too.

"Kristina is Don Lucho's family," Ochoa argued. "The daughter of his wife's cousin."

"So let Julio kill her," Mendoza reasoned. "They are cousins too, *si*? And the policeman was part of *his* plan."

Ochoa was clearly uncomfortable with leaving any

woman's killing in Julio's too-capable hands. "Your brother recruited them both, Teo."

Mendoza was out of bed and standing with his hands clasped behind his back, staring out into the back garden at the rain. "So I should do it? I don't think I am quite ready for this, Eddie. You send Julio, your hands are clean. He make this mess, let him take care of the garbage." He turned away from the window. "The storm, it is finish tonight, Eddie. I hear this on CNN."

Ochoa shrugged, staying noncommittal. "Maybe, the weather clears, we call the pilot."

"No maybe, Eddie. Tonight."

Ochoa stood firm. "We see, Teo. Already, I lost one pilot. You want to go today, and the storm is not cleared? Call Avianca."

At three that Monday afternoon, Dante, Rosa, and Oscar were killing time playing pool in the Losada game room when the phone rang. Esmerelda called on the intercom to say it was Chief Lieberman and Joe picked up. He asked Gus if he could put him on the speaker phone.

"We've got Detective Cobian with us, boss. I'm doing my best to recruit him, but I don't think he'd like our winters."

"Detective," Gus greeted Oscar. He sounded tired, emotionally beat up. "Thanks for your help."

Cobian looked toward the speaker phone. "My pleasure, Chief." He had a shot lined up and sank the two ball in a corner pocket.

"What you got going?" Joe asked.

"Frank left for lunch and never came back. Phone company tapped the woman's phone. She booked them both on a Delta flight to Detroit. It left fifty minutes ago. There's a Delta connecting flight to Miami that gets them to you about six. Her full name is Kristina Abrantes."

Rosa leaned toward the phone from the depths of her leather club chair. "You've got someone on them?"

"A policewoman, name of Vickers, with a change of clothes and a wig for the Motown-Miami leg. Beasley's headed your way, too, on a direct flight that just left."

"When's he arrive?" Joe asked.

"Should be in plenty of time to lend a hand. I'm hoping your native guide there can walk point for you at Miami International. Last thing you need is for Frank to spot you." He paused. "I just got off the phone with his wife, Joey. Ginny tells me he's been actin' strange lately. She figured it was just some midlife thing that'd blow over."

"This had to hit her pretty hard," Dante replied. "A topless hostess?"

"Oh, yeah."

Joe looked to Rosa. She was up and chalking the tip of her cue but ignoring the table. "The man was your partner, Gus. Your friend. I don't know how, but he's managed to blow it as bad as any cop can. He probably doesn't know, either."

"I do," Rosa offered. "He tried to think with his dick."

The tail vibration of the 737, combined with Frank Bryce's jitters, made it hard to dump coke from his little vial onto the back of his hand. He did it quickly, hoping for the best, lifting his hand to his face in a move that by now had become second nature. Then he raised his head to stare in the mirror over the cramped little washstand. Bits of white powder were caught in his mustache. He wiped them away while sweat trickled from his hairline to burn his eyes.

The first time Kristina snorted coke off his erection and licked away the residue, he'd nearly come in her face. Hell, he was harder than he'd been since he was twenty. Then she dumped a little pile on herself, asked him to do the same to her, and Frank Bryce became a stud buck. Instead of just laying there the way Ginny had for years, Kristina humped him back, her nails raking his flexing butt and back. When she came, she screamed in his ear, her whole body shuddering. *He'd* made her do that, and Frank thought he'd died and gone to heaven. When, minutes later, he came crashing down as the drug wore off, he wanted another snort more than anything in the world. Right then. It was never quite as good after that. Nothing could be, but by then he was on board for the ride, for better or worse.

This time, when the drug hit his brain, it did little to alleviate the panic that gripped his bowels. He asked himself what he was doing. Who he was kidding? He wanted to deny it, but Frank knew it had been a setup from the beginning. He knew it down in the deepest part of himself, where the truth was trapped and couldn't run. She'd hooked him, and not for money, but for his soul.

Frank felt for his weapon and caught himself. Fearful of airport security, he'd packed his .38 and holster in his luggage. He wondered if he could really pull the trigger anyway, or was he kidding himself there too? He dumped another pile of coke on the back of his hand, and snorted it quickly before that voice from down deep could answer.

At six-twenty Monday evening, Dante and Rosa waited forty yards down the sidewalk from the door to the Delta Airlines baggage claim area. When Frank Bryce and a dark-complected woman emerged from the terminal, they were dressed as tourists. The rain had fallen off, and the winds were starting to die when Jumbo Richardson's flight landed a half hour ago. Beasley was now seated behind the wheel of a drug-confiscated stretch Cadillac, a chauffeur's cap perched atop his massive head. As Bryce and the woman hurried toward the cab rank, luggage in hand, Oscar Cobian and Mel Sullivan sauntered out the terminal door and headed Jumbo's way. Mel's garment bag, stuffed hastily with magazines and crumpled paper, looked good enough to travel.

"I wonder if that bastard knows how ridiculous he looks?" Rosa asked, eyeing Bryce.

Frank was wearing an Hawaiian shirt, with palm trees and flying fish leaping from a frothy sea. Dante didn't mind the shirt, but wondered where he'd found the lime-green slacks, white loafers, and broad-brimmed straw hat. He was even more curious about the woman, with her high brow, long nose, and sensual lips. She had the sort of look and build that Dallas Direct would require of an employee: a pert little fanny in a tight skirt, legs a mile long, and almost no waist. While Frank was slightly hesitant, she had purpose in her stride. She reached the cab rank to beat a geriatric couple to the next car in line, jerked the back door open and tossed her luggage onto the seat.

"We're close now," Joe murmured. "I can smell the blood on their hands."

Rosa had the wheel of Joe's 300ZX, unwilling to let him drive after Saturday night's episode. She reached for the key. Ahead of them, Oscar and Mel climbed into the backseat of the limo. The fleeing cop and his girlfriend pulled away from the curb. In the limousine, Jumbo gave them a hundred feet, then followed.

Kristina Abrantes had orders from Eddie Ochoa that were specific. When they landed, she wasn't to bring Bryce anywhere near Eddie. Instead, a room had been reserved for them at the Coral Gables Holiday Inn on LeJuene Road, between Majorca and Navarre. There she would keep Bryce on ice. When it was certain they hadn't been followed, Ochoa would decide what to do with them. Frankie still knew plenty about NYPD Narcotics and OCCB operations, and could be of value to Lucho Esparza. On the other hand, once New York discovered he'd fled, he would be so hot he smoked.

As they rode south from the airport along rainswept LeJuene, Frankie huddled against the opposite door, his face troubled and mind wandering. Kristina's thoughts hadn't strayed anywhere. They were on her stash and how that last bag of cocaine her cousin Julio had given her was almost gone now. She'd had enough left to fill one vial for Frankie, to keep his string tight, and one for herself. The way he'd run back and forth to the bathroom during their flights, she couldn't imagine he had much left. And once it ran out, he was going to be trouble.

Sergeant Mel Sullivan watched from the backseat of the limousine as the cab carrying their quarry turned into the driveway of the Coral Gables Holiday Inn. "A limo is a little more the Biltmore's style, but pull up beneath the canopy, Lieutenant. I'll be ready to hop out as soon as our lovebirds have gone inside."

Richardson glanced back at Sullivan in the rearview. "Anybody in there might recognize you?"

"I doubt it. I spend too much time chained to a desk these days. Right, Oscar?

"It's best you go this leg alone, Sarge," Cobian replied. "The bartenders in Greenstreets all know me. The cocktail waitresses too. One of them walks through the lobby, I'm made."

Mel tugged his garment bag closer. "If this isn't some kinda ruse, and they really are checking in, I'll try to get a room either next door or across from them."

Eddie Ochoa was in the living room of the new safe house, still arguing with Teo, when a scrambled call was received from the suburban Kendall communications center. They had Kristina Abrantes on the line. Ochoa told them to have her hold.

"To land a seaplane in the Everglades at night, in the

rain? It is crazy, Teo. Too dangerous. If the rain stops altogether, yes. I won't make the call before it stops."

Mendoza jerked a heavy curtain aside and pointed out to where security lights cut the gloom. "Look!" he shouted. "*What* rain? It's like piss from a mouse. Who is this pilot, with no *cojones*? I *spit* on him!" He cleared his throat and hawked a glob of phlegm at the floor. It landed only inches from Eddie's shoes. "He is *maricon*!"

Nonplussed, Eddie smiled. It was true, his pilot waiting in Freeport didn't have any balls. But neither was the Alaskan native a coward or homosexual. Karen Winston had cut her eyeteeth flying supplies between Aleutian salmon canneries and the Bering Sea trawler fleets. Now that Eddy Sandts was gone, she was the best pilot Ochoa had, and he'd be damned if Mendoza was going to get her killed too. "We wait and see, Teo. What can the difference be? Two, three hours?" Eddie beckoned for the radio in his bodyguard's hand. Patched through to the Holiday Inn, he projected the calm of command. "*Hola*, Kristina. Good flight?"

"How long we wait here?" she demanded.

"Your friend. How is he?"

"*Nervoso*. What you expect?"

Ochoa still hadn't made up his mind to kill Bryce, as Teo had suggested. He might want to take him somewhere and squeeze him a little first. Then again, if Eddie angered Teo much further, he risked angering Lucho Esparza too. Neither man was an enemy he wanted to have. Meanwhile, this bitch was Bryce's control. As long as he was getting whiff and pussy, he was stable.

"Nobody follow you, *si*?"

"Nobody knows we go," she growled. Her voice dropped to a whisper. "Lissen. He's in the shower now, but when he come out, he gonna want more coca, and it jus' about gone. He carry his fucking gun with him everywhere."

Of course Bryce would be armed. He was a cop. Eddie

wondered if the captain had taken his gun into the shower with him. "Until I decide what to do, how about I send Julio with more coke? I think he like to see you."

"That be good," she replied. "Frankie know him. Maybe he won' be so jumpy."

Ochoa pressed the disconnect button and looked across to where Mesa was sulking on one of the sofas. God, he longed to be rid of this beast—this dangerous, predatory infant. "Your cousin Kristina, she wan' you to bring her more coca. Bryce, he snort it all up."

"And then what?" Julio asked. "After what I promised him, he's gonna want me to bring him back."

Eddie glanced to Mendoza, who averted his gaze. "You think your uncle wants a pet, and there is room on the plane, I leave it for you to decide."

It wasn't raining at all when Dante and Rosa joined Cobian and Richardson in the limousine, parked at the curb across LeJuene from the Holiday Inn. They'd left Joe's car on Navarre, the side street running east-west past the south side of the hotel. From one of the jump seats, Joe peered out through the smoked glass toward the front of the building.

"Any news yet?"

Oscar had a radio with scrambler capability in hand. "Mel just called. He's got a room next to them. Three twenty-six. He heard the toilet flush, then the shower start, maybe ten minutes ago. Soon as the water went on, he thinks the woman got on the phone."

Dante pointed diagonally across LeJuene toward Avenida Majorca, behind them. "We just drove around the block, back of the hotel. There's a service area on the south side with two slots for hotel courtesy vans and a couple garbage Dumpsters parked behind a low brick wall."

"So you saw the back entrance to Greenstreets?" Cobian asked.

"Uh-huh. Under that canopy. If you back up to the other side of the intersection, you'd have a good view of the parking lot back there, and could still see the front of the hotel."

Richardson started the car and backed slowly up LeJuene until the well-lit parking lot behind the hotel came into view.

"Perfect," Cobian told him. "Stop." He looked to Dante. "You got that phone in your car, right?"

"As long as the batteries last. I brought two, and one's dead now."

His waist wrapped in a towel, Frank Bryce stepped from the bath to find Kristina at the table across the room. Her coke vial, nearly half full when they landed at Miami International, was empty now. It was lying on the table with its cap off as she studiously touched up her nails. All that remained of their stash was a residue of dust on a hand mirror at her elbow.

"Hey," he complained. "You left nothing for me?"

Kristina looked up from her nail painting with barely disguised contempt. "I talk to Eddie Ochoa. My cousin, he be here with more. Soon."

A tiny ray of sunshine broke through the gloom depressing Bryce. He'd unpacked his toilet kit and again had access to his weapon. But as he stared at his reflection in the bathroom mirror, he couldn't bring himself to believe that death was his only way out. Maybe he was a coward, but Frank had convinced himself he was still of great value to the Cali cartel. He was, after all, the executive officer to the New York City chief of detectives. Or had been, until that noon. That made him a treasure trove of crucial information. How much trouble would it be for Lucho Esparza to provide him a simple existence in exile?

That glimmer of hope alive in his breast, Bryce moved to Kristina's side. He dragged a finger through the dust on the mirror and rubbed it into his gums. "Gimme your hand," he said.

"Wha'?" She held up her wet nails to display them.

He grabbed that hand, and against her attempt to pull free, forced it beneath his towel. "What'sa matter, baby? A week ago, I wouldn't have had to ask."

"When my nails, they are wet? You always gotta ask, Frankie. Look what you do to them." She tugged the hand free to show the damage now, fingers splayed.

A knock at the door saw Frank back away fast to grab his pistol. Gun arm crooked before him, the weapon held high, he crept to the door to check the security peep. It was Mesa.

A light rain had started to fall again as two cars, a black Mercedes that Oscar was sure belonged to Eddie Ochoa, and a pale blue Honda Civic, glided in tandem around the corner from LeJuene onto Majorca. At the curb alongside the back parking lot, two men in guayabera shirts emerged from the Mercedes to hurry toward the hotel. As soon as they were out of view, the Civic pulled past the Benz and turned right behind the hotel on Salzedo Street.

Cobian lifted his radio to call Sullivan in room 326. "We got action, Sarge."

"Ten four," Sullivan replied. Then, two minutes later, he came back at them. "Somebody just knocked on their door."

Still seated with Rosa in the back of the limousine, Dante was keeping an eye on Navarre Street where it crossed LeJuene, south of the hotel. That little Honda had acted exactly the way a security rover would, covering the lead car on the approach, then scouting for trouble over the planned exit route. So why hadn't it reappeared to join the Mercedes? Too much time had passed.

"I don't like this, Oscar. Ask him how many came upstairs?"

Oscar asked.

"Bad angle from here," Mel replied. "I think only one."

"Two went inside the hotel, Sarge."

"Like I said, I can't really see much."

Dante already had the door handle. "We're gonna take a stroll, back toward our car. I want to know where that Civic went."

"What happens, the Benz pulls out, Joey?" Beasley asked.

Dante had the door open now, and one foot on the street. Rosa was right behind him. "You've got the number of my cellular. Mel's got a phone up there. Have him call us."

As Julio Mesa entered the room, the first thing he saw was the gun in Frank Bryce's hand. It was a snub-nose S&W Chief's Special, cocked and ready.

"What's this, Jim? Paranoia is paradise?"

Bryce showed no sign of easing off. "You set me up, you little prick!"

Mesa looked over at Kristina and clucked his tongue. "Uh-oh. We ain't been telling tales outta school, have we?" He turned back to Bryce. "Put the gun away, Jim. It's a little late for this shit, ain't it? I'm the only chance you got."

"Chance of what?" Bryce stepped back to maintain his distance as Julio took a step toward him. "I've just flushed my whole fucking life down the toilet."

Julio smiled brightly. "C'mon. Colombia ain't so bad. It's warm, like here, with beautiful senoritas like this one, a peso a pound. Before you go and shoot me, you might want to think about it."

Bryce advanced, wrapped in his towel, to open his suitcase and grope inside for a pair of boxer shorts. With the gun still leveled at Mesa, he stooped to lift one foot through a leg hole, and then the other. "You bring any fucking coke?"

Julio patted his pants. "Nice fat bag, right here in my front pocket. You gonna shoot me, I reach in there to pull it out?"

"Not if you go nice and slow."

Mesa produced a Ziploc sandwich bag half full of shiny product, sparkling in chunks. He turned and tossed it onto the table alongside Kristina's mirror, where it hit the bottle of fingernail polish. "Go ahead, Jim. Do yourself. I know you got to be hurting. That was one *fuck* of a long flight, right?"

Frank edged around him.

"At least take the hammer off, Jim. You sneeze, you could shoot yourself in the dick."

At the table, Bryce got the bag open one-handed and dumped more coke onto the mirror than a rock band could do at one sitting. He used the bottom of the nail polish bottle to crush the coke up fine, lifted the mirror to his face, and stuck his nose to it like a pig in a trough. He let his gun hand fall to his side as he snorted, and Mesa saw his window of opportunity. Julio darted a hand to his Beretta, tucked into his waistband beneath his guayabera shirt, and cleared it, noise suppressor and all. Frank saw the movement from the corner of his eye and started to react. It was his last conscious act. A single slug tore through the left ventrical of his heart. He was already dead when he shot himself in the right knee.

While the report of Mesa's gun was no louder than a hand clap, Bryce's .38 was deafening in that confined space. Suddenly panicked, Julio hurried to the window to draw back the curtain and jerk the window open.

Kristina was at the table, frantically trying to scoop the coke dumped from the bag back into it. "Wha' you doing? We got to *go*, Julio."

"Checkout ain't till noon," he replied. "Why not get some rest?" He kicked the screen out and lifted one leg over the sill as he leveled the gun and fired. The shot took her midchest and drove her hard into the wall behind.

Dante and Rosa found the blue Civic on Avenida Navarre, where it idled adjacent to a low brick wall off the hotel service area. They strolled past, hand in hand, and crossed slowly toward their own parked car, across the street.

"Didn't we see *two* people in it, following the Mercedes?" Dante asked.

"And now there's one." Rosa was thoughtful as she inserted the key into the driver's side door and opened it to climb in. Once both of them were seated, they wondered how long they could stay there without arousing suspicion. They could see the back corner of the hotel. The service area garage was quiet. Frank Bryce and his woman friend were in a room on the third floor, facing east, with Sullivan in another, alongside. That meant two of the lit windows visible above some kind of first-floor terrace area were theirs. "Something strange is going down, Joe."

"Maybe a bait and switch? Two guys leave the Mercedes, one guy is missing from this car, and only one knocks on Frank's door."

"Call Sullivan," she suggested. "Ask what Jumbo and Oscar can see."

Dante had his field glasses out of the glove box and was studying the back of the hotel. Before he could reach for his phone, he saw an occupant of one of those third-floor rooms pull back the curtain and open the window. Backlit, the silouette of a man was clearly visible as he punched out the screen, threw a leg over the sill, and aimed a pistol back into the room. The gun jumped, and then he did, disappearing from view for an instant. When he reappeared, he leaped from the first-level terrace onto a hotel courtesy van. Joe tracked him as he scrambled from the van onto the pavement. He'd seen too many pictures the past couple days to be mistaken.

"That's Mesa!"

The lights of the Civic came on as the gunman opened the

passenger's side door. The car started to roll before he was all the way inside.

"Go!" Joe told Rosa. "No lights. Not till there's a car between us and them." He had his phone in his lap and dialed Sullivan's room as fast as his fingers would fly. Mel picked up mid-ring. "It's Dante, Mel. Julio Mesa just jumped from up there. He's in the blue Civic, on the fly. You heard the shots?"

"Just one, I think, but . . ." Mel's voice was faint. Joe checked the *display window* on his handset. It read: *Lo Bat*.

"Damn!"

"What's wrong?" The Civic hadn't turned the corner onto LeJuene, but had shot straight across it, aimed west into a quiet residential neighborhood. Rosa was being forced to hang way back.

"Battery's gone." Joe removed the handset from his ear and dropped it into his lap. To stay in touch with Gus as he drove south from Gainesville, he'd been forced to leave the phone on *roam*. It had cost him precious battery life. Without access to a charger, his communications link was broken.

"How about the CB?"

"Locked in the trunk. Besides, it's way too public. We might as well open the sunroof, stand up, and scream."

TWENTY-SIX

Sergeant Mel Sullivan could see the screen punched out next door as he leaned out his window, radio in hand. "What've you got down there?" he demanded of Cobian. "I had a gunshot up here. Just lost contact with Dante."

"Quiet out front, boss." There was a hesitation. "No. Wait. We've got two in guayabera shirts, walking toward the Benz."

"Someone just jumped out the window up here. Onto the pool deck. Left in that Civic."

"Don't have it on our screen, Sarge. Just the Benz."

"Stick to it, Oscar." Mel had a partial view of the room next door through an opening in the curtains. He could see a table, an overturned chair, and a lot of powder dumped on the carpet near a woman's outstretched hand. The hand didn't move. "At least one down up here. I'm calling for backup."

Mesa's driver headed west while a gasping Julio leaned forward, one hand on the dash. "Wha' happen?" the driver asked. "You suppose to bring somebody down, no?" The rain had started again, not a steady downpour with gusts of winds, but a drizzle strong enough to demand wipers.

"I walk in there, he wants to shoot me. The fucking wheels came off."

The radio on the console between the seats crackled and the driver picked up. "Wha'?"

It was one of the cartel soldiers in the Mercedes. "We jus' grown a tail. You wan' we shake it, or drag it along awhile?"

Mesa leaned over to check the rearview mirror. Through the rain, he saw no headlights and was satisfied the ruse had worked. Perhaps it was routine DEA surveillance, lucky enough to stumble on one of Ochoa's cars. Still, it made him nervous that the cops had come so close. Was Bryce followed? Had someone in New York smelled a rat? Julio might not agree with Teo about much, but he did agree it was time for Eddie to call his pilot, have him fly over, rain or not. He grabbed the radio from the driver. "You two, are you clean?" he asked the man in the Mercedes.

"*Sí, hermano*. They roust us, they won't find shit."

"Okay. There's been a problem. I couldn't bring Bryce back with me. Take your time. Drive over to the Grove or someplace. They pop you, stay cool." He handed the radio back.

"You still don' tell me why you run from there," the man said.

"He shot himself in the fucking knee, Jim. Made so much noise your buddies in the bar prob'ly heard it. Eddie told me whether I brought him out or not was *my* choice. So what choice did I have?"

"An' your good-looking cousin? You shoot her too?"

"Bet your ass. She'd rat out my uncle's whole show for her next snort. The cops got dope too, Jim."

Six blocks west of the Holiday Inn, the blue Civic turned south on Granada Boulevard. When Rosa reached the intersection, she let a car get between them and went to headlights. Four blocks later, the Civic swung west again on

Castile, then north two blocks on Columbus. Once they made that turn, she and the Civic were the only two cars moving on the street. She had no choice but to go past when the Civic turned into a driveway, three houses up Columbus on the left. As they went by, Dante craned around in his seat to see what he could.

The house, like most other residential structures in the area, was Spanish in influence. Small for the neighborhood, its stucco exterior was overgrown with vines—probably bougainvillea—the yard in front studded with palmettos. There were security lights on, up under the eaves, and other lights could be seen behind curtains covering a large arched window.

"Looks like we're running back into that golf course we crossed a minute ago," Rosa announced. "Right or left?"

Joe was kneeling in his seat to get the view out the rear window. "Go right. We'll circle around, park on that corner back there."

"What could you see?"

"Hard to say. Both Mesa and the driver were getting out. There's another car in the driveway. A black Mercedes. Identical with the one we saw outside the hotel except the plate."

"Oscar says Ochoa's got four." Rosa swung the wheel to turn right at the corner. The Granada Golf Course was on their left now. "Whenever he leaves his house on Krome Avenue, they all leave, each headed in a different direction."

They turned right on Castile again, and Rosa killed the lights to crawl toward the corner of Columbus. From where she pulled to the curb, they had a good view of the front of that house with the Civic in the drive.

"I'm going in for a closer look. Give me fifteen minutes. I'm not back by then, go for help." Dante reached over to switch the ignition key to *accessory* and ran his window down. His weapon left behind, he crawled out, then reached back inside to retrieve it. Before he could withdraw his hand, Rosa grabbed his wrist.

"Careful, Joe, Please."

"It's my middle name. Wish me luck."

The cartel man seated in shadow behind the wheel of the Mercedes in the safe house driveway reported the reappearance of a Nissan 300ZX. It had driven past the house as the Civic arrived, and was parked now on the corner of Columbus and Castile. After receiving this report, Julio Mesa and a cartel sentry equipped with Cyclops night-vision goggles stepped to the window of a darkened bedroom to peer out past the draperies.

"Where?" Mesa asked.

The sentry pointed. "There. The black one." He stripped off the goggles and handed them across.

Julio scanned the landscape with the lightweight device until he focused on the car in question. At only 1X magnification, it appeared the car had one occupant, seated behind the wheel. What? A Fed? "It's got a front plate." Florida cars carried only a rear license plate, while many out-of-state and all federal agency cars had them both fore and aft. He handed the goggles back to the sentry. "I'll need one of your guys to cover me. I'm gonna go take a look. You better call Eddie, tell him to have that pilot shift ass."

Once he reached the same side of the street as the target house, Dante moved from tree to tree. The house next door was quite a bit larger, with a BMW and Saab parked in the drive, and Christmas "chaser" lights outlining the roof. They seemed strange to a guy who associated them with a chill in the air. Together with the lights behind the front windows, they illuminated so much front lawn that Joe could see no way to cross it without risk of discovery.

Instead, he tried the latch on the gate to the pool area and gardens behind, and found it unsecured.

The floods lighting the pool terrace reached only fifty feet back into the shadows of ornamental shrubs and trees. Thankful that he hadn't encountered a dog, Joe skulked along a side wall to melt into the gloom. His clothes soaked through from the rain, he was halfway over the wall into the yard next door when he saw the glow of a cigarette fifteen feet away. Seated beneath him, in a white plastic patio chair, was a lone figure in a camouflage poncho, hood up, assault rifle laid across his knees.

It was anybody's guess what the man who sauntered down the driveway from the target house was up to. Rosa felt a slight flutter of panic as he looked in her direction. But then he looked the other way too. When he walked across the street, she followed him up the driveway opposite, as far as she could see. Then the bulk of a huge banyan tree hid him from view, and her imagination went into overdrive. The cartel had a second safe house across the street. They owned the entire block, as a sort of stronghold. Eddie Ochoa's mother was baking a cake and had run low on sugar.

Rosa was still trying to make sense of that figure's movement when a shadow fell between her and the streetlight behind her left shoulder. She twisted in her seat with a start, and found the muzzle of a noise suppressor aimed at her face.

Dante was idly calculating his chances of jumping that sentry, overwhelming him and commandeering the assault rifle cradled in his lap, when an unseen radio spewed muffled Spanish in a faint, rapid staccato. The sentry removed the radio from the folds of his poncho, growled something into it, and stood to advance on the house. But instead of entering, he stopped, turned, and looked outward. The yard was suddenly flooded with light. Fortunately, Joe was pressed flat in the overgrowth atop the wall. As slowly as he could manage it, and still be moving, he eased to the edge and slid back down.

Something had set them off. Had Beasley and Cobian followed that other Mercedes here? That didn't make sense. Why set up that kind of deception, then turn it back on yourself? It had to be something else. Had the neighbors reported seeing movement, here in this yard? He'd seen no security cameras, nor even a flicker of movement from the draperies covering the back windows.

Dante retraced his steps back through the depths of that garden without incident. Same story, as he slid along the wall past the shimmering pool to the gate. When he let himself out onto the walk alongside the drive, the bright Christmas lights drove him deep into the shadows of an avocado tree. From there, he studied the landscape.

A gun pointed at her face, Rosa had no choice but to open the door. Jerked out onto the street in the rain, she'd found herself face-to-face with the man she'd seen countless times in a Gainesville Police booking photograph.

Now his close-set green eyes regarded her again, in the living room of the house she was forced to enter, the muzzle of that noise-suppressed gun jammed painfully between her neck and jaw. Mesa had the stubble of four days trimmed into the beginnings of a sparse beard. In one hand he held her shield case as he stood over the contents of her purse, dumped on the coffee table at her knees.

"New York plates on the car. Picture right here on the fucking ID. I wouldn't believe it, I didn't see it with my own fucking eyes. Good-looking Latina bitch like this, a New York police *captain*, Teo."

It was hard for her to believe that the man Mesa addressed, standing by the front window and looking removed, could be Mateo Mendoza. He was on his feet, looking a little pinched maybe, but otherwise every bit as dangerous as his reputation suggested. Rosa wondered how it could be.

Mendoza stepped across to stand staring down at Rosa where she'd been shoved onto the sofa. "How you fin' this place, *Capitán*?"

Rosa nodded toward Mesa. "You should tell your friend, when he leaves a hotel, he should use the door."

In rapid-fire Spanish, Mendoza asked one of the cartel men in the room, all of whom brandished machine pistols, what the status of the pilot was. When the man replied that the plane was in the air, Teo turned to Mesa. "We go, *sobrino. Pronto.*" There was a definite sneer in his voice when he said *nephew*. He then faced Rosa again, his focus as clear and cold as a snow-melt stream. "You are alone here, *Capitán*? You drive here, from *Nueva York*, jus' to catch Teo Mendoza? By yourself?"

"I came here to kill the man who killed my brother," she replied, and saw the confusion it created.

"Wha'?"

"At the parking lot, by the river? When you changed vans?" How much could he remember about an anonymous parking attendant, shot in the dark? "His name was Enrique Olivera. He was my brother."

"It says here, your name's Losada," Julio Mesa countered.

"My married name. I'm divorced."

Mesa blurted a laugh. "*He* didn't kill your fucking brother, bitch. I did. You want to kill *me*."

"She ain' going to get that chance, *sobrino*," Mendoza growled. "Freeport to Miami, it take only one hour. We must go now."

"We're taking her with us," Mesa replied. "On your feet, Rosita. I can't bring my uncle one New York police captain, I'll bring him another."

* * *

The Raymond brothers, Tim and Artie, had been cruising the quiet residential streets of affluent Coral Gables since sunset, hunting for the new Infiniti J30 ordered by a chop shop in West Wood Lakes. So far they'd seen three, but none of them was in a situation they felt comfortable trying to tackle. All three were parked in driveways and alarmed. The occupants of each house seemed very much at home.

Tim Raymond had already done one stretch at Raiford for grand theft auto. He believed his time in stir had made him smarter, teaching him patience, but he had no desire to return. His younger brother, Artie, was the kind of hothead who could get them in trouble, but so long as Tim had him in harness, no rash moves would be made. Tim saw car boosting as a social skill, like comparative shopping. He hoped that one day, when Artie grew up a little, he'd learn patience too.

"Lookit that!" Artie yelped, pointing with excitement.

Tim, who had the wheel of their Acura Legend—it paid to look like you belonged where you were—slowed. He had to peer out the side window past Artie's shoulder to see what had caught his brother's interest. The car, tucked beneath a big banyan at the curb alongside, wasn't the Infiniti the chop shop had ordered, but a dark gray Nissan 300ZX, late model, in cherry condition.

"Back up," Artie urged. "I think the plate is outta state."

Rather than put it into reverse and draw undue attention to themselves, Tim went a block west and circled two blocks back for another pass. It wasn't their standing order, but a 300ZX, unencumbered, was too pretty a prize to pass up.

"Keep your shirt on, now," he growled at his brother. "Car like that, parked out here? Could be a setup." They'd swung back around onto Castile and were easing to the curb, a safe distance back from the Nissan.

"With New York plates?" Artie argued. "Only a fool

New Yorker, prob'ly stoned, would park wheels like them on the street."

"Looks good, don't it?" Tim drawled. He'd watched his rearview and checked every shadowed driveway and side alley they passed on this approach. Could Artie be right? That some doper visiting people here had gotten cocky? That was sure how it looked.

Artie reached beneath his seat to retrieve his spring steel window wand. The lock puller followed. He got so eager at moments like these that Tim would swear he could smell the musk ooze off him. "Like pickin' peaches, Timmy. Clock me. I'll have her rollin' inside thirty seconds. Bet you twenty bucks."

"Just watch your ass," Tim warned him. "You see anything, anything at *all*, I want you outta there, understand?"

Artie already had the door open and was out before Tim finished his sentence.

The rain was picking up again as Dante peered through the gloom at his car, or at least at his front bumper, tucked beneath the canopy of that overhanging tree. Then, as he considered a dash back across the next property and the street to rejoin Rosa, a figure hurried from the target house. The man held some kind of automatic weapon close to his side, and after scanning the street in both directions, rounded the backside of the parked Mercedes. Seconds later, he was behind the wheel and had started the engine. Three more people rushed from the house; two men and a woman. The lead man opened a rear door while another forced the woman inside, a gun to her head. The woman was Rosa.

Dante suddenly understood the floodlights. How long had she been sitting in the car before they discovered her? The fifteen minutes he'd allotted himself were only now exhausted. Doors slammed. The car started backward into the street, and Joe moved as quickly through shadow as his battered body allowed. He always carried a spare key in his wallet, lest he lock himself out of his car. He dug for it now, one eye on the progress of the Benz as it straightened and aimed for the golf course.

As he rounded the corner where his car was parked, he came upon a man with a jimmying wand slipped down between the door and window glass of his car. Less than ten feet away, an Acura Legend idled, another man behind the wheel. The car thief looked up as he worked the wand with one hand and the door release handle with the other to swing it open. He found Dante's Walther in his face.

"Perfect timing, asshole," Joe snarled. He used the distraction of the gun to move inside on the man and knock him ass over elbow with a vicious forearm thrust. Without looking back, Joe slid into the driver's seat and jammed his spare key home in the ignition. The car thieves were still trying to figure out what had hit them when Dante rocketed away from the curb.

Vivid pictures of Audrey Stumpf, stretched out on that mortuary slab in Martinsburg, flashed in memory as he turned the corner to accelerate up Columbus. Two blocks ahead, at the intersection with the golf course, he glimpsed the taillights of a car going west. Joe prayed to any deity who would listen that the car was a black Mercedes.

For the first few minutes of this nightmare, Rosa tried to sustain herself by believing that Joe had seen them grab her. Then the pragmatist at the core of her reared its unwelcome head. It insisted that Julio Mesa had no intention of making a gift of her to his uncle. Not a chance.

"So," Mesa purred. He sat close on the backseat, with Mendoza and the driver up front. The noise suppressor screwed onto the barrel of his gun was cool on her cheek as he traced a line with it from ear to chin. "I ain't never had a cop before. We got a few minutes before our plane leaves. Maybe you'll show me why they call you fuzz the *finest*."

His free hand closed on her left breast, then traveled to the buttons of her blouse. Her impulse was to fight him. The eyes of the driver, glancing up to watch the action in his rearview mirror, added to her rage. But to fight would be just what Mesa wanted, and would be suicide. Death was the one option she would hold in reserve.

Julio's rough fingers loosed buttons to plunge inside her blouse. Rosa forced herself to study how he held the gun, and to calculate the distance between the heel of her hand and the end of his nose. In her practice sessions with Dante, he'd shown her how much force it would take to shove the bridge of that nose back into Mesa's brain. She gasped when a thumb and forefinger pinched her.

"*Alto*, Julio!"

The fingers froze. There was no doubting the authority in that command. Mesa looked to the passenger seat with a mixture of irritation and surprise, the barrel of his gun ceasing to exert pressure on the underside of Rosa's jaw. Mateo Mendoza was turned in his seat to face them.

"Find your own action, Jim," Julio retorted. "This one's mine."

Teo sighed and clucked his tongue. "Let her go, *sobrino*."

Julio remained frozen, with a growing rage causing him to tremble slightly. Rosa felt the vibration of it in his gun hand, rested now against her chest. "You don't ever tell me what to do, Jim."

Mendoza surprised Rosa by smiling. "Check it out, *sobrino*." His gaze flicked down to the gap between the two front seats. Rosa looked to where he indicated at the same time Julio did. Mateo had a machine pistol wedged into that gap, aimed at Mesa's groin.

They remained deadlocked for only seconds before Mesa backed his hand out of Rosa's blouse and lowered his gun hand to the seat. She reached to button her blouse as she started to inch away.

"Who said you could move, bitch?" Julio snarled.

"I say," Mendoza answered for her. "And I think you pull the clip from your gun, put it in your pocket while you cool off."

Mesa was so reddened with fury as he complied with Teo's request that Rosa thought he might pop an artery. When he spoke, his voice quavered. "Don't think I'll ever forget this, Jim."

"There is still one in the chamber, *sí, sobrino*? You think I forget?"

At eight P.M. there was enough traffic on SW Eighth Street going west that Dante felt comfortable using headlights once the black Mercedes turned onto it. Two blocks later, he noticed the first Tamiami Trail, Route 41, and Florida 90 signs. He recalled from his map that Route 41 ran west from Miami into the Everglades, eventually crossing the whole bottom of the state. He had no recollection of a 90, nor where it and 41 parted ways.

There was no doubt in his mind that he was following the right car. How many Mercedes 600 sedans could there have been within three blocks of Columbus Avenue, at that hour on a Monday night? He followed with three cars between them while listening to WINZ news radio 940 for a weather update. Earlier, the forecast had predicted clearing by this hour. Instead, the same slower but steady drizzle persisted. On city streets it provided good cover, distracting the driver of the Benz and preventing him from spending too much time with his eyes on the rearview mirror. But as they pressed on farther west and traffic started to thin, Joe was forced to hang back farther and farther to avoid detection. They'd seen his car when they dragged Rosa from it. If they were headed into the Everglades, he would have no choice but to drive without lights.

* * *

As they sped past Miami International University, and beneath the Florida Turnpike, all Rosa could do to determine where they were going was read the meager signs visible along their route. They were on the Tamiami Trail, with a canal paralleling them on the right. There weren't many streetlights anymore, suggesting they were headed away from the city, going west. Beside her, Julio had sulked awhile before deciding to bolster his sagging self-esteem with cocaine. He was ten minutes into an orgy of snorting and grunting now, his sneer gone. Instead, he grinned and dumped a little pile of coke onto the back of his hand to extend it across the seat toward Rosa. If his keeper wouldn't let him carve her and chew her nipples off, maybe he could try to make a friend? Rosa swallowed her revulsion to shake her head.

"No thanks."

Mesa grunted his contempt and snorted the pile himself. "You gotta loosen up, baby. I'm the only *real* friend you got here." He gestured toward Mendoza. "Teo there, the only reason he ain't dumped you on the roadside is that you managed to find him. My uncle Lucho's gonna want to know how." His tone became confiding now. "You'll tell him too. Ten thousand Feds and all the cops in Miami can't find us, but you can? He'll tear your fingernails out, one at a time, until you tell him." He paused to dump another pile of coke onto his hand and run it up his nose. That was at least ten. "Me? You give me what I want, ain't nobody gonna hurt you. The woman gives me what I want, lives like a queen in Colombia."

Rosa suspected that what he wanted was what no woman could give him. She'd read the pathology reports. Neither Audrey Stumpf nor Kimberly Trammel had shown signs of penile penetration. The semen in both of those autopsies was found in traces outside their bodies and in their mouths.

Before being shot, the latter woman was penetrated only with a knife.

Maybe it was the giddiness of stress, but Rosa felt suddenly emboldened. "What is it this woman's got to give you, Julio? Your queen."

He smirked toward Teo, and chuckled. "You hear that, Jim? I *knew* she'd come around." He turned back to grin at her. "It's simple, mama. All you gotta do is make my dick hard."

Bingo, Rosa thought. What a surprise.

TWENTY-SEVEN

Five miles beyond the Florida Turnpike, the Tamiami Trail narrowed crossing Route 997. The Everglades were all around Dante now as he followed those taillights, almost a quarter mile distant. The rain had finally quit, but the night sky remained obscured by low clouds. Except for the dim red glow he followed, running without headlights would leave him blind. Then again, if he didn't risk it soon, the driver of that Mercedes was sure to notice him. In his favor, the road had run dead straight, clear out from where he first got on it. How long that would last, he had no idea, but the time had come to find out.

He feigned a turn by signaling right and swinging onto the shoulder. At the same instant he killed the signal and his lights, then swerved back until his tires ran smooth on pavement. That red smudge locked on again, dead ahead, he was otherwise enveloped in total blackness. He felt his hands go clammy on the wheel while he tromped the accelerator to close on his quarry. He realized that, to this right, he still paralleled the same canal he'd followed all the way out of town. One jog in the road and he would learn how long a 300ZX could float.

As he approached within seventy yards of the other car,

Dante was thankful that his own was dark gray, almost black. Slung low to the road, the Nissan would be virtually invisible, so long as the cloud cover held and an oncoming car didn't betray him. In anticipation of such an event, Joe drove with one hand on the parking brake, prepared to hit the shoulder as soon as he saw headlights on the horizon. So far, his luck was holding. The headlights of the Benz were now lighting his way too.

Julio had never before felt a paranoia like this when he had a headful of coke. It had hold of his bowels with icy fingers and was squeezing each time he looked in Teo's direction. It insisted he would not reach the seaplane alive, that Teo wouldn't let him. To save that ungrateful dog's life, he'd risked his own, and what did he get? He'd wanted to have a little fun with a cop bitch, and Teo had threatened to kill him. His fear insisted that Teo still wanted to kill him. If he didn't succeed in doing that, Teo would surely denounce him to his uncle Lucho.

There were those who said that Mendoza literally had eyes in the back of his head. Right now, Julio believed them. He could feel those eyes boring into him through the headrest. They watched as he dumped more coke onto the back of his hand and snorted again. They said he had met his match. The pistol wedged between the seats was gone now, but Julio could still see it there, aimed at his manhood.

"Here," the driver murmured. The car slowed and swung left across the road into an open gravel lot. The headlights illuminated wooden fencing and the thatched roof of a low, ramshackle building, its facade overgrown.

Mesa had been out this road several times in daylight. There wasn't much on it; a Miccosukee village and a variety of airboat tours, mostly run by enterprising Indians. This place looked like one of them, failed for some reason and abandoned. The driver pulled up to a gate to the right of the building, hopped out, and fit a key into a padlock. A chain fell away and the gates were swung wide. Beyond, a junk-strewn levee ran fifty yards into the darkness, a row of scraggly trees lining each side. The clouds had thinned to allow an occasional glimpse of stars as the driver resumed his seat. He eased them forward ten feet onto the levee, stopped, and got out again to close the gate. Teo ran his window down.

"Where is the boat?" he asked.

The driver pointed down past the junk airboat parts littering the levee, and Julio realized with another wave of fear that they would walk it from here. Teo at his back wasn't the only danger. There were alligators lurking in shadow.

With Teo's window down, Julio was being eaten by mosquitoes. "When's this plane s'posed to get here, Jim? I thought Eddie said an hour from the time he called. I don't hear a fucking thing."

Mendoza turned to face him through the gap between the seats. "Patience, *sobrino*." He crooked an ear and pointed toward the ceiling. "There."

As much as he wanted to demand that Teo raise his window, Julio listened. Far off, no louder than the mosquito buzzing in his ear, he heard the faint drone of an aircraft engine. His paranoia eased. High atop the crest of a new wave of coke-induced confidence, he could see his uncle's hideaway in the *Amazonas* now. He could see himself and this beautiful *cubana* bitch, him forcing her to his will.

"You hear, *sobrino*?"

Julio tapped the driver on the shoulder. "Go keep an eye on the road, Jim."

The brake lights of the Mercedes had brightened just as Dante was growing uncomfortable with the clearing sky. He wasn't sure what phase the moon was in, but with each peek through gaps in the clouds, he thought he could detect a pale glow. Out here in the 'Glades, twenty miles from Miami, the light of a clear night sky could be his undoing.

Joe strained to watch the landscape illuminated by the headlights of the Benz while he took his foot off the gas and used the handbrake to avoid closing the gap between them. They were turning left across the highway. Rather than go past, he steered for the right shoulder and idled a hundred feet away while the quarry swung through the parking area of an abandoned roadside attraction. They drew up in front of a gate, and Joe switched off his engine. Before the driver could climb out, Dante ran his window down, and for the second time that night, crawled out the window rather than open the door. This time, he banged his head.

For the past fifteen minutes, Rosa had been mesmerized by the drama engaging Julio Mesa and Teo Mendoza. Now her attention turned to how they meant to effect their escape. Earlier, when they'd spoken of a pilot, she assumed they would head for some remote, private airstrip. The Everglades had confused her until mention was made of a boat and she heard the far-off drone of a plane engine on the night breeze. In an area where swampland ran on for hundreds of square miles, the water in most places was less than a foot or two deep. Still, some amphibious aircraft drew very little water. The pilot wouldn't have to worry about power lines. And in this remote area, one could fly in and out with impunity.

Within minutes she would be airborne, bound for Colombia. That reality forced home another, more final one. Within hours, she would also be dead. Rosa felt a detached clarity. She wondered if this was how her parents had felt before they met their fates. She had a picture in her mind of Dante returning to his car to find it empty. She felt sorry for him, and what he would go through. She wondered if he would continue on to Colombia in pursuit of Mendoza, and knew it was likely that he would.

The driver disappeared into the gloom by the gates, while Rosa and the others sat in the car, listening to the thrum of the airplane engine grow louder. Then, probably by some radio-controlled means, a line of lights lit to glow soft in the distant grass. The plane engine roared in thundering crescendo as it swept low to make a pass, directly over that light line in the swamp. It faded away again, going west, and banked into a turn to make its approach.

"Showtime," Mesa announced as he opened his door. Instead of allowing Rosa to depart the car through her own door, he reached across to grab a handful of her hair. "Let's dance, Captain."

The flood of moonlight through parting clouds left Dante feeling totally exposed as he crossed the road and parking lot. After all that time spent driving in the dark, his night vision was so acute he could see deep into shadow. When he saw a lone man squatted near the fence, to one side of the gate, he was confused at first. Why had the man failed to see him? Only after he forced his heart from his throat did he realize the other man's eyes hadn't yet adjusted. It was apparent, from the way the guy fidgeted, that he'd just arrived there. From deep in shadow beneath the overgrowth outside the abandoned building, Joe studied him. The airplane engine, first heard at a distance, was loud now. He needed to get past this sentry in a hurry, with a minimum of noise. He watched a pack of cigarettes come out of the man's shirt pocket. To dig out his lighter, the sentry was forced to juggle the weapon in his lap and finally set it on the ground. One hand was occupied swatting mosquitoes, while he flicked the igniter. Joe realized the flash of his lighter flame would only further impede the man's night sight, and made the split-second decision to rush him.

Dante's good leg took the initial weight as he launched to race the thirty feet between him and his target. The weaker knee screamed in protest each time he planted his left foot. It made his run through shadow along the building front awkward as he drove everything but his objective from his mind. The roar of the plane engine notwithstanding, he couldn't risk a shot. He had to do this quietly.

The sentry wasn't aware of Dante until Joe had closed within five feet. He threw himself to one side and opened his mouth to yell. The force of the impact from Joe's elbow blow snapped his head back as the plane swept low over the swamp, not a hundred yards behind the gate, and his cry was crushed in his throat. Joe felt the hot breath of the man's grunt and clamped his hands on the sentry's head to give a quick, sideways jerk. The whole body beneath him began to convulse once that neck snapped.

Rather than land, the pilot started to climb after making a pass, presumably to inspect the terrain. Dante hauled himself to his feet with the aid of a gatepost, his left knee burning now, and stopped to retrieve the dead sentry's Uzi. He eased the gate open and slipped through. The Mercedes had been left parked on an overgrown verge, thirty feet deep, which ran east-west along the edge of the swamp. Its engine was running, with headlights left on to illuminate a tree-lined and debris-strewn earthen promenade that ran twenty yards south like a finger probing the Everglades grasses. There were three figures moving toward that levee's far end. One pulled Rosa along by the hair.

Joe watched as they stopped at the end of the promenade. He knew he would risk getting Rosa killed with a shot at seventy feet. He saw the man who'd been dragging Rosa disappear down out of sight, and seconds later a powerful engine roared to life. Dante recognized the semicircular top of a fan cage now. It was the business end of an airboat. His heart sank.

* * *

The airboat's engine was left to idle with its deep, throaty thrum as Julio Mesa climbed the levee to cast free the first of two mooring lines. Overhead, the seaplane had circled and was now on its approach. The boat swung loose, only one line holding it, as Julio crossed to the *cubana* and sent her staggering down the embankment with a forearm thrust. "Let's do it, Jim," he hollered to Mendoza.

Teo started down behind the woman as Julio untied the bow line. Mendoza had one foot on shore and one on the gunwale when Mesa threw all his weight against the line. Caught by surprise, Teo lost his balance and toppled into the swamp as Julio grabbed the ammunition clip from his pocket, slapped it home, and chambered a round. Mendoza reached frantically for his gun and was trying to find his feet when Julio shot him once, and then again. The first bullet knocked him flat on his back. The second drilled him, mid-chest. Without pausing to watch him die, Julio jumped aboard. He grinned at the *cubana* with bright-eyed malevolence, and whooped.

"Some gator's gonna think he died and went to heaven!"

The combined noise of the plane and the idling airboat engine were almost deafening. "One word to my uncle?" Julio hollered over the din. "About what you just saw? I'll cut your fucking tits off!"

When she just stared at him, Julio whipped the mooring line at the cop bitch's face. It caught her flush and he would swear she didn't even blink. Across the swamp, following the soft line of lights that described the landing area, the plane set down to skim through the reeds. Mesa climbed into the airboat's cockpit chair as the first strains of screaming salsa, floating on the heavy swamp air, broke through the thrum of the engine at his back.

Confused by the blare of trumpets and hot Latin beat. Mesa studied the pedals and throttle control, trying to figure how to make this buggy go. He looked up to frown toward the plane, where it had come to a stop, and then realized the music came from behind him; that it was growing louder. He glanced over his shoulder while increasing power to the engine by twisting the throttle. Above him on the levee, the Mercedes was plowing through all that scattered debris at good speed, bearing down on him like a runaway bulldozer, its radio cranked loud enough to shred the speakers.

A sudden surge of panic saw Julio tromp the wrong rudder pedal. The boat lurched hard into the bank rather than toward the open swamp, the impact sending the woman toppling over the side. Julio continued to struggle with the pedals, trying to get the boat to come about. Had Eddie's driver seen him shoot Mendoza? The car was on a course to ram him, and the boat refused to budge. He had to fight past his dread of alligators to jump clear, seconds before the Mercedes surged over the lip of the embankment.

Before he started the Mercedes to drive it forward, Dante had run down all the windows and opened the power sunroof. There was a Tito Puente CD already in the player, and once he had aimed the wheels straight ahead down the levee and set the shift lever in *drive*, he cranked the volume clear on up and accelerated. A new surge of rage gave him purpose. He'd heard gunfire. Two shots. They'd killed Rosa.

The plane landed, its engine noise now secondary to the roar of the airboat engine and to Tito Puente's ear-splitting Latin beat. For some reason, the fugitives in the airboat hadn't gotten under way, and that was just fine by Joe. The closer it was to shore, the quicker the airboat would burn.

He jumped clear, fifteen feet before the Mercedes reached the end of the levee. Once the car started to nose over the edge of the embankment, Joe dropped to his good knee and sighted in on the gas tank, tucked up beneath the rear bumper. The Uzi jumped in his hands as the rear of the car exploded. Engulfed in flames, it continued to roll downward until it disappeared from view, the bright orange gasoline fireball illuminating the landscape across the swamp well past where the seaplane idled.

Dante was on his feet and limping forward again. Holding the Uzi at hip level, he emptied the clip at the plane. One moment it sat there as placidly as a great blue heron, and the next it burst into flames. Joe saw a figure struggle from the cockpit door and fail to jump clear before the craft disintegrated with a concussed *whump*. Still brighter images burned in his mind's eye as he watched. There was Janet, so surprised as she turned. Audrey Stumpf, dead on that slab. The Chapel family in their dining room chairs. Rosa in his arms last night. The clip of the Uzi spent, he threw the weapon aside and reached to the small of his back for his Walther.

Atop of the embankment, Joe saw the burning airboat, nose to nose with the molten Mercedes. Flaming gasoline spread across the surface of the swamp toward the body of Mateo Mendoza. The dreaded hit-man floated face-up, a gaping hole torn in his chest and another black splotch high up on his left shoulder. Panic gripped Joe as he searched the flaming swamp. Any second now, the gas tank on the airboat would go. Already, the heat was so intense he was being driven back. Where was Rosa?

TWENTY-EIGHT

Julio was on his feet in eighteen inches of water, scrambling for the levee bank, when automatic fire erupted and the Benz burst into flame. Teo was dead and the *cubana* was unarmed, wherever she was. Reality hit Julio like an Andean avalanche. Eddie Ochoa had never intended for them to leave Miami. As Lucho Esparza's nephew and sole heir, Julio was the future king; a threat to Ochoa's rule in Miami. Why risk war later when the threat could be eliminated now?

Automatic fire continued to hammer the night, and the seaplane caught fire. Ochoa could claim this was an ambush by a rival faction, or the clandestine operation of some law enforcement agency. There would be no survivors to argue the veracity of his claim.

Mesa scrambled for the tree-lined levee bank while tugging the Beretta from his waistband. He released the clip to shake water from it and chastized himself for being so careless. After shooting Sonny and wasting five more rounds trying to bring down Bebe, he'd failed to reload. Two more bullets for Teo, which left him with only seven now.

The clip slapped home, Julio headed for deep shadow beneath a tree. He spotted movement on the bank above, and in a firelight bright enough to see color, there was no mistaking what he saw. The man looming above him had light hair, not dark. He was taller than Ochoa's driver, and he was Anglo. It wasn't an Uzi he held trained and sweeping the landscape, but a pistol. Julio was to the left of where this stranger prowled the levee bank, and used his advantage to raise the Beretta and take careful aim. Locked on his target's chest, he waited for him to turn before he fired. He wanted the man to see the muzzle of his gun before oblivion embraced his sorry ass.

The target came around, as predictable as the sweep second hand of Julio's Rolex. Mesa's grin widened when those eyes met the muzzle of his gun. Then the gas tank on the swamp buggy blew.

Rosa had crawled all the way up behind a log on the muddy levee bank before she realized it wasn't a log at all, but an eight-foot alligator. She froze. Hardly able to breathe, she lay there, waiting for the thing to smell her, or feel the panicked thundering of her heart, or whatever it was that alerted these beasts to the presence of prey. She wondered why it was still here after all the gunfire, the blaring salsa, and the explosion of the Mercedes, forty feet away. Reason argued feebly that it had to be either dead or on Prozac.

An eternity elapsed before the gas tank on the airboat went up with a concussed *whoosh*. Without so much as a sideward look, the monster lizard simply backpedaled, slithering in reverse through the mud to the water. Rosa exhaled hard and sucked the fetid Everglades air deep into her lungs. An instant later, Julio Mesa kicked that air back out again as he blundered into her while sprinting along the bank. She gasped in agony as he went down in a heap atop her. Before she could recover, he had the barrel of that Beretta jammed up beneath her chin again.

If Dante ever doubted the concept of divine intervention, he doubted no longer. With his deliverance came the harsh, cold slap of reality he needed. He'd let his rage get the better of him; let his passion overrule good sense. Yes, Teo Mendoza was dead, but at some point Mendoza had ceased to be the primary target. Julio Mesa had killed those prison guards, and Audrey Stumpf, and Kimberly Trammel. Mesa had probably killed Rosa, too, and because Joe was blind with the pain of it, Mesa had nearly killed him too. "Round one's yours, asshole," he growled at the night.

With the airboat destroyed and fire raging out across the water, there was only one path of escape, and Dante hurried to seal off the end of the levee. In control of where the promenade intersected the overgrown east-west verge, he would have the advantage and meant to use it. When he reached the head of the levee, he scooped mud to smear it on his bared face, neck, and arms, the mosquitoes trying to eat him alive. He had no idea where Mesa was, or how fast he was moving. The area that fronted the swamp to the left of the levee, directly behind the thatch-roofed building, was choked with mangrove along the waterline and strewn with more rusting pieces of machinery. Mesa was on that left side and had no choice but to come up it, unless he wanted to risk a dash across the levee. On this bank he would have the cover of a dozen stout, vine-shrouded trees, rare in this vast flatness. They'd probably been planted to create a picturesque approach to the swamp buggy mooring, but tonight they hulked scraggly and forlorn in the moonlight.

Joe was crouched and smearing mud inside his shirt when a voice, surprisingly thin and papery, called out to him.

"Yo, Jim! You know a good-looking police lady from New York? I got her here, my dick in her mouth!"

It took all of Dante's control to keep from charging down the levee. Instead, he rose slowly among the mangrove shadows, kicked off his shoes, and slid in the direction of that voice, one soundless, gliding stride at a time. "Keep talking," he whispered.

"Dig it, Jim! This bitch cop's gonna be my ticket outta here! Yo! You listening?"

When Mesa stopped talking, Joe stopped moving. He'd covered a third of the twenty-yard promenade that last burst, and guessed that Julio was now less than thirty feet away.

"Talk to me, you limp-dick hump! I mean *business* here!"

Fifteen feet away, Dante froze. From the cover of vines wrapping a tree trunk, mud oozing between his bare toes, and one fist wrapped tight around the butt of his Walther, he saw Rosa. She was alive, her blouse ripped to shreds, and Mesa standing behind her, one arm around her neck. He had a pistol in that hand and a knife in the other.

"I'll cut her tits off! You *know* I will!" Mesa yelled.

The glinting blade of his knife was held flat against her bare stomach.

The smell of the bitch's fear filled Julio's nostrils and made it hard for him to think clearly. Why wasn't the tall dude answering? And who the fuck was he? Had Eddie found a gringo freelancer to do his dirty work? Someone who didn't give a shit about this police bitch? God, he wished he had another snort right now. The cold sweat of her fear made him ache to do her, but what if the tall dude *did* care? What if she *was* his ticket?

A crash in the underbrush on the far side of the levee failed to penetrate at first. Julio had been listening for a voice, and suddenly, there his adversary was, trying to sneak up on him. He realized in an instant he couldn't kill her now. Not the way he wanted to. Not the way she deserved.

Like he'd awakened from a dream, Mesa hooked a leg in front of the bitch's ankles to drive her face-first into the mud. Backlit by the fire, he would be easy meat standing upright. Down in the undergrowth he could maneuver unseen. He grabbed a fistful of hair again and dragged her along beside him. That fool was thinking he could flank him by working down the opposite bank of the levee, but now he'd just blown his advantage. If he hadn't stumbled and given himself away, it could have worked, but it wouldn't work now.

Rosa had no idea who Jim was, but it was clear that he wanted Julio Mesa dead too. She was numb. Each passing second seemed like borrowed time, and when she heard that crash in the brush across the levee, she expected to be gutted on the spot. Now, as he dragged her by the hair, his knife twice slicing into her shoulder, she wondered how much longer she could last. If Jim hadn't appeared, she would have provoked Mesa to end it quickly.

While they crawled beneath the next tree up the levee, there was a sudden rustle in the clump of mangrove across from them. Julio froze, released her hair, and reared up on his knees, both hands on his automatic as he fired. A hot shell ejected to land between Rosa's bare shoulder blades. She screamed and twisted, sure that it was Mesa's knife. Rolled over on her side, she watched a gun emerge from the shadows of a vine-covered branch overhead. The gun muzzle spat flame, and Julio Mesa pitched forward, the back of his head a bloody pulp.

Dante dropped to the ground and collapsed onto his back at Rosa's side, mud coating his face and arms. "It's over," he gasped. "Are you hurt?"

"Joe?" She'd scrambled to cover her naked breasts with her hands and was suddenly on her knees, coming toward him. "Oh my God!"

He managed to get himself up on one elbow and saw the blood running down from her shoulder, colorless in the moonlight, but in dark contrast to her skin. "You're cut."

She touched the spots where Mesa's knife had gouged her, and winced. "He killed Mendoza, Joe."

"I saw." Dante looked over at the corpse of Julio Mesa, so near at hand he could touch it. Rosa was alive, and he felt a strange mixture of relief and exhaustion. Tears began to stream down his cheeks, cutting tracks through the drying mud. In the distance, he heard the wail of sirens. Those fires lighting the night were probably visible from Key West.

"Hold me?" Rosa asked.

Joe struggled to his knees and took her into his arms. He was afraid at first that he might hurt her, but the fierceness of her own hug allayed his fear. She was stronger than she looked. Always had been.

"Don't ever do that to me again," he whispered into her hair.

She squeezed even harder. "I love you too. Let's get the hell out of here."

Halfway up the levee, Dante removed his shirt and helped Rosa into it. She noticed that he was limping badly again and pulled his arm over her shoulder to take some of the weight. The fire trucks were less than a mile away by the time they reached the gate and passed into the parking lot out front. He led her to the edge of the road and began walking toward where he'd left his car. They'd gone thirty yards when he stopped abruptly.

"Shit."

"What?"

"My wheels. They're gone."

She looked up from beneath his arm. "You're sure this is where you left them?"

"Sure, I'm sure." He pointed diagonally across the road, then dug into his pocket to produce his keys. "Right over there. I don't believe it. *They* followed *me*. Those assholes stole my car."

Joe collapsed to sit on the ground, mosquitoes swarming around him, and started to laugh.